Stuart Johnson Reid

Lord John Russell

Stuart Johnson Reid

Lord John Russell

ISBN/EAN: 9783337168025

Printed in Europe, USA, Canada, Australia, Japan

Cover: Foto ©Raphael Reischuk / pixelio.de

More available books at **www.hansebooks.com**

LORD JOHN RUSSELL

BY

STUART J. REID

*I have looked to the happiness of my countrymen as the object
to which my efforts ought to be directed*

Recollections and Suggestions

NEW YORK

HARPER & BROTHERS, FRANKLIN SQUARE

1895

TO THE

LADY MARY AGATHA RUSSELL

THIS RECORD

OF

HER FATHER'S CAREER

IS

WITH TRUE REGARD

DEDICATED

PREFACE

THIS monograph could not have been written—in the intimate sense—if the Dowager Countess Russell had not extended a confidence which, I trust, has in no direction been abused. Lady Russell has not only granted me access to her journal and papers as well as the early note-books of her husband, but in many conversations has added the advantage of her own reminiscences.

I am also indebted in greater or less degree to Mrs. Warburton, Lady Georgiana Peel, Lady Agatha Russell, the Hon. Rollo Russell, Mr. G. W. E. Russell, and the Hon. George Elliot. Mr. Elliot's knowledge, as brother-in-law, and for many years as private secretary, touches both the personal and official aspects of Lord John's career, and it has been freely placed at my disposal. Outside the circle of Lord John's relatives I have received hints from the Hon. Charles Gore and Sir Villiers Lister, both of whom, at one period or another in his public life, also served him in the capacity of secretary.

I have received some details of Lord John's official life from one who served under him in a more public capacity—not, however, I hasten to add, as Chancellor of the Exchequer—but I am scarcely at liberty in this instance to mention my authority.

My thanks are due, in an emphatic sense, to my friend Mr. Spencer Walpole, who, with a generosity rare at all times, has not only allowed me to avail myself of facts contained in his authoritative biography of Lord John Russell, but has also glanced at the proof sheets of these pages, and has given me, in frank comment, the benefit of his own singularly wide and accurate knowledge of the historical and political annals of the reign. It is only right to add that Mr. Walpole is not in any sense responsible for the opinions expressed in a book which is only partially based on his own, is not always in agreement with his conclusions, and which follows independent lines.

The letter which the Queen wrote to the Countess Russell immediately after the death of one of her ' first and most distinguished Ministers' is now printed with her Majesty's permission.

The late Earl of Selborne and Mr. Lecky were sufficiently interested in my task to place on record for the volume some personal and political reminiscences which speak for themselves, and do so with authority.

I am also under obligations of various kinds to the Marquis of Dufferin and Ava, the Earl of Durham, Lord Stanmore, Dr. Anderson of Richmond, and the Rev. James Andrews of Woburn. I desire also to acknowledge the courtesy of Mr. Gladstone, Mr. Andrew Lang, Mr. James Knowles, Mr. Percy Bunting, Mr. Edwin Hodder, Messrs. Longmans, and the proprietors of ' Punch,' for liberty to quote from published books and journals.

In Montaigne's words, ' The tales I borrow, I charge upon the consciences of those from whom I have them.' I have gathered cues from all quarters, but in almost every case my indebtedness stands recorded on the passing page.

The portrait which forms the frontispiece is for the first time reproduced, with the sanction of the Countess Russell and Mr. G. F. Watts, from an original crayon drawing which hangs on the walls at Pembroke Lodge.

It may be as well to anticipate an obvious criticism by stating that the earlier title of the subject of this memoir is retained, not only in deference to the strongly expressed wish of the family at Pembroke Lodge, but also because it suggests nearly half a century spent in the House of Commons in pursuit of liberty.   In the closing days of Earl Russell's life his eye was accustomed to brighten, and his manner to relax, when some new acquaintance, in the eagerness of conversation, took the liberty of familiar friendship by addressing the old statesman as ' Lord John.'

STUART J. REID.

CHISLEHURST : *June* 4, 1895.

CONTENTS

CHAPTER I

EARLY YEARS, EDUCATION, AND TRAVEL

1792-1813

CHAPTER II

IN PARLIAMENT AND FOR THE PEOPLE

1813-1826

CHAPTER III

WINNING HIS SPURS

1826-1830

CHAPTER IV

A FIGHT FOR LIBERTY

1830-1832

CHAPTER V

THE DAWN OF A NEW ERA

1833-1838

CHAPTER VI

THE TWO FRONT BENCHES

1840-1845

CHAPTER X

DOWNING STREET AND CONSTANTINOPLE

1853

CHAPTER XI

WAR HINDERS REFORM

1854-1855

CHAPTER XII

THE VIENNA DIFFICULTY

1855

CHAPTER XIII

LITERATURE AND EDUCATION

CHAPTER XIV

COMING BACK TO POWER

1857–1861

CHAPTER XV

UNITED ITALY AND THE DIS-UNITED STATES

1861–1865

CHAPTER XVI

SECOND PREMIERSHIP

1865–1866

CHAPTER XVII

OUT OF HARNESS

1867–1874

CHAPTER XVIII

PEMBROKE LODGE

1847–1878

LORD JOHN RUSSELL

CHAPTER I

EARLY YEARS, EDUCATION, AND TRAVEL

1792–1813

Rise of the Russells under the Tudors—Childhood and early surroundings of Lord John—Schooldays at Westminster—First journey abroad with Lord Holland—Wellington and the Peninsular campaign—Student days in Edinburgh and speeches at the Speculative Society—Early leanings in Politics and Literature—Enters the House of Commons as member for Tavistock.

GOVERNMENT by great families was once a reality in England, and when Lord John Russell's long career began the old tradition had not yet lost its ascendency. The ranks of privilege can at least claim to have given at more than one great crisis in the national annals leaders to the cause of progress. It is not necessary in this connection to seek examples outside the House of Bedford, since the name of Lord William Russell in the seventeenth century and that of Lord John in the nineteenth stand foremost amongst the champions of civil and religious liberty. Hugh du Rozel, according to the Battle Roll, crossed from

Normandy in the train of the Conqueror. In the reign of Henry III. the first John Russell of note was a small landed proprietor in Dorset, and held the post of Constable of Corfe Castle. William Russell, in the year of Edward II.'s accession, was returned to Parliament, and his lineal descendant, Sir John Russell, was Speaker of the House of Commons in the days of Henry VI. The real founder, however, of the fortunes of the family was the third John Russell who is known to history. He was the son of the Speaker, and came to honour and affluence by a happy chance. Stress of weather drove Philip, Archduke of Austria and, in right of his wife, King of Castile, during a voyage from Flanders to Spain in the year 1506, to take refuge at Weymouth. Sir Thomas Trenchard, Sheriff of Dorset, entertained the unexpected guest, but he knew no Spanish, and Philip of Castile knew no English. In this emergency Sir Thomas sent in hot haste for his cousin, Squire Russell, of Barwick, who had travelled abroad and was able to talk Spanish fluently. The Archduke, greatly pleased with the sense and sensibility of his interpreter, insisted that John Russell must accompany him to the English Court, and Henry VII., no mean judge of men, was in turn impressed with his ability. The result was that, after many important services to the Crown, John Russell became first Earl of Bedford, and, under grants from Henry VIII. and Edward VI., the rich monastic lands of Tavistock and Woburn passed into his possession. The part which the Russells as a family have played in history of course lies outside the province of this volume, which is exclusively concerned with the character and career in recent times of one of the most distinguished statesmen of the present century.

Lord John Russell was born on August 18, 1792, at Hertford Street, Mayfair. His father, who was second son of Lord Tavistock, and grandson of the fourth Duke of Bedford, succeeded his brother Francis, as sixth Duke, in 1802, at the age of thirty-six, when his youngest and most famous son was ten years old. Long before his accession to the title, which was, indeed, quite unexpected, the sixth Duke had married the Hon. Georgiana Byng, daughter of Viscount Torrington, and the statesman with whose career these pages are concerned was the third son of this union. He spent his early childhood at Stratton Park, Hampshire. When he was a child of eight, Stratton Park was sold by the Duke of Bedford, and Oakley House, which he never liked so well, became the residence of his father. Although a shy, delicate child, he was sent in the spring of 1800, when only eight, to a private school at Sunbury—only a mile or two away from Richmond, where nearly eighty years later he died. In the autumn of 1801 he lost his mother, to whom he was deeply attached, and almost before the bewildered child had time to realise his loss, his uncle Francis also died, and his father, in consequence, became Duke of Bedford.

From Sunbury the motherless boy was sent with his elder brother to Westminster, in 1803, and the same year the Duke married Lady Georgiana Gordon, a daughter of the fourth Duke of Gordon, and her kindness to her step-children was marked and constant. Westminster School at the beginning of the century was an ill-disciplined place, in which fighting and fagging prevailed, and its rough and boisterous life taxed to the utmost the mettle of the plucky little fellow. He seems to have made no complaint, but to have taken his full share in the rough-and-tumble sports of his comrades in a school which has given many distinguished

men to the literature and public life of England : as, for
instance, the younger Vane—whom Milton extolled—Ben
Jonson and Dryden, Prior and Locke, Cowper and Southey,
Gibbon and Warren Hastings.

He learnt Latin at Westminster, and was kept to the
work of translation, but he used to declare somewhat rue-
fully in after-days that he had as a schoolboy to devote
the half-holidays to learning arithmetic and writing, and
these homely arts were taught him by a pedagogue who
seems to have kept a private school in Great Dean's Yard.
Many years later Earl Russell dictated to the Countess some
reminiscences of his early days, and since Lady Russell has
granted access to them, the following passages transcribed
from her own manuscript will be read with interest :—
' My education, for various reasons, was not a very regular
one. It began, indeed, in the usual English way by my
going to a very bad private school at Sunbury, and my being
transferred to a public school at Westminster at ten or eleven.
But I never entered the upper school. The hard life of a
fag—for in those days it was a hard life—and the unwhole-
some food disagreed with me so much that my stepmother,
the Duchess of Bedford, insisted that I should be taken
away and sent to a private tutor.' At Westminster School
physical hardihood was always encouraged. ' If two boys
were engaged to fight during the time of school, those boys
who wanted to see the fight had to leave school for the
purpose.' At this early period a passion for the theatre
possessed him, drawing him to Drury Lane or Covent Garden
whenever an opportunity occurred ; and this kind of relaxation retained a considerable hold upon him throughout the
greater portion of his life. Even as a child he was a bit of
a philosopher. In the journal which he began to keep in

the year he went to Westminster School is the following
entry :—'October 28, 1803.—Very great mist in the morning,
but afternoon very fine.   There was a grand review to-day
by the King in Hyde Park of the Volunteers.   I did not go,
as there was such a quantity of people that I should have
seen nothing, and should have been knocked down.'   Most
of the entries in the boy's journal are pithy statements of
matter of fact, as, for instance :—'Westminster, Monday,
October 10.—I was flogged to-day for the first time.'   A few
days later the young diarist places on record what he calls
some of the rules of the school.   He states that lessons
began every morning at eight, and that usually work was
continued till noon, with an interval at nine for breakfast.
Lessons were resumed at two on ordinary days, and finished
for the day at five.   'All the fellows have verses on Thurs-
days and Saturdays.   We go on Sundays to church in the
morning in Henry VII.'s Chapel, and in the evening have
prayers in the school.'

His 'broken and disturbed' education was next resumed
at Woburn Abbey under Dr. Cartwright, the Duke's domestic
chaplain, and brother to Major Cartwright, the well-known
political reformer.   The chaplain at Woburn was a many-
sided man.   He was not only a scholar and a poet, but
also possessed distinct mechanical skill, and afterwards won
fame as the inventor of the power-loom.   He was quick-
witted and accomplished, and it was a happy circumstance
that the high-spirited, impressionable lad, who by this
time was full of dreams of literary distinction, came under
his influence.   'I acquired from Dr. Cartwright,' declared
Lord John, 'a taste for Latin poetry which has never left
me.'   Not merely at work but at play, his new friend came
to his rescue.   'He invented the model of a boat which was

moved by clockwork and acted upon the water by a paddle underneath. He gave me the model, and I used to make it go across the ponds in the park.' Meanwhile literature was not forgotten, and before long the boy's juvenile effusions filled a manuscript book, which with an amusing flourish of trumpets was dedicated to 'the Right Hon. William Pitt, Chancellor of the Exchequer.' A couple of sentences will reveal its character, and the dawning humour of the youthful scribe :—'This little volume, being graced with your name, will prosper ; without it my labour would be all in vain. May you remain at the Helm of State long enough to bestow a pension on your very humble and obedient servant, John Russell.'

Between the years 1805 and 1808 Lord John pursued his education under a country parson in Kent. He was placed under the care of Mr. Smith, Vicar of Woodnesborough, near Sandwich, an ardent Whig, who taught a select number of pupils, amongst whom were several cadets of the aristocracy ; and to this seminary Lord John now followed his brothers, Lord Tavistock and Lord William Russell. Amongst his schoolfellows at Woodnesborough was the Lord Hartington of that generation, Lord Clare, Lord William Fitzgerald, and a future Duke of Leinster. The vicar in question, worthy Mr. Smith, was nicknamed 'Dean Smigo' by his pupils, but Lord John, looking back in after-years, declared that he was an excellent man, well acquainted with classical authors, both Greek and Latin, though 'without any remarkable qualities either of character or understanding.' He evidently won popularity amongst the boys by joining in their indoor amusements and granting frequent holidays, particularly on occasions when the Whig cause was triumphant in the locality or in Parliament.

Rambles inland and on the seashore, pony riding, shooting small birds, cricket, and other sports, as well as winter evening games, filled up the ample leisure from the duties of the schoolroom. One or two extracts from his journal are sufficient to show that, although still weakly, he was not lacking in boyish vivacity and in a healthy desire to emulate his elders. When Grenville and Fox joined their forces and so brought about the Ministry of ' All the Talents' the lads obtained a holiday—a fact which is thus recorded in sprawling schoolboy hand by Lord John in his diary. 'Saturday, February 8, 1806.— . . . We did no business on Mr. Fox's coming into the Ministry. I shot a couple of larks beyond Southerden. . . . I went out shooting for the first time with Mr. Smith's gun. I got eight shots at little birds and killed four of them.' On November 5 in the same year we find him writing :—' Eliza's [Miss Smith's] birthday. No business. I went out shooting, but only killed some little birds. I used to shoot much better than I do at present. Always miss now ; have not killed a partridge yet.' Poor boy ! But he lived to kill two deer and a wild boar. 'Similarity of age led me,' states Lord John, in one of his unpublished notes, ' to form a more intimate friendship with Clare than with any of the others, and our mutual liking grew into a strong attachment on both sides. I only remark this fact as Lord Byron, who had been a friend of Clare's at Harrow, appears to have shown some boyish jealousy when the latter expressed his sorrow at my departure for Spain.'

Now and then he turned his gift for composing verses in the direction of a satire on some political celebrity. He also wrote and spoke the prologue at private dramatic performances at Woburn during the holiday season, and took the part of 'Lucy' in 'The Rivals.'   A little later, in the brief period of his father's viceroyalty, he wrote another prologue, and on this occasion amused an Irish audience by his assumption of the part of an old woman.

The political atmosphere of Woburn and Woodnesborourgh as well as his father's official position, led the boy of fourteen to take a keen interest in public affairs.   His satirical verses on Melville, Pitt, Hawkesbury, and others, together with many passages in his journal, showed that his attention was frequently diverted from grammar and lexicon, field sports and footlights, to politics and Parliament, and the struggle amongst statesmen for place and power.   Although little is known of the actual incidents of Lord John's boyhood, such straws at least show the direction in which the current of his life was setting.

Whilst Lord John was the guest of Mr. Fox at Stable Yard, the subject of Lord Melville's acquittal by the Peers came up for discussion.   Next day the shrewd young critic wrote the following characteristic remark in his journal : 'What a pity that he who steals a penny loaf should be hung, whilst he who steals thousands of the public money should be acquitted !'   The brilliant qualities of Fox made a great impression on the lad, and there can be little doubt that his intercourse with the great statesman, slight and passing though it was, did much to awaken political ambition.   He also crossed the path of other men of light and leading in the political world, and in this way, boy though he was, he grew familiar with the strife of parties and the great questions of the hour.   Holland House opened its hospitable gates to him, and there he met a young clergyman of an unconventional type—the Rev. Sydney Smith—with whom he struck up a friendship that was destined to endure. The young schoolboy has left it on record in that inevitable 'journal' that he found his odd clerical acquaintance 'very amusing.'

In the summer of 1807 we learn from his journal that he passed three months with his father and stepmother at the English lakes and in the West of Scotland. With boyish glee he recounts the incidents of the journey, and his delight in visiting Inverary, Edinburgh, and Melrose. Yet it was his rambles and talks with Sir Walter Scott, whom he afterwards described as one of the wonders of the age, that left the most abiding impression upon him. On his way back to Woodnesborough he paid his first visit to the House of Lords, and heard a debate on the Copenhagen expedition, an affair in which, he considered, 'Ministers cut a most despicable figure.' On quitting school life at Woodnesborough, an experience was in store for him which enlarged his mental horizon, and drew out his sympathies for the weak and oppressed. Lord and Lady Holland had taken a fancy to the lad, and the Duke of Bedford consented to their proposal that he should accompany them on their visit to the Peninsula, then the scene of hostilities between the French and the allied armies of England and Spain. The account of this journey is best told in Lord John's own words : —

'In the autumn of 1808, when only sixteen years of age, I accompanied Lord and Lady Holland to Corunna, and afterwards to Lisbon, Seville, and Cadiz, returning by Lisbon to England in the summer of 1809. They were eager for the success of the Spanish cause, and I joined to sympathy for Spain a boyish hatred of Napoleon, who had treacherously obtained possession of an independent country by force and fraud—force of immense armies, fraud of the lowest kind.' There is in existence at Pembroke Lodge a small parchment-bound volume marked 'Diary, 1808,' which records in his own handwriting Lord John's first impressions of foreign travel. The notes are brief, but they show that the writer even then was keenly alive to the picturesque. The journal ends somewhat abruptly, and Lord John confesses in so many words that he gave up this journal in despair, a statement which is followed by the assertion that the record at least possesses the 'merit of brevity.'

Spain was in such a disturbed condition that the tour was full of excitement. War and rumours of war filled the air, and sudden changes of route were often necessary in order to avoid perilous encounters with the French. The travellers were sometimes accompanied by a military escort, but were more frequently left to their devices, and evil tidings of disaster to the Allies—often groundless, but not less alarming—kept the whole party on the alert, and proved, naturally, very exciting to the lad, who under such strange and dramatic circumstances gained his first experience of life abroad. Lord John had, however, taken with him his Virgil, Tacitus, and Cicero, and now and then, forgetful of the turmoil around him, he improved his acquaintance with the classics. He also studied the Spanish language, with the result that he acquired an excellent conversational knowledge of it. The lad had opinions and the courage of them, and when he saw the cause of the Spanish beginning to fail he was exasperated by the apathy of the Whigs at home, and accordingly, with the audacity of youth, wrote to his father :—

' I take the liberty of informing you and your Opposition friends that the French have not conquered the whole of Spain. . . . Lord Grey's speech appears to me either a mere attempt to plague Ministers for a few hours or a declaration against the principle of the people's right to depose an infamous despot. . . . It seems to be the object of the Opposition to prove that Spain is conquered, and that the Spaniards like being robbed and murdered.' It seems, therefore, that Lord John, even in his teens, was inclined to be dogmatic and oracular, but the soundness of his judgment, in this particular instance at least, is not less remarkable than his sturdy mental independence. Like his friend Sydney Smith, he was already becoming a lover of justice and of sympathy towards the oppressed.

In the summer of 1809, after a short journey to Cadiz, Lord Holland and his party crossed the plains of Estremadura on mules to Lisbon and embarked for England, though not without an unexpected delay caused by a slight attack of fever on the part of Lord John. On the voyage back Lord Holland and his secretary, Mr. Allen, pointed out to him the advantages of going to Edinburgh for the next winter, and in a letter to his father, dated Spithead, August 10, 1809, he adds : 'They say that I am yet too young to go to an English university ; that I should learn more there [Edinburgh] in the meantime than I should anywhere else.'

He goes on to state that he is convinced by their arguments, in spite of the fact that he had previously expressed ' so much dislike to an academical career in Edinburgh.' The truth is, Lord John wished to follow his elder brother, Lord Tavistock, to Cambridge ; but the Duke would not hear of the idea, and bluntly declared that nothing at that time was to be learnt at the English universities.

On his return to England it was decided to send Lord John to continue his studies at Edinburgh University. The

Northern Athens at that time was full of keen and varied intellectual life, and the young student could scarcely have set foot in it at a more auspicious moment. Other cadets of the English aristocracy, such as Lord Webb Seymour and Lord Henry Petty, were attracted at this period to the Northern university, partly by the restrictive statutes of Oxford and Cambridge, but still more by the genius and learning of men like Dugald Stewart and John Playfair.

The Duke of Bedford placed his son under the roof of the latter, who at that time held the chair of mathematics in the university, with the request that he would take a general oversight of his studies. Professor Playfair was a teacher who quickened to a remarkable extent the powers of his pupils, and at the same time by his own estimable qualities won their affection. Looking back in after-years, Lord John declared that ' Professor Playfair was one of the most delightful of men and very zealous lover of liberty.' He adds that the simplicity of the distinguished mathematician, as well as the elevation of his sentiments, was remarkable.

It is interesting to learn from Professor Playfair's own statement that he was quickly impressed with the ability of Lord John. Ambition was stirring in the breast of the young Whig, and though he could be idle enough at times, he seems on the whole to have lent his mind with increasing earnestness to the tasks of the hour. He also attended the classes of Professor Dugald Stewart during the three years he spent in the grey metropolis of the North, and the influence of that remarkable man was not merely stimulating at the time, but materially helped to shape his whole philosophy of life. After he had left Edinburgh, Lord John wrote some glowing lines about Dugald Stewart, which follow —afar off, it must be admitted—the style of Pope. We have only space to quote a snatch :

'Twas he gave laws to fancy, grace to thought,
Taught virtue's laws, and practised what he taught.

Intellectual stimulus came to him through another channel. He was elected in the spring of 1810 a member of the Edinburgh Speculative Society, and during that and the two following years he was zealous in his attendance at its weekly meetings. The Speculative Society was founded early in the reign of George III., and no less distinguished a man than Sir Walter Scott acted for a term of years as its secretary. It sought to unite men of different classes and pursuits, and to bring young students and more experienced thinkers and men of affairs together in friendly but keen debate on historical, philosophical, literary, and political questions.

It is certain that Lord John first discovered his powers of debate in the years when he took a prominent part in the Tuesday night discussions in the hall which had been erected for the Speculative Society in 1769 in the grounds of the university. The subjects about which he spoke are at least of passing interest even now as a revelation of character, for they show the drift of his thoughts. He was not content with merely academic themes, such as Queen Elizabeth's treatment of Mary Queen of Scots, or the policy of Alcibiades. Topics of more urgent moment, like the war of 1793, the proceedings of the Spanish Cortes in 1810, the education of the poor, the value of Canada to Great Britain, and one at least of the burning subjects of the day—the imprisonment of Gale Jones in Newgate by order of the House of Commons—claimed his attention and drew forth his powers of argument and oratory. His mind was already turning in the direction of the subject of Parliamentary Reform, and from Edinburgh he forwarded to his father an essay on that subject, which still exists among the family papers. It shows that he was preparing to vindicate even then on a new field the liberal and progressive traditions of the Russells.

The Duke of Bedford was never too busy or preoccupied to enter into his son's political speculations. He encouraged him to continue the habit of reasoning and writing on the great questions of the day, and Lord John, who in spite of uncertain health had no lack of energy, cheered by such kindly recognition, was not slow to respond to his father's sensible advice.

Meanwhile the war in the Peninsula was progressing, and it appealed to the Edinburgh undergraduate now with new and even painful interest. His brother, Lord William Russell, had accompanied his regiment to Spain in the summer of 1809, and had been wounded at the battle of Talavera. In the course of the following summer, Lord John states, in a manuscript which is in Lady Russell's possession : ' I went to Cadiz to see my brother William, who was then serving on the staff of Sir Thomas Graham. The head-quarters was in a small town on the Isle of Leon, and the General, who was one of the kindest of men, gave me a bed in his house during the time that I remained there.' Cadiz was at the moment besieged by the French, and Lord John proceeds to describe the strategical points in its defence. Afterwards he accompanied Colonel Stanhope, a member of General Graham's staff, to the head-quarters of Lord Wellington, who had just occupied with his army the lines of Torres Vedras. He thus records his impressions of the great soldier, and of the spectacle which lay before him :—

'Standing on the highest point, and looking around him on every side, was the English General, his eyes bright and searching as those of an eagle, his countenance full of hope, beaming with intelligence as he marked with quick perception every movement of troops and every change of circumstance within the sweep of the horizon. On each side of the fort of Sobral rose the entrenchments of the Allies, bristling with guns and alive with the troops who formed the garrison of this fortified position. Far off, on the left, the cliffs rose to a moderate elevation, and the lines of Torres Vedras were prominent in the distance. . . . There stood the advanced guard of the conquering legions of France ; here was the living barrier of England, Spain, and Portugal, prepared to stay the destructive flood, and to preserve from the deluge the liberty and independence of three armed nations. The sight filled me with admiration, with confidence, and with hope.'

Wellington told Colonel Stanhope that there was nothing he should like better than to attack the enemy, but since the force which he commanded was England's only army, he did not care to risk a battle. 'In fact, a defeat would have been most disastrous, for the English would have been obliged to retreat upon Lisbon and embark for England, probably after suffering great losses.' Within a fortnight Lord John was back again in London, and over the dinner table at Holland House the enterprising lad of eighteen was able to give Lord Grey an animated account of the prospects of the campaign, and of the appearance of Wellington's soldiers. The desire for Cambridge revived in Lord John with the conclusion of his Edinburgh course. His wishes were, however, overruled by his father, who, as already hinted, held extremely unfavourable views in regard to the characteristics at that period of undergraduate life in the English universities. The 'sciences of horse-racing, fox-hunting, and giving extravagant entertainments' the Duke regarded as the 'chief studies of our youths at Cambridge,' and he made no secret of his opinion that his promising son was better without them. Lord John's father is described by those who knew him as a plain, unpretending man, who talked well in private life, but was reserved in society. He was a great patron of the fine arts, and one of the best farmers in England, and was, moreover, able to hold his own in the debates of the House of Lords.

Meanwhile, at Woburn, Lord John's military ardour, which at this time was great, found an outlet in the command of a company of the Bedfordshire Militia. But the life of a country gentleman, even when it was varied by military drill, was not to the taste of this roving young Englishman. The passion for foreign travel, which he never afterwards wholly lost, asserted itself, and led him to cast about for congenial companions to accompany him abroad. Mr. George Bridgeman, afterwards Earl of Bradford, and Mr. Robert Clive, the second son of Earl Powis, agreed to accompany him, and with light hearts the three friends started in August 1812, with the intention of travelling through Sicily, Greece, Egypt, and Syria. They had not proceeded far, however, on their way to Southern Italy when tidings reached them that the battle of Salamanca had been fought and that Wellington had entered Madrid. The plans for exploring Sicily, Egypt, and Syria were instantly thrown to the winds, and the young enthusiasts at once bent their steps to the Spanish capital, in order to take part in the rejoicings of the populace at the victory of the Allies. They made the best of their way to Oporto, but were chagrined to find on arriving there that although Salamanca had been added to the list of Wellington's triumphs, the victor had not pushed on to the capital. Under these circumstances, Lord John and his companions determined to make a short tour in the northern part of Portugal before proceeding to Wellington's head-quarters at Burgos. They met with a few mild adventures on the road, and afterwards crossed the frontier and reached the field of Salamanca. The dead still lay unburied, and flocks of vultures rose sullenly as the travellers threaded their way across that terrible scene of carnage. However, neither Lord John's phlegm nor his philosophy deserted him, though the awfulness of the spectacle was not lost upon him. 'The blood spilt on that day will become a real saving of life if it become the means of delivering Spain from French dominion,' was his remark.

At Burgos the young civilian renewed his acquaintance with the Commander-in-Chief, and added to his experience of war by being for a short time under fire from the French, who held the neighbouring fortress. Wellington, however, like other good soldiers, did not care for non-combatants at the front, and accordingly the youths started for Madrid. Finding that the French were in possession, they pushed southwards, and spent Christmas at Cadiz. The prolonged campaign decided them to carry out their original scheme. Leaving Cadiz at the end of January they set off, *via* Gibraltar, Cordova, and Cartagena, for Alicante, where they proposed to embark for Sicily. But on the way reports reached them of French reverses, and they were emboldened once more to move towards Madrid. They had hardly started when other and less reassuring rumours reached them, and Lord John's two companions resolved to return to Alicante ; but he himself determined to ride across the country to the head-quarters of the army, at Frenida, a distance of 150 miles. We are indebted to Mr. Bridgeman's published letters for the following account of Lord John's plucky ride :- 'Finding the French did not continue the retreat, John Russell, my strange cousin and your ladyship's mad nephew, determined to execute a plan which he had often threatened, but it appeared to Clive and me so very injudicious a one that we never had an idea of his putting it into execution. However, the evening previous to our leaving Almaden, he said, "Well, I shall go to the army and see William, and I will meet you either at Madrid or Alicante." We found he was quite serious, and he then informed us of his intentions. . . . He would not take his servant, but ordered him to leave out half-a-dozen changes of linen, and his gun loaded. He was dressed in a blue greatcoat, overalls, and sword, and literally took nothing else except his dressing-case, a pair of pantaloons and shoes, a journal and an account book, pens and ink, and a bag of money. He woul not carry anything to reload his gun, which he said his principal reason for taking was to sell, should he be short of money, for we had too little to spare him any. The next morning he sold his pony. bought a young horse, and rode the first league with us. Here we parted with each other with much regret, and poor John seemed rather forlorn. God grant he may have reached head-quarters in safety and health, for he had been far from well the last few days he was with us. . . . Clive and I feel fully persuaded that we shall see him no more till we return to England.'

The fears entertained for Lord John's safety were well founded. Difficulties of many kinds had to be encountered on the journey, and there was always the risk of being arrested and detained by French piquets. But the 150 miles were traversed without mishap, and in twelve days the 'mad nephew' entered the English quarters. He stayed at Frenida more than a month, probably waiting for an opportunity to see a great battle. But the wish was not gratified. Dictating to Lady Russell in his later life the narrative of his journey in Spain, he said : 'When Lord Wellington left his head-quarters on the frontier of Spain and Portugal for his memorable campaign of Vittoria, I thought that as I was not a soldier I might as well leave Lord Wellington and proceed on a journey of amusement to Madrid.'

General Alava gave him introductions, and in the course of his journey he was entertained at dinner by a merry canon at Plasencia, who pressed upon him a liberal supply of wine. When Lord John declined taking any more, his host exclaimed : 'Do you not know the syllogism, " Qui bene bibit, bene dormit ; qui bene dormit, non peccat ; qui non peccat, salvatus erit"?' At this stage Lord John found it necessary to hire a servant who was capable of acting as guide. He used to say that his whole appearance on these journeys was somewhat grotesque, and in proof of this assertion he was accustomed in relating his adventures to add the following description :—'I wore a blue military cloak and a military cocked hat ; I had a sword by my side ; my whole luggage was carried in two bags, one on each side of the horse. In one of these I usually carried a leg of mutton, from which I cut two or three slices when I wished to prepare my dinner. My servant had a suit of clothes which had never been of the best, and was then mostly in rags. He, too, wore a cocked hat, and, being tall and thin, stalked before me with great dignity.' Such a description reads almost like a page from Cervantes.

Thus attended, Lord John visited the scene of the battle

of Talavera, in which his brother had been wounded, and on June 5, two days after the departure of the French, entered Madrid. Before the end of the month news arrived of the battle of Vittoria ; and the young Englishman shared in the public rejoicings which greeted the announcement. 'From Talavera,' adds Lord John, 'I proceeded to Madrid, where I met my friends George Bridgeman and Robert Clive. With them I travelled to Valencia, and with them in a ship laden with salt fish to Majorca.'

At Palma the travellers found hospitable quarters at the Bishop's palace, and after a brief stay crossed in an open boat to Port Mahon in Minorca—a rather risky trip, as the youths, with their love of adventure, made it by night, and were overtaken on the way by an alarming thunderstorm. Whilst in Minorca Lord John received a letter from his father, informing him of the death of his old friend General Fitzpatrick, and also stating that the Duke meant to use his influence at Tavistock to obtain for his son a seat in the House of Commons. 'He immediately flew home,' remarks his friend Mr. Bridgeman, 'on what wings I know not, but I suppose on those of political ambition.'

The Duke's nomination rendered his election in those days of pocket-boroughs a foregone conclusion. As soon as Lord John set foot in England he was greeted with the tidings that he had already been elected member for Tavistock, and so began, at the age of one-and-twenty, a career in the House of Commons which was destined to last for nearly fifty years.

CHAPTER II

The political outlook when Lord John entered the House of Commons —The 'Condition of England' question—The struggle for Parliamentary Reform—Side-lights on Napoleon Bonaparte—The Liverpool Administration in a panic—Lord John comes to the aid of Sir Francis Burdett—Foreign travel—First motion in favour of Reform—Making headway

LORD LIVERPOOL was at the head of affairs when Lord John Russell entered Parliament. His long tenure of power had commenced in the previous summer, and it lasted until the Premier was struck down by serious illness in the opening weeks of 1827. In Lord John's opinion, Lord Liverpool was a 'man of honest but narrow views,' and he probably would have endorsed the cynical description of him as the 'keystone rather than the capital' of his own Cabinet. Lord Castlereagh was at the Foreign Office, Lord Sidmouth was Home Secretary, Mr. Vansittart Chancellor of the Exchequer, Lord Palmerston Secretary at War, and Mr. Peel Secretary for Ireland. The political outlook on all sides was gloomy and menacing. The absorbing subject in Parliament was war and the sinews of war; whilst outside its walls hard-pressed taxpayers were moodily speculating on the probable figures in the nation's 'glory bill.' The two years' war with America was in progress. The battle between the *Shannon* and the *Chesapeake* was still the talk of the hour ; but there seemed just then no prospect of peace. Napoleon still struggled for the dictatorship of Europe, and Englishmen were wondering to what extent they would have to share in the attempt to foil his ambition. The Peninsular campaign was costly enough to the British taxpayer ; but his chagrin vanished—for the moment, at least—when Wellington's victories appealed to his pride. Since the beginning of the century the attention of Parliament and people had been directed mainly to foreign affairs. Domestic legislation was at a standstill. With one important exception—an Act for the Abolition of the Slave Trade—scarcely any measure of note, apart from military matters and international questions, had passed the House of Commons.

Parliamentary government, so far as it was supposed to be representative of the people, was a delusion. The number of members returned by private patronage for England and Wales amounted to more than three hundred. It was publicly asserted, and not without an appeal to statistics, that one hundred and fifty-four persons, great and small, actually returned no less than three hundred and seven members to the House of Commons. Representation in the boroughs was on a less worthy scale in the reign of George III. than it had been in the days of the Plantagenets, and whatever changes had been made in the franchise since the Tudors had been to the advantage of the privileged rather than to that of the people.

Parliament was little more than an assembly of delegates sent by large landowners. Ninety members were returned by forty-six places in which there were less than fifty electors ; and seventy members were returned by thirty-five places containing scarcely any electors at all.

Places such as Old Sarum—consisting of a mound and a few ruins—returned two members ; whilst Manchester, Leeds, and Birmingham, in spite of their great populations, and in spite, too, of keen political intelligence and far-reaching commercial activity, were not yet judged worthy of the least voice in affairs.   At Gatton the right of election lay in the hands of freeholders and householders paying scot and lot ; but the only elector was Lord Monson, who returned two members.   Many of the boroughs were bought at a fancy price by men ambitious to enter Parliament—a method which seems, however, to have had the advantage of economy when the cost of some of the elections is taken into account.   An election for Northampton cost the two candidates 30,000*l.* each, whilst Lord Milton and Mr. Lascelles, in 1807, spent between them 200,000*l.* at a contested election for the county of York.

Bribery and corruption were of course practised wholesale, and publicans fleeced politicians and made fortunes out of the pockets of aspirants for Westminster. In the 'People's Book' an instance is cited of the way some borough elections were 'managed.'   'The patron of a large town in Ireland, finding, on the approach of an election, that opposition was to be made to his interest, marched a regiment of soldiers into the place from Lough-rea, where they were quartered, and caused them to be elected freemen.   These military freemen then voted for his friend, who was, of course, returned !'   Inequality, inadequacy, unreality, corruption—these were the leading traits of the House of Commons.   The House of Commons no more represented the people of the United Kingdom than the parish council of Little Peddleton mirrors the mind of Europe.

The statute-book was disfigured by excessive penalities. Men were put in the pillory for perjury, libel, and the like. Forgers, robbers, incendiaries, poachers, and mutilators of cattle were sent to the gallows. Ignorance and brutality prevailed amongst large sections of the people both in town and country, and the privileged classes, in spite of vulgar ostentation and the parade of fine manners, set them an evil example in both directions. Yet, though the Church of England had no vision of the needs of the people and no voice for their wrongs, the great wave of religious life which had followed the preaching of Whitfield and Wesley had not spent its force, nor was it destined to do so before it had awakened in the multitude a spirit of quickened intelligence and self-respect which made them restive under political servitude and in the presence of acknowledged but unredressed grievances. Education, through the disinterested efforts of a group of philanthropists, was, moreover, beginning—in some slight degree, at least— to leaven the mass of ignorance in the country, the power of the press was making itself felt, and other agencies were also beginning to dispel the old apathy born of despair.

The French Revolution, with its dramatic overthrow of tyranny and its splendid watchword, 'Liberty, Equality, Fraternity,' made its own appeal to the hope as well as the imagination of the English people, although the sanguinary incidents which marked it retarded the movement for Reform in England, and as a matter of fact sent the Reformers into the wilderness for the space of forty years.

More than a quarter of a century before the birth of Lord John Russell, who was destined to carry the first Reform Bill through the House of Commons, Lord Chatham had not hesitated to denounce the borough representation of the country as the 'rotten part of our constitution,' which, he said, resembled a mortified limb; and he had added the significant words, 'If it does not drop, it must be amputated.' He held that it was useless to look for the strength and vigour of the constitution in little pocket-boroughs, and that the nation ought rather to rely on the 'great cities and counties.' Fox, in a debate in 1796, declared that peace could never be secured until the Constitution was amended. He added : 'The voice of the representatives of the people must prevail over the executive ministers of the Crown ; the people must be restored to their just rights.' These warnings fell unheeded, until the strain of long-continued war, bad harvests, harsh poor laws, and exorbitant taxes on the necessities of life conspired to goad the people to the verge of open rebellion.

Wilkes, Pitt, Burdett, Cartwright, and Grey, again and again returned to the charge, only to find, however, that the strongholds of privilege were not easily overthrown. The year 1792, in which, by a noteworthy coincidence, Lord John Russell was born, was rendered memorable in the history of a movement with which his name will always be associated by the formation of the society of the 'Friends of the People,' an influential association which had its place of meeting at the Freemasons' Tavern. Amongst its first members were Mr. Lambton (father of the first Earl of Durham), Mr (afterwards Sir James) Mackintosh, Mr. Sheridan, Mr. (afterwards Lord) Erskine, Mr. Charles (afterwards Earl) Grey, and more than twenty other members of Parliament. In the following year Mr. Grey brought forward the celebrated petition of the Friends of the People in the House of Commons. It exposed the abuses of the existing electoral system and presented a powerful argument for Par-

liamentary Reform. He moved that the petition should
be referred to the consideration 'of a committee'; but
Pitt, in spite of his own measure on the subject in 1785,
was now lukewarm about Reform, and accordingly opposed
as 'inopportune' such an inquiry. 'This is not a time,'
were his words, 'to make hazardous experiments.' The
spirit of anarchy, in his view, was abroad, and Burke's
'Reflections,' had of course increased the panic of the
moment. Although Grey pressed the motion, only 141
members supported it, and though four years later he
moved for leave to bring in a bill on the subject, justice
and common sense were again over-ridden, and, so far as
Parliament was concerned, the question slept until 1809,
when Sir Francis Burdett revived the agitation.

Meanwhile, men of the stamp of Horne Tooke, William
Cobbett, Hone, 'Orator' Hunt, and Major Cartwright—
brother of Lord John Russell's tutor at Woburn, and the
originator of the popular cry, 'One man, one vote' - were in
various ways keeping the question steadily before the minds
of the people.   Hampden Clubs and other democratic associations were also springing up in various parts of the
country, sometimes to the advantage of demagogues of
damaged reputation rather than to the advancement of the
popular cause.   Sir Francis Burdett may be said to have
represented the Reformers in Parliament during the remainder of the reign of George III., though, just as the old
order was changing, Earl Grey, in 1819, publicly renewed his
connection with the question, and pledged himself to support
any sound and judicious measure which promised to deal
effectively with known abuses. In spite of the apathy of
Parliament and the sullen opposition of the privileged classes
to all projects of the kind, whether great or small, sweeping

or partial, the question was slowly ripening in the public mind. Sydney Smith in 1819 declared, ' I think all wise men should begin to turn their minds Reformwards. We shall do it better than Mr. Hunt or Mr. Cobbett. Done it *must* and *will* be.' In the following year Lord John Russell, at the age of twenty-eight, became identified with the question of Parliamentary Reform by bringing before the House of Commons a measure for the redress of certain scandalous grievances, chiefly at Grampound. When Lord John's Parliamentary career began, George III. was hopelessly mad and blind, and, as if to heighten the depressing aspect of public affairs, the scandalous conduct of his sons was straining to the breaking-point the loyalty of men of intelligence to the Throne.

Lord John's maiden speech in Parliament was directed against the proposal of the Liverpool Administration to enforce its views in regard to the union of Norway and Sweden. It escaped the attention of Parliamentary reporters and has passed into oblivion. The pages of ' Hansard,' however, give a brief summary of his next speech, which, like its predecessor, was on the side of liberty. It was delivered on July 14, 1814, in opposition to the second reading of the Alien Acts, which in spite of such a protest quickly became law. His comments were concise and characteristic. ' He considered the Act to be one which was very liable to abuse. The present time was that which least called for it ; and Ministers, in bringing forward the measure now because it had been necessary before, reminded him of the unfortunate wag mentioned in ' Joe Miller,' who was so fond of rehearsing a joke that he always repeated it at the wrong time.' During the first months of his Parliamentary experience Lord John was elected a member of Grillion's Club, which had been established in Bond Street about twelve months previously, and which became in after-years a favourite haunt of many men of light and leading. It was founded on a somewhat novel basis. Leading members of the Whig and Tory parties met for social purposes. Political discussion was strictly tabooed, and nothing but the amenities of life were cultivated. In after-years the club became to Lord John Russell, as it has also been to many distinguished politicians, a welcome haven from the turmoil of Westminster.

Delicate health in the autumn quickened Lord John's desire to renew the pleasures of foreign travel. He accordingly went by sea to Italy, and arrived at Leghorn in the opening days of December. He was still wandering in Southern Europe when Parliament reassembled, and the Christmas Eve of that year was rendered memorable to him by an interview with Napoleon in exile at Elba.

Through the kindness of Lady Russell it is possible here to quote from an old-fashioned leather-bound volume in her husband's handwriting, which gives a detailed account of the incidents of his Italian tour in 1814–15, and of his conversation on this occasion with the banished despot of Europe. Part of what follows has already been published by Mr. Walpole, but much of it has remained for eighty years in the privacy of Lord John's own notebook, from the faded pages of which it is now transcribed :—'Napoleon was dressed in a green coat, with a hat in his hand, very much as he is painted ; but, excepting the resemblance of dress, I had a very mistaken idea of him from his portrait. He appears very short, which is partly owing to his being very fat, his hands and legs being quite swollen and unwieldy. That makes him appear awkward, and not unlike the whole-length figure of Gibbon the historian. Besides this, instead of the bold-marked countenance that I expected, he has fat cheeks and rather a turn-up nose, which, to bring in another historian, makes the shape of his face resemble the portraits of Hume. He has a dusky grey eye, which would be called vicious in a horse, and the shape of his mouth expresses contempt and decision. His manner is very good-natured, and seems studied to put one at one's ease by its familiarity ; his smile and laugh are very agreeable ; he asks a number of questions without object, and often repeats them, a habit which he has, no doubt, acquired during fifteen years of supreme command. He began asking me about my family, the allowance my father gave me, if I ran into debt, drank, played, &c. He asked me if I had been in Spain, and if I was not imprisoned by the Inquisition. I told him that I had seen the abolition of the Inquisition voted, and of the injudicious manner in which it was done.'

Napoleon told Lord John that Ferdinand was in the hands of the priests. Spain, like Italy, he added, was a fine country, especially Andalusia and Seville. Lord John admitted this, but spoke of the uncultivated nature of the land. 'Agriculture,' replied Napoleon, 'is neglected because the land is in the hands of the Church.' 'And of the grandees,' suggested his visitor. 'Yes,' was the answer, 'who have privileges contrary to the public prosperity.' Napoleon added that he thought the evil might be remedied by divided property and abolishing hurtful privileges, as was done in France. Afterwards Napoleon asked many questions about the Cortes, and when Lord John told him that many of the members made good speeches on abstract questions, but they failed when any practical debate on finance or war took place, Napoleon drily remarked : 'Oui, faute de l'habitude de gouverner.' Presently the talk drifted to Wellington, or rather Napoleon adroitly led it thither. He described the man who had driven the French out of Spain as a 'grand chasseur,' and asked if Wellington liked Paris. Lord John replied that he thought not, and added that Wellington had said that he should find himself much at a loss as to what to do in time of peace, as he seemed scarcely to like anything but war. Whereupon Napoleon exclaimed, 'La guerre est un grand jeu, une belle occupation.' He expressed his surprise that England should have sent the Duke to Paris, and he added, evidently with a touch of bitterness, 'On n'aime pas l'homme par qui on a été battu.'

The Emperor's great anxiety seemed to be to get reliable tidings of the condition of France. Lord John's own words are : 'He inquired if I had seen at Florence many Englishmen who came from there, and when I mentioned Lord Holland, he asked if he thought things went well with the Bourbons. When I answered in the negative he seemed delighted, and asked if Lord Holland thought they would be able to stay there.' On this point Lord John was not able to satisfy him, and Napoleon said that he understood that the Bourbons had neglected the Englishmen who had treated them well in England, and particularly the Duke of Buckingham, and he condemned their lack of gratitude. Lord John suggested that the Bourbons were afraid to be thought to be dependent on the English, but Napoleon brushed this aside by asserting that the English in general were very well received. In a mocking tone he expressed his wish to know whether the army was much attached to the Bourbons. The Vienna Congress was, of course, just then in progress, and Napoleon showed himself nothing loth to talk about it.   He said : 'The Powers will disagree, but they will not go to war.'   He spoke of the Regent's conduct to the Princess as very impolitic, and he added that it shocked the *bienséances* by the observance of which his father George III. had become so popular.   He declared that our struggle with America was 'une guerre de vengeance,' as the frontier question could not possibly be of any importance.   According to Napoleon, the great superiority of England to France lay in her aristocracy.

Napoleon stated that he had intended to create a new aristocracy in France by marrying his officers to the daughters of the old nobility, and he added that he had reserved a fund from the contributions which he levied when he made treaties with Austria, Prussia, &c., in order to found these new families.   Speaking of some of the naval engagements, 'he found great fault with the French admiral who fought the battle of the Nile, and pointed out what he ought to have done ; but he found most fault with the admiral who fought Sir R. Calder for not disabling his fleet, and said that if he could have got the Channel clear then, or at any other time, he would have invaded England.'   Talleyrand, he declared, had advised the war with Spain, and Napoleon also made out that he had prevented him from saving the Duc d'Enghien.   Spain ought to have been conquered, and Napoleon declared that he would have gone there himself if the war with Russia had not occurred.   England would repent of bringing the Russians so far, and he added in this connection the remarkable words, 'They will deprive her of India.'

After lingering for a while in Vienna, Florence, Rome, Naples, and other cities, Lord John returned home by way of Germany, and on June 5 he spoke in Parliament against the renewal of hostilities.   He was one of the small minority in Parliament who refused to regard Napoleon's flight from Elba as a sufficient *casus belli*.   Counsels of peace, however, were naturally just then not likely to prevail, and Wellington's victory a fortnight later falsified Lord John's fears. He did not speak again until February 1816, when, in seconding an amendment to the Address, he protested against the continuance of the income-tax as a calamity to the country.   He pointed out that, although there had been repeated victories abroad, prosperity at home had vanished; that farmers could not pay their rents nor landlords their taxes ; and that everybody who was not paid out of the public purse felt that prosperity was gone.   A few weeks later he opposed the Army Estimates, contending that a standing army of 150,000 men 'must alarm every friend of his country and its constitution.'

It was probably owing in a measure to the hopelessness of the situation, but also partly to ill-health, that Lord John absented himself to a great extent from Parliament.   He was, in truth, chagrined at the course of affairs and discouraged with his own prospects, and in consequence he lapsed for a time into the position of a silent member of the House of Commons.   Meanwhile, the summer of 1816 was wet and cold and the harvest was in consequence a disastrous failure.   Wheat rose to 103s. a quarter, and bread riots broke out in the Eastern Counties.   The Luddites, who commenced breaking up machinery in manufacturing towns in 1811, again committed great excesses.   Tumults occurred in London, and the Prince Regent was insulted in the streets on his return from opening Parliament.

The Liverpool Cabinet gave way to panic, and quickly

resorted to extreme measures. A secret committee was appointed in each House to investigate the causes of the disaffection of a portion of his Majesty's subjects. Four bills were, as the result of their deliberations, swiftly introduced and passed through Parliament. The first enacted penalties for decoying sailors and soldiers ; the second was a pitiful exhibition of lack of confidence, for it aimed at special measures for the protection of the Prince Regent ; the third furnished magistrates with unusual powers for the prevention of seditious meetings ; and the fourth suspended the Habeas Corpus Act till July 1, giving the Executive authority 'to secure and detain such persons as his Majesty shall suspect are conspiring against his person and Government.'

The measures of the Government filled Lord John with indignation, and he assailed the proposal to suspend the Habeas Corpus Act in a vigorous speech, which showed conclusively that his sympathies were on the side of the weak and distressed classes of the community. 'I had not intended,' he said, 'to trouble the House with any observations of mine during the present session of Parliament. Indeed, the state of my health induced me to resolve upon quitting the fatiguing business of this House altogether. But he must have no ordinary mind whose attention is not roused in a singular manner when it is proposed to suspend the rights and liberties of Englishmen, though even for a short period. I am determined, for my own part, that no weakness of frame, no indisposition of body, shall prevent my protesting against the most dangerous precedent which this House ever made. We talk much— I think, a great deal too much—of the wisdom of our ancestors. I wish we could imitate the courage of our ancestors. They were not ready to lay their liberties at the foot of the Crown upon every vain or imaginary alarm.' He begged the majority not to give, by the adoption of a policy of coercion, the opponents of law and order the opportunity of saying, ' When we ask for redress you refuse all innovation ; when the Crown asks for protection you sanction a new code.'

All protests, as usual, were thrown away, and the bill was passed. Lord John resumed his literary tasks, and as a matter of fact only once addressed the House in the course of the next two years. He repeatedly declared his intention of entirely giving up politics and devoting his time to literature and travel. Many friends urged him to relinquish such an idea. Moore's poetical ' Remonstrance,' which gladdened Lord John not a little at the moment, is so well known that we need scarcely quote more than the closing lines :

> Thus gifted, thou never canst sleep in the shade ;
>   If the stirring of genius, the music of fame,
> And the charm of thy cause have not power to persuade,
>   Yet think how to freedom thou'rt pledged by thy name.
> Like the boughs of that laurel, by Delphi's decree
>   Set apart for the fane and its service divine,
> All the branches that spring from the old Russell tree
>   Are by Liberty claimed for the use of her shrine.'

Lord John's literary labours began at this time to be considerable. He also enlarged his knowledge of the world by giving free play to his love of foreign travel.

A general election occurred in the summer of 1818, and it proved that though the Tories were weakened they still had a majority. Lord John, with his uncle Lord William Russell, were, however, returned for Tavistock. Public affairs in 1819 were of a kind to draw him from his retirement, and as a matter of fact it was in that year that his speeches began to attract more than passing notice. He spoke briefly in favour of reducing the number of the Lords of the Admiralty, advocated an inquiry into domestic and foreign policy, protested against the surrender of the town of Parga, on the coast of Epirus, to the Turks, and made an energetic speech against the prevailing bribery and corruption which disgraced contested elections. The summer of that year was also rendered memorable in Lord John's career by his first speech on Parliamentary Reform. In July, Sir Francis Burdett, undeterred by previous overwhelming defeats, brought forward his usual sweeping motion demanding universal suffrage, equal electoral districts, vote by ballot, and annual Parliaments. Lord John's criticism was level-headed, and therefore characteristic. He had little sympathy with extreme measures, and he knew, moreover, that it was not merely useless but injurious to the cause of Reform to urge them at such a moment. The opposition was too powerful and too impervious to anything in the nature of an idea to give such proposals just then the least chance of success. Property meant to fight hard for its privileges, and the great landowners looked upon their pocket-boroughs as a goodly heritage as well as a rightful appanage of rank and wealth. As for the great unrepresented towns, they were regarded as hot-beds of sedition, and therefore the people were to be kept in their place, and that meant without a voice in the affairs of the nation. The close corporations and the corrupt boroughs were meanwhile dismissed with a shrug of the shoulders or a laugh of scorn.

Lord John was as yet by no means a full-fledged Reformer, but it was something in those days for a duke's son to take sides, even in a modified way, with the party of progress. His speech represented the views not so much of the multitude as of the middle classes. They were alarmed at the truculent violence of mob orators up and down the country : their fund of inherited reverence for the aristocracy was as yet scarcely diminished. They had their own dread of spoliation, and they had not quite recovered from their fright over the French Revolution. They were law abiding, moreover, and the blood and treasure which it had cost the nation to crush Napoleon had allayed in thousands of them the thirst for glory, and turned them into possibly humdrum but very sincere lovers of peace. Lord John's speech was an appeal to the average man in his strength and in his limitations, and men of cautious common-sense everywhere rejoiced that the young Whig—who was liked none the less by farmer and shopkeeper because he was a lord—had struck the nail exactly on the head. The growth of Lord John's influence in Parliament was watched at Woburn with keen interest. 'I have had a good deal of conversation,' wrote the Duke, 'with old Tierney at Cassiobury about you. . . . I find with pleasure that he has a very high opinion of your debating powers ; and says, if you will stick to one branch of politics and not range over too desultory a field, you may become eminently useful and conspicuous in the House of Commons. . . . The line I should recommend for your selection would be that of foreign politics, and all home politics bearing on civil and religious liberty—a pretty wide range. . . .'

As soon as the end of the session brought a respite from his Parliamentary duties Lord John started for the Continent with Moore the poet. The author of 'Lalla Rookh' was at that moment struggling, after the manner of the majority of poets at any moment, with the three-headed monster pounds, shillings, and pence, through the failure of his deputy in an official appointment at Bermuda. The poet's journal contains many allusions to Lord John, and the following passage from it, dated September 4, 1819, speaks for itself :—'Set off with Lord John in his carriage at seven ; breakfasted and arrived at Dover to dinner at seven o'clock ; the journey very agreeable. Lord John mild and sensible ; took off Talma very well. Mentioned Buonaparte having instructed Talma in the part of Nero ; correcting him for being in such a bustle in giving his orders, and telling him they ought to be given calmly, as coming from a person used to sovereignty.[1] After a fortnight in Paris the travellers went on to Milan, where they parted company, Moore going to Venice to visit Byron, and Lord John to Genoa, to renew a pleasant acquaintance with Madame Durazzo, an Italian lady of rank who was at one time well known in English society.

Madame Durazzo was a quick-witted and accomplished woman, and her vivacious and sympathetic nature was hardly less remarkable than her personal charm. There is evidence enough that she made a considerable impression upon the young English statesman, who, indeed, wrote a sonnet about her. Lord John's verdict on Italy and the Italians is pithily expressed in a hitherto unpublished extract from his journal :—'Italy is a delightful country for a traveller—every town full of the finest specimens of art, even now, and many marked by remains of antiquity near one another—all different. Easy travelling, books in plenty, living cheap and tolerably good—what can a man wish for but a little grace and good taste in dress amongst women ? Men of science abound in Italy—the Papal Government discouraged them at Rome ; but the country

---

[1] *Memoirs, Journal, and Correspondence of Thomas Moore.* Edited by the Right Hon. Lord John Russell, M.P.

cannot be said to be behind the world in knowledge.
Poets, too, are plenty; I never read their verses.'

Meanwhile, the condition of England was becoming
critical. Birmingham, Leeds, Manchester, and other great
towns were filled with angry discontent, and turbulent mass
meetings of the people were held to protest against any
further neglect of their just demands for political representation. Major Cartwright advised these great unrepresented
communities to 'send a petition in the form of a living man
instead of one on parchment or paper,' so that he might
state in unmistakable terms their demands to the Speaker.
Sir Charles Wolseley, a Staffordshire baronet and a friend
of Burdett, was elected with a great flourish of trumpets at
Birmingham to act in this capacity, and Manchester determined also to send a representative, and on August 16, 1819,
a great open-air meeting was called to give effect to this
resolution. The multitude were dispersed by the military,
and readers of Bamford's 'Passages in the Life of a Radical'
will remember his graphic and detailed description of the
scene of tumult and bloodshed which followed, and which
is known as the Peterloo Massacre. The carnage inspired
Shelley's magnificent 'Mask of Anarchy' : --

> . . . One fled past, a maniac maid,
> And her name was Hope, she said :
> But she looked more like Despair,
> And she cried out in the air :
>
> ' My father Time is weak and grey
> With waiting for a better day.'

In those days Parliament did not sit in August, and the
members of the Cabinet were not at hand when the crisis
arose. The Prince Regent expressed his approbation of the
conduct of the magistrates of Manchester as well as of that

of the officers and troops of the cavalry, whose firmness and effectual support of the civil power preserved the peace of the town. The Cabinet also lost no time in giving its emphatic support to the high-handed action of the Lancashire magistrates, and Major Cartwright and other leaders of the popular movement became the heroes of the hour because the Liverpool Administration was foolish enough to turn them into political martyrs by prosecuting them on the charge of sedition. Lord John at this crisis received several letters urging his return home immediately. That his influence was already regarded as of some importance is evident from the terms in which Sir James Mackintosh addressed him. ' You are more wanted than anybody, not only for general service, but because your Reform must be immediately brought forward—if possible, as the act of the party, but at all events as the creed of all Whig Reformers.' Writing to Moore from Genoa on November 9, Lord John says : 'I am just setting off for London. Mackintosh has written me an oily letter, to which I have answered by a vinegar one ; but I want you to keep me up in acerbity.'

Soon after Parliament met, the famous Six Acts—usually termed the ' Gagging Acts '—were passed, though not without strenuous opposition. These measures were intended to hinder delay in the administration of justice in the case of misdemeanour, to prevent the training of persons to the use of arms, to enable magistrates to seize and detain arms, to prevent seditious meetings, and to bring to punishment the authors of blasphemous and seditious libels. No meeting of more than fifty people was to be held without six days' notice to a magistrate ; only freeholders or inhabitants were to be allowed even to attend ; and adjournments were forbidden. The time and place of meeting were, if deemed advisable, to be changed by the local authorities, and no banners or flags were to be displayed. The wisdom of Lord Eldon, the patriotism of Lord Castlereagh, and the panic of Lord Sidmouth were responsible for these tyrannical enactments. On December 14 Lord John brought forward his first resolutions in favour of Reform. He proposed (1) that all boroughs in which gross and notorious bribery and corruption should be proved to prevail should cease to return members to Parliament ; (2) that the right so taken away should be given to some great town or to the largest counties ; (3) that it is the duty of the House to consider of further means to detect and to prevent corruption in Parliamentary elections ; (4) that it is expedient that the borough of Grampound should be disfranchised. Even Castlereagh complimented him on the manner in which he had introduced the question, and undertook that, if Lord John would withdraw the resolutions and bring in a bill to disfranchise Grampound, he would not oppose the proposition, and to this arrangement Lord John consented. Shortly before the dissolution of Parliament, consequent upon the death of the King, in January 1820, Lord John obtained leave to bring in a bill for suspending the issue of writs to the corrupt boroughs of Penryn, Camelford, Grampound, and Barnstaple. But the alarm occasioned by the Cato Street Conspiracy threw back the movement and awakened all the old prejudices against even the slightest concession.

At the general election of 1820 Lord John was returned for the county of Huntingdon. As soon as possible Lord John returned to the charge, and brought forward his measure for dealing with Grampound and to transfer the right of voting to Leeds, the franchise to be given to occupiers of houses rated at 5*l.* and upwards. In his 'Recollections and Suggestions' Lord John says: 'With a view to work my way to a change, not by eloquence—for I had none—but by patient toil and a plain statement of facts, I brought before the House of Commons the case of Grampound. I obtained an inquiry, and, with the assistance of Mr. Charles Wynn, I forced the solicitors employed in bribery to reveal the secrets of their employers : the case was clear ; the borough was convicted.' Whilst the debate was proceeding Queen Caroline arrived in England from the Continent, and was received with much popular enthusiasm. Hostile measures were at once taken in the House of Commons against her, and though the despicable proceedings eventually came to nought, they effectually stopped all further discussion of the question of Reform for the time being.

Like Canning and Brougham, Lord John took the side of the injured Queen, and he drew up a petition to George IV. begging him to end the further consideration of the Bill of Pains and Penalties against Caroline by proroguing Parliament. Such a request was entirely thrown away on a man of the character of George IV., for the King was bent on a policy of mean revenge ; and as only the honour of a woman was concerned, the 'first gentleman of Europe' found the Liverpool Administration obsequious enough to do his bidding. When at length public opinion prevailed and the proceedings against the Queen were withdrawn in November, and whilst rejoicings and illuminations were going on in London at the Queen's deliverance, Lord John went to Paris, remaining there till January. Moore was in Paris, and he was much in his company, and divided the rest of his time between

literature and society. He wrote his now forgotten novel,
'The Nun of Arrouca,' during the six weeks which he spent
in Paris. A Frenchman, visiting the poet, 'lamented that
his friend Lord John showed to so little advantage in
society from his extreme taciturnity, and still more from
his apparent coldness and indifference to what is said by
others. Several here to whom he was introduced had been
much disappointed in consequence of this manner.'

Lady Blessington, who was at that time living abroad,
states that Lord John came and dined with herself and the
Earl, and the comments of so beautiful and accomplished a
woman of fashion are at least worthy of passing record.
'Lord John was in better health and spirits than when I
remember him in England. He is exceedingly well read, and
has a quiet dash of humour, that renders his observations
very amusing. When the reserve peculiar to him is thawed,
he can be very agreeable. Good sense, a considerable power
of discrimination, a highly cultivated mind, a great equality
of temper, are the characteristics of Lord John Russell, and
these peculiarly fit him for taking a distinguished part in
public life.' Lady Blessington adds that the only obstacle,
in her opinion, to Lord John's success lays in the natural
reserve of his manners, which might lead people 'to think
him cold and proud.' This is exactly what happened, and
only those who knew Lord John intimately were aware of
the delicate consideration for others which lurked beneath
his somewhat frigid demeanour.

Early in the year 1821 Lord John reintroduced his bill
for the disfranchisement of Grampound. Several amendments were proposed, and one, brought forward by Mr.
Stuart Wortley, limiting the right to vote to 20*l.* householders,
was carried. Thereupon Lord John declined to take further

charge of the measure. After being altered and pruned by both Houses the bill was passed, in spite of Lord Eldon, 'with tears and doleful predictions,' urging the peers 'to resist this first turn of the helm towards the whirlpool of democracy.' Grampound ceased to exist as a Parliamentary borough, and the county of York gained two members. Although Lord John supported the amended bill—on the principle that half a loaf is better than no bread—he at the same time announced that 'in a future session he proposed to call attention to the claims of large towns to send members to this House.' He was determined to do all in his power to deprive what he termed the 'dead bones of a former state of England' of political influence, and to give representation to what he termed the 'living energy and industry of the England of the nineteenth century, with its steam-engines and its factories, its cotton and woollen cloths, its cutlery and its coal-mines, its wealth and its intelligence.' Whilst the bill about Grampound was being discussed by the Lords he took further action in this direction, and presented four resolutions for the discovery and punishment of bribery, the disfranchisement of corrupt boroughs, and the enfranchisement of wealthy and populous towns. On a division his proposals were defeated by thirty-one votes in a House of 279 members, and this, under all the circumstances, was a better result than he expected.

On April 25, 1822, Lord John again tested the feeling of Parliament with his motion 'that the present state of the representation requires serious consideration.' In the course of a speech of three hours he startled the House by proposing that 100 new members should be added, and, in order that the Commons should not be overcrowded, he added another resolution, to the effect that a similar number of the small boroughs should be represented by one member instead of two. Mr. Canning opposed such a scheme, but complimented Lord John on the ability he had displayed in its advocacy, and then added : 'That the noble lord will carry his motion this evening I have no fear ; but with the talents which he has shown himself to possess, and with (I sincerely hope) a long and brilliant career of Parliamentary distinction before him, he will, no doubt, renew his efforts hereafter. If, however, he shall persevere, and if his perseverance shall be successful, and if the results of that success shall be such as I cannot help apprehending, his be the triumph to have precipitated those results, be mine the consolation that, to the utmost and to the latest of my power, I have opposed them.'[1]

Little persuasion was necessary to win a hostile vote, and in a House of 433 members Lord John found himself in a minority of 164. Next year he renewed his attempt, but with the same result, and in 1826 he once more brought forward his proposals for Reform, to be defeated. Two months afterwards, however —May 26, 1826—undaunted by his repeated failures, he brought in a bill for the discovery and suppression of bribery at elections. The forces arrayed against him again proved too formidable, and Lord John, deeming it useless to proceed, abandoned the bill. He made one more attempt in the expiring Parliament, in a series of resolutions, to arrest political corruption, and when the division was taken the numbers were equal, whereupon the Speaker recorded his vote on Lord John's side. In June the House was dissolved.

The Whigs of the new generation were meanwhile dreaming of projects which had never entered into the cal-

[1] Canning's Speeches.

culations of their predecessors. Lord John long afterwards gave expression to the views which were beginning to prevail, such as non-interference in the internal government of other nations, the necessity of peace with America and the acknowledgment of her Independence, the satisfaction of the people of Ireland by the concession of political equality, the advancement of religious liberty, parliamentary reform, and the unrestricted liberty of the press. 'Had these principles,' he declares, 'prevailed from 1770 to 1820, the country would have avoided the American War and the first French Revolutionary War, the rebellion in Ireland in 1798, and the creation of three or four millions of national debt.'[1] Whenever opportunity allowed, Lord John sought in Parliament during the period under review to give practical effect to such convictions. He spoke in favour of the repeal of the Foreign Enlistment Bill, on the question of the evacuation of Spain by the French army, on the Alien Bill, on an inquiry into labourers' wages, on the Irish Insurrection Bill, on Roman Catholic claims and Roman Catholic endowment, and on agricultural distress.

During the closing years of George III.'s reign and the inglorious days of his successor, Lord John Russell rose slowly but steadily towards political influence and power. His speeches attracted growing attention, and his courage and common sense were rewarded with the deepening confidence of the nation. Although he was still regarded with some little dread by his 'betters and his elders,' to borrow his own phrase, the people hailed with satisfaction the rise of so honest, clear-headed, and dogged a champion of peace, retrenchment, and Reform. Court and Cabinet might look askance at the young statesman, but the great towns were

---

[1] *Recollections and Suggestions,* p. 43.

at his back, and he knew—in spite of all appearances to the contrary—that they, though yet unrepresented, were in reality stronger than all the forces of selfish privilege and senseless prejudice. Lord John had proved himself to be a man of action. The nation was beginning to dream that he would yet prove himself to be a man of mark.

CHAPTER III

WINNING HIS SPURS

1826–1830

Defeated and out of harness—Journey to Italy—Back in Parliament—
Canning's accession to power—Bribery and corruption—The re-
peal of the Test and Corporation Acts—The struggle between the
Court and the Cabinet over Catholic Emancipation—Defeat of
Wellington at the polls—Lord John appointed Paymaster-General.

WHIG optimists in the newspapers at the General Election of
1826 declared that the future welfare of the country would
depend much on the intelligence and independence of the
new Parliament. Ordinary men accustomed to look facts
in the face were not, however, so sanguine, and Albany
Fonblanque expressed the more common view amongst
Radicals when he asserted that if the national welfare turned
on the exhibition in an unreformed House of Commons of
such unparliamentary qualities as intelligence and independence, there would be ground not for hope but for despair.
He added that he saw no shadow of a reason for supposing
that one Parliament under the existing system would differ
in any essential degree from another. He maintained that,
while the sources of corruption continued to flow, legislation
would roll on in the same course.

Self-improvement was, in truth, the last thing to be expected from a House of Commons which represented vested
rights, and the interests and even the caprices of a few

individuals, rather than the convictions or needs of the nation. The Tory party was stubborn and defiant even when the end of the Liverpool Administration was in sight. The Test Acts were unrepealed, prejudice and suspicion shut out the Catholics from the Legislature, and the sacred rights of property triumphed over the terrible wrongs of the slave. The barbarous enactments of the Criminal Code had not yet been entirely swept away, and the municipal corporations, even to contemporary eyes, appeared as nothing less than sinks of corruption.

Lord John was defeated in Huntingdonshire, and, to his disappointment, found himself out of harness. He had hoped to bring in his Bribery Bill early in the session, and under the altered circumstances he persuaded Lord Althorp to press the measure forward. In a letter to that statesman which was afterwards printed, he states clearly the evils which he wished to remedy. A sentence or two will show the need of redress : 'A gentleman from London goes down to a borough of which he scarcely before knew the existence. The electors do not ask his political opinions ; they do not inquire into his private character ; they only require to be satisfied of the impurity of his intentions. If he is elected, no one, in all probability, contests the validity of his return. His opponents are as guilty as he is, and no other person will incur the expense of a petition for the sake of a public benefit. Fifteen days after the meeting of Parliament (this being the limit for the presentation of a petition), a handsome reward is distributed to each of the worthy and independent electors.'

In the early autumn Lord John quitted England, with the intention of passing the winter in Italy. The Duke of Bedford felt that his son had struck the nail on the head

with his pithy and outspoken letter to Lord Althorp on
political bribery, and he was not alone in thinking that Lord
John ought not to throw away such an advantage by a prolonged absence on the Continent. Lord William accordingly
wrote to his brother to urge a speedy return, and the letter
is worth quoting, since incidentally it throws light on another
aspect of Lord John's character : ' If you feel any ambition
—which you have not ; if you give up the charms of Genoa
—which you cannot ; if you could renounce the dinners and
tea-tables and gossips of Rome—which you cannot ; if you
would cease to care about attending balls and assemblies, and
dangling after ladies—which you cannot, there is a noble
field of ambition and utility opened to a statesman. It is Ireland, suffering, ill-used Ireland ! The gratitude of millions,
the applause of the world, would attend the man who would
rescue the poor country. The place is open, and must soon
be filled up. Ireland cannot remain as she is. The Ministers
feel it, and would gladly listen to any man who would point
out the way to relieve her. Undertake the task ; it is one
of great difficulty, but let that be your encouragement. See
the Pope's minister ; have his opinion on the Catholic
question ; go to Ireland ; find out the causes of her
suffering ; make yourself master of the subject. Set to work,
as you did about Reform, by curing small evils at first. . . .
I am pointing to the way for you to make your name immortal, by doing good to millions and to your country.
But you will yawn over this, and go to some good dinner
to be agreeable, the height of ambition with the present
generation.'

Meanwhile, through the influence of the Duke of Devonshire, Lord John was elected in November for the Irish
borough of Bandon Bridge, and in February, fresh from

prologue-writing for the private theatricals which Lord Normanby was giving that winter in Florence, he took his seat in the House of Commons. Lord Liverpool was struck down with paralysis on February 18, and it quickly became apparent that his case was hopeless. After a few weeks of suspense, which were filled with Cabinet intrigues, Mr. Canning received the King's commands to reconstruct the Ministry; but this was more easily said than done. 'Lord Liverpool's disappearance from the political scene,' says Lord Russell, 'gave rise to a great *débâcle*. The fragments of the old system rushed against each other, and for a time all was confusion.' Six of Canning's colleagues flatly refused to serve under him in the new Cabinet—Peel, Wellington, Eldon, Westmoreland, Bathurst, and Bexley—though the latter afterwards took advantage of his second thoughts and returned to the fold. Although an opponent of Parliamentary reform and of the removal of Nonconformist disabilities, Canning gave his support to Catholic emancipation, to the demand for free trade, and the abolition of slavery. Canning's accession to power threw the Tory ranks into confusion. 'The Tory party,' states Lord Russell, 'which had survived the follies and disasters of the American war, which had borne the defeats and achieved the final glories of the French war, was broken by its separation from Mr. Canning into fragments, which could not easily be reunited.'

Sydney Smith—who, by the way, had no love for Canning, and failed to a quite noteworthy extent to understand him—like the rest, took a gloomy view of the situation, which he summed up in his own inimitable fashion. 'Politics, domestic and foreign, are very discouraging; Jesuits abroad, Turks in Greece, "No Poperists" in England! A panting to burn B ; B fuming to roast C ; C miserable that he can't reduce D to ashes ; and D consigning to eternal perdition the first three letters of the alphabet.' Canning's tenure of power was brief and uneasy. His opponents were many, his difficulties were great, and, to add to all, his health was failing. 'My position,' was his own confession, 'is not that of gratified ambition.' His Administration only lasted five months, for at the end of that period death cut short the brilliant though erratic and disappointed career of a states-man of courage and capacity, who entered public life as a follower of Pitt, and refused in after years to pin his faith blindly to either political party, and so incurred the suspicions alike of uncompromising Whigs and unbending Tories.

During the Canning Administration, Lord John's influence in the House made itself felt, and always along progressive lines. When the annual Indemnity Bill for Dissenters came up for discussion, he, in answer to a taunt that the Whigs were making political capital out of the Catholic question, and at the same time neglecting the claims of the Nonconformists, declared that he was ready to move the repeal of restrictions upon the Dissenters as soon as they themselves were of opinion that the moment was ripe for action. This virtual challenge, as will be presently seen, was recognised by the Nonconformists as a call to arms. Meanwhile cases of flagrant bribery at East Retford and Penryn—two notoriously corrupt boroughs—came before the House, and it was proposed to disenfranchise the former and to give in its place two members to Birmingham. The bill, however, did not get beyond its second reading. Lord John, nothing daunted, proposed in the session of 1828 that Penryn should suffer disenfranchisement, and that Manchester should take its place. This was ultimately carried in the House of Commons ; but the Peers fought shy of Manchester, and preferred to 'amend' the bill by widening the right of voting at Penryn to the adjacent Hundred. This refusal to take occasion by the hand and to gratify the political aspirations of the most important unrepresented town in the kingdom, did much to hasten the introduction of a wider scheme of reform.

Power slipped for the moment on the death of Canning into the weak hands of Lord Goderich, who tried ineffectually to keep together a Coalition Ministry. Lord John's best friends appear to have been apprehensive at this juncture lest the young statesman, in the general confusion of parties, should lapse into somewhat of a political Laodicean. 'I feel a little anxious,' wrote Moore, 'to know exactly the colour of your politics just now, as from the rumours I hear of some of your brother " watchmen," Althorp, Milton, and the like, I begin sometimes to apprehend that you too may be among the fallers off. Lord Lansdowne tells me, however, you continue quite staunch, and for his sake I hope so.' But Lord John was not a 'faller off.' His eyes were fully open to the anomalous position in which he in common with other members of the party of reform had been placed under Canning and Goderich. Relief, however, came swiftly. Lord Goderich, after four months of feeble semblance of authority, resigned, finding it impossible to adjust differences. As a subaltern, declared one who had narrowly watched his career, Lord Goderich was respectable, but as a chief he proved himself to be despicable. The Duke of Wellington became Prime Minister, with a Tory Cabinet at his back, and with Peel as leader in the House of Commons. Thus the 'great *débâcle*,' which commenced with Canning's accession to power—in spite of the presence in the Cabinet of Palmerston and Huskisson—drew to an end, and a line of cleavage was once more apparent between the Whigs and the Tories. With Wellington, Lord John had of course neither part nor lot, and when the Duke accepted office he promptly ranged himself in the opposite camp.

Ireland was on the verge of rebellion when Wellington and Peel took office, and in the person of O'Connell it possessed a leader of splendid eloquence and courage, who pressed the claims of the Roman Catholics for immediate relief from religious disabilities. Whilst the Government was deliberating upon the policy which they ought to pursue in presence of the stormy and menacing agitation which had arisen in Ireland, the Protestant Dissenters saw their opportunity, and rallied their forces into a powerful organisation for the total repeal of the Test and Corporation Acts. Their cause had been quietly making way, through the Press and the platform, during the dark years for political and religious liberty which divide 1820 from 1828, and the Protestant Society had kept the question steadily before the public mind. Meanwhile that organisation had itself become a distinct force in the State. 'The leaders of the Whig party now formally identified themselves with it. In one year the Duke of Sussex took the chair ; in another Lord Holland occupied the same position ; Sir James Mackintosh delivered from its platform a defence of religious liberty, such as had scarcely been given to the English people since the time of Locke ; and Lord John Russell, boldly identifying himself and his party with the political interests of Dissenters, came forward as chairman in another year, to advocate the full civil and religious rights of the three millions who were now openly connected with one or other of the Free Churches. The period of the Revolution, when

Somers, Halifax, Burnet, and their associates laid the foundations of constitutional government, seemed to have returned.'[1] Immediately Parliament assembled, Lord John Russell—backed by many petitions from the Nonconformists—gave notice that on February 26 it was his intention to move the repeal of the Test and Corporation Acts.

The Test Act compelled all persons holding any office of profit and trust under the Crown to take the oath of allegiance, to partake of the Sacrament according to the rites of the Church of England, and to subscribe the declaration against Transubstantiation. It was an evil legacy from the reign of Charles II., and became law in 1673. The Corporation Act was also placed on the statute-book in the same reign, and in point of time twelve years earlier— namely, in 1661. It was a well-directed blow against the political ascendency of Nonconformists in the cities and towns. It required all public officials to take the Sacrament according to the rites of the Church of England, within twelve months of their appointment, and, whilst it excluded conscientious men, it proved no barrier to unprincipled hypocrites. The repeal of the Test and Corporation Acts had been mooted from time to time, but the forces of prejudice and apathy had hitherto proved invincible. Fox espoused the cause of the Dissenters in 1790, and moved for a committee of the whole House to deal with the question. He urged that men were to be judged not by their opinions, but by their actions, and he asserted that no one could charge the Dissenters with ideas or conduct dangerous to the State. Parliament, he further contended, had practically admitted the injustice of such disqualifications by passing annual Acts

[1] *History of the Free Churches of England*, pp. 457-458, by H. S. Skeats and C. S. Miall.

of Indemnity. He laid stress on the loyalty which the Dissenters had shown during the Jacobite risings of 1715 and 1745, when the High Church party, which now resisted their just demands, had been 'hostile to the reigning family, and active in exciting tumults, insurrections, and rebellions.' The authority of Pitt and the eloquence of Burke were put forth in opposition to the repeal of the Test Acts, and the panic awakened by the French Revolution threw Parliament into a reactionary mood, which rendered reform in any direction impossible. The result was that the question, so far as the House of Commons was concerned, was shirked from 1790 until 1828, when Lord John Russell took up the advocacy of a cause in which, nearly forty years earlier, the genius of Charles James Fox had been unavailingly enlisted.

In moving the repeal of the Test and Corporation Acts, Lord John recapitulated their history and advanced cogent arguments on behalf of the rights of conscience. It could not, he contended, be urged that these laws were necessary for the security of the Church, for they were not in force either in Scotland or in Ireland. The number and variety of offices embraced by the Test Act reduced the measure, so far as its practical working was concerned, to a palpable absurdity, as non-commissioned officers, as well as commissioned excisemen, tide-waiters, and even pedlars, were embraced in its provisions. In theory, at least, the penalties incurred by these different classes of men were neither few nor slight—forfeiture of the office, disqualification for any other under Government, incapacity to maintain a suit at law, to act as guardian or executor, or to inherit a legacy, and even liability to a pecuniary penalty of 500*l.*! Of course, such ridiculous penalties were in most cases suspended, but the law which imposed them still disgraced the statute-book, and was acknowledged by all unprejudiced persons to be indefensible. Besides, the most Holy Sacrament of the Christian Church was habitually reduced to a mere civil form imposed by Act of Parliament upon persons who either derided its solemn meaning or might be spiritually unfit to receive it. Was it decent, asked Cowper in his famous 'Expostulation,' thus—

> To make the symbols of atoning grace
> An office-key, a pick-lock to a place?

To such a question, put in such a form, only one answer was possible. Under circumstances men took the Communion, declared Lord John, for the purpose of qualifying for office, and with no other intent, and the least worthy were the most unscrupulous. 'Such are the consequences of mixing politics with religion. You embitter and aggravate political dissensions by the venom of theological disputes, and you profane religion with the vices of political ambition, making it both hateful to man and offensive to God.'

Peel opposed the motion, and professed to regard the grievances of the Dissenters as more sentimental than real. Huskisson and Palmerston followed on the same side, whilst Althorp and Brougham lent their aid to the demand for religious liberty. The result of the division showed a majority of forty-four in favour of the motion, and the bill was accordingly brought in and read a second time without discussion. During the progress of the measure through the House of Lords, the two Archbishops—less fearful for the safety of the Established Church than some of their followers—met Lord John's motion for the repeal of the Acts in a liberal and enlightened manner. 'Religious tests,' said Archbishop Harcourt of York, 'imposed for political purposes, must in themselves be always liable more or less to endanger religious sincerity.'   Such an admission, of course, materially strengthened Lord John Russell's hands, and prepared the way for a speedy revision of the law. Many who had hitherto supported the Test Act began to see that such measures were, after all, a failure and a sham. If their terms were so lax that any man could subscribe to them with undisturbed conscience, then they ceased to be any test at all.   On the contrary, if they were hard and rigid, then they forced men to the most odious form of dissimulation.   A declaration, if required by the Crown, was therefore substituted for the sacramental test, by which a person entering office pledged himself not to use its influence as a means for subverting the Established Church.   On the motion of the Bishop of Llandaff, the words 'on the true faith of a Christian' were inserted in the declaration—a clause which, by the way, had the effect, as Lord Holland perceived at the time, of excluding Jews from Parliament until the year 1858.

Lord Winchilsea endeavoured by an amendment to shut out Unitarians from the relief thus afforded to conscience, but, happily, such an intolerant proceeding, even in an unreformed Parliament, met with no success.   Lord Eldon fiercely attacked the measure—'like a lion,' as he said, 'but with his talons cut off'—but met with little support.   It was felt that the great weight of authority as well as argument was in favour of the liberal policy which Lord John Russell advocated, and hence, after a protracted debate, the cause of religious freedom triumphed, and on May 9, 1828, the Test and Corporation Acts were finally repealed. A great and forward impulse was thus given to the cause of religious equality, and under the same energetic leadership the party of progress set themselves with fresh hope to invade other citadels of privilege.

The victory came as a surprise not merely to Lord John but also to the Nonconformists. The fact that a Tory Government was in power was responsible for the widespread anticipation of a bitter and protracted struggle. Amongst the congratulations which Lord John received, none perhaps was more significant than Lord Grey's generous admission that 'he had done more than any man now living' on behalf of liberty. 'I am a little anxious,' wrote Moore, 'to know that your glory has done you no harm in the way of health, as I see you are a pretty constant attendant on the House. There is nothing, I fear, worse for a man's constitution than to trouble himself too much about the constitution of Church and State. So pray let me have one line to say how you are.' 'My constitution, wrote back Lord John, ' is not quite so much improved as the Constitution of the country by late events, but the joy of it will soon revive me. It is really a gratifying thing to force the enemy to give up his first line—that none but Churchmen are worthy to serve the State ; I trust we shall soon make him give up the second, that none but Protestants are.'

Lord Eldon had predicted that Catholic Emancipation would follow on the heels of the repeal of the Test and Corporation Acts, and the event proved that he was right. The election of Daniel O'Connell for Clare had suddenly raised the question in an acute form. Although the followers of Canning had already left the Ministry, the Duke of Wellington and Peel found themselves powerless to quell the agitation which O'Connell and the Catholic Associa-

tion had raised in Ireland by any means short of civil war.
'What our Ministry will do,' wrote Lord John, ' Heaven
only knows, but I cannot blame O'Connell for being a
little impatient, after twenty-seven years of just expectation
disappointed.' The allusion was, of course, to Pitt's
scheme at the beginning of the century to enable Catholics
to sit in Parliament and so to reconcile the Irish people to
the Union—a generous project which was brought to nought
by the obstinate attitude of George III. Lord John was
meditating introducing a measure for Catholic Emancipation,
when Peel took the wind from his sails. George IV., however, supported by a majority of the Lords Spiritual and
Temporal, was as stoutly opposed to concession as George III.
Lord John Russell's words on this point are significant
'George III.'s religious scruples, and even his personal
prejudices, were respected by the nation, and formed real
barriers so long as he did not himself waive them ; the
religious scruples of George IV. did not meet with ready
belief, nor did his personal dislikes inspire national respect
nor obtain national acquiescence.' The struggle between
the Court and the Cabinet was, however, of brief duration,
and Wellington bore down the opposition of the Lords, and
on April 13, 1829, the Roman Catholic Emancipation Bill
became law.

In June the question of Parliamentary reform was
brought before Parliament by Lord Blandford, but his resolutions—which were the outcome of Tory panic concerning
the probable result of Roman Catholic Emancipation—met
with little favour, either then or when they were renewed at
the commencement of the session of 1830. Lord Blandford
had in truth made himself conspicuous by his opposition to
the Catholic claims, and the nation distrusted the sudden

zeal of the heir to Blenheim in such a cause. On February 23, 1830, Lord John Russell sought leave to bring in a bill for conferring the franchise upon Manchester, Birmingham, and Leeds, on the plea that they were the three largest unrepresented towns in the country. The moderate proposal was, however, rejected in a House of three hundred and twenty-eight members by a majority of forty-eight. Three months later Mr. O'Connell brought forward a motion for Triennial Parliaments, Universal Suffrage, and the adoption of the Ballot; but this was rejected. But in a House of three hundred and thirty-two members, only thirteen were in favour of it, whilst an amendment by Lord John stating that it was ' expedient to extend the basis of the representation of the people ' was also rejected by a majority of ninety-six. On June 26 George IV. died, and a few weeks later Parliament was dissolved. At the General Election, Lord John stood for Bedford, and, much to his chagrin, was defeated by a single vote. After the declaration of the poll in August, he crossed over to Paris, where he prolonged his stay till November. The unconstitutional ordinances of July 25, 1830, had brought about a revolution, and Lord John Russell, who was intimate with the chief statesman concerned, was wishful to study the crisis on the spot, and in the recital of its dramatic incidents to find relief from his own political disappointment.

During this visit he used his influence with General Lafayette for the life of Prince de Polignac, who was connected by marriage with a noble English family, and was about to be put on his trial. Lord John was intimately acquainted, not only with Lafayette, but with other leaders in the French political world, and his intercession, on which his friends in England placed much reliance, seems to have carried effectual weight, for the Prince's life was spared.

With distress at home and revolution abroad, signs of the coming change made themselves felt at the General Election.   Outside the pocket boroughs, the Ministerialists went almost everywhere to the wall, and 'not a single member of the Duke of Wellington's Cabinet obtained a seat in the new Parliament by anything approaching to free and open election.'[1]   The first Parliament of William IV. met on October 26, and two or three days later, in the debate on the King's Speech, Wellington made his now historic statement in answer to Earl Grey, who resented the lack of reference to Reform : 'I am not prepared to bring forward any measure of the description alluded to by the noble lord.   I am not only not prepared to bring forward any measure of this nature, but I will at once declare that, as far as I am concerned, as long as I hold any station in the government of the country, I shall always feel it my duty to resist such measures when proposed by others.'

This statement produced a feeling of dismay even in the calm atmosphere of the House of Lords, and the Duke, noticing the scarcely suppressed excitement, turned to one of his colleagues and whispered : 'What can I have said which seems to have made so great a disturbance?' Quick came the dry retort of the candid friend : ' You have announced the fall of your Government, that is all.'   The consternation was almost comic.   'Never was there an act of more egregious folly, or one so universally condemned,' says Charles Greville.   'I came to town last night (five days after the Duke's speech), and found the town ringing with

1 *The Three Reforms of Parliament*, by William Heaton, chap. ii. p. 38.

his imprudence and everybody expecting that a few days would produce his resignation.' Within a fortnight the general expectation was fulfilled, for on November 16 the Duke, making a pretext of an unexpected defeat over Sir H. Parnell's motion regarding the Civil List, threw up the sponge, and Lord Grey was sent for by the King and entrusted with the new Administration. The irony of the situation became complete when Lord Grey made it a stipulation to his acceptance of office that Parliamentary Reform should be a Cabinet measure.

Lord John, meanwhile, was a candidate for Tavistock, and when the election was still in progress the new Premier offered him the comparatively unimportant post of Paymaster-General, and, though he might reasonably have expected higher rank in the Government, he accepted the appointment. He was accustomed to assert that the actual duties of the Paymaster were performed by cashiers ; and he has left it on record that the only official act of any importance that he performed was the pleasant task of allotting garden-plots at Chelsea to seventy old soldiers, a boon which the pensioners highly appreciated.

CHAPTER IV

A FIGHT FOR LIBERTY

1830–1832

Lord Grey and the cause of Reform—Lord Durham's share in the
Reform Bill—The voice of the people—Lord John introduces the
Bill and explains its provisions—The surprise of the Tories—
'Reform, Aye or No'—Lord John in the Cabinet—The Bill thrown
out—The indignation of the country—Proposed creation of Peers
—Wellington and Sidmouth in despair—The Bill carried—Lord
John's tribute to Althorp.

EARL GREY was a man of sixty-six when he was called to
power, and during the whole of his public career he had
been identified with the cause of Reform. He, more than
any other man, was the founder, in 1792—the year in which
Lord John Russell was born—of 'The Friends of the People,'
a political association which united the forces of the patriotic
societies which just then were struggling into existence in
various parts of the land. He was the foe of Pitt and the
friend of Fox, and his official career began during the
short-lived but glorious Administration of All the Talents.
During the dreary quarter of a century which succeeded,
when the destinies of England were committed to men of
despotic calibre and narrow capacity like Sidmouth, Liverpool, Eldon, and Castlereagh, he remained, through good
and evil report, in deed as well as in name, a Friend of the
People. As far back as 1793, he declared : 'I am more

convinced than ever that a reform in Parliament might now be peaceably effected. I am afraid that we are not wise enough to profit by experience, and what has occasioned the ruin of other Governments will overthrow this—a perseverance in abuse until the people, maddened by excessive injury and roused to a feeling of their own strength, will not stop within the limits of moderate reformation.' The conduct of Ministers during the dark period which followed the fall of the Ministry of All the Talents in 1807, was, in Grey's deliberate opinion, calculated to excite insurrection, since it was a policy of relentless coercion and repression.

He made no secret of his conviction that the Government, by issuing proclamations in which whole classes of the community were denounced as seditious, as well as by fulminating against insurrections that only existed in their own guilty imaginations, filled the minds of the people with false alarms, and taught every man to distrust if not to hate his neighbour. There was no more chance of Reform under the existing *régime* than of ' a thaw in Zembla,' to borrow a famous simile. Cobbett was right in his assertion that the measures and manners of George IV.'s reign did more to shake the long-settled ideas of the people in favour of monarchical government than anything which had happened since the days of Cromwell. The day of the King's funeral—it was early in July and beautifully fine—was marked, of course, by official signs of mourning, but the rank and file of the people rejoiced, and, according to a contemporary record, the merry-making and junketing in the villages round London recalled the scenes of an ordinary Whit Monday.

On the whole, the nation accepted the accession of the Sailor King with equanimity, though scarcely with enthusiasm, and for the moment it was not thought that the new reign would bring an immediate change of Ministry. The dull, uncompromising nonsense, however, which Wellington put into the King's lips in the Speech from the Throne at the beginning of November, threatening with punishment the seditious and disaffected, followed as it quickly was by the Duke's own statement in answer to Lord Grey, that no measure of Parliamentary reform should be proposed by the Government as long as he was responsible for its policy, awoke the storm which drove the Tories from power and compelled the King to send for Grey. The distress in the country was universal—riots prevailed, rick-burning was common. Lord Grey's prediction of 1793 seemed about to be fulfilled, for the people, 'maddened by excessive injury and roused to a feeling of their own strength,' seemed about to break the traces and to take the bit between their teeth. The deep and widespread confidence alike in the character and capacity of Lord Grey did more than anything else at that moment to calm the public mind and to turn wild clamour into quiet and resistless enthusiasm.

Yet in certain respects Lord Grey was out of touch with the new spirit of the nation. If his own political ardour had not cooled, the lapse of years had not widened to any perceptible degree his vision of the issues at stake. He was a man of stately manners and fastidious tastes, and, though admirably qualified to hold the position of leader of the aristocratic Whigs, he had little in common with the toiling masses of the people. He was a conscientious and even chivalrous statesman, but he held himself too much aloof from the rank and file of his party, and thin-skinned Radicals were inclined to think him somewhat cold and even condescending. Lord Grey lacked the warm heart of Fox, and his speeches, in consequence, able and philosophic though they were, were destitute of that unpremeditated and magical eloquence which led Grattan to describe Fox's oratory as 'rolling in, resistless as the waves of the Atlantic.' On one memorable occasion—the second reading of the Reform Bill in the House of Lords—Lord Grey entirely escaped from such oratorical restraints, and even the Peers were moved to unwonted enthusiasm by the strong emotion which pervaded that singularly outspoken appeal.

His son-in-law, Lord Durham, on the other hand, had the making of a great popular leader, in spite of his imperious manners and somewhat dictatorial bearing. The head of one of the oldest families in the North of England, Lord Durham entered the House of Commons in the year 1813, at the age of twenty-one, as Mr. John George Lambton, and quickly distinguished himself by his advanced views on questions of foreign policy as well as Parliamentary reform. He married the daughter of Lord Grey in 1816, and gave his support in Parliament to Canning. On the formation of his father-in-law's Cabinet in 1830, he was appointed Lord Privy Seal. His popular sobriquet, 'Radical Jack,' itself attests the admiration of the populace, and when Lambton was raised to the peerage in 1828 he carried to the House of Lords the enthusiastic homage as well as the great expectations of the crowd. Lord Durham was the idol of the Radicals, and his presence in the Grey Administration was justly regarded as a pledge of energetic action.

He would unquestionably have had the honour of introducing the Reform Bill in the House of Commons if he had still been a member of that assembly, for he had made the question peculiarly his own, and behind him lay the enthusiasm of the entire party of Reform. Althorp, though leader of the House, and in spite of the confidence which his character inspired, lacked the power of initiative and the Parliamentary courage necessary to steer the Ship of State through such rough waters. When Lord Grey proposed to entrust the measure to Lord John, Brougham pushed the claims of Althorp, and raised objections to Lord John on the ground that the young Paymaster-General was not in the Cabinet ; but Durham stoutly opposed him, and urged that Lord John had the first claim, since he had last been in possession of the question.

An unpublished paper of Lord Durham's, in the possession of the present Earl, throws passing light on the action, at this juncture, of the Ministry, and therefore it may be well to quote it. 'Shortly after the formation of the Government, Lord Grey asked me in the House of Lords if I would assist him in preparing the Reform Bill. I answered that I would do so with the greatest pleasure. He then said, " You can have no objection to consult Lord John Russell ? " I replied, "Certainly not, but the reverse." ' In consequence of this conversation, Lord Durham goes on to state, he placed himself in communication with Lord John, and they together agreed to summon to their councils Sir James Graham and Lord Duncannon. Thus the famous Committee of Four came into existence. Durham acted as chairman, and in that capacity signed the daily minutes of the proceedings. The meetings were held at his house in Cleveland Row, and he there received, on behalf of Lord Grey, the various deputations from different parts of the kingdom which were flocking up to impress their views of the situation on the new Premier. Since the measure had of necessity to originate in the House of Commons, and Lord John, it was already settled, was to be its first spokesman, Lord Durham suggested that Russell should draw up a plan. This was done, and it was carefully discussed and amended in various directions, and eventually the measure as finally agreed upon was submitted to Lord Grey, with a report which Lord Durham, as chairman, drew up, and which was signed not only by him but by his three colleagues. Lord Durham states, in speaking of the part he took as chairman of the Committee on Reform, that Lord Grey intrusted him with the preparation in the first instance of the measure, and that he called to his aid the three other statesmen. He adds : 'This was no Cabinet secret, for it was necessarily known to hundreds, Lord Grey having referred to me all the memorials from different towns and bodies.' Lord Durham was in advance of his colleagues on this as upon most questions, for he took his stand on household suffrage, vote by ballot and triennial Parliaments, and if he could have carried his original draft of the Reform Bill that measure would have been far more revolutionary than that which became law. His proposals in the House of Commons in 1821 went, in fact, much further than the measure which became law under Lord Grey.

Lord Grey announced in the Lords on February 3 that a Reform measure had been framed and would be introduced in the House of Commons on March 1 by Lord John Russell, who, ' having advocated the cause of Parliamentary Reform, with ability and perseverance, in days when it was not popular, ought, in the opinion of the Administration, to be selected, now that the cause was prosperous, to bring forward a measure of full and efficient Reform, instead of the partial measures he had hitherto proposed.'

Petitions in favour of Reform from all parts of the kingdom poured into both Houses. The excitement in the country rose steadily week by week, mingled with expressions of satisfaction that the Bill was to be committed to the charge of such able hands. In Parliament speculations were rife as to the scope of the measure, whilst rumours of dissension in the Cabinet flew around the clubs. Even as late as the middle of February, the Duke of Wellington went about predicting that the Reform question could not be carried, and that the Grey Administration could not stand. Ministers contrived to keep their secret uncommonly well, and when at length the eventful day, March 1, arrived, the House of Commons was packed by a crowd such as had scarcely been seen there in its history. Troops of eager politicians came up from the country and waited at all the inlets of the House, whilst the leading supporters of the Whigs in London society gathered at dinner-parties, and anxiously awaited intelligence from Westminster.

Lord John's speech began at six o'clock, and lasted for two hours and a quarter. Beginning in a low voice, he proceeded gradually to unfold his measure, greeted in turns by cheers of approval and shouts of derision. Greville says it was ludicrous to see the faces of the members for those places doomed to disfranchisement, as they were severally announced. Wetherell, a typical Tory of the no-surrender school, began to take notes as the plan was unfolded, but after various contortions and grimaces he threw down his paper, with a look of mingled despair, ridicule, and horror. Lord Durham, seated under the gallery, doubted the reality of the scene passing before his eyes. 'They are mad, they are mad!' was one of the running comments to Lord John's statement. The Opposition, on the whole, seemed inclined to laugh out of court such extravagant proposals, but Peel, on the contrary, looked both grave and angry, for he saw further than most, and knew very well that boldness was the best chance. 'Burdett and I walked home together,' states Hobhouse, 'and agreed that there was very little chance of the measure being carried. We thought our friends in Westminster would oppose the ten-pound franchise.'

'I rise, sir,' Lord John commenced, 'with feelings of the deepest anxiety to bring forward a question which, unparalleled as it is in importance, is as unparalleled in points of difficulty. Nor is my anxiety, in approaching this question, lessened by reflecting that on former occasions I have brought this subject before the consideration of the House. For if, on other occasions, I have invited the attention of the House of Commons to this most important subject, it has been upon my own responsibility—unaided by anyone—and involving no one in the consequences of defeat . . . But the measure which I have now to bring forward, is a measure, not of mine but of the Government. . . . It is, therefore, with the greatest anxiety that I venture to explain their intentions to this House on a subject, the interest of which is shown by the crowded audience who have assembled here, but still more by the deep interest which is felt by millions out of this House, who look with anxiety, with hope, and with expectation, to the result of this day's debate.'

In the course of his argument, setting forth the need of Reform, he alluded to the feelings of a foreigner, having heard of British wealth, civilisation, and renown, coming to England to examine our institutions. 'Would not such a foreigner be much astonished if he were taken to a green mound, and informed that it sent two members to the British Parliament; if he were shown a stone wall, and told that it also sent two members to the British Parliament; or, if he walked into a park, without the vestige of a dwelling, and was told that it, too, sent two members to the British Parliament? But if he were surprised at this, how much more would he be astonished if he were carried into the North of England, where he would see large flourishing towns, full of trade, activity, and intelligence, vast magazines of wealth and manufactures, and were told that these places sent no representatives to Parliament. But his wonder would not end here; he would be astonished if he were carried to such a place as Liverpool, and were there told that he might see a specimen of a popular election, what would be the result? He would see bribery employed in the most unblushing manner, he would see every voter receiving a number of guineas in a box as the price of his corruption; and after such a spectacle would he not be indeed surprised that representatives so chosen could possibly perform the functions of legislators, or enjoy respect in any degree?' In speaking of the reasons for giving representatives to Manchester, Leeds, Birmingham, and other large towns, Lord John argued: 'Because Old Sarum sent members to Parliament in the reign of Edward III., when it had a population to be benefited by it, the Government on the same principle deprived that forsaken place of the franchise in order to bestow the privilege where the population was now found.

Lord John explained that by the provisions of the bill sixty boroughs with less than 2,000 inhabitants were to lose the franchise; forty-seven boroughs, returning ninety-four members, were to lose one member each. Of the seats thus placed at the disposal of the Government eight were to be given to London, thirty-four to large towns, fifty-five to English counties, five to Scotland, three to Ireland, and one to Wales. The franchise was to be extended to inhabitants of houses rated at ten pounds a year, and to leaseholders and copyholders of counties. It was reckoned that about half a million persons would be enfranchised by the bill; but the number of members in the House would be reduced by sixty-two. Lord John laid significant stress on the fact that they had come to the deliberate opinion that 'no half-measures would be sufficient, that no trifling, no paltry reform could give stability to the Crown, strength to the Parliament, or satisfaction to the country.' Long afterwards Lord John Russell declared that the measure when thus first placed before the House of Commons awoke feelings of astonishment mingled with joy or with consternation according to the temper of the hearers. 'Some, perhaps many, thought that the measure was a pre-lude to civil war, which, in point of fact, it averted. But incredulity was the prevailing feeling, both among the moderate Whigs and the great mass of the Tories. The Radicals alone were delighted and triumphant. Joseph Hume, whom I met in the streets a day or two afterwards, as-sured me of his hearty support of the Government.' There were many Radicals, however, who thought that the measure scarcely went far enough, and one of them happily summed up the situation by saying that, although the Reform Bill did not give the people all they wanted, it broke up the old system and took the weapons from the hands of the enemies of progress.

Night after night the debate proceeded, and it became plain that the Tories had been completely taken by surprise Meanwhile outside the House of Commons the people fol-lowed the debate with feverish interest. 'Nothing talked of, thought of, dreamt of but Reform,' wrote Greville.

'Every creature one meets asks, " What is said now ? How will it go ? What is the last news ? What do you think ? " And so it is from morning till night, in the streets, in the clubs, and in private houses.' After a week of controversy, leave was given to bring in the bill. On March 21, Lord John moved the second reading, but was met by an amendment, that the Reform Bill be read a second time that day six months. The House divided at three o'clock on the morning of the 23rd, and the second reading was carried by a majority of one—333-332—in the fullest House on record. 'It is better to capitulate than to be taken by storm,' was the comment of one of the cynics of the hour. Illuminations took place all over the country. The people were good-humoured but determined, and the Opposition began to recover from its fright and to declare that the Government could not proceed with the measure and were certain to resign. Peel's action—and sometimes his lack of it—was severely criticised by many of his own followers, and not a few of the Tories, unable to forgive the surrender to the claims of the Catholics, met the new crisis in the time-honoured spirit of Gallio. They seemed to have thought not only that the country was fast going to the dogs, but that under all the circumstances, it did not much matter.

Parliament met after the usual Easter recess, and on April 18 General Gascoigne moved as an instruction to the committee that the number of members of Parliament ought not to be diminished, and after a debate which lasted till four o'clock in the morning the resolution was carried in a House of 490 members by a majority of eight. The Government thus suddenly placed in a minority saw their opportunity and took it. Lord Grey and his colleagues had begun

to realise that it was impossible for them to carry the Reform
Bill in the existing House of Commons without modifica-
tions which would have robbed the boon of half its worth.
The Tories had made a blunder in tactics over Gascoigne's
motion, and their opponents took occasion by the forelock,
with the result that, after an extraordinary scene in the Lords,
Parliament was suddenly dissolved by the King in person.
Brougham had given the people their cry, and ' the bill,
the whole bill, and nothing but the bill,' was the popular
watchword during the tumult of the General Election.   On
the dissolution of Parliament the Lord Mayor sanctioned
the illumination of London, and an angry mob, forgetful of
the soldier in the statesman, broke the windows of Apsley
House.

Speaking at a political meeting two days after the dissolution, Lord John Russell said that the electors in the approach-
hing struggle were called on not merely to select the best
men to defend their rights and interests, but also to give a
plain answer to the question, put to the constituencies by the
King in dissolving Parliament, Do you approve, aye or no, of
the principle of Reform in the representation ? Right through
the length and breadth of the kingdom his words were caught
up, and from hundreds of platforms came the question, ' Reform : Aye or No ? ' and the response in favour of the measure
was emphatic and overwhelming.   The country was split into
the opposing camps of the Reformers and anti-Reformers,
and every other question was thrust aside in the struggle.
The political unions proved themselves to be a power in
the land, and the operatives and artisans of the great manufacturing centres, though still excluded from citizenship, left
no stone unturned to ensure the popular triumph.   Lord
John was pressed to stand both for Lancashire and Devon-

shire ; he chose the latter county, with which he was closely associated by family traditions as well as by personal friendships, and was triumphantly returned, with Lord Ebrington as colleague. Even in the agricultural districts the ascendency of the old landed families was powerless to arrest the movement, and as the results of the elections became known it was seen that Lord Sefton had caught the situation in his dry remark : 'The county members are tumbling about like ninepins.' Parliament assembled in June, and it became plain at a glance that democratic ideas were working like leaven upon public opinion in England. In spite of rotten boroughs, close corporations, the opposition of the majority of the territorial aristocracy, and the panic of thousands of timid people, who imagined that the British Constitution was imperilled, the Reformers came back in strength, and at least a hundred who had fought the Bill in the late Parliament were shut out from a renewal of the struggle, whilst out of eighty-two county members that were returned, only six were hostile to Reform.

On June 24, Lord John Russell, now raised to Cabinet rank, introduced the Second Reform Bill, which was substantially the same as the first, and the measure was carried rapidly through its preliminary stage, and on July 8 it passed the second reading by a majority of 136. The Government, however, in Committee was met night after night by an irritating cross-fire of criticism ; repeated motions for adjournment were made ; there was a systematic division of labour in the task of obstruction. In order to promote delay, the leaders of the Opposition stood up again and again and repeated the same statements and arguments, and often in almost the same words. 'If Mr. Speaker,' wrote Jekyll, 'outlives the Reform debate, he may defy *la grippe* and the cholera. I can recommend no books, for the book-sellers declare nobody reads or buys in the present fever. The newspapers are furious, the Sunday papers are talking treason by wholesale. . . . Peel does all he can to make his friends behave like gentlemen. But the nightly vulgarities of the House of Commons furnish new reasons for Reform, and not a ray of talent glimmers among them all. Double-distilled stupidity!'[1] In the midst of it all Russell fell ill, worn out with fatigue and excitement, and as the summer slipped past the people became alarmed and indignant at the dead-lock, and in various parts of the kingdom the attitude of the masses grew not merely restless but menacing. At length the tactics of the Opposition were exhausted, and it was possible to report progress. 'On September 7,' is Lord John's statement, 'the debate was closed, and after much labour, and considerable sacrifice of health, I was able on that night to propose, amid much cheering, that the bill should be reported to the House.' The third reading was carried on September 19 by a majority of fifty-five. Three days later, at five in the morning on September 22, the question was at length put, and in a House of five hundred and eighty-one members the majority for Ministers was one hundred and nine.

The bill was promptly sent up to the Peers, and Lord Grey proposed the second reading on October 3 in a speech of sustained eloquence. Lord Grey spoke as if he felt the occasion to be the most critical event in a political career which had extended to nearly half a century. He struck at once the right key-note, the gravity of the situation, the

---

[1] *Correspondence of Mr. Joseph Jekyll,* 1818–1838. Edited, with a brief Memoir, by the Hon. Algernon Bourke. Pp. 272–273.

magnitude of the issues involved, the welfare of the nation. He made a modest but dignified allusion to his own life-long association with the question. 'In 1786 I voted for Reform. I supported Mr. Pitt in his motion for shortening the duration of Parliaments. I gave my best assistance to the measure of Reform introduced by Mr. Flood before the French Revolution.[1] On one or two occasions I originated motions on the subject.' Then he turned abruptly from his own personal association with the subject to what he finely termed the 'mighty interests of the State,' and the course which Ministers felt they must take if they were to meet the demands of justice, and not to imperil the safety of the nation. He laid stress on the general discontent which prevailed, on the political agitation of the last twelve months, on the distress that reigned in the manufacturing districts, on the influence of the numerous political associations which had grown powerful because of that distress, on the suffering of the agricultural population, on the 'nightly alarms, burnings, and popular disturbances,' as well as on the 'general feeling of doubt and apprehension observable in every countenance.' He endeavoured to show that the measure was not revolutionary in spirit or subversive of the British Constitution, as many people proclaimed.

Lord Grey contended that there was nothing in the measure that was not founded on the principles of English government, nothing that was not perfectly consistent with the ancient practices of the Constitution, and nothing that might not be adopted with absolute safety to the rights and privileges of all orders of the State. He made a scathing allusion

---

[1] Flood's Reform proposals were made in 1790. His idea was to augment the House of Commons by one hundred members, to be elected by the resident householders of every county.

to the 'gross and scandalous corruption practised without disguise' at elections, and he declared that the sale of seats in the House of Commons was a matter of equal notoriety with the return of nominees of noble and wealthy persons to that House. He laid stress on the fact that a few individuals under the existing system were able to turn into a means of personal profit privileges which had been conferred in past centuries for the benefit of the nation. 'It is with these views that the Government has considered that the boroughs which are called nomination boroughs ought to be abolished. In looking at these boroughs, we found that some of them were incapable of correction, for it is impossible to extend their constituency. Some of them consisted only of the sites of ancient boroughs, which, however, might perhaps in former times have been very fit places to return members to Parliament ; in others, the constituency was insignificantly small, and from their local situation incapable of receiving any increase ; so that, upon the whole, this gangrene of our representative system bade defiance to all remedies but that of excision.'

After several nights' debate, in which Brougham, according to Lord John, delivered one of the greatest speeches ever heard in the House of Lords, the bill was at length rejected, after an all-night sitting, at twenty minutes past six o'clock on Saturday morning, October 8, by a majority of forty-one (199 to 158), in which majority were twenty-one bishops. Had these prelates voted the other way, the bill would have passed the second reading. As the carriages of the nobility rattled through the streets at daybreak, artisans and labourers trudging to their work learnt with indignation that the demands of the people had been treated with characteristic contempt by the Peers.

The next few days were full of wild excitement. The people were exasperated, and their attitude grew suddenly menacing. Even those who had hitherto remained calm and almost apathetic grew indignant. Wild threats prevailed, and it seemed as if there might be at any moment a general outbreak of violence. Even as it was, riots of the most disquieting kind took place at Bristol, Derby, and other places. Nottingham Castle was burnt down by an infuriated mob; newspapers appeared in mourning; the bells of some of the churches rang muffled peals; the Marquis of Londonderry and other Peers who had made themselves peculiarly obnoxious were assaulted in the streets; and the Bishops could not stir abroad without being followed by the jeers and execrations of the multitude. Quiet middle-class people talked of refusing to pay the taxes, and showed unmistakably that they had caught the revolutionary spirit of the hour. Birmingham, which was the head-quarters of the Political Union, held a vast open-air meeting, at which one hundred and fifty thousand people were present, and resolutions were passed, beseeching the King to create as many new Peers as might be necessary to ensure the triumph of Reform. Lord Althorp and Lord John Russell were publicly thanked at this gathering for their action, and the reply of the latter is historic: 'Our prospects are obscured for a moment, but, I trust, only for a moment; it is impossible that the whisper of a faction should prevail against the voice of a nation.'

Meanwhile Lord Ebrington, Lord John's colleague in the representation of Devonshire, came to the rescue of the Government with a vote of confidence, which was carried by a sweeping majority. Two days later, on Wednesday, October 12, many of the shops of the metropolis were closed in token of political mourning, and on that day sixty thousand men marched in procession to St. James's Palace, bearing a petition to the King in favour of the retention of the Grey Administration. Hume presented it, and when he returned to the waiting crowd in the Park, he was able to tell them that their prayer would not pass unheeded. No wonder that Croker wrote shortly afterwards : 'The four M's—the Monarch, the Ministry, the Members, and the Multitude—all against us. The King stands on his Government, the Government on the House of Commons, the House of Commons on the people. How can we attack a line thus linked and supported?' Indignation meetings were held in all parts of the country, and at one of them, held at Taunton, Sydney Smith delivered the famous speech in which he compared the attempt of the House of Lords to restrain the rising tide of Democracy to the frantic but futile battle which Dame Partington waged with her mop, during a storm at Sidmouth, when the Atlantic invaded her threshold. 'The Atlantic was roused. Mrs. Partington's spirit was up. But I need not tell you that the contest was unequal. The Atlantic Ocean beat Mrs. Partington. Gentlemen, be at your ease, be quiet and steady ; you will beat—Mrs. Partington.' The newspapers carried the witty allusion everywhere. It tickled the public fancy, and did much to relax the bitter mood of the nation, and vapouring heroics were forgotten in laughter, and indignation gave way to amused contempt.

Parliament, which had been prorogued towards the end of October, reassembled in the first week of December, and on the 12th of that month Lord John once more introduced —for the third time in twelve months—the Reform Bill. A few alterations had been made in its text, the outcome chiefly of the facts which the new census had brought to light. In order to meet certain anomalies in the original scheme, Ministers, with the help of Thomas Drummond, who shortly afterwards honourably distinguished himself in Irish affairs, drew up two lists of boroughs, one for total disenfranchisement and the other for semi-disenfranchisement; and the principle on which fifty-six towns were included in the first list, and thirty in the second, was determined by the number of houses in each borough and the value of the assessed taxes. Six days later the second reading was passed, after three nights' discussion, by a majority of 324 to 162. The House rose immediately for the Christmas recess, and on January 20 the bill reached the committee stage, and there it remained till March 14. The third reading took place on March 23, and the bill was passed by a majority of 116. Althorp, as the leader of the Commons, and Russell, as the Minister in charge of the measure, carried the Reform Bill promptly to the House of Lords, and made formal request for the 'concurrence of their lordships to the same.' Other men had laboured to bring about this result; but the nation felt that, but for the pluck and persistency of Russell, and the judgment and tact of Althorp, failure would have attended their efforts.

It is difficult now to understand the secret of the influence which Althorp wielded in the Grey Administration, but it was great enough to lead the Premier to ask him to accept a peerage, in order—in the crisis which was now at hand—to bring the Lords to their senses. Althorp was.in no sense of the word a great statesman; in fact, his career was the triumph of character rather than capacity. All through the struggle, when controversy grew furious and passion rose high, Althorp kept a cool head, and his adroitness in conciliatory speech was remarkable. He was a moderate man, who never failed to do justice to his opponent's case, and his influence was not merely in the Commons ; it made itself felt to good purpose in the Court, as well as in the country. He was a man of chivalrous instincts and unchallenged probity. It was one of his political opponents, Sir Henry Hardinge, who exclaimed, 'Althorp carried the bill. His fine temper did it !'

Lord John Russell, like his colleagues, was fully alive to the gravity of the crisis. He made no secret of his conviction that, if another deadlock arose, the consequence would be bloodshed, and the outbreak of a conflict in which the British Constitution would probably perish. Twelve months before, the cry in the country had been, 'What will the Lords do ?' but now an altogether different question was on men's lips, 'What must be done with the Lords ?' Government knew that the real struggle over the bill would be in Committee, and therefore they refused to be unduly elated when the second reading was carried on April 14 with a majority of nine, in spite of the Duke of Wellington's blustering heroics. Three weeks later, Lord Lyndhurst carried, by a majority of thirty-five, a motion for the mutilation of the bill, in spite of Lord Grey's assurance that it dealt a fatal blow at the measure. The Premier immediately moved the adjournment of the debate, and the situation grew suddenly dramatic. The Cabinet had made its last concession ; Ministers determined, in Lord Durham's words, that a 'sufficient creation of Peers was absolutely necessary' if their resignation was not to take immediate effect, and they laid their views before the King. William IV., like his predecessor, lived in a narrow world ; he was surrounded by gossips who played upon his fears of revolution, and took care to appeal to his prejudices. His zeal for Reform had already cooled, and Queen Adelaide was hostile to Lord Grey's measure.

When, therefore, Lord Grey and Lord Brougham went down to Windsor to urge the creation of new Peers, they met with a chilling reception. The King refused his sanction, and the Ministry had no other alternative than to resign. William IV. took counsel with Lord Lyndhurst, and summoned the Duke of Wellington. Meanwhile the House of Commons at the instance of Lord Ebrington, again passed a vote of confidence in the Grey Administration, and adopted an address to His Majesty, begging him to call to his councils such persons only as ' will carry into effect unimpaired in all its essential provisions that bill for reforming the representation of the people which has recently passed the House of Commons.' Wellington tried to form a Ministry in order to carry out some emasculated scheme of Reform, but Peel was inexorable, and refused to have part or lot in the project.

Meanwhile the cry rang through the country, 'The bill, the whole bill, and nothing but the bill !' William IV. was hissed as he passed through the streets, and the walls blazed with insulting lampoons and caricatures. Signboards which displayed the King's portrait were framed with crape, and Queen Adelaide's likeness was disfigured with lampblack. Rumours of projected riots filled the town, and whispers of a plot for seizing the wives and children of the aristocracy led the authorities to order the swords of the Scots Greys to be rough-sharpened. At the last moment, when the attitude of the country was menacing, the King yielded, on May 17, and sent for Lord Grey. 'Only think,' wrote Joseph Parkes on May 18, 'that at three yesterday all was gloomy foreboding in the Cabinet, and at twenty-five minutes before five last night Lord Althorp did not know the King's answer till Lord Grey returned at half-past five—

"All right." Thus on the decision of one man rests the fate of nations.'[1]

Instead of creating new Peers, the King addressed a letter to members of the House of Lords who were hostile to the bill, urging them to withdraw their opposition. A hint from Windsor went further with the aristocracy in those days than any number of appeals, reasonable or just, from the country. About a hundred of the Peers, in angry sullen mood, shook off the dust of Westminster, and, in Lord John's words, 'skulked in clubs and country houses.' Sindbad, to borrow Albany Fonblanque's vigorous simile, was getting rid of the old man of the sea, not permanently, alas ! but at least for the occasion. During the progress of these negotiations, the nation, now confident of victory, stood not merely at attention but on the alert. 'I say,' exclaimed Attwood at Birmingham—and the phrase expressed the situation—' the people of England stand at this moment like greyhounds on the slip !' Triumph was only a matter of time. ' Pray beg of Lord Grey to keep well,' wrote Sydney Smith to the Countess ; ' I have no doubt of a favourable issue. I see an open sea beyond the icebergs.' At length the open sea was reached, and on June 7 the Reform Bill received the Royal Assent and became the law of the land, and with it the era of government by public opinion began. The mode by which the country at last obtained this great measure of redress did not commend itself to Lord John's judgment. He did not disguise his opinion that the creation of many new Peers favourable to Reform would have been a more dignified proceeding than the request from Windsor to noble lords to dissemble and cloak their disappointment. ' Whether twelve or one hundred be the number requisite to enable

[1] *Life of George Grote*, by Mrs. Grote, p. 80.

the Peers to give their votes in conformity with public opinion,' were his words, ' it seems to me that the House of Lords, sympathising with the people at large, and acting in concurrence with the enlightened state of the prevailing wish, represents far better the dignity of the House, and its share in legislation, than a majority got together by the long supremacy of one party in the State, eager to show its ill-will by rejecting bills of small importance, but afraid to appear, and skulking in clubs and country houses, in face of a measure which has attracted the ardent sympathy of public opinion.'

'God may and, I hope, will forgive you for this bill,' was Lord Sidmouth's plaintive lament to Earl Grey, ' but I do not think I ever can !' There lives no record of reply. The last protest of the Duke of Wellington, delivered just before the measure became law, was characteristic in many respects, and not least in its blunt honesty. ' Reform, my lords, has triumphed, the barriers of the Constitution are broken down, the waters of destruction have burst the gates of the temple, and the tempest begins to howl. Who can say where its course should stop? who can stay its speed ? For my own part, I earnestly hope that my predictions may not be fulfilled, and that my country may not be ruined by the measure which the noble earl and his colleagues have sanctioned.' Lord John Russell, on the contrary, held then the view which he afterwards expressed : ' It is the right of a people to represent its grievances : it is the business of a statesman to devise remedies.' In the first quarter of the present century the people made their grievances known. Lord Grey and his Cabinet in 1831–2 devised remedies, and, in Lord John's memorable phrase, ' popular enthusiasm rose in its strength and converted them into law.'

The Reform Bill, as Walter Bagehot has shown, did nothing to remove the worst evils from which the nation suffered, for the simple reason that those evils were not political but economical. But if it left unchallenged the reign of protection and much else in the way of palpable and glaring injustice, it ushered in a new temper in regard to public questions. It recognised the new conditions of English society, and gave the mercantile and manufacturing classes, with their wealth, intelligence, and energy, not only the consciousness of power, but the sense of responsibility.

The political struggle under Pitt had been between the aristocracy and the monarchy, but that under Grey was between the aristocracy and the middle classes, for the claims of the democracy in the broad sense of the word lay outside the scope of the measure. In spite of its halting confidence in the people, men felt that former things of harsh oppression had passed away, and that the Reform Bill rendered their return impossible. It was at best only a half measure, but it broke the old exclusive traditions and diminished to a remarkable degree the power of the landed interest in Parliament. It has been said that it was the business of Lord John Russell at that crisis to save England from copying the example of the French Revolution, and there can be no doubt whatever that the measure was a safety-valve at a moment when political excitement assumed a menacing form. The public rejoicings were inspired as much by hope as by gladness. A new era had dawned, the will of the nation had prevailed, the spirit of progress was abroad, and the multitudes knew that other reforms, less showy perhaps but not less substantial, were at hand. ' Look at England before the Reform Bill, and look at it now,' wrote Mr. Froude in in 1874. ' Its population

almost doubled ; its commerce quadrupled ; every individual in the kingdom lifted to a high level of comfort
and intelligence—the speed quickening every year ; the
advance so enormous, the increase so splendid, that language
turns to rhetoric in describing it.' When due allowance is
made for the rhetoric of such a description—for alas ! the
' high level of comfort' for every individual in the kingdom
is still unattained—the substantial truth of such a statement
cannot be gainsaid. When the battle was fought, Lord
John was generous enough to say that the success of the
Reform Bill in the House of Commons was due mainly to
the confidence felt in the integrity and sound judgment of
Lord Althorp. At the same time he never concealed his
conviction that it was the multitude outside who made the
measure resistless.

CHAPTER V

The turn of the tide with the Whigs—The two voices in the Cabinet—
Lord John and Ireland—Althorp and the Poor Law—The Melbourne Administration on the rocks—Peel in power—The question
of Irish tithes—Marriage of Lord John—Grievances of Nonconformists—Lord Melbourne's influence over the Queen—Lord
Durham's mission to Canada—Personal sorrow.

HIGH-WATER mark was reached with the Whigs in the spring
of 1833, and before the tide turned, two years later, Lord
Grey and his colleagues had, in various directions, done
much to justify the hopes of their followers. The result of
the General Election in the previous December was seen
when the first Reformed Parliament assembled at Westminster, on January 29, 1833. Lord Althorp, as Leader of
the House of Commons, found himself with 485 members
at his back, whilst Sir Robert Peel confronted him with
about 170 stalwart Tories. After all, the disparity was
hardly as great as it looked, for it was a mixed multitude
which followed Althorp, and in its ranks were the elements
of conflict and even of revolt. The Whigs had made common
cause with the Radicals when the Reform Bill stood in
jeopardy every hour, but the triumph of the measure
imperilled this grand alliance. Not a few of the Whigs had
been faint-hearted during the struggle, and were now some-

what alarmed at its overwhelming success. Their inclination
was either to rest on their laurels or to make haste slowly.
The Radicals, on the contrary, longed for new worlds to
conquer. They were full of energy and enthusiasm, and
desired nothing so much as to ride abroad redressing human
wrongs. The traditions of the past were dear to the Whigs,
but the Radicals thrust such considerations impatiently
aside, and boasted that 1832 was the Year 1 of the people.
It was impossible that such warring elements should permanently coalesce ; the marvel is that they held together so
long.

Even in the Cabinet there were two voices. The Duke
of Richmond was at heart a Tory masquerading in the
dress of a Whig. Lord Durham was a Radical of an outspoken and uncompromising type, in spite of his aristocratic
trappings and his great possessions. Nevertheless, the new
era opened, not merely with a flourish of trumpets, but with
notable work in the realm of practical statesmanship.
Fowell Buxton took up the work of Wilberforce on behalf
of the desolate and oppressed, and lived to bring about
the abolition of slavery ; whilst Shaftesbury's charity began
at home with the neglected factory children. Religious
toleration was represented in the Commons by the
Jewish Relief Bill, and its opposite in the Lords by the
defeat of that measure. Althorp amended the Poor
Laws, and, though neither he nor his colleagues would
admit the fact, the bill rendered, by its alterations in the
provisions of settlement and the bold attack which it made
on the thraldom of labour, the repeal of the Corn Laws
inevitable. Grant renewed the charter of the East India
Company, but not its monopoly of the trade with the East.
Roebuck brought forward a great scheme of education, whilst

Grote sought to introduce the ballot, and Hume, in the interests of economy, but at the cost of much personal odium, assailed sinecures and extravagance in every shape and form. Ward drew attention to the abuses of the Irish Church, and did much by his exertions to lessen them ; and Lord John Russell a year or two later brought about a civic revolution by the Municipal Reform Act—a measure which, next to the reform of Parliament, did more to broaden and uplift the political life of the people than any other enactment of the century.   Ireland blocked the way of Lord Grey's Ministry, and the wild talk and hectoring attitude of O'Connell, and his bold bid for personal ascendency, made it difficult for responsible statesmen to deal calmly with the problems by which they were confronted.

It is true that Lord John was not always on the side of the angels of progress and redress. He blundered occasionally like other men, and sometimes even hesitated strangely to give effect to his convictions, and therefore it would be idle as well as absurd to attempt to make out that he was consistent, much less infallible. The Radicals a little later complained that he talked of finality in reform, and supported the coercive measures of Stanley in Ireland, and opposed Hume in his efforts to secure the abolition of naval and military sinecures. He declined to support a proposed investigation of the pension list. He set his face against Tennyson's scheme for shortening the duration of Parliaments, and Grote had to reckon with his hostility to the adoption of the ballot. But in spite of it all, he was still, in Sydney Smith's happy phrase, to all intents and purposes 'Lord John Reformer.' No one doubted his honesty or challenged his motives. The compass by which Russell steered his course through political life might tremble, but men felt that it remained true.

Ireland drew forth his sympathies, but he failed to see any way out of the difficulty. 'I wish I knew what to do to help your country,' were his words to Moore, 'but, as I do not, it is of no use giving her smooth words, as O'Connell told me, and I must be silent.' It was not in his nature, however, to sit still with folded hands. He held his peace, but quietly crossed the Channel to study the problem on the spot. It was his first visit to the distressful country for many years, and he wished Moore to accompany him as guide, philosopher, and friend. He assured the poet that he would allow him to be as patriotic as he pleased about 'the first flower of the earth and first gem of the sea' during the proposed sentimental journey. 'Your being a rebel,' were his words, 'may somewhat atone for my being a Cabinet Minister.' Moore, however, was compelled to decline the tempting proposal by the necessity of making ends meet by sticking to the hack work which that universal provider of knowledge, Dr. Lardner, had set him in the interests of the 'Cabinet Encyclopædia'—an enterprise to which men of the calibre of Mackintosh, Southey, Herschell, and even Walter Scott had lent a helping hand.

Lord John landed in Ireland in the beginning of September 1833, and went first to Lord Duncannon's place at Bessborough. Afterwards he proceeded to Waterford to visit Lord Ebrington, his colleague in the representation of Devonshire. He next found his way to Cork and Killarney, and he wrote again to Moore urging him to 'hang Dr. Lardner on his tree of knowledge,' and to join him at the eleventh hour. Moore must have been in somewhat reduced circumstances at the moment—for he was a luxurious, pleasure-loving man, who never required much persuasion to throw down his work—since such an appeal availed nothing. Meanwhile Lord John had carried Lord Ebrington back to Dublin, and they went together to the North of Ireland. The visit to Belfast attracted considerable attention ; Lord John's services over the Reform Bill were of course fresh in the public mind, and he was entertained in orthodox fashion at a public dinner. This short tour in Ireland did much to open his eyes to the real grievances of the people, and, fresh from the scene of disaffection, he was able to speak with authority when the late autumn compelled the Whig Cabinet to throw everything else aside in order to devise if possible some measure of relief for Ireland. Stanley was Chief Secretary, and, though one of the most brilliant men of his time alike in deed and word, unfortunately his haughty temper and autocratic leanings were a grievous hindrance if a policy of coercion was to be exchanged for the more excellent way of conciliation. O'Connell opposed his policy in scathing terms, and attacked him personally with bitter invective, and in the end there was open war between the two men.

Lord Grey, now that Parliamentary Reform had been conceded, was developing into an easy-going aristocratic Whig of somewhat contracted sympathies, and Stanley, though still in the Cabinet, was apparently determined to administer the affairs of Ireland on the most approved Tory principles. Althorp, Russell, and Duncannon were men whose sympathies leaned more or less decidedly in the opposite direction, and therefore, especially with O'Connell thundering at the gates with the Irish people and the English Radicals at his back, a deadlock was inevitable. Durham, in ill health and chagrin, and irritated by the stationary, if not reactionary, attitude of certain members of the Grey Administration, resigned office in the spring of

1833. Goderich became Privy Seal, and this enabled Stanley
to exchange the Irish Secretaryship for that of the Colonies.
He had driven Ireland to the verge of revolt, but he had
nevertheless made an honest attempt to grapple with many
practical evils, and his Education Bill was a piece of constructive statesmanship which placed Roman Catholics on
an equality with Protestants.   Early in the session of
1834 Althorp introduced the Poor Law Amendment
Act, and the measure was passed in July.   The changes
which it brought about were startling, for its enactments were drastic.   This great economic measure came
to the relief of a nation in which 'one person in every
seven was a pauper.'   The new law limited relief to
destitution, prohibited out-door help to the able-bodied,
beyond medical aid, instituted tests to detect imposture,
confederated parishes into unions, and substituted large
district workhouses for merely local shelters for the destitute.
In five years the poor rate was reduced by three millions,
and the population, set free by the new interpretation of
'Settlement,' were able, in their own phrase, to follow the
work and to congregate accordingly wherever the chance of
a livelihood offered.   One great question followed hard
on the heels of another.

In the King's Speech at the opening of Parliament, the
consideration of Irish tithes was recommended, for extin-
guishing 'all just causes of complaint without injury to the
rights and property of any class of subjects or to any institution in Church or State.'   Mr. Littleton (afterwards Lord
Hatherton), who had succeeded Stanley as Irish Secretary
accordingly introduced a new Tithe Bill, the object of which
was to change the tithe first into a rent-charge payable by
the landlord, and eventually into land tax.   The measure also

proposed that the clergy should be content with a sum which fell short of the amount to which they were entitled by law, so that riot and bloodshed might be avoided by lessened demands. On the second reading of the bill, Lord John frankly avowed the faith that was in him, a circumstance which led to unexpected results. He declared that, as he understood it, the aim of the bill was to determine and secure the amount of the tithe. The question of appropriation was to be kept entirely distinct. If the object of the bill was to grant a certain sum to the Established Church of Ireland, and the question was to end there, his opinion of it might be different. But he understood it to be a bill to secure a certain amount of property and revenue destined by the State to religious and charitable purposes, and if the State should find that it was not appropriated justly to the purposes of religious and moral instruction, it would then be the duty of Parliament to consider the necessity of a different appropriation. His opinion was that the revenues of the Church of Ireland were larger than necessary for the religious and moral instruction of the persons belonging to that Church, and for the stability of the Church itself.

Lord John did not think it would be advisable or wise to mix the question of appropriation with the question of amount of the revenues ; but when Parliament had vindicated the property in tithes, he should then be prepared to assert his opinion with regard to their appropriation. If, when the revenue was once secured, the assertion of that opinion should lead him to differ and separate from those with whom he was united by political connection, and for whom he entertained the deepest private affection, he should feel much regret ; yet he should, at whatever cost and sacrifice, do what he should consider his bounden duty — namely, do justice to Ireland.

He afterwards explained that this speech, which produced a great impression, was prompted by the attitude of
Stanley concerning the permanence and inviolability of the
Irish Church. He was, in fact, afraid that if Stanley's
statement was allowed to pass in silence by his colleagues,
the whole Government would be regarded as pledged to the
maintenance in their existing shape of the temporalities of
an alien institution. Lord John accordingly struck from his
own bat, amid the cheers of the Radicals. Stanley expressed
to Sir James Graham his view of the situation in the now
familiar phrase, ' Johnny has upset the coach.' The truth
was, divided counsels existed in the Cabinet on this question
of appropriation, and Lord John's blunt deliverance, though
it did not wreck the Ministry, placed it in a dilemma. He
was urged by some of his colleagues to explain away what
he had said, but he had made up his mind and was in no
humour to retract.

Palmerston, with whom he was destined to have many an
encounter in coming days, thought he ought to have been
turned out of the Cabinet, and others of his colleagues were
hardly less incensed. The independent member, in the person
of Mr. Ward, who sat for St. Albans, promptly took advantage
of Russell's speech to bring forward a motion to the effect
that the Church in Ireland ' exceeds the wants of the population, and ought to be reduced.' This proposition was
elbowed out of the way by the appointment of a Royal Commission of Inquiry into the revenues of the Irish Church ; but
Stanley felt that his position in the Cabinet was now untenable, and therefore retired from office in the company of the
Duke of Richmond, Lord Ripon, and Sir James Graham. The
Radicals made no secret of their glee. Ward, they held, had
been a benefactor to the party beyond their wildest dreams,
for he had exorcised the evil spirits of the Grey Administration.

Lord Grey had an opportunity at this crisis of infusing fresh vigour into his Ministry by raising to Cabinet rank men of progressive views who stood well with the country. Another course was, however, taken, for the Marquis of Conyngham became Postmaster-General, the Earl of Carlisle Privy Seal, whilst Lord Auckland went to the Admiralty, and Mr. Spring Rice became Colonial Secretary, and so the opportunity of a genuine reconstruction of the Government was lost. The result was, the Government was weakened, and no one was satisfied. 'Whigs, Tories, and Radicals,' wrote Greville, 'join in full cry against them, and the "Times," in a succession of bitter vituperative articles very well done, fires off its contempt and disgust at the paltry patching-up of the Cabinet.'

Durham's retirement, though made on the score of ill-health, had not merely cooled the enthusiasm of the Radicals towards the Grey Administration, but had also awakened their suspicions. Lord John was restive, and inclined to kick over the traces ; whilst Althorp, whose tastes were bucolic, had also a desire to depart. 'Nature,' he exclaimed, 'intended me to be a grazier ; but men will insist on making me a statesman.' He confided to Lord John that he detested office to such an extent that he 'wished himself dead' every morning when he awoke. Meanwhile vested interests here, there, and everywhere, were uniting their forces against the Ministry, and its sins of omission as well as of commission were leaping to light on the platform and in the Press. Wellington found his reputation for political sagacity agreeably recognised, and he fell into the attitude of an oracle whose jeremiads had come true. When Lord Grey proposed the renewal of the Coercion Act without alteration, Lord Althorp

expressed a strong objection to such a proceeding.   He had
assured Littleton that the Act would not be put in force
again in its entirety, and the latter, with more candour than
discretion, had communicated the intimation to O'Connell,
who bruited it abroad.

Lord John had come to definite convictions about
Ireland, and he was determined not to remain in the Cabinet
unless he was allowed to speak out.   On June 23 the Irish
Tithe Bill reached the stage of committee, and Littleton
drew attention to the changes which had been introduced
into the measure—slight concessions to public opinion which
Lord John felt were too paltry to meet the gravity of the
case.   O'Connell threw down the gauntlet to the Ministry,
and asked the House to pass an amendment asserting that
the surplus revenues of the Church ought to be applied to
purposes of public utility.   Peel laid significant stress on
the divided counsels in the Ministry, and accused Lord John
of asserting that the Irish Church was the greatest grievance
of which the nation had ever had to complain.   The latter
repudiated such a charge, and explained that what he had
said was that the revenues of the Church were too great for
its stability, thereby implying that he both desired and contemplated its continued existence.   Although not unwilling
to support a mild Coercion Bill, if it went hand in hand with
a determined effort to deal with abuses, he made it clear
that repressive enactments without such an effort at Reform
were altogether repugnant to his sense of justice.   He
declared that Coercion Acts were 'peculiarly abhorrent to
those who pride themselves on the name of Whigs ;' and he
added that, when such a necessity arose, Ministers were confronted with the duty of looking 'deeper into the causes of
the long-standing and permanent evils' of Ireland.   I am

not prepared to continue the government of Ireland without fully probing her condition ; I am not prepared to propose bills for coercion, and the maintenance of a large force of military and police, without endeavouring to improve, so far as lies in my power, the condition of the people. I will not be a Minister to carry on systems which I think founded on bigotry and prejudice. Be the consequence what it may, I am content to abide by these opinions, to carry them out to their fullest extent, not by any premature declaration of mere opinion, but by going on gradually, from time to time improving our institutions, and, without injuring the ancient and venerable fabrics, rendering them fit and proper mansions for a great, free, and intelligent people.' Such a speech was worthy of Fox, and it recalls a passage in Lord John's biography of that illustrious statesman. Fox did his best in the teeth of prejudice and obloquy to free Ireland from the thraldom which centuries of oppression had created : 'In 1780, in 1793, and in 1829, that which had been denied to reason was granted to force. Ireland triumphed, not because the justice of her claims was apparent, but because the threat of insurrection overcame prejudice, made fear superior to bigotry, and concession triumphant over persecution.' [1]

Even O'Connell expressed his admiration of this bold and fearless declaration, and the speech did much to increase Lord John's reputation, both within and without the House of Commons. In answer to a letter of congratulation, he said that his friends would make him, by their encouragement—what he felt he was not by nature— a good speaker. 'There are occasions,' he added, ' on which one must express one's feelings or sink into contempt.

[1] Russell's *Life of Fox*, vol. i. p. 242.

I own I have not been easy during the period in which I thought it absolutely necessary to suspend the assertion of my opinions in order to secure peace in this country.' Lord John's attitude on this occasion threw into relief his keen sense of political responsibility, no less than the honesty and courage which were characteristic of the man. A day or two later the Cabinet drifted on to the rocks. The policy of Coercion was reaffirmed in spite of Althorp's protests, and in spite also of Littleton's pledge to the contrary to O'Connell. Generosity was not the strong point of the Irish orator, and, to the confusion of Littleton and the annoyance of Grey, he insisted on taking the world into his confidence from his place in Parliament. This was the last straw. Lord Althorp would no longer serve, and Lord Grey, harassed to death, determined no longer to lead. After all, ' Johnny ' was only one of many who upset the coach, which, in truth, turned over because its wheels were rotten. On the evening of June 29 a meeting of the Cabinet was held, and, in Russell's words, ' Lord Grey placed before us the letters containing his own resignation and that of Lord Althorp, which he had sent early in the morning to the King. He likewise laid before us the King's gracious acceptance of his resignation, and he gave to Lord Melbourne a sealed letter from his Majesty. Lord Melbourne, upon opening this letter, found in it an invitation to him to undertake the formation of a Government. Seeing that nothing was to be done that night, I left the Cabinet and went to the Opera.'

Lord Melbourne was sent for in July, and took his place at the head of a Cabinet which remained practically unaltered. He had been Home Secretary under Grey, and Duncannon was now called to fill that post. The first Melbourne Administration was short-lived, for when it had existed four months Earl Spencer died, and Althorp, on his succession to the peerage, was compelled to relinquish his leadership of the House of Commons. William IV. cared little for Melbourne, and less for Russell, and, as he wished to pick a quarrel with the Whigs, since their policy excited his alarm, he used Althorp for a pretext. Lord Grey had professed to regard Althorp as indispensable to the Ministry, and the King imagined that Melbourne would adopt the same view. Although reluctant to part with Althorp, who eagerly seized the occasion of his accession to an earldom to retire from official life, Melbourne refused to believe that the heavens would fall because of that fact.

There was no pressing conflict of opinion between the King and his advisers, but William IV. nevertheless availed himself of the accident of Althorp's elevation to the peerage to dismiss the Ministry. The reversion of the leadership in the Commons fell naturally to Lord John, and Melbourne was quick to recognise the fact. 'Thus invited,' says Lord John Russell, 'I considered it my duty to accept the task, though I told Lord Melbourne that I could not expect to have the same influence with the House of Commons which Lord Althorp had possessed. In conversation with Mr. Abercromby I said, more in joke than in earnest, that if I were offered the command of the Channel Fleet, and thought it my duty to accept, I should not refuse it.' It was unlike Sydney Smith to treat the remark about taking command of the Channel Fleet seriously, when 'he elaborated a charge' against Lord John on the Deans and Chapters question ; but even the witty Canon could lose his temper sometimes.

The King, however, had strong opinions on the subject

of Lord John's qualifications, and he expressed in emphatic terms his disapproval. The nation trusted Lord John, and had come to definite and flattering conclusions about him as a statesman, but at Windsor a different opinion prevailed. The King, in fact, made no secret to Lord Melbourne, in the famous interview at Brighton, of his conviction that Lord John Russell had neither the ability nor the influence to qualify him for the task ; and he added that he would 'make a wretched figure' when opposed in the Commons by men like Peel and Stanley. His Majesty further volunteered the remark that he did not 'understand that young gentleman,' and could not agree to the arrangement proposed. William, moreover, took occasion to pose as a veritable, as well as titular, Defender of the Faith, for, on the authority of Baron Stockmar, the King 'considered Lord John Russell to have pledged himself to certain encroachments on the Church, which his Majesty had made up his mind and expressed his determination to resist.' As Russell was clearly quite out of the reckoning, Melbourne suggested two other names. But the King had made up his mind on more subjects than one, and next morning, Lord Melbourne found himself in possession of a written paper, which informed him his Majesty had no further occasion either for his services or for those of his colleagues.

William IV. acted within his constitutional rights, but such an exercise of the royal prerogative was, to say the least, worthy of George III. in his most uninspired mood. Althorp regarded the King's action as the 'greatest piece of folly ever committed,' and Lord John, in reply to the friendly note which contained this emphatic verdict, summoned his philosophy to his aid in the following characteristic rejoinder : 'I suppose everything is for the best in this world ; otherwise the only good which I should see in this event would be that it saves me from being sadly pommelled by Peel and Stanley, to say nothing of O'Connell.' Wellington, who was hastily summoned by the King, suggested that Sir Robert Peel should be entrusted with the formation of a new Government.

Sir Robert Peel was accordingly sent for in hot haste from Rome to form a new Ministry.   On his arrival in London in December 1834, he at once set about the formation of a Cabinet.   This is Jekyll's comment : ' Our crisis has been entertaining, and Peel is expected to-day.   I wish he could have remained long enough at Rome to have learnt mosaic, of which parti-coloured materials our Cabinets have been constructed for twenty years, and for want of cement have fallen to pieces.   The Whigs squall out, " Let us depart, for the Reformers grow too impatient."   The Tories squall out, " Let us come in, and we will be very good boys, and become Reformers ourselves."   However, the country is safe by the Reform Bill, for no Minister can remain in office now by corrupt Parliaments ; he must act with approbation of the country or lose his Cabinet in a couple of months.'   At the General Election which followed, Peel issued his celebrated address to the electors of Tamworth, in which he declared himself favourable to the reform of ' proved abuses,' and to the carrying out of such measures ' gradually, dispassionately, and deliberately,' in order that it might be lasting.   Lord John was returned again for South Devon ; but on the re-assembling of Parliament the Liberal majority had dwindled from 314 to 107.   It was during his election tour that he delivered an address at Totnes, which Greville described as not merely ' a very masterly performance,' but ' one of the cleverest and most appropriate speeches ' he had ever read, and for which his friends warmly complimented him. It was a powerful and humorous examination of the Tories' professed anxiety for Reform, and of the prospects of any Reform measures being carried out by their instrumentality.

Lord John now became leader of the Opposition, though the Duke of Bedford dreaded the strain, and expostulated with his son on his acceptance of so irksome and laborious a task. 'You will have to conduct and keep in order a noisy and turbulent pack of hounds which, I think, you will find it quite impossible to restrain.' The Duke of Bedford's fears were not groundless, and Lord John afterwards confessed that, in the whole period during which he had led the Liberal party in the House of Commons, he never had so difficult a task. The forces under his command consisted of a few stalwart Radicals, a number of Whigs of the traditional and somewhat stationary type, and some sixty Irish members. Nevertheless, he promptly assumed an aggressive attitude, and his first victory as leader of the Opposition was won on the question of the choice of a new Speaker, when Mr. Abercromby was placed in the chair in preference to the Ministerial candidate. As the session went on, Lord John's resources in attack grew more and more marked, but he was foiled by the lack of cohesion amongst his followers. It became evident that, unless all sections of the Opposition were united as one man, the Government of Sir Robert Peel could not be overthrown. Alliance with the Radicals and the Irish party, although hateful to the old-fashioned Whigs, was in fact imperative. Lord John summoned a meeting of the Opposition at Lord Lichfield's house ; the support of the Radicals and Irish was secured, and then the leader marshalled his forces for what he hoped would prove a decisive victory. His expectations were not disappointed, for early in April he brought forward a motion for the appropriation of the surplus revenues of the Irish Church to general moral and religious purposes, and won with a majority of twenty-seven votes (285 to 258). Sir Robert Peel forthwith resigned, and the Whigs were avenged for their cavalier dismissal by the King.

On the day after the Prime Minister's resignation, Lord John Russell was married—April 11, 1835, at St. George's, Hanover Square—to Adelaide, Lady Ribblesdale, the widow of the second bearer of that title. The respite from political strife was of short duration, for at the end of forty-eight hours he was summoned from Woburn to take the seals of the Home Office in the second Melbourne Administration. The members of the new Cabinet presented themselves to their constituents for re-election, and Lord John suffered defeat in Devonshire. A seat was, however, found for him at Stroud, and in May he was back again in the House of Commons. The first measure of importance introduced by him, on June 5, was the Municipal Reform Act—a measure which embodied the results of the Commission on the subject appointed by Lord Grey. The bill swept away a host of antiquated and absurd privileges of corporate cities and towns, abolished the authority of cliques of freemen, rectified a variety of abuses, and entrusted municipal government to the hands of all taxpayers. Lord John piloted the measure through the Commons, and fought almost single-handed the representatives of vested rights. After a long contest with the Opposition and the Lords, he had the satisfaction of passing the bill, in a somewhat modified form, through its final stages in September, though the Peers, as usual, opposed it as long as they dared, and only yielded at last when Peel in the one House and Wellington in the other recommended concession.

The Irish Tithes Bill was subsequently introduced, and, though it now included the clauses for the appropriation of certain revenues, it passed the Commons by a majority of thirty-seven. The Lords, however, struck out the appropriation clauses, and the Government in consequence abandoned the measure. The Irish Municipal Bill shared a similar fate, and Lord John's desire to see justice done in Ireland was brought for the moment to naught. The labours of the session had been peculiarly arduous, and in the autumn his health suffered from the prolonged strain. His ability as a leader of the House of Commons, in spite of the dismal predictions of William IV. and the admonitions of paternal solicitude, was now recognised by men of all shades of opinion, though, of course, he had to confront the criticism alike of candid friends and equally outspoken foes. He recruited his energies in the West of England, and, though he had been so recently defeated in Devonshire, wherever he went the people, by way of amends, gave him an ovation. Votes of thanks were accorded to him for his championship of civil and religious liberty, and in November he was entertained at a banquet at Bristol, and presented with a handsome testimonial, raised by the sixpences of ardent Reformers.

Parliament, in the Speech from the Throne, when the session of 1836 began, was called upon to take into early consideration various measures of Reform. The programme of the Ministry, like that of many subsequent administrations, was not lacking in ambition. It was proposed to deal with the antiquated and vexatious manner in which from time immemorial the tithes of the English Church had been collected. The question of Irish tithes was also once more to be brought forward for solution ; the municipal corporations of Ireland and the relief of its poor were to be dealt with in the light of recent legislation for England in the same direction. Improvements in the practical working of the administration of justice, 'more especially in the Court of Chancery,' were foreshadowed, and it was announced that the early attention of Parliament would also be called to certain 'grievances which affect those who dissent from the doctrines or discipline of the Established Church.' Such a list of measures bore on its very face the unmistakeable stamp of Lord John Russell's zeal for political redress and religious toleration. Early in the session he brought forward two measures for the relief of Nonconformists. One of them legalised marriages in the presence of a registrar in Nonconformist places of worship, and the other provided for a general civil registration of births, marriages, and deaths. His original proposal was that marriage in church as well as chapel should only take place after due notice had been given to the registrar. The bishops refused to entertain such an idea, and the House of Lords gave effect to their objections, with the result that the registrar was bowed out of church, though not out of chapel, where indeed he remains to this day. The Tithe Commutation Act and three other measures—one for equalising the incomes of prelates, rearranging ancient dioceses and creating new sees ; another for the better application of the revenues of the Church to its general purposes ; and a third to diminish pluralities—bore witness to his ardour for ecclesiastical reform. The first became law in 1836, and the other two respectively in 1838 and 1839. He lent his aid also to the movement for the foundation on a broad and liberal basis of a new university in London with power to confer degrees—a concession to Nonconformist scholarship and liberal culture generally, which was the more appreciated since Oxford and Cambridge still jealously excluded by their religious tests the youth of the Free Churches.

The Tithe Commutation Act was passed in June; it provided for the exchange of tithes into a rent-charge upon land payable in money, but according to a sliding scale which varied with the average price of corn during the seven preceding years. In the opinion of Lord Farnborough, to no measure since the Reformation has the Church owed so much peace and security. The Irish Municipal Bill was carried in the course of the session through the Commons, but the Lords rendered the measure impossible; and though the Irish Poor Law Bill was carried, a different fate awaited Irish Tithes. This measure was introduced for the fifth time, but in consequence of the King's death, on June 20, and the dissolution of Parliament which followed, it had to be abandoned. Between 1835 and 1837 Lord John, as Home Secretary, brought about many changes for the better in the regulation of prisons, and especially in the treatment of juvenile offenders. By his directions prisoners in Newgate, from metropolitan counties, were transferred to the gaol of each county. Following in the steps of Sir Samuel Romilly, he also reduced the number of capital crimes, and, later on, brought about various prison reforms, notably the establishment of a reformatory for juvenile offenders.

The rejoicings over Queen Victoria's accession in the summer of 1837 were quickly followed by a General Election. The result of this appeal to the country was that the Liberal majority in the House of Commons was reduced to less than forty. Lord John was again returned for Stroud, and on that occasion he delivered a speech in which he cleverly contrasted the legislative achievements of the Tories with those of the Whigs. He made a chivalrous allusion to the 'illustrious Princess who has ascended the Throne with purest intentions and the justest desires.' One passage from his speech merits quotation : 'We have had glorious female reigns. Those of Elizabeth and Anne led us to great victories. Let us now hope that we are going to have a female reign illustrious in its deeds of peace—an Elizabeth without her tyranny, an Anne without her weakness. . . . I trust that we may succeed in making the reign of Victoria celebrated among the nations of the earth and to all posterity, and that England may not forget her precedence of teaching the nations how to live.'

Lord Melbourne had never been a favourite with William, but from the first he stood high in the regard of the young Queen. Her Majesty was but eighteen when she ascended the throne upon which her reign has shed so great a lustre ; she had been brought up in comparative seclusion, and her knowledge of public affairs was, of necessity, small. Lord Melbourne at that time was approaching sixty, and the respect which her Majesty gave to his years was heightened by the quick recognition of the fact that the Prime Minister was one of the most experienced statesmen which the country at that moment possessed. He was also a man of ready wit, and endowed with the charm of fine manners, and under his easy nonchalance there lurked more earnest and patriotic conviction than he ever cared to admit. ' I am sorry to hurt any man's feelings,' said Sydney Smith, 'and to brush aside the magnificent fabric of levity and gaiety he has reared ; but I accuse our Minister of honesty and diligence.' Ridiculous rumours filled the air during the earliest years of her Majesty's reign concerning the supposed undue influence which Lord Melbourne exerted at Court. The more advanced Radicals complained that he sought to render himself indispensable to the sovereign, and that his plan was to surround her with his friends, relations, and creatures, and so to obtain a prolonged tenure of power. The Tories also grumbled, and made no secret of the same ungenerous suspicions. They knew neither her Majesty nor Lord Melbourne who thus spoke. At the same time, it must be admitted that Lord Melbourne was becoming more and more out of touch with popular aspirations, and the political and social questions which were rapidly coming to the front were treated by him in a somewhat cavalier manner.

Russell had his own misgivings, and was by no means inclined to lay too much stress on the opinions of philosophical Radicals of the type of Grote. At the same time, he urged upon Melbourne the desirability of meeting the Radicals as far as possible, and he laid stress on the fact that they, at least, were not seeking for grounds of difference with the Premier. 'There are two things which I think would be more acceptable than any others to this body—the one to make the ballot an open question, the other to remove Tories from the political command of the army.' Lord Melbourne, however, believed that the ballot would create many evils and cure none. Lord John yielded to his chief, but in doing so brought upon himself a good deal of angry criticism, which was intensified by an unadvised declaration in the House of Commons. In his speech on the Address he referred to the question of Reform, and declared that it was quite impossible for him to take part in further measures of Reform. The people of England might revise the Act of 1832, or agitate for a new one ; but as for himself, he refused to be associated with any such movement. A storm of expostulation and angry protest broke out ; but the advanced Reformers failed to move Lord John from the position which he had taken. So they concentrated their hostility in a harmless nickname, and Lord John for some time forward was called in Radical circles and certain journalistic publications, ' Finality Jack.' This honest but superfluous and embarrassing deliverance brought him taunts and reproaches, as well as a temporary loss of popularity. It was always characteristic of Lord John to speak his mind, and he sometimes did it not wisely but too well. Grote wrote in February 1838 : ' The degeneracy of the Liberal party, and their passive acquiescence in everything, good or bad, which emanates from the present Ministry, puts the accomplishment of any political good out of the question ; and it is not worth while to undergo the fatigue of a nightly attendance in Parliament for the simple purpose of sustaining Whig Conservatism against Tory Conservatism. I now look back wistfully to my unfinished Greek history.' Yet Lord Brougham, in the year of the Queen's accession, declared that Russell was the ' stoutest Reformer of them all.'

The rebellion in Canada was the first great incident in the new reign, and the Melbourne Cabinet met the crisis by proposals—which were moved by Lord John in the Commons, and adopted—for suspending the Canadian Constitution for the space of four years. The Earl of Durham, at the beginning of 1838, was appointed Governor-General with extraordinary powers, and he reluctantly accepted the difficult post, trusting, as he himself said, to the confidence and support of the Government, and to the forbearance of those who differed from his political views. No one doubts that Durham acted to the best of his judgment, though everyone admits that he exceeded at least the letter of his authority ; and no one can challenge, in the light of the subsequent history of Canada, the greatness and far-reaching nature of his services, both to the Crown and to the Dominion. Relying on the forbearance and support, in the faith of which he had accepted his difficult commission, the Governor-General took a high hand with the rebels ; but his ordinances were disallowed, and he was practically discredited and openly deserted by the Government. When he was on the point of returning home, a broken-hearted man, in failing health, it was Lord John Russell who at length stood up in Durham's defence. Speaking on the Durham Indemnity Bill, Lord John said : ' I ask you to pass this Bill of Indemnity, telling you that I shall be prepared when the time comes, not indeed to say that the terms or words of the ordinances passed by the Earl of Durham are altogether to be justified, but that, looking at his conduct as a whole, I shall be ready to take part with him. I shall be ready to bear my share of any responsibility which is to be incurred in these difficult circumstances.' The generous nature of this declaration was everywhere recognised, and by none more heartily than Lord Durham. ' I do not conceal from you that my feelings have been deeply wounded by the conduct of the Ministry. From you, however, and you alone of them all, have I received any cordial support personally ; and I feel, as I have told you in a former letter, very grateful to you.'

Meanwhile Lord John Russell had been called upon

to oppose Mr. Grote's motion in favour of the ballot. Although the motion was lost by 315 to 198 votes, the result was peculiarly galling to Lord John, for amongst the majority were those members who were usually opposed to the Government, whilst the minority was made up of Lord Melbourne's followers. But the crisis threatening the Ministry passed away when a motion of want of confidence in Lord Glenelg, the head of the Colonial Office, was defeated by twenty-nine votes. The Irish legislation of the Government as represented by the Tithe Bill did not prosper, and it became evident that, in order to pass the measure, the Appropriation Clause must be abandoned. Although Lord John Russell emphatically declared in 1835 that no Tithe Bill could be effective which did not include an Appropriation Clause, he gave way to the claims of political expediency, and further alienated the Radicals by allowing a measure which had been robbed of its potency to pass through Parliament. Lord Melbourne's Government accomplished during the session something in the direction of Irish Reform by the passage of the Poor Law, but it failed to carry the Municipal Bill, which in many respects was the most important of the three.

The autumn, which witnessed on both sides of the Atlantic the excitement over Lord Durham's mission to Canada, was darkened in the home of Lord John by the death at Brighton, on November 1, of his wife. His first impulse was to place the resignation of his office and of leadership in the Commons in the hands of his chief. Urgent appeals from all quarters were made to him to remain at his post, and, though his own health was precarious, cheered by the sympathy of his colleagues and of the country, he resumed his work after a few weeks of quiet at Cassiobury.

CHAPTER VI

THE TWO FRONT BENCHES

1840–1845

Lord John's position in the Cabinet and in the Commons—His services to Education—Joseph Lancaster—Lord John's Colonial Policy—Mr. Gladstone's opinion—Lord Stanmore's recollections—The mistakes of the Melbourne Cabinet—The Duke of Wellington's opinion of Lord John—The agitation against the Corn Laws—Lord John's view of Sir Robert Peel—The Edinburgh Letter—Peel's dilemma—Lord John's comment on the situation.

THE truth was, Lord John could not be spared, and his strong sense of duty triumphed over his personal grief. One shrewd contemporary observer of men and movements declared that Melbourne and Russell were the only two men in the Cabinet for whom the country cared a straw. The opinion of the man in the street was summed up in Sydney Smith's assertion that the Melbourne Government could not possibly exist without Lord John, for the simple reason that five minutes after his departure it would be dissolved into 'sparks of liberality and splinters of reform.' In 1839 the Irish policy of the Government was challenged, and, on the motion of Lord Roden, a vote of censure was carried in the House of Lords. When the matter came before the Commons, Lord John delivered a speech so adroit and so skilful that friends and foes alike were satisfied, and even pronounced Radicals forgot to grumble.

Lord John's speech averted a Ministerial crisis, and on a division the Government won by twenty-two votes. A month later the affairs of Jamaica came up for discussion, for the Government found itself forced, by the action of the House of Assembly in refusing to adopt the Prisons Act which had been passed by the Imperial Legislature, to ask Parliament to suspend the Constitution of the colony for a period of five years ; and on a division they gained their point by a majority of only five votes. The Jamaica Bill was an autocratic measure, which served still further to discredit Lord Melbourne with the party of progress. Chagrined at the narrow majority, the Cabinet submitted its resignation to her Majesty, who assured Lord John that she had 'never felt more pain' than when she learnt the decision of her Ministers. The Queen sent first for Wellington, and afterwards, at his suggestion, for Peel, who undertook to form an Administration ; but when her Majesty insisted on retaining the services of the Whig Ladies-in-Waiting, Sir Robert declined to act, and the former Cabinet was recalled to office, though hardly with flying colours.

Education, to hark back for a moment, was the next great question with which Lord John dealt, for, in the summer of 1839, he brought in a bill to increase the grant to elementary schools from 20,000*l.* a year to 30,000*l.*—first made in 1833—and to place it under the control of the Privy Council, as well as to subject the aided schools to inspection. 'I explained,' was his own statement, 'in the simplest terms, without any exaggeration, the want of education in the country, the deficiencies of religious instruction, and the injustice of subjecting to the penalties of the criminal law persons who had never been taught their duty to God and man.' His proposals, particularly with regard to the establishment of a Normal school, were met with a storm of opposition. This part of the scheme was therefore abandoned ; 'but the throwing out of one of our children to the wolf,' remarks Lord John, 'did little to appease his fury !' At length the measure, in its modified shape, was carried in the Commons ; but the House of Lords, led on this occasion by the Archbishop of Canterbury, by a majority of more than a hundred, condemned the scheme entirely. Dr. Blomfield, Bishop of London, at this juncture came forward as peacemaker, and, at a private meeting at Lansdowne House, consisting of the Archbishop of Canterbury, the Bishops of London and Salisbury, Lord Lansdowne, and Lord John Russell, the dispute was amicably adjusted, on the basis of the reports of the Inspectors of Schools being sent to the Bishops as well as to the Committee of Privy Council, and co-operation between the Bishops and the Committee in the work of education.

The Duke of Bedford was one of the first men of position in the country to come to the aid of Joseph Lancaster—a young Quaker philanthropist, who, in spite of poverty and obscurity, did more for the cause of popular education in England in the early years of the century than all the privileged people in the country.[1] Here a floating straw of reminiscence may be cited, since it throws momentary light on the mischievous instincts of a quick-witted boy. Lord John, looking back towards the close of his life, said : 'One of my earliest recollections as a boy at Woburn Abbey is that of putting on Joseph Lancaster's broad hat and mimicking his mode of salutation.'

---

[1] Justice has never yet been done to the founder of the Lancasterian system of education. Joseph Lancaster was a remarkable man who aroused the conscience of the nation, and even the dull intelligence of George III., to the imperative need of popular education.

Other changes were imminent. Lord Normanby had proved himself to be a popular Viceroy of Ireland ; indeed, O'Connell asserted that he was one of the best Englishmen that had ever been sent across St. George's Channel in an official capacity. He was now Colonial Secretary ; and, in spite of his virtues, he was scarcely the man for such a position—at all events, at a crisis in which affairs required firm handling. He managed matters so badly that the Under-Secretary (Mr. Labouchere, afterwards Lord Taunton) was in open revolt. The cards were accordingly shuffled in May 1839, and, amongst other and less significant changes, Normanby and Russell changed places. Lord John quickly made his presence felt at the Colonial Office. He was a patient listener to the permanent officials ; indeed, he declared that he meant to give six months to making himself master of the new duties of his position. Like all men of the highest capacity, Lord John was never unwilling to learn. He held that the Imperial Government was bound not merely by honour, but by enlightened self-interest, to protect the rights and to advance the welfare of the Colonies. His words are significant, and it seems well to quote them, since they gather up the policy which he consistently followed : 'If Great Britain gives up her supremacy from a niggardly spirit of parsimony, or from a craven fear of helplessness, other Powers will soon look upon the Empire, not with the regard due to an equal, as she once was, but with jealousy of the height she once held, without the fear she once inspired. To build up an empire extending over every sea, swaying many diverse races, and combining many forms of religion, requires courage and capacity ; to allow such an empire to fall to pieces is a task which may be performed by the poor in intellect, and the pusillanimous in conduct.'

When Lord John was once asked at the Colonial Office by an official of the French Government how much of Australia was claimed as the dominion of Great Britain, he promptly answered, ' The whole.' The visitor, quite taken aback, found it expedient to take his departure. Lord John vigorously assailed the view that colonies which had their own parliaments, framed on the British model, were virtually independent, and, therefore, had no right to expect more than moral help from the Mother Country. During his tenure of office New Zealand became part of the British dominions. By the treaty of Waitangi, the Queen assumed the sovereignty, and the new colony was assured of the protection of England. Lord John assured the British Provinces of North America that, so long as they wished to remain subjects of the Queen, they might confidently rely on the protection of England in all emergencies.

Mr. Gladstone has in recent years done justice to the remarkable prescience, and scarcely less remarkable administrative skill, which Lord John brought to bear at a critical juncture in the conduct of the Colonial policy of the Melbourne Government. He lays stress on the ' unfaltering courage ' which Russell displayed in meeting, as far as was then possible, the legitimate demand for responsible self-government. It is not, therefore, surprising that, to borrow Mr. Gladstone's words, ' Lord John Russell substituted harmony for antagonism in the daily conduct of affairs for those Colonies, each of which, in an infancy of irrepressible vigour, was bursting its swaddling clothes. Is it inexcusable to say that by this decision, which was far ahead of the current opinion of the day, he saved the Empire, possibly from disruption, certainly from much em-

barrassment and much discredit.'[1]   Lord John was a man of
vision.   He saw, beyond most of his contemporaries, the
coming magnitude of the Empire, and he did his best to
shape on broad lines and to far-reaching issues the policy of
England towards her children beyond the seas.   Lord John
recognised in no churlish or half-hearted spirit the claims
of the Colonies, nor did he stand dismayed by the vision
of Empire.   'There was a time when we might have stood
alone,' are his words.   'That time has passed.   We conquered and peopled Canada, we took possession of the
whole of Australia, Van Dieman's Land, and New Zealand.
We have annexed India to the Crown.   There is no
going back.   For my part, I delight in observing the imitation of our free institutions, and even our habits and
manners, in colonies at a distance from the Palace of Westminster.'   He trusted the Colonies, and refused to believe
that all the wisdom which was profitable to direct their
affairs was centred in Downing Street.   His attitude was sympathetic and generous, and at the same time it was candid
and firm.

Lord Stanmore's recollections of his father's colleague
go back to this period, and will be read with interest : 'As
a boy of ten or twelve I often saw Lord John.   His half-
sister, Lady Louisa Russell, was the wife of my half-brother,
Lord Abercorn, and Lord John was a frequent guest at Lord
Abercorn's villa at Stanmore, where my father habitually
passed his Saturdays and Sundays during the session, and
where I almost wholly lived.   My first conscious remembrance of Lord John dates from the summer of 1839, and

---

[1] 'The Melbourne Government : its Acts and Persons,' by the
Right Hon. W. E. Gladstone, M.P. *The Nineteenth Century*, January
1890, p. 50.

in that and the following years I often saw him at the Priory. Towards the close of 1839 Lord John lost his first wife, and the picture of his little figure, in deep mourning, walking by the side of my father on the gravel walks about the house in the spring and summer of 1840 is one vividly impressed on my recollection. His manner to children was not unpleasant, and I well remember his pausing, an amused listener to a childish and vehement political discussion between his step-daughter, Miss Lister, and myself—a discussion which he from time to time stirred up to increased animation by playfully mischievous suggestions.'

Early in the session of 1840, the Ministry was met by a vote of want of confidence, and in the course of the discussion Sir James Graham accused Lord John of encouraging sedition by appointing as magistrate one of the leaders of the Chartist agitation at Newport. Lord John, it turned out, had appointed Mr. Frost, the leader in question, on the advice of the Lord-Lieutenant, and he was able to prove that his own speech at Liverpool had been erroneously reported. The hostile resolution was accordingly repelled, and the division resulted in favour of the Government. For six years Turkey and Egypt had been openly hostile to each other, and in 1839 the war had been pushed to such extremities that Great Britain, Austria, Russia, and Prussia entered into a compact to bring about—by compulsion if necessary—a cessation of hostilities. Lord Holland and Lord Clarendon objected to England's share in the Treaty of July 1840, but Lord Palmerston compelled the Cabinet to acquiesce by a threat of resignation, and Lord John, at this crisis, showed that he was strongly in favour of his colleague's policy. The matter, however, was by no means settled, for once more a grave division of opinion in the party arose as to the wisdom of practically throwing away our alliance with France. Althorp—now Lord Spencer—reminded his former colleagues that that nation was most fitted to be our ally of any in Europe, on the threefold ground of situation, institutions, and civilisation.

Lord John drew up a memorandum and submitted it to his colleagues, in which he recognised the rights of France, and proposed to summon her, under given conditions, to take measures with the other Powers to preserve the peace of Europe. The personal ascendency of Lord Palmerston on questions of foreign policy was, however, already so marked that Lord Melbourne—now his brother-in-law, was reluctant to insist on moderation. Lord John, however, stood firm, and the breaking up of the Government seemed inevitable. During the crisis which followed, Lord Palmerston, striking, as was his wont, from his own bat, rejected, under circumstances which Mr. Walpole has explained in detail in his Life of Lord John Russell, a proposal for a conference of the allied Powers. Lord John had already entered his protest against any one member of the Cabinet being allowed to conduct affairs as he pleased, without consultation or control, and he now informed Lord Melbourne in a letter dated November 1, 1840—which Mr. Walpole prints—that Palmerston's reply to Austria compelled him to once more consider his position, as he could not defend in the House of Commons measures which he thought wrong. Lord Melbourne promptly recognised that Russell was the only possible leader in the Commons, and he induced Lord Palmerston to admit his mistake over the despatch to Metternich, and in this way the misunderstanding was brought to an end. Meanwhile, the fortunes of the war in the East turned against Ibrahim Pasha, and Palmerston's policy, though not his manner of carrying it out, was justified.

The closing years of the Melbourne Administration were marked not only by divided counsels, but by actual blunders of policy, and in this connection it is perhaps enough to cite the Opium war against China and the foolhardy invasion of Afghanistan. At home the question of Free Trade was coming rapidly to the front, and the Anti-corn Law League, which was founded in Manchester in 1838, was already beginning to prove itself a power in the land. As far back as 1826, Hume had taken up his parable in Parliament against the Corn Laws as a blight on the trade of the country; and two years after the Reform Bill was passed he had returned to the attack, only to find, however, that the nation was still wedded to Protection. Afterwards, year after year, Mr. Villiers drew attention to the subject, and moved for an inquiry into the working of the Corn Laws. He declared that the existing system was opposed by the industry, the intelligence, and the commerce of the nation, and at length, in a half-hearted fashion, the Government found itself compelled, if it was to exist at all, to make some attempt to deal with the problem. Lord Melbourne, and some at least of his colleagues, were but little interested in the question, and they failed to gauge the feeling of the country.

In the spring of 1841 action of some kind grew inevitable, and the Cabinet determined to propose a fixed duty of eight shillings per quarter on wheat, and to reduce the duty on sugar. Lord John opened the debate on the latter proposal in a speech which moved even Greville to enthusiasm; but neither his arguments nor his eloquence produced the desired impression on the House, for the Government was defeated by thirty-six votes. Everyone expected the Ministry at once to face the question of dissolution or resignation ; but Melbourne was determined to cling to office as long as possible, in spite of the growing difficulties and even humiliations of his position. On June 4, the day on which Lord John was to bring forward his proposal for a fixed duty on wheat, Sir Robert Peel carried a vote of want of confidence by a majority of one, and, as an appeal to the country was at length inevitable, Parliament was dissolved a few days later. The Melbourne Ministry had outstayed its welcome. The manner in which it had left Lord Durham in the lurch over his ill-advised ordinances had aroused widespread indignation, for the multitude at least could not forget the greatness of his services to the cause of Reform. If the dissolution had come two or three years earlier, the Government might have gone to the country without fear ; but in 1841, both at home and abroad, their blunders and their vacillation had alienated confidence, and it was not difficult to forecast the result. The General Election brought Lord John a personal triumph. He was presented with a requisition signed by several thousand persons, asking him to contest the City of London, and after an exciting struggle he was returned, though with only a narrow majority ; and during the political vicissitudes of the next eighteen years London was faithful to him.

Lord John Russell was essentially a home-loving man and the gloom which bereavement had cast over his life in the autumn of 1839 was at best only partially dispelled by the close and sympathetic relations with his family. It was, therefore, with satisfaction that all his friends, both on his own account and that of his motherless young children, heard of his approaching second marriage. Immediately after the election for the City, Lord John was married to Lady Fanny Elliot, second daughter of the Earl of Minto, a union which brought him lasting happiness.

Parliament met in the middle of August, and the Government were defeated on the Address by a majority of ninety-one, and on August 28 Lord John found himself once more out of harness. In his speech in the House of Commons announcing the resignation of the Government, he said that the Whigs under Lord Grey had begun with the Reform Act, and that they were closing their tenure of power by proposals for the relief of commerce. The truth was, the Melbourne Administration had not risen to its opportunities. Its fixed duty on corn was a paltry compromise. The leaders of the party needed to be educated up to the level of the national demands. Opposition was to bring about unexpected political combinations and new political opportunities, and the years of conflict which were dawning were also to bring more clearly into view Lord John Russell's claims to the Liberal leadership. When the Melbourne Administration was manifestly losing the confidence of the nation, Rogers the poet was walking one day with the Duke of Wellington in Hyde Park, and the talk turned on the political situation. Rogers remarked, 'What a powerful band Lord John Russell will have to contend with ! There's Peel, Lord Stanley, Sir James Graham——;' and the Duke interrupted him at this point with the laconic reply, 'Lord John Russell is a host in himself.'

Protection had triumphed at the General Election, and Sir Robert Peel came to power as champion of the Corn Laws. The Whigs had fallen between two stools, for the country was not in a humour to tolerate vacillation. The Melbourne Cabinet had, in truth, in the years which had witnessed its decline and fall, spoken with the voice of Jacob, but stretched forth the hands of Esau. The Radicals shook their heads, scouted the Ministry's deplorable efforts at finance, and felt, to say the least, lukewarm about their spirited foreign policy. 'I don't thank a man for supporting me when he thinks me right,' was the cynical confession of a statesman of an earlier generation ; 'my gratitude is with the man who supports me when he thinks me wrong.' Melbourne was doubtless of the same mind ; but the man in the crowd, of Liberal proclivities, was, for the most part, rather disgusted with the turn which affairs had taken, and the polling booths made it plain that he thought the Prime Minister wrong, and, that being the case, he was not obliging enough to return him to power. The big drum had been successfully beaten, moreover, at the General Election by the defenders of all sorts and sizes of vested interests, sinecures, monopolies, and the like, and Sir Robert Peel—though not without personal misgivings—accordingly succeeded Melbourne as First Lord, whilst Stanley, now the hope of stern unbending Tories, took Russell's place as Secretary for the Colonies.

The annals of the Peel Administration of course lie outside the province of this monograph ; they have already been told with insight and vigour in a companion volume, and the temptation to wander at a tangent into the history of the Queen's reign—especially with Lord John out of office—must be resisted in deference to the exigencies of space. In the Peel Cabinet the men who had revolted under Melbourne, with the exception of the Duke of Richmond, were rewarded with place and power. Lord Ripon, who was spoken of at the time with scarcely disguised contempt as a man of tried inefficiency, became President of the Board of Trade. Sir James Graham, a statesman who was becoming somewhat impervious to new ideas, and who as a Minister displayed little tact in regard to either movements or men, was appointed Home Secretary. Stanley, who had proved himself to be a strong man in the wrong camp, and therefore the evil genius of his party, now carried his unquestionable skill, and his brilliant powers of debate, as well as his imperious temper and contracted views, to the service of the Tories. One other man held a prominent place in Peel's Cabinet, and proved a tower of strength in it—Lord Aberdeen, who was Secretary for Foreign Affairs, and who did much to maintain the peace of Europe when the Tahiti incident and the Spanish marriages threatened embroilment. Lord Aberdeen, from 1841 to 1846, guided the foreign policy of England with ability and discretion, and, as a matter of fact, steered the nation through diplomatic quarrels which, if Lord Palmerston had been at the Foreign Office, would probably have ended in war. This circumstance heightens the irony of his subsequent career.

The outlook, political and social, when Peel took office and Russell confronted him as leader of the Opposition, was gloomy and full of hazard. The times, in Peel's judgment, were ' out of joint,' and this threw party Government out of joint and raised issues which confused ordinary minds. The old political catchwords ' Peace, retrenchment, and reform,' no longer awoke enthusiasm. Civil and religious liberty were all very well in their way, but they naturally failed to satisfy men and women who were ground down by economic oppression, and were famished through lack of bread. The social condition of England was deplorable, for, though the Reform Bill had brought in its wake measures of relief for the middle classes, it had left the artisans and the peasants almost where it found them. In spite of the new Poor Law and other enactments, the people were burdened with the curse of bitter and hopeless poverty, and the misery and squalor in which they were permitted to live threw a menacing shadow over the fair promise of the opening years of the young Queen's reign.   The historians of the period are responsible for the statement that in Manchester, for example, one-tenth of the population lived in cellars ; even in the rural districts, the overcrowding, with all its attending horrors in the direction of disease and vice, was scarcely less terrible, for in one parish in Dorset thirty-six persons dwelt, on an average, in each house.   The wonder is, not that the Anti-Corn Law League under such circumstances grew strong and the demand for the People's Charter rang through the land, but that the masses in town and country alike bore the harsh servitude of their lot with the patience that was common, and with the heroism that was not rare.

Lord John Russell never refused to admit the ability of Peel's Administration.   He described it as powerful, popular, and successful.   He recognised the honesty of his great rival, his openness of mind, the courage which he displayed in turning a deaf ear to the croakers in his own Cabinet, and the genuine concern which he manifested for the unredressed grievances of the people.   In his 'Recollections' he lays stress on the fact that Sir Robert Peel did not hesitate, when he thought such a step essential to the public welfare, to risk the fate of his Ministry on behalf of an unpopular measure.   Ireland was a stone of stumbling in his path, and long after he had parted with his old ideas of Protestant ascendency he found himself confronted with the suspicion of the Roman Catholics, who, in Lord John's words, 'obstinately refused favours at Peel's hands, which they would have been willing to accept from a Liberal Administration.' The allusion is, of course, to the Maynooth Grant—a measure of practical relief to the Irish Catholics, which would, without doubt, have thrown Sir Robert Peel out of office if he had been left to the tender mercies of his own supporters. Disraeli was fond of asserting that Peel lacked imagination, and there was a measure of truth in the charge. He was a great patriotic statesman, haunted by no foolish bugbear of consistency, but willing to learn by experience, and courageous enough to follow what he believed to be right, with unpolitical but patriotic scorn of consequence. Men with stereotyped ideas, who persisted in interpreting concession, however just, as weakness, and reform, however urgent, as revolution, were unable to follow such a leader.

Peel might lack imagination, but he never lacked courage, and the generosity of vision which imposed on courage great and difficult tasks of statesmanship. He could educate himself—for he kept an open mind—and was swift to seize and to interpret great issues in the affairs of the nation ; but it was altogether a different matter for him to educate his party. In the spring of 1845, Sir Robert Peel determined to meet the situation in Ireland by bold proposals for the education of the Catholic priesthood. Almost to the close of the eighteenth century the Catholics were compelled by the existing laws to train young men intended for the work of the priesthood in Ireland in French colleges, since no seminary of the kind was permitted in Ireland. The French Revolution overthrew this arrangement, and in 1795, by an Act of the Irish Parliament, Maynooth College was founded, and was supported by annual grants, which were continued, though not without much opposition, by the Imperial Parliament after the Union. On April 3, Sir Robert Peel brought forward his measure for dealing in a generous manner with the needs and claims of this great institution. He proposed that the annual grant should be raised from 9,000*l.* to upwards of 26,000*l.*, that a charter of incorporation should be given, and that the trustees should be allowed to hold land to the value of 3,000*l.* a year. He also proposed that the new endowment should be a charge upon the Consolidated Fund, so that angry discussions of the kind in which bigotry and prejudice delight might be avoided. Moreover, in order to restore and enlarge the college buildings, Sir Robert finally proposed an immediate and separate grant of 30,000*l.* Few statesmen were more sensitive than Peel, but, convinced of the justice of such a concession, he spoke that day amid the angry opposition of the majority of his usual supporters and the approving cheers of his ordinary opponents.

Peel was not the man to falter, although his party was in revolt. He had gauged the forces which were arrayed in Ireland against the authority of Parliament ; he stated in his final words on the subject that there was in that country a formidable confederacy, which was prepared to go any lengths against a hard interpretation of the supremacy of England. ' I do not believe that you can break it up by force ; I believe you can do much by acting in a spirit of kindness, forbearance, and generosity.' At once a great storm of opposition arose in Parliament, on the platform, and in the Press. The Carlton Club found itself brought into sudden and unexpected agreement with many a little Bethel up and down the country, for the champions of ' No Surrender' in Pall Mall were of one mind with those of ' No

Popery' in Exeter Hall. Society for the moment, according to Harriet Martineau, seemed to be going mad, and she saw enough to convince her that it was not the extent of the grant that was deprecated so much as an advance in that direction at all. Public indignation ran so high that in some instances members of Parliament were called upon to resign their seats, whilst Dublin—so far at least as its sentiments were represented by the Protestant Operative Association—was for nothing less than the impeachment of the unhappy Prime Minister. Sectarian animosity, whipped into fury by rhetorical appeals to its prejudices, encouraged the paper trade by interminable petitions to Parliament ; and three nights were spent in debate in the Lords and six in the Commons over the second reading of the bill.

Lord John Russell was assailed with threatening letters as soon as it was known that he intended to help Peel to outweather the storm of obloquy which he was called to encounter. Sir Robert's proposals were welcomed by him as a new and worthy departure from the old repressive policy. It was because he thought that such a measure would go far to conciliate the Catholics of Ireland, as well as to prove to them that any question which touched their interests and welfare was not a matter of unconcern to the statesmen and people of England, that he gave—with a loyalty only too rare in public life—his powerful support to a Minister who would otherwise have been driven to bay by his own followers. It was, in fact, owing to Lord John's action that Peel triumphed over the majority of his own party, and his speech in support of the Ministry, though not remarkable for eloquence, was admirable alike in temper and in tact, and was hailed at the moment as a presage of victory. 'Peel lives, moves, and has his being through

Lord John Russell,' was Lord Shaftesbury's comment at the moment. Looking back at the crisis from the leisure of retirement, Lord John Russell declared that the Maynooth Act was a work of wisdom and liberality, and one which ought always to be remembered to the honour of the statesman who proposed and carried it. The controversy over the Maynooth Grant revealed how great was the gulf between Peel and the majority of the Tories, and Greville, as usual, in his own incisive way hit off the situation. 'The truth is that the Government is Peel, that Peel is a Reformer and more of a Whig than a Tory, and that the mass of his followers are prejudiced, ignorant, obstinate, and selfish.' Peel declared that he looked with indifference on a storm which he thought partly fanatical and partly religious in its origin, and he added that he was careless as to the consequences which might follow the passing of the Maynooth Bill, so far at least as they concerned his own position.

Meanwhile another and far greater question was coming forward with unsuspected rapidity for solution. The summer of 1845 was cold and wet, and its dark skies and drenching showers were followed by a miserable harvest. With the approach of autumn the fields were flooded and the farmers in consequence in despair. Although England and Scotland suffered greatly, the disaster fell with still greater force on Ireland. As the anxious weeks wore on, alarm deepened into actual distress, for there arose a mighty famine in the land. The potato crop proved a disastrous failure, and with the approach of winter starvation joined its eloquence to that of Cobden and Bright in their demand for the repeal of the Corn Laws. In speaking afterwards of that terrible crisis, and of the services which Cobden and himself were enabled to render to the nation, John Bright used these memorable words : 'Do not suppose that I wish you to imagine that he and I were the only persons engaged in this great question. We were not even the first, though afterwards, perhaps, we became before the public the foremost, but there were others before us, and we were joined, not by scores, but by hundreds, and afterwards by thousands, and afterwards by countless multitudes, and afterwards famine itself, against which we had warred, joined us, and a great Minister was converted, and minorities became majorities, and finally the barrier was entirely thrown down.'

Quite early in the history of the Anti-Corn-Law League, Cobden had predicted, in spite of the apathy and opposition which the derided Manchester school of politics then encountered, at a time when Peel and Russell alike turned a deaf ear to its appeals, that the repeal of the Corn Laws would be eventually carried in Parliament by a 'statesman of established reputation.' Argument and agitation prepared the way for this great measure of practical relief, but the multitude were not far from the mark when they asserted that it was the rain that destroyed the Corn Laws.[1] The imperative necessity of bringing food from abroad if the people were not to perish for lack of bread brought both Sir Robert Peel and Lord John Russell almost at the same moment to the conclusion that this great economic problem must at once be faced. Peel declared in 1847 that towards the end of 1845 he had reached the conclusion that the repeal of the Corn Laws was indispensable to the public welfare.

---

[1] 'The Corn Law of 1815 was a copy of the Corn Law of 1670—so little had economic science grown in England during all those years. The Corn Law of 1670 imposed a duty on the importation of foreign grain which amounted almost literally to a prohibition.'—*Sir Robert Peel*, by Justin M'Carthy, M.P., chapter xii. p. 136.

If that was so, he seems to have kept his opinion to himself, for as late as November 29, in the memorandum which he sent to his colleagues, there is no hint of abolition. On the contrary, Sir Robert, who was always fond of setting forth three alternatives of action, wrote as follows : 'Time presses, and on some definite course we must decide. Shall we undertake without suspension to modify the existing Corn Law? Shall we resolve to maintain the existing Corn Law? Shall we advise the suspension of that law for a limited period? My opinion is for the last course, admitting as I do that it involves the necessity for the immediate consideration of the alterations to be made in the existing Corn Law ; such alterations to take effect after the period of suspension. I should rather say it involves the question of the principle and degree of protection to agriculture.'[1] As to the justice of the demand for Free Trade, Peel, there can be no doubt, was already convinced ; but his party was regarded as the stronghold of Protection, and he knew enough of the men who sat behind him to be fully alive to the fact that they still clung tenaciously to the fallacies which Adam Smith had exploded. 'We had ill luck,' were Lord Aberdeen's words to the Queen ; 'if it had not been for the famine in Ireland, which rendered immediate measures necessary, Sir Robert would have prepared the party gradually for the change.'[2]

Cobden, it is only fair to state, made no secret of his conviction that the question of the repeal of the Corn Laws was safer in the hands of Sir Robert than of Lord John. Peel might be less versed in constitutional questions,

---

[1] *The Croker Papers*, edited by Louis Jennings, vol. iii. p. 35.
[2] *Life of the Prince Consort*, by Sir Theodore Martin, vol. i. p. 317.

but he was more in touch with the manufacturing classes, and more familiar with economic conditions. Sir Robert, however, was sore let and hindered by the weaklings of his own Cabinet, and the rats did not disguise their intention of quitting the ship. Lord John Russell, who was spending the autumn in Scotland, was the first 'responsible statesman' to take decisive action, for whilst Peel, hampered by the vacillation and opposition of his colleagues, still hesitated, Russell took the world into his confidence in his historic 'Edinburgh Letter,' dated November 22, 1845, to his constituents in London. It was a bold and uncompromising declaration of policy, for the logic of events had at length convinced Lord John that any further delay was dangerous. He complained that Her Majesty's Ministers had not only met, but separated, without affording the nation any promise of immediate relief. He pointed out that the existing duties on corn were so contrived that, the worse the quality of the wheat, the higher was the duty. 'When good wheat rises to seventy shillings a quarter, the average price of all wheat is fifty-seven or fifty-eight shillings, and the duty fourteen or fifteen shillings a quarter. Thus the corn barometer points to fair, while the ship is bending under a storm.' He reviewed the course of recent legislation on the subject, and declared that he had for years endeavoured to obtain a compromise. He showed that Peel had opposed in 1839, 1840, and 1841, even qualified concession, and he added the stinging allusion to that statesman's attitude on other great questions of still earlier date. 'He met the proposition for diminished Protection in the same way in which he had met the offer of securities for Protestant interests in 1817 and 1825—in the same way in which he met the proposal to allow Manchester, Leeds, and

Birmingham to send members to Parliament in 1830.' Finally, Lord John announced his conviction that it was no longer worth while to contend for a fixed duty, and his vigorous attack on the Ministry ended with a call to arms. ' Let us unite to put an end to a system which has been proved to be the blight of commerce, the bane of agriculture, the source of bitter divisions among classes, the cause of penury, fever, mortality, and crime among the people. The Government appear to be waiting for some excuse to give up the present Corn Law Let the people, by petition, by address, by remonstrance, afford them the excuse they seek.'

Sir Robert, when this manifesto appeared, had almost conquered the reluctance of his own Cabinet to definite action ; but his position grew now untenable in consequence of the panic of Stanley and the Duke of Buccleuch. Lord John's speech was quickly followed by a Ministerial crisis, and Peel, beset by fightings without and fears within his Cabinet, had no alternative but resignation. He accordingly relinquished office on December 5, and three days later Lord John, much to his own surprise, was summoned to Windsor and entrusted with the task of forming a new Ministry. He was met by difficulties which, in spite of negotiations, proved insurmountable, for Howick, who had succeeded in the previous summer to his distinguished father's earldom, refused to serve with Palmerston. Lord Grey raised another point which might reasonably have been conceded, for he urged that Cobden, as the leader of the Anti-Corn-Law League, ought to have the offer of a seat in the Cabinet. Lord John was unable to bring about an amicable understanding, and therefore, as the year was closing, he was compelled to inform her Majesty of the fact, and to hand back what Disraeli theatrically described as the 'poisoned chalice' to Sir Robert. 'It is all at an end,' wrote Lord John to his wife. 'Power may come, some day or other, in a less odious shape.'

CHAPTER VII

FACTION AND FAMINE

1846-1847

Peel and Free Trade—Disraeli and Lord George Bentinck lead the
attack—Russell to the rescue—Fall of Peel—Lord John summoned
to power—Lord John's position in the Commons and in the country—The Condition of Ireland question—Famine and its deadly
work—The Russell Government and measures of relief—Crime and
coercion—The Whigs and Education—Factory Bill—The case of
Dr. Hampden.

LORD STANLEY's place in the 'organised hypocrisy,' as the
Protectionists termed the last Ministry of Sir Robert Peel,
was taken by Mr. Gladstone. Sir Robert Peel resumed
office in the closing days of December, and all the members
of his old Cabinet, on the principle of bowing to the inevitable, returned with him, except the Duke of Buccleuch
and Lord Stanley, who resolutely declined to have part or lot
in the new departure which the Premier now felt called upon
to make. The Duke of Wellington, though hostile to Free
Trade, determined to stand by Peel; but he did not disguise
the fact that his only reason for remaining in office was for
the sake of the Queen. He declared that he acted as the
'retained servant of the monarchy,' for he did not wish her
Majesty to be placed under the necessity of taking members
of the Anti-Corn-Law League, or, as he put it, 'Cobden
& Co.,' for her responsible advisers.

The opening days of 1846 were full of political excitement, and were filled with all kinds of rumours. Wellington, on January 6, wrote : 'I don't despair of the Corn Laws,' and confessed that he did not know what were the intentions of Sir Robert Peel concerning them.[1] Peel kept his own counsel, though the conviction grew that he had persuaded himself that in boldness lay the chance as well as the duty of the hour. Peel, like Russell, was converted to Free Trade by the logic of events, and he determined at all hazards to avow the new faith that was in him. Parliament was opened by the Queen in person on January 22, and the Speech from the Throne laid stress on the privation and suffering in Ireland, and shadowed forth the repeal of prohibitive and the relaxation of protective duties. The debate on the Address was rendered memorable by Peel's explanations of the circumstances under which the recent crisis had arisen. He made a long speech, and the tone of it, according to Lord Malmesbury, was half threatening and half apologetic. It was a manly, straightforward statement of the case, and Sir Robert made it plain that he had accepted the views of the Manchester school on the Corn Laws, and was prepared to act without further hesitation on his convictions. One significant admission was added. He stated before he sat down that it was 'no easy task to insure the harmonious and united action of an ancient monarchy, a proud aristocracy, and a reformed House of Commons.'

New interests were, in fact, beginning to find a voice in Parliament, and that meant the beginning of the principle of readjustment which is yet in' progress. A few days later the Prime Minister explained his financial

---

[1] *The Croker Papers*, vol. iii. ch. xxiv. p. 53.

plans for the year, and in the course of them he proposed the gradual repeal of the Corn Laws. Free trade in corn was, in fact, to take final effect after an interval of three years. Meanwhile the sliding scale was to be abandoned in favour of a fixed duty of ten shillings the quarter on corn, and other concessions for the relief not only of agriculture but of manufactures and commerce were announced. The principle of Free Trade was, in fact, applied not in one but in many directions, and from that hour its legislative triumph was assured. In the course of the protracted debate which followed, Disraeli, with all the virulence of a disappointed place-hunter, attacked Sir Robert Peel with bitter personalities and barbed sarcasm. On this occasion, throwing decency and good taste to the winds, and, to borrow a phrase of his own, 'intoxicated with the exuberance of his own verbosity,' and with no lack of tawdry rhetoric and melodramatic emphasis, he did his best to cover with ridicule and to reduce to confusion one of the most chivalrous and lofty-minded statesmen of the Queen's reign.

Disraeli's audacity in attack did much to revive the drooping courage of the Protectionist party, the leadership of which fell for the moment into the hands of Lord George Bentinck, a nobleman more renowned at Newmarket than at Westminster. Once saddled with authority, Lord George developed some capacity for politics ; but his claims as a statesman were never serious, though Disraeli, in the polical biography which he published shortly after his friend's sudden death, gives him credit for qualities of mind of which the nation at large saw little evidence. After long and tedious discussion, extending over some twenty nights, the Free Trade Bill was carried through the Commons by a majority of ninety-eight votes, and in the Lords it passed the second reading by forty-seven votes. Croker—true to the dismal suggestion of his name—promptly took up his parable against Sir Robert. He declared that the repeal of the Corn Laws meant a schism in the great landed interest and broad acres, in his view, were the only solid foundation on which the government of the nation could possibly be based. He asked, how was it possible to resist the attack on the Irish Church and the Irish Union after the surrender of the Corn Laws? He wanted to know how primogeniture, the Bishops, the House of Lords, and the Crown itself were to be maintained, now that the leader of the Conservative party had truckled to the League. Sir Robert Peel, he added, had imperilled these institutions of the country more than Cobbett or O'Connell; he had broken up the old interests, divided the great families, and thrown personal hostility into the social life of half the counties of England —and all to propitiate Richard Cobden. Such was the bitter cry of the outcast Protectionist, and similar vapourings arose in cliques and clubs all over the land. The abolition of the Corn Laws was the last measure of Sir Robert Peel's political life, and he owed the victory, which was won amid the murmurs and threats of his own followers, to the support which his political antagonists gave him, under the leadership of Lord John Russell, who recognised both the wisdom and the expediency of Sir Robert's course.

Meanwhile the dark winter of discontent which privation had unhappily brought about in Ireland had been marked by many crimes of violence, and at length the Government deemed it imperative to ask Parliament to grant them additional powers for the suppression of outrage. The measure met with the opposition alike of Lord John

Russell and Daniel O'Connell. The Government moved the second reading of the Irish Coercion Bill, and the Protectionists, who knew very well not only the views of Daniel O'Connell, but of Smith O'Brien, saw their opportunity and promptly took it. Lord George Bentinck had supported the Coercion Bill on its introduction in the spring, and had done so in the most unmistakable terms. He was not the man, however, to forego the mean luxury of revenge, and neither he nor Disraeli could forgive what they regarded as Sir Robert's great betrayal of the landed interest. He now had the audacity to assert that Peel had lost the confidence of every honest man both within and without the House of Commons, and in spite of his assurances of support he ranged himself for the moment with Russell and O'Connell to crush the Administration. The division took place on June 25, and in a House of 571 members the Ministry was defeated by a majority of 73. The defeat of the Government was so crushing that Whigs and Protectionists alike, on the announcement of the figures, were too much taken aback to cheer. ' Anything,' said Sir Robert, ' is preferable to maintaining ourselves in office without a full measure of the confidence of this House.'

Lord John had triumphed with the help of the Irish, whom Peel had alienated ; but the great Minister's downfall had in part been accomplished by the treachery of those who abandoned him with clamour and evil-speaking in the hour of need. Defeat was followed within a week by resignation, and on July 4 Peel, writing from the leisured seclusion of Drayton Manor, ' in the loveliest weather,' was magnanimous enough to say, ' I have every disposition to forgive my enemies for having conferred on me the blessing of the loss of power.' Lord John was summoned to

Windsor, and kissed hands on July 6. He became Prime Minister when the condition of affairs was gloomy and menacing, and the following passage from his wife's journal, written on July 14, conjures up in two or three words a vivid picture of the difficulties of the hour : 'John has much to distress him in the state of the country. God grant him success in his labours to amend it ! Famine, fever, trade failing, and discontent growing are evils which it requires all his resolution, sense of duty, and love for the public to face.' Lord Palmerston was, of course, inevitable as Foreign Secretary in the new Administration ; Sir Charles Wood became Chancellor of the Exchequer, and Sir George Grey, Home Secretary. Earl Grey's scruples were at length satisfied, and he became Secretary to the Colonies ; whilst Lord Clarendon took office as President of the Board of Trade, and Lord Lansdowne became President of the Council. Among the lesser lights of the Ministry were Sir J. C. Hobhouse, Mr. Milner Gibson, Mr. Fox Maule, Lord Morpeth, and Mr. (afterwards Lord) Macaulay. Sir James Graham was offered the Governor-Generalship of India, but he had aspirations at Westminster, which, however, were never fulfilled, and declined the offer. The Tory party was demoralised and split up into cliques by suspicion and indignation. Stanley was in the House of Lords by this time, Peel was in disgrace, and Lord George Bentinck was already beginning to cut a somewhat ridiculous figure, whilst nobody as yet was quite prepared to take Disraeli seriously. 'We are left masters of the field,' wrote Palmerston, with a touch of characteristic humour, 'not only on account of our own merits, which, though we say it ourselves, are great, but by virtue of the absence of any efficient competitors.'

The new Ministry began well. Lord John's address to

his constituents in the City made an excellent impression,
and was worthy of the man and the occasion. 'You may be
assured that I shall not desert in office the principles to
which I adhered when they were less favourably received.
I cannot indeed claim the merit either of having carried measures of Free Trade as a Minister, or of having so prepared
the public mind by any exertions of mine as to convert
what would have been an impracticable attempt into a certain
victory. To others belong those distinctions. But I have
endeavoured to do my part in this great work according to
my means and convictions, first by proposing a temperate
relaxation of the Corn Laws, and afterwards, when that
measure has been repeatedly rejected, by declaring in favour
of total repeal, and using every influence I could exert to
prevent a renewal of the struggle for an object not worth
the cost of conflict. The Government of this country ought
to behold with an impartial eye the various portions of the
community engaged in agriculture, in manufactures, and in
commerce. The feeling that any of them is treated with
injustice provokes ill-will, disturbs legislation, and diverts
attention from many useful and necessary reforms. Great
social improvements are required : public education is manifestly imperfect ; the treatment of criminals is a problem
yet undecided ; the sanitary condition of our towns and villages has been grossly neglected. Our recent discussions
have laid bare the misery, the discontent, and outrages of
Ireland ; they are too clearly authenticated to be denied,
too extensive to be treated by any but the most comprehen-
sive means.'

Lord John had been thirty-three years in the House of
Commons when he became for the first time Prime Minister.
The distinction of rank and of an historic name gave him in

1813, when government by great families was still more than a phrase, a splendid start. The love of liberty which he inherited as a tradition grew strong within him, partly through his residence in Edinburgh under Dugald Stewart, partly through the generous and stimulating associations of Holland House, but still more, perhaps, because of the tyranny of which he was an eye-witness during his travels as a youth in Italy and Spain at a period when Europe lay under the heel of Napoleon. Lord John was ever a fighter, and the political conflicts of his early manhood against the triple alliance of injustice, bigotry, and selfish apathy in the presence of palpable social abuses lent ardour to his convictions, tenacity to his aims, and boldness to his attitude in public life. Although an old Parliamentary hand, he was in actual years only fifty-four when he came to supreme office in the service of the State, but he had already succeeded in placing great measures on the Statute Book, and he had also won recognition on both sides of the House as a leader of fearless courage, open mind, and great fertility of resource alike in attack and in defence. Peel, his most formidable rival on the floor of the Commons, hinted that Lord John Russell was small in small things, but, he added significantly that, when the issues grew great, he was great also. Everyone who looks at Lord John's career in its length and breadth must admit the justice of such a criticism. On one occasion he himself said, in speaking of the first Lord Halifax, that the favourite of Charles II. had 'too keen a perception of errors and faults to act well with others,' and the remark might have been applied to himself. There were times when Lord John, by acting hastily on the impulse of the moment, landed his colleagues in serious and unlooked for difficulties, and sometimes it happened that in his anxiety to clear his own soul by taking an independent course, he compromised to a serious extent the position of others.

Lord Melbourne's cynical remark, to the effect that nobody did anything very foolish except from some strong principle, carries with it a tribute to motive as well as a censure on action, and it is certain that the promptings to which Lord John yielded in the questionable phases of his public career were not due to the adroit and calculating temper of self-interest. His weaknesses were indeed, after all, trivial in comparison to his strength. He rose to the great occasion and was inspired by it. All that was formal and hesitating in manner and speech disappeared, and under the combined influence of the sense of responsibility and the excitement of the hour 'languid Johnny,' to borrow Bulwer Lytton's phrase, 'soared to glorious John.' Palmerston, like Melbourne, was all things to all men. His easy nonchalance, sunny temper, and perfect familiarity with the ways of the world and the weaknesses of average humanity, gave him an advantage which Lord John, with his nervous temperament, indifferent health, fastidious tastes, shy and rather distant bearing, and uncompromising convictions, never possessed. Russell's ethical fervour and practical energetic bent of mind divided him sharply from politicians who lived from hand to mouth, and were never consumed by a zeal for reform in one direction or another ; and these qualities sometimes threw him into a position of singular isolation. The wiles and artifices by which less proud and less conscientious men win power, and the opportune compliments and unwatched concessions by which too often they retain it, lay amongst the things to which he refused to stoop.

Men might think Lord John taciturn, angular, abrupt,

tenacious, and dogmatic, but it was impossible not to recognise his honesty, public spirit, pluck in the presence of difficulty, and high interpretation of the claims of public duty which marked his strenuous and indomitable career. His qualifications for the post of Prime Minister were not open to challenge. He was deeply versed in constitutional problems, and had received a long and varied training in the handling of great affairs. He possessed to an enviable degree the art of lucid exposition, and could render intricate proposals luminous to the public mind. He was a shrewd Parliamentary tactician, as well as a statesman who had worthily gained the confidence of the nation. He was ready in debate, swift to see and to seize the opportunity of the hour. He was full of practical sagacity, and his personal character lent weight to his position in the country. In the more militant stages of his career, and especially when he was fighting the battles of Parliamentary reform and religious liberty, he felt the full brunt of that 'sullen resistance to innovation,' as well as that ' unalterable perseverance in the wisdom of prejudice,' which Burke declared was characteristic of the English race. The natural conservatism of growing years, it must be frankly admitted, led eventually in Lord John's case, as in that of the majority of mankind, to the slackening of interest in the new problems of a younger generation, but to the extreme verge of life he remained far too great a statesman and much too generous a man ever to lapse into the position of a mere *laudator temporis acti.* Lord John did not allow the few remaining weeks of a protracted and exhaustive session to elapse without a vigorous attempt to push the principle of Free Trade to its logical issues. He passed a measure which rendered the repeal of the Corn Laws total and immediate, and he carried, with the support of Peel and in spite of the opposition of Bentinck and Disraeli, the abolition of protection to sugar grown in the British Colonies.

Ireland quickly proved itself to be a stone of stumbling and a rock of offence to the new Administration. Lord John's appointment of Lord Bessborough—his old colleague, Duncannon, in the Committee on Reform in 1830—as viceroy was popular, for he was a resident Irish landlord, and a man who was genuinely concerned for the welfare of the people. O'Connell trusted Lord Bessborough, and that, in the disturbed condition of the country, counted for much. The task of the new viceroy was hard, even with such support, and though Bessborough laboured manfully and with admirable tact to better the social condition of the people and to exorcise the spirit of discord, the forces arrayed against him proved resistless when famine came to their aid. As the summer slipped past, crime and outrage increased, and the prospect for the approaching winter grew not merely gloomy but menacing. Peel had been turned out of office because of his Irish Arms Bill, and Bessborough was no sooner installed in Dublin than he made urgent representations to the Cabinet in Downing Street as to the necessity of adopting similar repressive measures, in view of the prevailing lawlessness and the contempt for life and property which in the disaffected districts were only too common. In August the crisis was already so acute that the Government, yielding to the fears of its Irish advisers, stultified itself by proposing the renewal of the Arms Bill until the following spring. The step was ill advised, and provoked much hostile criticism. Lord John did not relish the measure, but Lord Bessborough declared that Ireland could not be governed for the moment without it, and as he also talked of throwing up his appointment, and was supported in this view of the situation by Mr. Labouchere (afterwards Lord Taunton), who at that time was Chief Secretary, the Prime Minister gave way and introduced in the House of Commons proposals which were out of keeping with his own antecedents, and which he personally disliked. In speaking of Sir Robert Peel's Coercion Bill in his published 'Recollections,' Lord John makes no secret of his own attitude towards the measure. 'I objected to the Bill on Irish grounds. I then thought, and I still think, that it is wrong to arrest men and put them in prison on the ground that they *may* be murderers and housebreakers. They may be, on the other hand, honest labourers going home from their work.' On the contrary, he thought that every means ought to be promptly taken for discovering the perpetrators of crime and bringing them to justice, and he also believed in giving the authorities on the spot ample means of dealing with the reign of terror which agrarian outrages had established.

If O'Connell had been at Lord John's side at that juncture, England might have sent a practical message of good-will to Ireland instead of falling back on the old policy of coercion. O'Connell had learnt to trust Russell—as far, at least, as it was possible for a leader of the Irish people to trust a Whig statesman—and Russell, on the other hand, was beginning to understand not merely O'Connell, but the forces which lay behind him, and which rendered him, quite apart from his own eloquence and gifts, powerful. Unfortunately, the Liberator was by this time broken in health, and the Young Ireland party were already in revolt against his authority, a circumstance which, in itself, filled the Premier with misgivings, and led him to give way, however reluctantly, to the demand of the viceroy for repressive measures. Lord John was, in fact, only too well aware that force was no remedy. He wished, as much as O'Connell, to root up the causes which produced crime. Young Ireland, however, seemed determined to kick over the traces at the very time when the Liberator was inducing the Whigs to look at the question in a practical manner. Lord John knew, to borrow his own expression, that the 'armoury of penal legislation was full of the weapons of past battles, and yet the victory of order and peace had not been gained.' The Liberal party set its face against coercion in any shape or form, and the Government withdrew a proposal which they ought never to have introduced. This course had scarcely been taken when a new and terrible complication of the social problem in Ireland arose.

Famine suddenly made its presence felt, and did so in a manner which threw the privation and scarcity of the previous winter altogether into the shade. The potato crop was a disastrous failure, and, as the summer waned, the distress of an impoverished and thriftless race grew acute. The calamity was as crushing as it was rapid. 'On July 27,' are Father Mathew's words, 'I passed from Cork to Dublin, and this doomed plant bloomed in all the luxuriance of an abundant harvest. Returning on August 3 I beheld with sorrow one wide waste of putrefying vegetation.' A million and a half of acres were at the moment under cultivation, and the blight only spared a quarter of them, whilst, to make matters worse, the oat crop, by an unhappy coincidence, proved to a startling extent insufficient. The financial loss in that disastrous harvest, in the reckoning of experts, amounted to between fifteen and sixteen millions sterling. Fever and dysentery made fatal inroads on the dwindling strength of the gaunt and famished peasantry, and in one district alone, out of a population of 62,000 inhabitants, no less than 5,000 persons died, directly or indirectly, of starvation in the course of three months. ' All our thoughts,' wrote O'Connell, ' are engrossed with two topics—endeavouring to keep the people from outbreaks, and endeavouring to get food for them.' In many instances the landlords seemed robbed of the characteristics of ordinary humanity, for the ruthless process of eviction was carried on with a high hand, and old men and children were left unsheltered as well as unfed.

Property had neglected its duties, but, as usual, did not neglect its rights, and in that terrible crisis it overrode the rights of humanity. Many of the landowners, however, manfully did their best to stay the plague, but anything which they could accomplish seemed a mockery amid the widespread distress. Readers of Sir Gavan Duffy's ' Four Years of Irish History' will recall his vivid description of the manner in which some of the landowners, however, saw their cruel opportunity, and accordingly ' closed on the people with ejectments, turned them on the road, and plucked down their roof-trees,' and also that still more painful passage which describes how women with dead children in their arms were seen begging for a coffin to bury them. Relief committees were, of course, started ; the Friends, in particular, busied themselves in practical efforts to cope with the distress, and Mr. W. E. Forster, who went to Ireland to distribute relief, declared that his wonder was, as he passed from village to village, not that the people died, but that so many contrived to live.

The Russell Government met the crisis with courage, though scarcely with adequate understanding. Ireland remembered with bitterness their Arms Bill and their repressive measures. Public feeling ran high over some of their proposals, for the people resented Lord John's modification of Sir Robert Peel's plan by which the cost of public works was to be defrayed by the State and district in which employment was given. Lord John determined that the cost should be met in the first instance by Government loans, which were to be repaid with an almost nominal interest by the people of the district. This was interpreted to mean that Ireland was to bear her own burdens, and in her impoverished state was to be saddled with the financial responsibilities inseparable from so pitiable a collapse of prosperity. Bread riots and agrarian disturbances grew common, and the Government met them with rather more than becoming sternness, instead of dealing promptly with the land-tenure system which lay at the root of so much of the misery. At the beginning of the session of 1847 it was stated that 10,000,000*l.* would be required to meet the exigencies of the situation. Lord George Bentinck proposed a grant of 16,000,000*l.* for the construction of Irish railways, but Lord John made the question one of personal confidence in himself, and threatened resignation if it passed. His chief objection to the proposal was based on the fact that seventy-five per cent. of the money spent in railway construction would not reach the labouring classes. Lord George Bentinck's motion was rejected by a sweeping majority, though at a subsequent stage in the session the Government consented to advance a substantial sum to three Irish railways— a concession which exposed them to the usual taunts of inconsistency.

Measures were also introduced for promoting emigration to the colonies, and for the suspension of certain clauses of the Navigation Laws which hindered the importation of foreign corn. At one time during the distress there were no less than six hundred thousand men employed on public works in Ireland, and the Government found it no easy task to organise this vast army of labour, or to prevent abuses. Lord Bessborough urged that the people should be employed in the improvement of private estates, but Lord John met this proposal with disapproval, though he at length agreed that the drainage of private land should come within the scope of public works. It was further determined to lend money in aid of the improvement of private property, the operation of the Irish Poor Law was also extended, and in other directions energetic measures were taken for the relief of the prevailing destitution. Lord John was a keen observer both of men and of movements, and the characteristics of the peasantry, and more particularly the personal helplessness of the people, and the lack of concerted action among them, impressed him. 'There are some things,' he declared, 'which the Crown cannot grant and which Parliament cannot enact—the spirit of self-reliance and the spirit of co-operation. I must say plainly that I should indeed despair of this task were it not that I think I see symptoms in the Irish people both of greater reliance on their own energies and exertions, and of greater intelligence to co-operate with each other. Happy will it be, indeed, if the Irish take for their maxim, " Help yourselves and Heaven will help you," and then I think they will find there is some use in adversity.'

Lord John Russell's Irish policy has often been misunderstood, and not seldom misrepresented, but no one who looks all the facts calmly in the face, or takes into account the difficulties which the famine threw in his path, will be inclined to harsh criticism.   Lady Russell's journal at this period reveals how great was her husband's anxiety in view of the evil tidings from Ireland, and one extract may be allowed to speak for itself.   After stating that her husband has much to distress him in the state of the country, these words follow : ' God grant him success in his labours to amend it—famine, fever, trade failing, and discontent growing are evils which it requires all his resolution, sense of duty, and love for the public to face.   I pray that he may, and believe that he will, one day be looked back to as the greatest benefactor of unhappy Ireland.'   When once the nature of the calamity became apparent, Lord John never relaxed his efforts to grapple with the emergency, and, though not a demonstrative man, there is proof enough that he felt acutely for the people, and laboured, not always perhaps wisely, but at least well, for the amelioration of their lot.   He was assailed with a good deal of personal abuse, and was credited with vacillation and apathy, especially in Ireland, where his opponents, acting in the capacity of jurymen at inquests on the victims of the famine, sometimes went so far as to bring in a verdict of wilful murder against the Prime Minister.   It is easy enough after the event to point out better methods than those devised at the imperious call of the moment by the Russell Administration, but there are few fair-minded people in the present day who would venture to assert that justice and mercy were not in the ascendent during a crisis which taxed to the utmost the resources of practical statesmanship.

The new Parliament assembled in November, and a Committee of both Houses was appointed to take into consideration the depressed condition of trade, for symptoms of unmistakable distress were apparent in the great centres of industry. Ireland, moreover, still blocked the way, and Lord Clarendon, who had succeeded to the viceroyalty, alarmed at the condition of affairs, pressed for extraordinary powers. The famine by this time was only a memory, but it had left a large section of the peasantry in a sullen and defiant mood. As a consequence stormy restlessness and open revolt made themselves felt. Armed mobs, sometimes five hundred and even a thousand strong, wandered about in lawless fashion, pounced upon corn and made raids on cattle, and it seemed indeed at times as if life as well as property was imperilled. Lord Clarendon was determined to make the disaffected feel that the law could not be set aside with impunity. He declared that the majority of these disturbers of the peace were not in actual distress, and he made no secret of his opinion that their object was not merely intimidation but plunder. 'I feel,' were his words as the autumn advanced, 'as if I was at the head of a provisional government in a half-conquered country.'

It is easy to assert that Lord Clarendon took a panic-stricken view of the situation, and attempts have again and again been made to mitigate, if not to explain away, the dark annals of Irish crime. The facts, however, speak for themselves, and they seemed at the moment to point to such a sinister condition of affairs that Lord John Russell felt he had no option but to adopt repressive measures. Sir George Grey stated in Parliament that the number of cases of fatal bloodshed during the six summer months of 1846 was sixty-eight, whilst in the corresponding period in 1847 it had increased to ninety-six. Shooting with intent to slay, which in the six months of 1846 had numbered fifty-five, now stood at 126. Robbery under arms had also grown with ominous rapidity, for in the contrasted half-years of 1846 and 1847 deeds of violence of this kind were 207 and 530 respectively, whilst outrage in another of its most cruel and despicable forms—the firing of dwelling-houses—revealed, under the same conditions of time, 116 acts of incendiarism in 1847, as against fifty-one in the previous year. The disaffected districts of Clare, Limerick, and Tipperary made the heaviest contribution to this dismal catalogue of crime ; but far beyond their borders though with diminished force, the lawless spirit prevailed.

Mr. Spencer Walpole, in his standard and authoritative ' Life of Lord John Russell,' has shown, by an appeal to his correspondence with Lord Clarendon, how reluctant the Prime Minister was to bring forward a new Arms Bill. He has also made it plain that it was only the logic of events which finally convinced the Prime Minister of the necessity in any shape for such a measure. Mr. Walpole has also vindicated, at considerable length, Lord John from the familiar charge of having adopted in power the proposals which led to the overthrow of the Peel Administration. He lays stress on the fact that the Arms Bill, which the Government carried at the close of 1847 by a sweeping majority, was, to a noteworthy extent, different from that which Sir Robert sought to impose on Ireland twelve months earlier, and which the Whigs met with strenuous and successful opposition. In Mr. Walpole's words, the new proposals ' did not contain any provision for compensating the victims of outrages at the expense of the ratepayers ; they did not render persons congregated in public-houses or carrying arms liable to arrest ; above all, they did not comprise the brutal clause which made persons out of doors at night liable to transportation.' The condition of Ireland was, indeed, so menacing that the majority of the English people of all

shades of political opinion were of one mind as to the
necessity for stern measures.   Sir Robert Peel, with no less
candour than chivalry, declared that the best reparation
which could be made to the last Government would be
to assist the present Government in passing such a law.
Perhaps still more significant were the admissions of Mr. John
Bright.   At the General Election the young orator had
been returned to Parliament, not for a Sleepy Hollow like
Durham, which had first sent him, but for the commanding constituency of Manchester, and almost at once he
found himself in opposition to the views of a vast number
of the inhabitants.   He was requested to present a petition
against the bill signed by more than 20,000 persons
in Manchester.   In doing so he took the opportunity of ex-
plaining in the House of Commons the reasons which made
it impossible for him—friend of peace and goodwill as he
assuredly was—to support its prayer.   He declared that the
unanimous statements of all the newspapers, the evidence
of men of all parties connected with Ireland, as well as the
facts which were placed before them with official authority,
made it plain beyond a doubt that the ordinary law was
utterly powerless, and, therefore, he felt that the case of the
Government, so far as the necessity for such a bill was
concerned, was both clear and perfect.

Mr. Bright drew attention to the fact that assassinations
in Ireland were not looked upon as murders, but rather as
executions ; and that some of them at least were not due
to sudden outbursts of passion, but were planned with
deliberation and carried out in cold blood.   He saw no
reason to doubt that in certain districts public sentiment
was 'depraved and thoroughly vitiated ;' and he added
that, since the ordinary law had failed to meet the emergency

the Government had a case for the demand they made
for an extension of their present powers, and he thought
that the bill before the House was the less to be opposed
since, whilst it strengthened the hands of the Executive, it
did not greatly exceed or infringe the ordinary law. Mr. Bright
at the same time, it is only fair to add, made no secret of his
own conviction that the Government had not grappled with
sufficient courage with its difficulties, and he complained of
the delay which had arisen over promised legislation of a
remedial character.

Lord John himself was persuaded, some time before
Mr. Bright made this speech, that it was useless to attempt
to meet the captious and selfish objections on the question of
agrarian reform of the landlord class ; and, as a matter of fact,
he had already drawn up, without consulting anyone, the
outline of a measure which he described to Lord Clarendon
as a 'plan for giving some security and some provision to
the miserable cottiers, who are now treated as brute beasts.'
Years before—to be exact, in the spring of 1844—he had declared in the House of Commons that, whilst the Government
of England was, as it ought to be, a Government of opinion,
the Government of Ireland was notoriously a Government
of force. Gradually he was forced to the view that centuries
of oppression and misunderstanding, of class hatred and
opposite aims, had brought about a social condition which
made it necessary that judicial authority should have a voice
between landlord and tenant in every case of ejectment.
Lord John's difficulties in dealing with Ireland were complicated by the distrust of three-fourths of the people of the
good intentions of English statesmanship. Political agitators,
great and small, of the Young Ireland school, did their best
to deepen the suspicions of an impulsive and ignorant

peasantry against the Whigs, and Lord John was personally assailed, until he became a sort of bogie-man to the lively and undisciplined imagination of a sensitive but resentful race.

Even educated Irishmen of a later generation have, with scarcely an exception, failed to do justice either to the dull weight of prejudice and opposition with which Lord John had to contend in his efforts to help their country, or to give him due credit for the constructive statesmanship which he brought to a complicated and disheartening task.[1] Lord John Russell was, in fact, in some directions not only in advance of his party but of his times ; and, though it has long been the fashion to cavil at his Irish policy, it ought not to be forgotten, in common fairness, that he not only passed the Encumbered Estates Act of 1848, but sought to introduce the principle of compensation to tenants for the improvements which they had made on their holdings. Vested interests proved, however, too powerful, and Ireland stood in her own light by persistent sedition. The revolutionary spirit was abroad in 1848 not only in France, but in other parts of Europe, and the Irish, under Mr. Smith O'Brien, Mr. John Mitchel, and less responsible men, talked at random, with the result that treasonable conspiracy prevailed, and the country was brought to the verge of civil war. The Irish Government was forced by hostile and armed movements to proclaim certain districts in which rebellion was already rampant. The Treason Felony Act made it illegal, and punishable with penal servitude, to write or speak in a manner calculated to provoke rebellion against the Crown. This extreme stipula-

---

[1] Judge O'Connor Morris, in his interesting retrospect, *Memories and Thoughts of a Life*, just published, whilst severely criticising the Whig attitude towards Ireland, admits that Russell's Irish policy was not only 'well-meant,' but in the main successful.

tion was made at the instance of Lord Campbell. Such an invasion of freedom of speech was not allowed to pass unchallenged, and Lord John, who winced under the necessity of repression, admitted the force of the objection, so far as to declare that this form of irksome restraint should not be protracted beyond the necessity of the hour. He was not the man to shirk personal danger, and therefore, in spite of insurrection and panic, and the threats of agitators who were seeking to compass the repeal of the Union by violent measures, he went himself to Dublin to consult with Lord Clarendon, and to gather on the spot his own impressions of the situation. He found the country once more overshadowed by the prospects of famine, and he came to the conclusion that the population was too numerous for the soil, and subsequently passed a measure for promoting aided emigration. He proposed also to assist from the public funds the Roman Catholic clergy, whose livelihood had grown precarious through the national distress ; but, in deference to strong Protestant opposition, this method of amelioration had to be abandoned The leaders of the Young Ireland party set the authorities at defiance, and John Mitchel, a leader who advocated an appeal to physical force, and Smith O'Brien, who talked wildly about the establishment of an Irish Republic, were arrested, convicted, and transported. O'Connell himself declared that Smith O'Brien was an exceedingly weak man, proud and self-conceited and 'impenetrable to advice.' 'You cannot be sure of him for half an hour.' The force of the movement was broken by cliques and quarrels, until the spirit of disaffection was no longer formidable. In August, her Majesty displayed in a marked way her personal interest in her Irish subjects by a State visit to Dublin. The Queen was received with enthusiasm, and her presence did much to weaken still further the already diminishing power of sedition.

The question of education lay always close to the heart of Lord John Russell, who found time even amid the stress of 1847 to advance it. The Melbourne Administration had vested the management of Parliamentary grants in aid of education in a committee of the Privy Council. In spite of suspicion and hostility, which found expression both in Parliament and in ecclesiastical circles, the movement extended year by year and slowly pervaded with the first beginnings of culture the social life of the people. Lord John had taken an active part in establishing the authority of the Privy Council in education ; he had watched the rapid growth of its influence, and had not forgotten to mark the defects which had come to light during the six years' working of the system. He therefore proposed to remodel it, and took steps in doing so to better the position of the teacher, as well as to render primary education more efficient. Paid pupil teachers accordingly took the place of unpaid monitors, and the opportunity of gaining admittance after this practical apprenticeship to training colleges, where they might be equipped for the full discharge of the duties of their calling, was thrown open to them. As a further inducement, teachers who had gone through this collegiate training received a Government grant in addition to the usual salary. Grants were also for the first time given to schools which passed with success through the ordeal of official inspection.

The passing of the Factory Bill was another effort in the practical redress of wrongs to which Lord John Russell lent his powerful aid. The measure, which will always be honourably associated with the names of Lord Shaftesbury and Mr. Fielden, was a victory for labour which was hailed with enthusiasm by artisans and operatives throughout the land. It came as a measure of practical relief, not merely to men, but to upwards of three hundred and sixty-three thousand women and children, employed in monotonous tasks in mill and manufactory. Another change which Lord John Russell was directly instrumental in bringing about was the creation of the Poor Law Commission into a Ministerial Department, responsible to Parliament, and able to explain its work and to defend its policy at Westminster, through the lips of the President of the Poor Law Board. Regulations were at the same time made for workhouse control, meetings of guardians, and the like. The great and ever-growing needs of Manchester were recognised in 1847 by the creation of the Bishopric. Parliament was dissolved on July 23, and as the adoption of Free Trade had left the country for the moment without any great question directly before it, no marked political excitement followed the appeal to the people. The Conservative party was in truth demoralised by the downfall of Peel, and the new forces which were soon to shape its course had as yet scarcely revealed themselves, though Lord Stanley, Lord George Bentinck, and Mr. Disraeli were manifestly the coming men in Opposition. If the general election was distinguished by little enthusiasm either on one side or the other, it yet brought with it a personal triumph to Lord John, for he was returned for the City at the head of the poll. The Government itself not only renewed its strength, but increased it as a result of the contest throughout the country. At the same time the hostility of the opponents of Free Trade was seen in the return of two hundred and twenty-six Protectionists, in addition to one hundred and five Conservatives of the new school of Bentinck and Disraeli.

In other directions, meanwhile, difficulties had beset the Government. The proposed appointment of a Broad Churchman of advanced views, in the person of Dr. Hampden, Regius Professor at Oxford, to the vacant see of Hereford filled the High Church party with indignant dismay. Dr. Newman, with the courage and self-sacrifice which were characteristic of the man, had refused by this time to hold any longer an untenable position, and, in spite of his brilliant prospects in the English Church, had yielded to conscience and submitted to Rome. Dr. Pusey, however, remained, and under his skilful leadership the Oxford Movement grew strong, and threw its spell in particular over devout women, whose æsthetic instincts it satisfied, and whose aspirations after a semi-conventual life it met.[1] Lord John had many of the characteristics of the plain Englishman. He understood zealous Protestants, and, as his rejected scheme for aiding the priests in Ireland itself shows, he was also able to apprehend the position of earnest Roman Catholics. He had, however, not so learnt his Catechism or his Prayer Book as to understand that the Reformation, if not a crime, was at least a blunder, and therefore, like other plain Englishmen, he was not prepared to admit the pretensions and assumptions of a new race of nondescript priests. Thirteen prelates took the unusual course of requesting the Prime Minister to reconsider his decision, but Lord John's reply was at once courteous and emphatic. 'I cannot sacrifice the reputation of Dr. Hampden, the rights of the Crown, and what I believe to be the true interests of the Church, to a feeling which I believe to have been founded on misapprehension and fomented by prejudice.' Although Dr. Pusey did not hesitate to de-

---

[1] The first Anglican Sisterhood was founded by Dr. Pusey in London in the spring of 1845.

clare that the affair was 'a matter of life and death,'[1] ecclesiastical protest availed nothing, and Dr. Hampden was in due time consecrated.

Neither agrarian outrages in Ireland nor clerical agitation in England hindered, in the session of 1848, the passing of measures of social improvement. The Public Health Act, which was based on the representations of Sir Edwin Chadwick and Dr. Southwood Smith, grappled with the sanitary question in cities and towns, and thus improved in a variety of directions the social life of the people. It had hitherto been the fashion of Whigs and Tories alike to neglect practical measures of this kind, even though they were so closely linked to the health and welfare of the community.

[1] *Life of E. B. Pusey*, D.D., by H. P. Liddon, D.D., vol. iii. p. 160

CHAPTER VIII

IN ROUGH WATERS

1848 1852

The People's Charter —Feargus O'Connor and the crowd—Lord Palmerston strikes from his own bat—Lord John's view of the political situation —Death of Peel—Palmerston and the Court —' No Popery '—The Durham Letter —The invasion scare—Lord John's remark about Palmerston —Fall of the Russell Administration.

ENGLAND in 1848 was not destined to escape an outbreak of the revolutionary spirit, though the Chartist movement, in spite of the panic which it awakened, was never really formidable. The overthrow and flight of Louis Philippe, the proclamation in March of the French Republic on the basis of universal suffrage and national workshops, and the revolutionary movements and insurrections in Austria and Italy, filled the artisans and operatives of this country with wild dreams, and led them to rally their scattered and hitherto dispirited forces. Within six years of the passing of the Reform Bill, in fact, in the autumn after the Queen's accession, the working classes had come to the conclusion that their interests had been largely overlooked, and that the expectations they had cherished in the struggle of 1831–32 had been falsified by the apathy and even the reaction which followed the victory. Not in one, but in all the great civil and religious struggles of the century, they had borne the brunt of the battle ; and yet they had been thrust aside when it came to the dividing of the spoil.

The middle classes were in a different position : their aspirations were satisfied, and they were quite prepared, for the moment at least, to rest and be thankful. The sleek complacency of the shopkeeper, moreover, and his hostility to further agitation, threw into somewhat dramatic relief the restless and sullen attitude of less fortunate conscripts of toil. Food was dear, wages were low, work was slack, and in the great centres of industry the mills were running half-time, and so keen was the struggle for existence that the operatives were at the mercy of their taskmasters, and too often found it cruel. Small wonder if social discontent was widespread, especially when it is remembered that the people were not only hopeless and ill-fed, but housed under conditions which set at defiance even the most elementary laws of health. More than to any other man in the ranks of higher statesmanship the people looked to Lord Durham, the idol of the pitmen of the North, for the redress of their wrongs, and no statesman of that period possessed more courage or more real acquaintance with the actual needs of the people. Lord Durham, though a man of splendid ability, swift vision, and generous sympathy, had, unhappily, the knack of making enemies, and the fiery impetuosity of his spirit brought him more than once into conflict with leaders whose temperament was cold and whose caution was great. The rebellion in Canada withdrew Lord Durham from the arena of English politics at the beginning of 1838. Then it was that the people recognised to the full the temper of the statesmen that were left, and the fact that, if deliverance was to come from political and social thraldom, they must look to themselves and organise their strength.

The representatives of the working classes in 1838 formulated their demand for radical political reform in the famous six points of the People's Charter. This declaration claimed manhood suffrage ; the division of the country into equal electoral districts ; vote by ballot ; annual Parliaments ; the abolition of property qualification for a seat in the House of Commons ; and payment of members of Parliament for their services. The People's Charter took the working classes by storm : it fired their imagination, inspired their hopes, and drew them in every manufacturing town and district into organised association.

The leader of the movement was Feargus O'Connor, an Irish barrister and journalist, who had entered Parliament in 1832 as a follower of O'Connell and as member for Cork. He quarrelled, however, with the Irish leader, a circumstance which was fatal to success as an agitator in his own country. Restless and reckless, he henceforth carried his energy and devoted his eloquence to the Chartist movement in England, and in 1847 the popular vote carried him once more to the House of Commons as member for Nottingham. He copied the tactics of O'Connell, but had neither the judgment nor the strength of the Irish dictator. He seems, indeed, to have been rather a poor creature of the vainglorious, bombastic type. A year or two later he became hopelessly insane, and in the vaporing heroics and parade of gasconade which marked him as the champion of the Chartists in the spring of 1848 it is charitable now to discover the first seeds of his disorder. However that may be, he was a nine-days' wonder, for from All Fools' Day to the morning of April 10 society in London was in a state of abject panic. The troubles in Ireland, the insurrections and rumours of insurrection on the Continent, the revolution in France, the menacing discontent in the provinces, and the threatening attitude of the working men in the metropolis, were enough to cause alarm among the privileged classes, and conscience made cowards, not certainly of them all, but of the majority.

Literature enough and to spare, explanatory, declamatory and the like, has grown around a movement which ran like an unfed river, until it lost itself in the sand. Three men of genius took up their parable about what one of them called the 'Condition of England Question,' and in the pages of Carlyle's 'Chartism' and 'Past and Present,' Disraeli's 'Sybil,' and last, but not least, in Kingsley's 'Alton Locke,' the reader of to-day is in possession of sidelights, vivid, picturesque, and dramatic, on English society in the years when the Chartists were coming to their power, and in the year when they lost it. Lord John was at first in favour of allowing the Chartists to demonstrate to their hearts' content. He therefore proposed to permit them to cross Westminster Bridge, so that they might deliver their petition at the doors of Parliament. He thought that the police might then prevent the re-forming of the procession, and scatter the crowd in the direction of Charing Cross. Lord John had done too much for the people to be afraid of them, and he refused to accept the alarmist view of the situation. But the consternation was so widespread, and the panic so general, that the Government felt compelled on April 6 to declare the proposed meeting criminal and illegal, to call upon all peaceably disposed citizens not to attend, and to take extraordinary precautions. It was, however, announced that the right of assembly would be respected ; but, on the advice of Wellington, only three of the leaders were to be allowed to cross the bridge. The Bank, the Tower, and the neighbourhood of Kennington Common meanwhile were protected by troops of cavalry and infantry, whilst the approaches to the Houses of Parliament and the Government offices were held by artillery.

The morning of the fateful 10th dawned brightly, but no one dared forecast how the evening would close, and for a few hours of suspense there was a reign of terror. Many houses were barricaded, and in the West End the streets were deserted except by the valiant special constables, who stood at every corner in defence of law and order. The shopkeepers, who were not prepared to take joyfully the spoiling of their goods, formed the great mass of this citizen army—one hundred and fifty thousand strong. There were, nevertheless, recruits from all classes, and in the excitement and peril of the hour odd men rubbed shoulders. Lord Shaftesbury, for instance, was on duty in Mount Street, Grosvenor Square, with a sallow young foreigner for companion, who was afterwards to create a more serious disturbance on his own account, and to spring to power as Napoleon III. Thomas Carlyle preferred to play the part of the untrammelled man in the street, and sallied forth in search of food for reflection. He wanted to see the 'revolution' for himself, and strode towards Hyde Park, determined, he tells us, to walk himself into a glow of heat in spite of the 'venomous cold wind' which called forth his anathemas. The Chelsea moralist found London, westward at least, safe and quiet, in spite of 'empty rumours and a hundred and fifty thousand oaths of special constables.' He noticed as he passed Apsley House that even the Duke had taken the affair seriously, in his private as well as his public capacity, for all the iron blinds were down. The Green

Park was closed. Mounted Guardsmen stood ready on Constitution Hill. The fashionable carriage had vanished from Piccadilly. Business everywhere was at a standstill, for London knew not what that day might bring forth. Presently the rain began to fall, and then came down in drenching showers. In spite of their patriotic fervour, the special constables grew both damp and depressed. Suddenly a rumour ran along the streets that the great demonstration at Kennington Common had ended in smoke, and by noon the crowd was streaming over Westminster Bridge and along Whitehall, bearing the tidings that the march to the House of Commons had been abandoned. Feargus O'Connor had, in fact, taken fright, and presently the petition rattled ingloriously to Westminster in the safe but modest keeping of a hackney cab. The shower swept the angry and noisy rabble homewards, or into neighbouring public-houses, and ridicule—as the evening filled the town with complacent special constables and their admiring wives and sweethearts—did even more than the rain to quench the Chartist agitation. It had been boldly announced that one hundred and fifty thousand people would meet at Kennington. Less than a third of that number assembled, and a considerable part of the crowd had evidently been attracted by curiosity. Afterwards, when the monster petition with its signatures was examined, it was found to fall short of the boasted 'five million' names by upwards of three millions. Many of those which did appear were palpably fictitious ; indeed the rude wit of the London apprentice was responsible for scores of silly signatures. Lord John's comment on the affair was characteristic. After stating that no great numbers followed the cab which contained the petition, and that there was no mob at the door of the House of Commons, he adds : 'London escaped the fate of Paris, Berlin, and Vienna. For my own part, I saw in these proceedings a fresh proof that the people of England were satisfied with the Government under which they had the happiness to live, did not wish to be instructed by their neighbours in the principles of freedom, and did not envy them either the liberty they had enjoyed under Robespierre, or the order which had been established among them by Napoleon the Great.'

Lord John's allusion to Paris, Berlin, and Vienna suggests foreign politics, and also the growing lack of harmony between Lord Palmerston on the one hand and the Court and Cabinet on the other. Although he long held the highest office under the Crown, Lord Palmerston's chief claim to distinction was won as Foreign Minister. He began his official career as a Tory in the Portland Administration of 1807, and two years later—at the age of five-and-twenty—was appointed Secretary at War in the Perceval Government. He held this post for the long term of eighteen years, and when Canning succeeded to power still retained it, with a seat in the Cabinet. Palmerston was a liberal Tory of the school of Canning, and, when Lord Grey became Premier in 1830, was a man of sufficient mark to be entrusted with the seals of the Foreign Office, though, until his retirement in 1834, Grey exercised a controlling voice in the foreign policy of the nation. It was not until Grey was succeeded by Melbourne that Palmerston began to display both his strength and his weakness in independent action.

He saw his opportunity and took it. He knew his own mind and disliked interference, and this made him more and more inclined to be heedless of the aid, and almost of the approval, of his colleagues. Under a provokingly pleasant manner lurked, increasingly, the temper of an autocrat. Melbourne sat lightly to most things, and not least to questions of foreign policy. He was easily bored, and believed in *laissez-faire* to an extent which has never been matched by any other Prime Minister in the Queen's reign. The consequence was that for seven critical years Palmerston did what was right in his own eyes, until he came to regard himself not merely as the custodian of English interests abroad, but almost as the one man in the Cabinet who was entitled to speak with authority concerning them. If the responsibility of the first Afghan war must rest chiefly on his shoulders, it is only fair to remember that he took the risk of a war with France in order to drive Ibrahim Pacha out of Syria. From first to last, his tenure at the Foreign Office covered a period of nearly twenty years. Though he made serious mistakes, he also made despots in every part of the world afraid of him ; whilst struggling nationalities felt that the great English Minister was not oblivious of the claims of justice, or deaf to the appeal for mercy. Early in the Russell Administration Lord Palmerston's high-handed treatment of other members of the Cabinet provoked angry comment, and Sir Robert Peel did not conceal his opinion that Lord John gave his impetuous colleague too much of his own way. The truth was, the Premier's hands, and heart also, were in 1846 and 1847 full of the Irish famine, and Lord Palmerston took advantage of the fact. Moreover, Lord John Russell was, broadly speaking, in substantial agreement with his Foreign Minister, though he cordially disliked his habit of taking swift and almost independent action.

At the beginning of 1848 Palmerston seemed determined to pick a quarrel with France, and in February drew up a threatening despatch on the difficulty which had arisen between our Ambassador (Lord Normanby) and Louis Philippe, which brought matters to a crisis. Louis Philippe had acted a dishonourable part over the Spanish marriages, and Palmerston was prepared to go out of his way to humiliate France. At the last moment, the affair came to Lord John's knowledge through Lord Clarendon, with the result that the communication was countermanded. Lord Palmerston appears to have taken the rebuff, humiliating as it was, with characteristic nonchalance, and it produced little more than a momentary effect. The ignominious flight of Louis Philippe quickly followed, and the revolution in France was the signal in Vienna for a revolt of the students and artisans, which drove Metternich to find refuge in England and the Emperor Ferdinand to seek asylum in the Tyrol. Austrians, Hungarians, and Slavs only needed an opportunity, such as the 'year of revolutions' afforded, to display their hostility to one another, and the racial jealousy brought Austria and Hungary to open war. In Milan, in Naples, and Berlin the revolutionary spirit displayed itself, and in these centres, as well as in Switzerland, changes in the direction of liberty took place.

Lord John Russell, in an important document, which Mr. Walpole has printed, and which bears date May 1, 1848, has explained his own view of the political situation in Europe at that moment. After a lucid and impressive survey of the changes that had taken place in the map of Europe since the Congress of Vienna, Lord John lays down the principle that it is neither becoming nor expedient for England to proclaim that the Treaties of 1815 were invalid. On the contrary, England ought rather to promote, in the interests of peace and order, the maintenance of the territorial divisions then made. At the same time, England, amid the storm, ought not to persist in clinging to a wreck if a safe spar is within her reach. He recognised that Austria could hardly restore her sway in Italy, and was not in a position to confront the cost of a protracted war, in which France was certain to take sides against her. He, therefore, thought it advisable that English diplomacy should be brought to bear at Vienna, so as to 'produce a frank abandonment of Lombardy and Venice on the part of Austria.' He declared that it was not to the advantage of England to meddle with the internal affairs of Spain ; but he thought there was a favourable chance of coming to an understanding with Germany, where the Schleswig-Holstein question already threatened disturbance. ' It is our interest,' are the final words of this significant State paper, ' to use our influence as speedily and as generally as possible to settle the pending questions and to fix the boundaries of States. Otherwise, if war once becomes general, it will spread over Germany, reach Belgium, and finally sweep England into its vortex. Should our efforts for peace succeed, Europe may begin a new career with more or less of hope and of concord ; should they fail, we must keep our sword in the scabbard as long as we can, but we cannot hope to be neutral in a great European war. England cannot be indifferent to the supremacy of France over Germany and Italy, or to the advance of Russian armies to Constantinople ; still less to the incorporation of Belgium with a new French Empire.'

As usual, Lord Palmerston had his own ideas and the courage of them. Within three weeks of the Russell Memorandum to the Cabinet he accordingly stood out in his true

colours as a frank opportunist. The guiding rule of his
foreign policy, he stated, was to promote and advance,
as far as lay in his power, the interests of the country as
opportunity served and as necessity arose. 'We have no
everlasting union with this or that country—no identifica-
tion of policy with another. We have no natural enemies
—no perpetual friends. When we find a Power pursuing
that course of policy which we wish also to promote, for
the time that Power becomes our ally; and when we find a
country whose interests are at variance with our own, we
are involved for a time with the Government of that country.
We find no fault with other nations for pursuing their interests ; and they ought not to find fault with us, if, in pursuing
our interests, our course may be different from theirs.'

Lord Palmerston held that the real policy of this
country was to be the champion of justice and right,
though professing no sympathy with the notion that England
ought to become, to borrow his own expression, the Quixote
of the world. 'I hold that England is a Power sufficiently
strong to steer her own course, and not to tie herself as an
unnecessary appendage to the policy of any other Government.' He declared that, if he might be allowed to gather
into one sentence the principle which he thought ought to
guide an English statesman, he would adopt the expression
of Canning, and say that with every British Minister the
interests of England ought to be the shibboleth of his policy.
Unfortunately, Lord Palmerston, in spite of such statements,
was too much inclined to throw the moral weight of England
into this or that scale on his own responsibility, and, as it
often seemed to dispassionate observers, on the mere caprice
of the hour. He took up the position that the interests of
England were safe in his hands, and magnified his office,

sometimes to the annoyance of the Court and often to the chagrin of the Cabinet. No matter what storm raged, Palmerston always contrived to come to the surface again like a cork. He never lost his self-possession, and a profound sense of his own infallibility helped him, under difficulties and rebuffs which would have knocked the spirit out of other men, to adopt the attitude of the patriotic statesman struggling with adversity. When the session of 1849 closed he was in an extremely difficult position, in consequence of the growing dislike in high quarters to his policy, and the coolness which had sprung up between himself and the majority of his colleagues ; yet we find him writing a jaunty note to his brother in the strain of a man who had not only deserved success but won it. ' After the trumpetings of attacks that were to demolish first one and then another of the Government—first me, then Grey, then Charles Wood—we have come triumphantly out of the debates and divisions, and end the session stronger than we began it.' [1]

Lord Palmerston's passion for personal ascendency was not to be repressed, and in the electric condition of Europe it proved perilous as well as embarrassing to the Russell Administration. Without the knowledge of the Queen or his colleagues, Lord Palmerston, for instance, sent a letter to Sir H. Bulwer advising an extension of the basis of the Spanish Government, an act of interference which caused so much irritation at Madrid that the Spanish Government requested the British Ambassador to leave the country. Happily, the breach with Madrid was repaired after a few months' anxiety on the part of Palmerston's colleagues. The Queen's

---

[1] *Life of Lord Palmerston*, by the Hon. Evelyn Ashley, vol. ii. p. 95.

sense of the indiscretion was apparent in the request to Lord Palmerston to submit in future all his despatches to the Prime Minister. Other occasions soon arose which increased distrust at Windsor, and further strained friendly relations between the Prime Minister and the Foreign Secretary. The latter's removal to some less responsible post was contemplated, for her Majesty appeared to disapprove of everything Lord Palmerston did. Without detailing the various circumstances which awakened the Queen's displeasure, it is sufficient to draw attention to one event—known in the annals of diplomacy as the 'Don Pacifico' affair—which threatened the overthrow of the Ministry.

Two British subjects demanded in vain compensation from the Greek Government for damage to their property. Lord Palmerston came to their defence, and sent private instructions to the Admiral of the British fleet at the Dardanelles to seize Greek vessels by way of reprisal, which was promptly done. The tidings fell like a thunderbolt upon Downing Street. France and Russia made angry protests, and war was predicted. At length an offer of mediation from Paris was accepted, and the matter was arranged in London. Lord Palmerston, however, omitted to inform the English Minister at Athens of the settlement, and, whilst everyone in England rejoiced that the storm had blown over, the Admiral was laying an embargo on other ships, and at last forced the Greek Government to grant compensation. France, indignant at such cavalier treatment, recalled M. Drouyn de Lhuys from London, and again the war-cloud lowered. Lord Palmerston had the audacity to state in the House of Commons that the French Minister had returned to Paris in order 'presumably to be the medium of communication between the two Governments as to these matters.' The truth came out on the morrow, and Lord John, in the discreet absence of his colleague, was forced to explain as best he might the position of affairs. Although he screened Lord Palmerston as far as he was able, he determined to make a change at the Foreign Office.

In June 1850, Lord Stanley challenged the foreign policy of Lord Palmerston in the House of Lords, and carried, by a majority of thirty-seven, a resolution of censure. Mr. Roebuck, in the Commons, met the hostile vote by a resolution of confidence, and, after four nights' debate, secured a majority of forty-six. Lord Palmerston made an able defence of his conduct of affairs, and Lord John Russell, who differed from him not so much in the matter as in the manner of his decisions, not merely refused to leave his colleague in the lurch, but came vigorously to his support. The debate was rendered memorable on other grounds. Sir Robert Peel, in the course of it, delivered his last speech in Parliament. The division, which gave Palmerston a fresh tenure of power, was taken at four o'clock on the morning of Saturday, June 29. Peel left the House to snatch a few hours' sleep before going at noon to a meeting which was to settle the disputed question as to the site of the Great Exhibition. He kept his appointment ; but later in the day he was thrown from his horse on Constitution Hill, and received injuries which proved fatal on the night of July 2. His death was a national calamity, for at sixty-two he was still in the fulness of his strength. There will always be a diversity of judgment concerning his career ; there is but one opinion about his character. Few statesmen have gone to their grave amid more remarkable expressions of regret. Old and young colleagues, from the Duke of Wellington to Mr. Gladstone, betrayed by their emotion no less than by their words, their grief over the loss of a leader who followed his conscience even at the expense of the collapse of his power. Lord John Russell, the most distinguished, without doubt, of Sir Robert's opponents on the floor of the House, paid a generous tribute to his rival's memory. He declared that posterity would regard Sir Robert Peel as one of the greatest and most patriotic of statesman. He laid stress on that 'long and large experience of public affairs, that profound knowledge, that oratorical power, that copious yet exact memory, with which the House was wont to be enlightened, interested, and guided.' When the offer of a public funeral was declined, in deference to Sir Robert's known wishes, Lord John proposed and carried a resolution for the erection of a statue in Westminster Abbey. He also marked his sense of the loss which the nation had sustained, in the disappearance of an illustrious man, by giving his noble-minded and broken-hearted widow the refusal of a peerage.

Meanwhile, Lord Palmerston, on the strength of the vote of confidence in the Commons, was somewhat of a popular hero. People who believe that England can do no wrong, at least abroad, believed in him. His audacity delighted the man in the club. His pluck took the plat-form and much of the press by storm. The multitude relished his peremptory despatches, and were delighted when he either showed fight or encouraged it in others. In course of time 'Pam' became the typical fine old English gentleman of genial temper but domineering instincts. Prince Albert disliked him ; he was too little of a courtier, too much of an off-handed man of affairs. Windsor, of course, received early tidings of the impression which was made at foreign Courts by the most independent and and cavalier Foreign Minister of the century. Occasionally he needlessly offended the susceptibilities of exalted personages abroad as well as at home. At length the Queen, determined no longer to be put in a false position, drew up a sharply-worded memorandum, in which explicit directions were given for the transaction of business between the Crown and the Foreign Office. 'The Queen requires, first, that Lord Palmerston will distinctly state what he proposes in a given case, in order that the Queen may know as distinctly to what she is giving her royal sanction ; secondly, having once given her sanction to a measure, that it be not arbitrarily altered or modified by the Minister. Such an act she must consider as failing in sincerity towards the Crown, and justly to be visited by the exercise of her constitutional right of dismissing that Minister. She expects to be kept informed of what passes between him and the Foreign Ministers before important decisions are taken, based upon that intercourse ; to receive the foreign despatches in good time ; and to have the drafts for her approval sent to her in sufficient time to make herself acquainted with their contents before they must be sent off.'

No responsible adviser of the Crown during the reign had received such emphatic censure, and in August 1850 people were talking as if Palmerston was bound to resign. He certainly would have done so if he had merely consulted his own feelings ; but he declared that to resign just then would be to play into the hands of the political adversaries whom he had just defeated, and to throw over his supporters at the moment when they had fought a successful battle on his behalf. Lord Palmerston, therefore, accepted the Queen's instructions with unwonted meekness. He assured her Majesty that he would not fail to attend to the directions which the memorandum contained, and for a while harmony was restored. In the autumn of 1851 Louis Kossuth arrived in England, and met with an enthusiastic reception, of the kind which was afterwards accorded in London to another popular hero, in the person of Garibaldi. Lord Palmerston received Kossuth at the Foreign Office, and, contrary to the wishes of the Queen and Prime Minister, deputations were admitted, and addresses were presented, thanking Palmerston for his services in the cause of humanity, whilst in the same breath allusions to the Emperors of Austria and Russia as 'odious and detestable assassins' were made. Almost before the annoyance created by this fresh act of indiscretion had subsided, Lord Palmerston was guilty of a still more serious offence.

Louis Napoleon had been elected President of the French Republic by five and a half million votes. He was thought to be ambitious rather than able, and he had pledged himself to sustain the existing Constitution. He worked for his own hand, however, and accordingly conciliated first the clergy, then the peasants, and finally the army, by fair promises, popular acts, and a bold policy. On December 2, 1851, when his term of office was expiring, Napoleon suddenly overthrew the Assembly, which had refused a month or two previously to revise the Constitution in order to make the President eligible for re-election, and next morning all Europe was startled with tidings of the *Coup d'État*. Both the English Court and Cabinet felt that absolute neutrality must be observed during the tumult which followed in Paris, and instructions to that effect were accordingly transmitted to Lord Normanby. But when that diplomatist made known this official communication, he was met with the retort that Lord Palmerston, in a conversation with the French Ambassador in London, had already declared that the *Coup d'État* was an act of self-defence, and in fact was the best thing under the circumstances for France. Lord Palmerston, in a subsequent despatch to Lord Normanby, which was not submitted either to the Queen or the Prime Minister, reiterated his opinion.

Under these circumstances, Lord John Russell had no alternative except to dismiss Lord Palmerston. He did so, as he explained when Parliament met in February, on the ground that the Foreign Secretary had practically put himself, for the moment, in the place of the Crown. He had given the moral approbation of England to the acts of the President of the Republic of France, though he knew, when he was doing so, that he was acting in direct opposition to the wishes of the sovereign and the policy of the Government. Lord John stated in the House of Commons that he took upon himself the sole and entire responsibility of advising her Majesty to require the resignation of Lord Palmerston. He added that, though the Foreign Secretary had neglected what was due to the Crown and his colleagues, he felt sure that he had not intended any personal disrespect. Greville declared that, in all his experience of scenes in Parliament, he could recall no such triumph as Lord Russell achieved on this occasion, nor had he ever witnessed a discomfiture more complete than that of Palmerston. Lord Dalling, another eye-witness of the episode, has described, from the point of view of a sympathiser with Palmerston, the manner in which he seemed completely taken by surprise by the 'tremendous assault' which Lord John, by a damaging appeal to facts, made against him. In his view, Russell's speech was one of the most powerful to which he had ever listened, and its effect was overwhelming. Disraeli, meeting Lord Dalling by chance next day on the staircase of the Russian Embassy, exclaimed as he passed, with significant emphasis, 'There *was* a Palmerston!' The common opinion at the clubs found expression in a phrase which passed from lip to lip, 'Palmerston is smashed;' but, though driven for the moment to bay, the dismissed Minister was himself of another mind.

Lord Palmerston was offered the Irish Viceroyalty, but he declined to take such an appointment. He accepted his dismissal with a characteristic affectation of indifference, and in the course of a laboured defence of his action in the House of Commons, excused his communication to the French Ambassador on the plea that it was only the expression of an opinion on passing events, common to that 'easy and familiar personal intercourse, which tends so usefully to the maintenance of friendly relations with foreign Governments.' Lady Russell wrote down at the time her own impressions of this crisis in her husband's Cabinet, and the following passage throws a valuable sidelight on a memorable incident in the Queen's reign : 'The breach between John and Lord Palmerston was a calamity to the country, to the Whig party, and to themselves ; and, although it had for some months been a threatening danger on the horizon, I cannot but feel that there was accident in its actual occurrence. Had we been in London or at Pembroke Lodge, and not at Woburn Abbey, at the time, they would have met, and talked over the subject of their difference ; words spoken might have been equally strong, but would have been less cutting than words written, and conciliatory expressions on John's part would have led the way to promises on Lord Palmerston's. ... They two kept up the character of England, as the sturdy guardians of her rights against other nations, and the champions of freedom and independence abroad.

They did so both before and after the breach of 1851, which was, happily, closed in the following year, when they were once more colleagues in office.   On matters of home policy Lord Palmerston remained the Tory he had been in his earlier days, and this was the cause of many a trial to John.'

The Russell Administration, as the Premier himself frankly recognised, was seriously weakened by the dismissal of Lord Palmerston; and its position was not improved when Lord Clarendon, on somewhat paltry grounds, refused the Foreign Office.   Lord John's sagacity was shown by the prompt offer of the vacant appointment to Lord Granville, who, at the age of thirty-six, entered the Cabinet, and began a career which was destined to prove a controlling force in the foreign policy of England in the Victorian era.

Meanwhile fresh difficulties had arisen.   In the autumn of 1850—a year which had already been rendered memorable in ecclesiastical circles by the Gorham case—Pius IX. issued a Bull by which England became a province of the Roman Catholic Church.   Dr. Wiseman was created Cardinal Archbishop of Westminster, and England was divided into twelve sees with territorial titles.   The assumption by Pius IX. of spiritual authority over England was a blunder ; indeed, no better proof in recent times of the lack of infallibility at Rome could well be discovered.   One swallow, proverbially, does not make a spring ; and when Newman took refuge in flight, other leaders of the Oxford Movement refused to accept his logic and to follow his example.   Englishmen have always resented anything in the shape of foreign dictation, and deep in the national heart there yet survives a rooted hostility to the claims of the Vatican.   Napoleon's *Coup d'État,* which followed quickly on the heels of this dramatic act of Papal aggression, scarcely took the nation more completely by surprise. No Vatican decree could well have proved more unpopular, and even Canon Liddon is obliged to admit that the bishops, with one solitary exception, 'threw the weight of their authority on the side of popular and short-sighted passion.'[1]

Pius IX. knew nothing of the English character, but Cardinal Wiseman, at least, could not plead ignorance of the real issues at stake ; and therefore his grandiloquent and, under all the circumstances, ridiculous pastoral letter, which he dated 'From out of the Flaminian Gate at Rome,' was justly regarded as an insult to the religious convictions of the vast majority of the English people. Anglicans and Nonconformists alike resented such an authoritative deliverance, and presently the old 'No Popery' cry rang like a clarion through the land. Dr. Newman, with the zeal of a pervert, preached a sermon on the revival of the Catholic Church, and in the course of it he stated that the 'people of England, who for so many years have been separated from the See of Rome, are about, of their own will, to be added to the Holy Church.' The words were, doubtless, spoken in good faith, for the great leader of the Oxford Movement naturally expected that those who had espoused his views, like honest men, would follow his example. Dr. Pusey, however, was a more astute ecclesiastical statesman than Cardinal Wiseman. He was in favour of a 'very moderate' declaration against Rome, for the resources of compromise were evidently in his eyes not exhausted. The truth was, Pusey and Keble, by a course of action which to this day remains a standing riddle to the Papacy on the one hand, and to Protestantism on the other, threw dust in the eyes of Pius IX., and were

---

[1] *Life of E. B. Pusey*, *D.D.*, by H. P. Liddon, D.D., vol. iii. p. 292. Longmans & Co.

the real authors of Papal aggression. Lord John Russell saw this quite clearly, and in proof of such an assertion it is only necessary to appeal to his famous Durham Letter. He had watched the drift of ecclesiastical opinion, and had seen with concern that the tide was running swiftly in the direction of Rome.

England had renounced the Papal supremacy for the space of 300 years, and had grown strong in the liberty which had followed the downfall of such thraldom. Oxford had taught Rome to tempt England ; the leaders of the so-called Anglican revival were responsible for the flourish of trumpets at the Vatican. Lord John's ecclesiastical appointments called forth sharp criticism. He was a Protestant of the old uncompromising type, with leanings towards advanced thought in Biblical criticism. He knew, moreover, what Puritanism had done for the English nation in the seventeenth century, and made no secret of his conviction that it was the Nonconformists, more than any other class, who had rendered civil and religious liberty possible. He moreover knew that in his own time they, more than any other part of the community, had carried the Reform Bill, brought about the abolition of slavery, and established Free Trade. He had been brought into contact with their leaders, and was beginning to perceive, with the nation at large, how paltry and inadequate were the claims of a rigid Churchmanship, since the true apostolical succession is a matter of altitude of spiritual devotion, and borrows none of its rights from the pretensions of clerical caste.

The Durham Letter was written from Downing Street, on November 4, 1850. It gained its name because it was addressed to the Premier's old friend Dr. Maltby, Bishop of

Durham, and appeared in the newspapers on the day on which it was dated. Lord John declared that he had not only promoted to the utmost of his power the claims of Roman Catholics to all civil rights, but had deemed it not merely just, but desirable, that that Church should impart religious instruction to the 'numerous Irish immigrants in London and elsewhere, who, without such help, would have been left in heathen ignorance.' He believed that this might have been accomplished without any such innovation as that which the Papacy now contemplated. He laid stress on the assumption of power made in all the documents on the subject which had come from Rome, and he protested against such pretensions as inconsistent with the Queen's supremacy, with the rights of the bishops and clergy, and with the spiritual independence of the nation. He confessed that his alarm was not equal to his indignation, since Englishmen would never again allow any foreign prince or potentate to impose a yoke on their minds and consciences. He hinted at legislative action on the subject, and then proceeded to take up his parable against the Tractarians in the following unmistakeable terms : 'There is a danger, however, which alarms me much more than the aggression of a foreign sovereign. Clergymen of our Church who have subscribed the Thirty-nine Articles and have acknowledged in explicit terms the Queen's supremacy, have been the most forward in leading their flocks, step by step, to the verge of the precipice. The honour paid to saints, the claim of infallibility for the Church, the superstitious use of the sign of the Cross, the muttering of the Liturgy so as to disguise the language in which it was written, the recommendation of auricular confession, and the administration of penance and absolution— all these things are pointed out by clergymen as worthy of adoption, and are now openly reprehended by the Bishop of London in his Charge to the clergy of his diocese. What, then, is the danger to be apprehended from a foreign prince of no power, compared to the danger within the gates from the unworthy sons of the Church of England herself? I have but little hope that the propounders and framers of these innovations will desist from their insidious course ; but I rely with confidence on the people of England, and I will not bate a jot of heart or life so long as the glorious principles and the immortal martyrs of the Reformation shall be held in reverence by the great mass of a nation, which look with contempt on the mummeries of superstition, and with scorn at the laborious endeavours which are now being made to confine the intellect and enslave the soul.'

Lord John's manifesto was as fuel to the flames. All over the kingdom preparations were in progress at the moment for a national carnival—now fallen largely into disrepute. Guy Fawkes was hastily dethroned, and the Pope and Cardinal Wiseman were paraded in effigy through the streets of London, Exeter, and other cities, and burnt at nightfall amid the jeers of the crowd. Petitions began to pour in against Papal aggression, and the literature of the subject, in controversial tract, pamphlet, and volume, grew suddenly not less bewildering than formidable. The arrival in London of Father Gavazzi, an ex-priest of commanding presence and impassioned oratory, helped to arouse still further the Protestant spirit of the nation. The Press, the pulpit, the platform, formed a triple alliance against the Vatican, and the indignant rejection of the Pope's claims may be said to have been carried by acclamation. Clamour ran riot through the land, and spent its force in noisy demonstrations. The Catholics met the tumult, on the whole, with praiseworthy moderation, and presently signs of the inevitable reaction began to appear. Lord John's colleagues were not of one mind as to the wisdom of the Durham Letter, for if there is one taunt before which an ordinary Englishman quails, it is the accusation of religious bigotry.

The Durham Letter was an instance in which Lord John's zeal outran his discretion.[1] Lord Shaftesbury, who was in the thick of the tumult, and has left a vivid description of it in his journal,[2] declared that Cardinal Wiseman's manifesto, in spite of its audacity, was likely to prove ' more hurtful to the shooter than to the target.' Looking back at the crisis, after an interval of more than forty years, the same criticism seems to apply with added force to the Durham Letter. Lord John overshot the mark, and his accusations wounded those whom he did not intend to attack, and in the recoil of public opinion his own reputation suffered. He resented, with pardonable warmth, the attitude of the Vatican, and was jealous of any infringement, from that or any other quarter, of the Queen's supremacy in her own realms. The most damaging sentences in the Durham Letter were not directed against the Catholics, either in Rome, England, or Ireland, but against the Tractarian clergymen—men whom he regarded as ' unworthy sons of the Church of England.' The Catholics, incensed at the denial of the Pope's supremacy, were, however, in no mood to make distinctions, and they have interpreted Lord John's strictures on Dr. Pusey and his followers as an attack on their own reli-

---

[1] Cobden described it as ' a Guy Fawkes outcry,' and predicted the fall of the Ministry.

[2] See *Life and Work of the Seventh Earl of Shaftesbury*, by Edwin Hodder, pp. 429-435.

gious faith. The consequence was that the manifesto was regarded, especially in Ireland, not merely as a protest against the politics of the Vatican, but as a sweeping censure on the creed of Rome. Lord John's character and past services might have shielded him from such a construction being placed upon his words, for he had proved, on more than one historic occasion, his devotion to the cause of religious liberty. Disraeli, writing to his sister in November, said : 'I think John Russell is in a scrape. I understand that his party are furious with him. The Irish are frantic. If he goes on with the Protestant movement he will be thrown over by the Papists ; if he shuffles with the Protestants, their blood is too high to be silent now, and they will come to us. I think Johnny is checkmated.'[1]

For the moment, however, passion and prejudice everywhere ran riot, and on both sides of the controversy common sense and common fairness were forgotten. A representative Irish politician of a later generation has not failed to observe the irony of the position. 'It was a curious incident in political history,' declares Mr. Justin McCarthy, 'that Lord John Russell, who had more than any Englishman then living been identified with the principles of religious liberty, who had sat at the feet of Fox, and had for his closest friend the Catholic poet Thomas Moore, came to be regarded by Roman Catholics as the bitterest enemy of their creed and their rights of worship.'[2] It is easy to cavil at Lord John Russell's interpretation of the Oxford Movement, and to assert that the accusations of the Durham Letter were due to bigotry and panic. He believed,

---

[1] *Lord Beaconsfield's Correspondence with his Sister* (1832-1852), p. 249. London : John Murray.

[2] *History of Our Own Times*, by Justin McCarthy, M.P. vol. ii. pp. 85, 86.

in common with thousands of other distressed Churchmen, that the Tractarians were foes within the gates of the Establishment.   He regarded them, moreover, as ministers of religion who were hostile to the work of the Reformation, and therefore he deemed that they were in a false position in the Anglican Church.   Their priestly claims and sacerdotal rites, their obvious sympathies and avowed convictions, separated them sharply from ordinary clergymen, and were difficult to reconcile with adherence to the principles of Protestantism. Like many other men at the time, and still more of to-day, he was at a loss to discover how ecclesiastics of such a stamp could remain in the ministry of the Church of England, when they seemed to ordinary eyes to be in league with Rome.   The prelates, almost to a man, were hotly opposed to the Tractarians when Lord John wrote the Durham Letter.   They shared his convictions and applauded his action.   Since then many things have happened.   The Oxford Movement has triumphed, and has done so largely by the self-sacrificing devotion of its adherents.   It has summoned to its aid art and music, learning and eloquence ; it has appealed to the æsthetic and emotional elements in human nature ; it has led captive the imagination of many by its dramatic revival of mediæval ideas and methods ; and it has stilled by its assumption of authority the restlessness of souls, too weary to argue, too troubled to rebel.   The bishops of to-day have grown either quite friendly towards the Oxford Movement, or else discreetly tolerant.   Yet, when all this is admitted, it does nothing towards proving that Lord John Russell was a mistaken alarmist.   The Durham Letter and its impassioned protest have been justified by the logic of events.   It is easy for men to be charitable who have slipped their convictions.

Possibly it was not judicious on Lord John's part to be so zealously affected in the matter. That is, perhaps, open to dispute, but the question remains : Was he mistaken in principle? He saw clergymen of the English Church, Protestant at least in name, 'leading their flocks step by step to the very verge of the precipice,' and he took up his parable against them, and pointed out the danger to the hitherto accepted faith and practice of the English Church. One of the most distinguished prelates of the Anglican Church in the Queen's reign has not hesitated to assert that the tenets against which Lord John Russell protested in the Durham Letter were, in his judgment, of a kind which are 'destructive of all reasonable faith, and reduce worship to a mere belief in spells and priestcraft.' Cardinal Vaughan, it is needless to say, does not sympathise with such a view. He, however, has opinions on the subject which are worthy of the attention of those who think that Lord John was a mere alarmist. His Eminence delivered a suggestive address at Preston on September 10, 1894, on the 'Re-Union of Christendom.' He thinks—and it is idle to deny that he has good ground for thinking—that, in spite of bishops, lawyers, and legislature, Delphic judgments at Lambeth, and spasmodic protests up and down the country, a change in doctrine and ritual is in progress in the Anglican Church which can only be described as a revolution. He asserts that the 'Real Presence, the sacrifice of the Mass, offered for the living and the dead, no infrequent reservation of the Sacrament, regular auricular confession, Extreme Unction, Purgatory, prayers for the dead, devotions to Our Lady, to her Immaculate Conception, the use of her Rosary, and the invocation of saints, are doctrines taught and accepted, with a growing desire and relish for them, in the Church of England.'

Cardinal Vaughan also declares that the present churches of the Establishment are 'often distinguishable only with extreme difficulty from those belonging to the Church of Rome.' Such statements are either true or false. If false, they are open to contradiction; if true, they justify in substance the position taken up in the Durham Letter. Towards the close of his life, Lord John told Mr. Lecky that he did not regret his action, and to the last he maintained that he was right in the protest which he made in the Durham Letter. Yet he acknowledged, as he looked back upon the affair, that he might have softened certain expressions in it with advantage. Parliament met on February 4, 1851, and the Queen's Speech contained the following passage: 'The recent assumption of certain ecclesiastical titles conferred by a foreign Power has excited strong feelings in this country; and large bodies of my subjects have presented addresses to me expressing attachment to the Throne, and praying that such assumptions should be resisted. I have assured them of my resolution to maintain the rights of my crown and the independence of the nation against all encroachments, from whatsoever quarter they may proceed.'

Three days later, Lord John introduced the Ecclesiastical Titles Bill. The measure prohibited the assumption of territorial titles by Roman Catholic bishops; but there is truth in the assertion that no enactment of the kind could prevent other persons from giving the dignitaries of the Catholic Church such titles, and, as a matter of fact, the attempt to deprive them of the distinction led to its ostentatious adoption. The proposal to render null and void gifts or religious endowments acquired by the new prelates was abandoned in the course of the acrimonious debates which followed. Other difficulties.

arose, and Ireland was declared to be exempt from the operation of the measure. The object of the bill, declared Lord John Russell, was merely to assert the supremacy of the Crown. Nothing was further from his thought than to play the part of a religious persecutor. He merely wished to draw a sharp and unmistakeable line of demarcation between the spiritual jurisdiction of the Pope over the adherents of the Roman Catholic Church in the Queen's realms, and such an act of Papal aggression as was involved in the claim of Pius IX. to grant ecclesiastical titles borrowed from places in the United Kingdom.

The bill satisfied neither the friends nor the foes of Roman Catholicism. It was persistently regarded by the one as an attack on religious liberty, and by the other as quite inadequate as a bulwark of Protestantism. Nevertheless it became law, but not before the summer of 1851, when the agitation had spent its force. It was regarded almost as a dead letter from the first, and, though it remained on the Statute-book for twenty years, its repeal was a foregone conclusion. When it was revoked in 1871 the temper of the nation had changed, and no one was inclined to make even a passing protest. John Leech, in a cartoon in *Punch*, caught the droll aspect of the situation with even more than his customary skill. Lord John relished the joke, even though he recognised that it was not likely to prove of service to him at the next General Election. In conversation with a friend he said : 'Do you remember a cartoon in *Punch* where I was represented as a little boy writing "No Popery" on a wall and running away?' The answer was a smile of assent. 'Well,' he added, 'that was very severe, and did my Government a great deal of harm, but I was so convinced that it was not maliciously meant that I sent for John Leech, and asked him what I could do for him. He said that he should like a nomination for his son to the Charterhouse, and I gave it to him. That is how I used my patronage.'

Meanwhile, when the Ecclesiastical Titles Bill was still under discussion, a Ministerial crisis had arisen. Finance was never the strong point of the first Russell Administration, and Sir Charles Wood's Budget gave widespread dissatisfaction. Mr. Locke King heightened the embarrassment of the moment by bringing forward a motion for placing the county and borough franchise on an equal basis ; and before the discussion of the Budget could be renewed this motion was carried against the Government, though in a small House, by a majority of almost two to one. Lord John Russell met the hostile vote by immediate resignation ; and Lord Stanley— who four months later became Earl of Derby—was summoned to Windsor and attempted to form a Ministry. His efforts were, however, unsuccessful, for Peel had left the Tory party not merely disorganised but full of warring elements. Lord John, therefore, returned to office in March, and Locke King's measure was promptly thrown out by a majority of more than two hundred. The London season of that year was rendered memorable by the opening of the Great Exhibition, amid universal plaudits and dreams of long-continued peace amongst the nations. As the year closed Lord Palmerston's ill-advised action over the *Coup d'État* in France brought about, as we have already seen, his dismissal, a circumstance which still further weakened the Russell Cabinet.

The year 1852 opened darkly for Lord John. Difficulties, small and great, seemed thickening around him. He had been called to power at a singularly trying moment, and no one who looks dispassionately at the policy which he pursued between the years 1846 and 1852 can fail to recognise that he had at least tried to do his duty. There is a touch of pathos in the harassed statesman's reply to a letter of congratulation which reached him on the threshold of the new year from a near relative, and it is worthy of quotation, since it reveals the attitude of the man on far greater questions than those with which he was beset at the moment : 'I cannot say that the new year is a happy one to me. Political troubles are too thick for my weak sight to penetrate them, but we all rest in the mercy of God, who will dispose of us as He thinks best.'[1] When Parliament met in February, Lord Palmerston's opportunity came. On the heels of the panic about Papal aggression came widespread alarm as to the policy which Napoleon III. might pursue towards this country. The fear of invasion grew strong in the land, and patriotic fervour restlessly clamoured for prompt legislative action. Forty years ago, in every town and village of England there were people who could speak from personal knowledge concerning the reign of terror which the first Napoleon, by his conquering march over Europe and his threatened descent on the English shores, had established, and, as a consequence, though with diminished force, the old consternation suddenly revived.

Lord John Russell had no more real fear of Napoleon than he had of the Pope, but he rose to the occasion and brought before Parliament a measure for the reorganisation of the local Militia. He believed that such a force, with national enthusiasm at its back, was sufficient to repel invasion—a contingency which, in common with other re-

[1] *Life of Lord John Russell*, by Spencer Walpole, vol. ii p. 143.

sponsible statesmen, he did not regard as more than remote. Lord Palmerston, however, posing as the candid friend of the nation, and the exceptionally well-informed ex-Foreign Minister, professed to see rocks ahead, and there were—at all events for the Russell Administration.   In England, any appeal to the Jingo instincts of the populace is certain to meet with a more or less hysterical welcome, and Palmerston more than once took advantage of the fact.   He expressed his dissatisfaction with Lord John's Militia Bill, and by a majority of eleven carried an amendment to it. Lord John met the hostile demonstration by resignation, and, though Palmerston professed to be surprised at such a result, his real opinion leaps to light in the historic sentence which he wrote to his brother on February 24 : 'I have had my tit-for-tat with John Russell, and I turned him out on Friday last.'   One hitherto unpublished reminiscence of that crisis deserves to be recorded, especially as it throws into passing relief Lord John's generosity of temper : 'I remember,' states his brother-in-law and at one time private secretary, the Hon. George Elliot, 'being indignant with Lord Palmerston, after he had been dismissed by Lord John, bringing forward a verbal amendment on the Militia Bill in 1852—a mere pretext by which the Government was overthrown.   But Lord John would not at all enter into my feelings, and said, "It's all fair.   I dealt him a blow, and he has given me one in return." '

Lord John's interest in the question of Parliamentary Reform was life-long.   It was one of the subjects on which his views were in complete divergence with those of Lord Palmerston.   Just before the 'tit-for-tat' amendment, the Premier brought forward a new scheme on the subject which he had reluctantly waived in 1849 in deference to the wishes of the majority of his colleagues, who then regarded such a proposal as premature. At the beginning of 1852 Lord John had overcome such obstacles, and he accordingly introduced his new Reform Bill, as if anxious to wipe out before his retirement from office the reproach which the sobriquet of 'Finality Jack' had unjustly cast upon him. He proposed to extend the suffrage by reducing the county qualification to 20*l.*, and the borough to 5*l.*, and by granting the franchise to persons paying forty shillings yearly in direct taxation. He also proposed to abolish the property qualification of English and Irish members of Parliament, and to extend the boundaries of boroughs having less than 500 electors. Lord Palmerston's hostile action of course compelled the abandonment of this measure, and it is worthy of passing remark that, on the night before his defeat, Lord John made a chivalrous and splendid defence of Lord Clarendon, in answer to an attack, not merely on the policy, but on the personal character of the Viceroy of Ireland.

Sudden as the fall of the Russell Administration was, it can hardly be described as unexpected, and many causes, most of which have already been indicated in these pages, contributed to bring it about. Albany Fonblanque, one of the shrewdest contemporary observers of men and movements, gathered the political gossip of the moment together in a paragraph which sets forth in graphic fashion the tumult of opinion in the spring of 1852. 'Lord John Russell has fallen, and all are agreed that he is greatly to blame for falling ; but hardly any two men agree about the immediate cause of his fall. "It was the Durham Letter," says one. "Not a jot," replies another ; "the Durham Letter was quite right, and would have strengthened him prodigiously if it had been followed up by a vigorous anti-Papal measure : it was the paltry bill that destroyed him." "The Ecclesiastical Titles Bill," interposes a third, "did just enough in doing next to nothing : no, it was the house tax in the Budget that did the mischief." "The house tax might have been got over," puts in another, "but the proposal of the income tax, with all its injustices unmitigated, doomed Lord John." "Not a whit," rejoins a Radical reformer, "the income tax is popular, especially with people who don't pay it ; Lord John's opposition to Locke King's motion sealed his fate." "Locke King's division was a flea-bite," cries a staunch Protestant, "the Pope has done it all."'

Stress has been laid in these pages on the attempts of the Russell Administration to deal with an acute and terrible phase of the eternal Irish problem, as well as to set forth in outline the difficulties which it encountered in regard to its foreign policy through the cavalier attitude and bid for personal ascendency of Lord Palmerston. The five or six years during which Lord John Russell was at the head of affairs were marked by a succession of panics which heightened immeasurably the difficulties of his position. One was purely commercial, but it threw gloom over the country, brought stagnation to trade, and political discontent followed in its train, which in turn reacted on the prospects of the Government. The Irish famine and the rebellion which followed in its wake taxed the resources of the Cabinet to the utmost, and the efforts which were made by the Ministry to grapple with the evil have scarcely received even yet due recognition. The Chartist movement, the agitation over the Papal claims and the fear of invasion, are landmarks in the turbulent and menacing annals of the time.

The repeal of the Navigation Act bore witness to Lord John's zealous determination to extend the principles of Free

Trade, and the Jewish Disabilities Bill—which was rejected by the House of Lords—is itself a sufficient answer to those who, because of his resistance, not to the spiritual claims, but to the political arrogance of the Vatican, have ventured to charge him with a lack of religious toleration.   He himself once declared that as a statesman he had received as much favour as he had deserved ; he added that, where his measures had miscarried, he did not attribute the failure to animosity or misrepresentation, but rather to errors which he had himself committed from mistaken judgment or an erroneous interpretation of facts.   No one who looks at Lord John Russell's career with simple justice, to say nothing of generosity, can doubt the truth of his words.   'I believe, I may say, that my ends have been honest.   I have looked to the happiness of my country as the object to which my efforts ought to be directed.'

CHAPTER IX

COALITION BUT NOT UNION

1852-1853

The Aberdeen Ministry—Warring elements—Mr. Gladstone's position
—Lord John at the Foreign Office and Leader of the House—Lady
Russell's criticism of Lord Macaulay's statement—A small cloud in
the East—Lord Shaftesbury has his doubts

THERE is no need to linger over the history of the next few
months, for in a political sense they were barren and un-
fruitful. The first Derby Administration possessed no elements of strength, and quickly proved a mere stop-gap
Cabinet. Its tenure of power was not only brief but inglorious. The new Ministers took office in February, and they
left it in December. Lord Palmerston may be said to have
given them their chance, and Mr. Gladstone gave them their
coup de grâce. The Derby Administration was summoned
into existence because Lord Palmerston carried his amendment on the Militia Bill, and it refused to lag superfluous on
the stage after the crushing defeat which followed Mr.
Gladstone's brilliant attack on the Budget of Mr. Disraeli.
The chief legislative achievement of this short-lived Government was an extension of the Bribery Act, which Lord John
Russell had introduced in 1841. A measure was now passed
providing for a searching investigation of corrupt practices
by commissioners appointed by the Crown. The affairs of
New Zealand were also placed on a sound political basis.

A General Election occurred in the summer, but before the new Parliament met in the autumn the nation was called to mourn the death of the Duke of Wellington. The old soldier had won the crowning victory of Waterloo four years before the Queen's birth, and yet he survived long enough to grace with his presence the opening ceremony of the Great Exhibition—that magnificent triumph of the arts of peace which was held in London in the summer of 1851. The remarkable personal ascendency which the Duke of Wellington achieved because of his splendid record as a soldier, though backed by high personal character, was not thrown on the side of either liberty or progress when the hero transferred his services from the camp to the cabinet. As a soldier, Wellington shone without a rival, but as a statesman he was an obstinate reactionary. Perhaps his solitary claim to political regard is that he, more than any other man, wrung from the weak hands of George IV. a reluctant consent to Catholic Emancipation—a concession which could no longer be refused with safety, and one which had been delayed for the lifetime of a generation through rigid adherence in high places to antiquated prejudices and unreasoning alarm.

The strength of parties in the new Parliament proved to be nearly evenly balanced. Indeed, the Liberals were only in a majority of sixteen, if the small but compact phalanx of forty Peelites be left for the moment out of the reckoning. The Conservatives had, in truth, gained ground in the country through the reverses of one kind and another which had overtaken their opponents. Lord Palmerston, always fond, to borrow his own phrase, of striking from his own bat, declared in airy fashion that Lord John had given him with dismissal independence, and, though Lord Derby offered him a seat in his Cabinet, he was too shrewd and far-seeing a statesman to accept it. The Liberal party was divided about Lord Palmerston, and that fact led to vacillation at the polling booths. Ardent Protestants were disappointed that the Durham Letter had been followed by what they regarded as weak and insufficient legislative action, whilst some of the phrases of that outspoken manifesto still rankled in the minds of ardent High Churchmen. The old Conservative party had been smashed by Peel's adoption of Free Trade, and the new Conservative party which was struggling into existence still looked askance at the pretensions of Mr. Disraeli, who, thanks to his own ability and to the persistent advocacy of his claims in earlier years by his now departed friend, Lord George Bentinck, was fairly seated in the saddle, and inclined to use both whip and spurs.

In the autobiography recently published of the late Sir William Gregory [1] a vivid description will be found of the way in which the aristocracy and the squires 'kicked at the supremacy of one whom they looked at as a mountebank;' and on the same page will be found the remarkable assertion that it was nothing but Mr. Disraeli's claim to lead the Conservative party which prevented Mr. Gladstone from joining it in 1852.[2] Disraeli's borrowed heroics in his pompous oration in the House of Commons on the occasion of the death of Wellington, and his errors in tactics

---

[1] *Sir William Gregory, K.C.M.G. : an Autobiography*, edited by Lady Gregory, pp. 92, 93.

[2] Mr. Gladstone's comment on this statement is that it is interesting as coming from an acute contemporary observer. At the same time it expresses an opinion and presents no facts. Mr. Gladstone adds that he is not aware that the question of re-union with the Conservative party was ever presented to him in such a way as to embrace the relations to Mr. Disraeli.

and taste as leader of the House, heightened the prevailing impression that, even if the result of the General Election had been different, the Derby Administration was doomed to failure. All through the autumn the quidnuncs at the clubs were busy predicting the probable course of events, and more or less absurd rumours ran round the town concerning the statesmen who were likely to succeed to power in the event of Derby's resignation. The choice in reality lay between Russell, Palmerston, and Aberdeen, for Lansdowne was out of health, and therefore out of the question.

As in a mirror Lady Russell's journal reflects what she calls the alarm in the Whig camp at the rumour of the intended resignation of the Derby Cabinet if Disraeli's financial proposals were defeated, and the hurried consultations which followed between Lord Lansdowne, Lord Aberdeen, and Lord John, Sir James Graham, Mr. Cobden, and Mr. Bright. Two days before the division which overthrew the Government on December 17, Lord John was at Woburn, and his brother, the Duke of Bedford, asked him what course he thought the Queen should adopt in case the Ministry was beaten. He replied that her Majesty, under such circumstances, ought to send for Lord Lansdowne and Lord Aberdeen. This was the course which the Queen adopted, but Lord Lansdowne, old and ill, felt powerless to respond to the summons. Meanwhile, Lord John, who certainly possessed the strongest claims—a circumstance which was recognised at the time by Mr. Gladstone—had determined from a sense of public duty not to press them, for he recognised that neither Palmerston nor the Peelites, who, for the moment, in the nice balance of parties, commanded the situation, would serve under him. He had led the Liberal forces for a long term of years, both in power and in opposition, and neither his devotion nor his ability was open to question, in spite of the offence which he had given, on the one hand to a powerful colleague, and on the other to powerful interests.

Lord Aberdeen was regarded by the followers of Peel as their leader. He was a favourite at Court, and a statesman of established reputation of the doctrinaire type, but he was not a man who ever excited, or probably was capable of exciting, popular enthusiasm. On the day after Disraeli's defeat Lord Aberdeen met Lord John by chance in the Park, and the latter, waiving personal ambition, told him that, though he could say nothing decisive for the moment, he thought he should accept office under him. On the morrow Lord Aberdeen was summoned to Osborne, and accepted the task of forming an Administration. Next day her Majesty wrote to Lord John announcing the fact, and the letter ended with the following passage : 'The Queen thinks the moment to have arrived when a popular, efficient, and durable Government could be formed by the sincere and united efforts of all professing Conservative and Liberal opinions. The Queen, knowing that this can only be effected by the patriotic sacrifice of personal interests and feelings to the public, trusts that Lord John Russell will, as far as he is able, give his valuable and powerful assistance to the realisation of this object.' This communication found Lord John halting between two opinions. Palmerston had declined to serve under him, and he might, with even greater propriety, in his turn have refused to serve under Aberdeen. His own health, which was never strong, had suffered through the long strain of office in years which had been marked by famine and rebellion. He had just begun to revel, to quote his own words, in 'all the delights of freedom from red boxes, with the privilege of fresh air and mountain prospects.'

He had already found the recreation of a busy man, and was engrossed in the preparation of the 'Memoirs and Journal' of his friend, Thomas Moore. The poet had died in February of that year, and Lord John, with characteristic goodwill, had undertaken to edit his voluminous· papers in order to help a widow without wounding her pride. In fact, on many grounds he might reasonably have stood aside, and he certainly would have done so if personal motives had counted most with him, or if he had been the self-seeker which some of his detractors have imagined. Here Lord Macaulay comes to our help with a vivid account of what he terms an eventful day—one of the dark days before Christmas—on which the possibility of a Coalition Government under Aberdeen was still doubtful. Macaulay states that he went to Lansdowne House, on December 20, on a hasty summons to find its master and Lord John in consultation over the Queen's letter. He was asked his opinion of the document and duly gave it. 'Then Lord John said that of course he should try to help Lord Aberdeen : but how? There were two ways. He might take the lead of the Commons with the Foreign Office, or he might refuse office, and give his support from the back benches. I adjured him not to think of this last course, and I argued it with him during a quarter of an hour with, I thought, a great flow of thoughts and words. I was encouraged by Lord Lansdowne, who nodded, smiled, and rubbed his hands at everything I said. I reminded him that the Duke of Wellington had taken the Foreign Office after having been at the Treasury, and I quoted his own pretty speech to the Duke. " You said, Lord John, that we could not all win battles of Waterloo, but that we might all imitate the old man's patriotism, sense of duty, and indifference to selfish interests ; and vanities when the public welfare was concerned ; and now is the time for you to make a sacrifice Your past services and your name give us a right to expect it." He went away, evidently much impressed by what had been said, and promising to consult others. When he was gone, Lord Lansdowne told me that I had come just as opportunely as Blücher did at Waterloo.'[1] It is only right to state that Lady Russell demurs to some parts of this account of her husband's attitude at the crisis. Nothing could be further from the truth than that Lord John's vacillation was due to personal motives, or that his hesitation arose from his reluctance to take any office short of the Premiership. Lady Russell adds 'this never for one moment weighed with him, so that he did not require Lord Macaulay or Lord Lansdowne to argue him out of the objection.' Lord John's difficulty was based upon the 'improbability of agreement in a Cabinet so composed, and therefore the probable evil to the country.' Letters written by Lady Russell at the moment to a relative, of too private a character to quote, give additional weight to this statement. One homely remark made at the time may, however, be cited. Lady Russell declared that her husband would not mind being ' shoeblack to Lord Aberdeen ' if it would serve the country.

The Aberdeen Ministry came into existence just as the year 1852 was ending. It was, in truth, a strange bit of mosaic work, fashioned with curious art, as the result

---

[1] *Life and Letters of Lord Macaulay*, by the Right Hon. Sir George Otto Trevelyan, M.P., vol. ii. p. 340.

of negotiations between the Whigs and the Peelites which had extended over a period of nearly six months. It represented the triumph of expediency, but it awakened little enthusiasm in spite of the much-vaunted ability and experience of its members. Derby and Disraeli were left out on the one side and Cobden and Bright on the other, a circumstance, however, which did not prevent men comparing the Coalition Government to the short-lived but famous Ministry of all the Talents. The nation rubbed its eyes and wondered whether good or evil was in store when it saw Peel's lieutenants rowing in the same boat with Russell. The vanished leader, however, was responsible for such a strange turn of the wheel, for everyone recognised that Sir Robert had ' steered his fleet into the enemy's port.' His followers came to power through the dilemma of the moment and the temporary eclipse of politicians of more resolute convictions. The Whigs were divided, and with Ireland they were discredited, whilst the Radicals were still clamouring at the doors of Downing Street with small chance of admission, in spite of their growing power in the country· The little clique of Peelites played their cards adroitly, and though they were, to a large extent, a party without followers, they were masters of the situation, and Russell and Palmerston, in consequence, were the only men of commanding personality, outside their own ranks, who were admitted to the chief seats in the new Cabinet. Russell became Foreign Secretary, whilst Palmerston took control of the Home Office.

So great was the rush for place that Lord Derby with a smile informed the Queen that, as so many former Ministers expected a seat, he thought that less than thirty-two could hardly be the number of the new Cabinet. Tories of the old school looked on with amazement, and Radicals of the new with suspicion. All things seemed possible in the excitement of parties. 'Tom Baring said to me last night,' Greville remarks, ' " Can't you make room for Disraeli in this Coalition Government ? " I said : " Why, will you give him to us ? " " Oh yes," he said, "you shall have him with pleasure." ' Great expectations were, however, ruthlessly nipped in the bud, and the Cabinet, instead of being unwieldy, was uncommonly small, for it consisted only of thirteen members—an unlucky start, if old wives' fables are to be believed. Five of Sir Robert Peel's colleagues—the Premier, the Duke of Newcastle, Sir James Graham, Mr. Sidney Herbert, and Mr. Gladstone—represented the moderately progressive views of their old leader. Russell and Palmerston represented the Whigs, but, thanks to one of life's little ironies, the statesman who passed the Reform Bill was installed for the moment at the Foreign Office, and the Minister who was a Liberal abroad and a Conservative at home was intrusted with the internal affairs of the nation. The truth was, Lord Palmerston was impossible at the Foreign Office if Lord Aberdeen was at the Treasury, for the two men were diametrically opposed in regard to the policy which England ought to adopt in her relations with Europe in general, and Russia in particular. In fact, if Lord John Russell was for the moment out of the reckoning as Premier, Lord Palmerston ought unquestionably to have had the reversion of power. Unfortunately, though growingly popular in the country, he had rendered himself unwelcome at Court, where Lord Aberdeen, on the contrary, had long been a trusted adviser.

Even if it be granted that neither Russell nor Palmerston was admissible as leader, it was a palpable blunder to exclude

from Cabinet rank men of clean-cut convictions like Cobden
and Bright. They had a large following in the country,
and had won their spurs in the Anti-Corn-Law struggle.
They represented the aspirations of the most active section
of the Liberal Party, and they also possessed the spell which
eloquence and sincerity never fail to throw over the imagination of the people. They were not judged worthy,
however, and Milner Gibson, in spite of his services as a
member of the Russell Cabinet, was also debarred from
office ; whilst Mr. Charles Villiers, whose social claims
could not be entirely overlooked, found his not inconsider-
able services to the people rewarded by subordinate rank.
The view which was taken at Court of the Aberdeen Ministry
is recorded in the ' Life of the Prince Consort.' The Queen
regarded the Cabinet as ' the realisation of the country's and
our own most ardent wishes ; ' [1] and in her Majesty's view the
words ' brilliant ' and ' strong ' described the new Government. Brilliant it might be, but strong it assuredly was not,
for it was pervaded by the spirit of mutual distrust, and circumstances conspired to accentuate the wide divergence
of opinion which lurked beneath the surface harmony.
However such a union of warring forces might be agreeable to the Queen, the belief that it realised the 'most
ardent wishes' of the nation was not widely held outside the
Court, for ' England,' to borrow Disraeli's familiar but significant phrase, ' does not love Coalitions.' In the Aberdeen
Cabinet, party interests were banded together in office ;
but the vivifying influences of unity of conviction and
common sentiment were absent from its deliberations.
After all, as Sir Edward Bulwer Lytton drily remarked when
the inevitable crisis arose, there is ' one indisputable element

[1] Sir Theodore Martin's *Life of the Prince Consort*, vol. ii. p. 483.

of a Coalition Government, and that is that its members
should coalesce.' As a matter of fact, they not only drifted
into war but drifted apart. ' It is a powerful team and will
require good driving,' was the comment of a shrewd political
observer. 'There are some odd tempers and queer ways
among them.'

Lord Aberdeen had many virtues, but he was not a
good driver, and when the horses grew restive and kicked
over the traces, he lacked nerve, hesitated, and was lost.
Trained for political life at the side of Pitt,[1] after a distinguished career in diplomacy, which made him known in all
the Courts of Europe, he entered the Cabinet of the Duke of
Wellington in 1828, and afterwards held the post of Secretary
for the Colonies in the first Peel Administration of 1834,
and that of Secretary for Foreign Affairs during Sir Robert's
final spell of power in the years 1841–46. He never sat in
the House of Commons, but, though a Tory peer, he voted
for Catholic Emancipation. He swiftly fell into line, however, with his party, and recorded his vote against the
Reform Bill. He never, perhaps, quite understood the
temper of a popular assembly, for he was a shy, reserved
man, sparing in speech and punctilious in manner. Close
association with Wellington and Peel had, of course, done
much to shape his outlook on affairs, and much acquaintance with the etiquette of foreign Courts had insensibly led
him to cultivate the habit of formal reserve. Born in the
same year as Palmerston, the Premier possessed neither
the openness to new ideas nor the vivacity of his masterful
colleague ; in fact, Lord Aberdeen at sixty-eight, unlike Lord
Palmerston, was an old man in temperament, as well as
conservative, in the sense of one not given to change. Yet,

---

[1] Pitt became guardian to the young Lord Haddo in 1792.

it is only fair to add that, if Aberdeen's views of foreign policy were of a somewhat stereotyped kind, he was, at all events at this period in their careers, more progressive on home policy than Palmerston, who was too much inclined not to move for the social welfare of the people before he was compelled.

The new Ministry ran well until it was hindered by complications in the East. In the middle of February, a few days after the meeting of Parliament, Lord John retired from the Foreign Office, and led the House through the session with great ability, but without taking office. It is important to remember that he had only accepted the Foreign Office under strong pressure, and as a temporary expedient. It was, however, understood that he was at liberty at any moment to relinquish the Foreign Office in favour of Lord Clarendon, if he found the duties too onerous to discharge in conjunction with the task of leadership in the Commons. The session of 1853 was rendered memorable by the display of Mr. Gladstone's skill in finance ; and the first Budget of the new Chancellor of the Exchequer was in every sense in splendid contrast with the miserable fiasco of the previous year, when Mr. Disraeli was responsible for proposals which, as Sir George Cornewall Lewis said, were of a kind that flesh and blood could not stand. The trade of the country had revived, and, with tranquility, some degree of prosperity had returned, even to Ireland. Lord John Russell, true to his policy of religious equality, brought forward the Jewish Disabilities Bill, but the House of Lords, with equal consistency, threw out the measure. The Law of Transportation was altered, and a new India Bill was passed, which threw open the Civil Service to competition. Many financial reforms were introduced, a new proposal was made for a wider extent of elementary education, and much legislative activity in a variety of directions was displayed.

Lord Aberdeen had taken office under pressure and from a sense of duty. It had few attractions for him, and he looked forward with quiet satisfaction to release from its cares. Lord Stanmore's authority can be cited for the statement that in the summer of 1853 his father deemed that the time had come when he might retire in Lord John Russell's favour, in accordance with an arrangement which had been made in general terms when the Cabinet was formed. There were members of the Coalition Government who were opposed to this step; but Lord Aberdeen anticipated no serious difficulty in carrying out the proposal. Suddenly the aspect of affairs grew not merely critical but menacing, and the Prime Minister found himself confronted by complications abroad, from which he felt it would be despicable to retreat by the easy method of personal resignation. There is not the slightest occasion, nor, indeed, is this the place, to recount the vicissitudes of the Aberdeen Administration in its baffled struggles against the alternative of war. The achievements of the Coalition Government, no less than its failures, with much of its secret history, have already been told with praiseworthy candour and intimate knowledge by Lord Stanmore, who as a young man acted as private secretary to his father, Lord Aberdeen, through the stress and storm of those fateful years. It is therefore only necessary in these pages to state the broad outlines of the story, and to indicate Lord John Russell's position in the least popular Cabinet of the Queen's reign.

Lord Shaftesbury jotted down in his journal, when the new Ministry came into office, these words, and they sum up pretty accurately the situation, and the common verdict

upon it : 'Aberdeen Prime Minister, Lord John Russell
Minister for Foreign Affairs.　Is it possible that this arrange-
ment should prosper?　Can the Liberal policy of Lord
John square with the restrictive policy of Lord Aberdeen?
I wish them joy and a safe deliverance.'

CHAPTER X

1853

Causes of the Crimean War—Nicholas seizes his opportunity—The Secret
Memorandum—Napoleon and the susceptibilities of the Vatican —
Lord Stratford de Redcliffe and the Porte—Prince Menschikoff shows
his hand—Lord Aberdeen hopes against hope—Lord Palmerston's
opinion of the crisis—The Vienna Note—Lord John grows restive
—Sinope arouses England—The deadlock in the Cabinet.

MANY causes conspired to bring about the war in the
Crimea, though the pretext for the quarrel—a dispute
between the monks of the Latin and Greek Churches concerning the custody of the Holy Places in Palestine—presents
no element of difficulty. It is, however, no easy matter to
gather up in a few pages the reasons which led to the war.
Amongst the most prominent of them were the ambitious
projects of the despotic Emperor Nicholas. The military
revolt in his own capital at the period of his accession, and
the Polish insurrections of 1830 and 1850, had rendered him
harsh and imperious, and disinclined to concessions on any
adequate scale to the restless but spasmodic demands for
political reform in Russia. Gloomy and reserved though the
Autocrat of All the Russias was, he recognised that it would
be a mistake to rely for the pacification of his vast empire on
the policy of masterly inactivity. His war with Persia, his
invasion of Turkey, and the army which he sent to help

Austria to settle her quarrel with Hungary, not only appealed to the pride of Russia, but provided so many outlets for the energy and ambition of her ruler. It was in the East that Nicholas saw his opportunity, and his policy was a revival, under the changed conditions of the times, of that of Peter the Great and Catherine II.

Nicholas had long secretly chafed at the exclusion of his war-ships—by the provisions of the treaty of 1841—from access through the Black Sea to the Mediterranean, and he dreamed dreams of Constantinople, and saw visions of India. Linked to many lawless instincts, there was in the Emperor's personal character much of the intolerance of the fanatic. Religion and pride alike made the fact rankle in his breast that so many of the Sultan's subjects were Sclavs, and professed the Russian form of Christianity. He was, moreover, astute enough to see that a war which could be construed by the simple and devout peasantry as an attempt to uplift the standard of the Cross in the dominions of the Crescent would appeal at once to the clergy and populace of Holy Russia. Nicholas had persuaded himself that, with Lord Aberdeen at the head of affairs, and Palmerston in a place of safety at the Home Office, England was scarcely in a condition to give practical effect to her traditional jealousy of Russia. In the weakness of her divided counsels he saw his opportunity. It had become a fixed idea with the Emperor that Turkey was in a moribund condition; and neither Orloff nor Nesselrode had been able to disabuse his mind of the notion.

Everyone is aware that in January 1853 the Emperor told the English Ambassador, Sir Hamilton Seymour, that Turkey was the 'sick man' of Europe, and ever since then the phrase has passed current and become historic. It was often on the lips of Nicholas, for he talked freely, and sometimes showed so little discretion that Nesselrode once declared, with fine irony, that the White Czar could not claim to be a diplomatist. The phrase cannot have startled Lord Aberdeen. It must have sounded, indeed, like the echo of words which the Emperor had uttered in London in the summer of 1844. Nicholas, on the occasion of his visit to England in that year, spoke freely about the Eastern Question, not merely to the Duke of Wellington, whose military prowess he greatly admired, but also to Sir Robert Peel and Lord Aberdeen, who was then Minister for Foreign Affairs. He told the latter in so many words that Turkey was a dying man, and did his best to impress the three English statesmen with the necessity for preparation in view of the approaching crisis. He stated that he foresaw that the time was coming when he would have to put his armies in movement, and added that Austria would be compelled to do the same. He protested that he made no claim to an inch of Turkish soil, but was prepared to dispute the right of anyone else to an inch of it —a palpable allusion to the French support of Mehemet Ali. It was too soon to stipulate what should be done when the 'sick man's' last hour had run its course. All he wanted, he maintained, was the basis of an understanding.

In Nicholas's opinion England ought to make common cause with Russia and Austria, and he did not disguise his jealousy of France. It was clear that he dreaded the growth of close union between England and France, and for Louis Philippe then, as for Louis Napoleon afterwards, his feeling was one of coldness if not of actual disdain. The Emperor Nicholas won golden opinions amongst all classes during his short stay in England. Sir Theodore Martin's 'Life of the Prince Consort,' and especially the letter which is published in its pages from the Queen to King Leopold, showed the marked impression which was made at Windsor by his handsome presence, his apparently unstudied confidences, the simplicity and charm of his manners, and the adroitness of his well-turned compliments. Whenever the Autocrat of All the Russias appeared in public, at a military review, or the Opera, or at Ascot, he received an ovation, and Baron Stockmar, with dry cynicism, has not failed to record the lavish gifts of ' endless snuff-boxes and large presents ' which made his departure memorable to the Court officials. Out of this visit grew, though the world knew nothing of it then, the Secret Memorandum, drawn up by Peel, Wellington, and Aberdeen, and signed by them as well as by the Emperor himself. This document, though it actually committed England to nothing more serious than the recognition in black and white of the desperate straits of the Porte, and the fact that England and Russia were alike concerned in maintaining the *status quo* in Turkey, dwelt significantly on the fact that, in the event of a crisis in Turkey, Russia and England were to come to an understanding with each other as to what concerted action they should take. The agreement already existing between Russia and Austria was significantly emphasised in the document, and stress was laid on the fact that if England joined the compact, France would have no alternative but to accept the decision.

There can be no question that Nicholas attached an exaggerated importance to this memorandum. It expressed his opinion rather than the determination of the Peel Administration ; but a half-barbaric despot not unnaturally imagined that when the responsible advisers of the Crown entered into a secret agreement with him, no matter how vague its terms might appear when subjected to critical analysis, England and himself were practically of one mind. When the Coalition Government was formed, two of the three statesmen, whom the Emperor Nicholas regarded as his friends at Court, were dead, but the third, in the person of Lord Aberdeen, had succeeded, by an unexpected turn of the wheel, to the chief place in the new Ministry. Long before the Imperial visit to London the Emperor had honoured Lord Aberdeen with his friendship, and, now that the Foreign Minister of 1844 was the Prime Minister of 1853, the opportune moment for energetic action seemed to have arrived. Nicholas, accordingly, now hinted that if the 'sick man' died England should seize Egypt and Crete, and that the European provinces of Turkey should be formed into independent states under Russian protection. He met, however, with no response, for the English Cabinet by this time saw that the impending collapse of Turkey, on which Nicholas laid such emphatic stress, was by no means a foregone conclusion. Napoleon and Palmerston had, moreover, drawn France and England into friendly alliance. There was no shadow of doubt that the Christian subjects of Turkey were grossly oppressed, and it is only fair to believe that Nicholas, as the head of the Greek Church, was honestly anxious to rid them of such thraldom. At the same time no one imagined that he was exactly the ruler to expend blood and treasure, in the risks of war, in the *rôle* of a Defender of the Faith.

Count Vitzthum doubts whether the Emperor really contemplated the taking of Constantinople, but it is plain that he meant to crush the Turkish Empire, and England, knowing that the man had masterful instincts and ambitious schemes

—that suggest, at all events, a passing comparison with Napoleon Bonaparte – took alarm at his restlessness, and the menace to India, which it seemed to suggest. ' If we do not stop the Russians on the Danube,' said Lord John Russell, ' we shall have to stop them on the Indus.' It is now a matter of common knowledge that, when the Crimean War began, Nicholas had General Duhamel's scheme before him for an invasion of India through Asia. Such an advance, it was foreseen, would cripple England's resources in Europe by compelling her to despatch an army of defence to the East. It certainly looks, therefore, as if Russia, when hostilities in the Crimea actually began, was preparing herself for a sudden descent on Constantinople. Napoleon III., eager to conciliate the religious susceptibilities of his own subjects, as well as to gratify the Vatican, wished the Sultan to make the Latin monks the supreme custodians of the Holy Places. Complications, the issue of which it was impossible to forecast, appeared inevitable, and for the moment there seemed only one man who could grapple with the situation at Constantinople. Lord Palmerston altogether, and Lord John Russell in part, sympathised with the clamour which arose in the Press for the return of the Great Elchi to the Porte.

In the entire annals of British diplomacy there is scarcely a more picturesque or virile figure than that of Lord Stratford de Redcliffe. Capacity for public affairs ran in the blood of the Cannings, as the three statues which to-day stand side by side in Westminster Abbey proudly attest. Those marble memorials represent George Canning, the great Foreign Minister, who in the famous, if grandiloquent, phrase ' called the New World into existence to redress the balance of the Old ;' his son Charles, Earl Canning, first

Viceroy of India ; and his cousin, Stratford Canning, Viscount
Stratford de Redcliffe, who for a long term of years sought
to quicken into newness of social and political life the broken
and demoralised forces of the Ottoman Empire, and who
practically dictated from Constantinople the policy of
England in the East.   He was born in 1786 and died in
1880.   He entered the public service as a *précis*-writer at
the Foreign Office, and rose swiftly in the profession of diplomacy.   His acquaintance with Eastern affairs began in 1808,
when he was appointed First Secretary to Sir Robert Adair,
whom he succeeded two years later at Constantinople as
Minister Plenipotentiary.   The Treaty of Bucharest, which
in 1812 brought the war, then in progress between Russia and
Turkey, to an end, was the first of a brilliant series of diplomatic triumphs, which established his reputation in all the
Councils of Europe, and made him, in Lord Tennyson's words,
'The voice of England in the East.'   After services in
Switzerland, in Washington, and at the Congress of Vienna,
Canning, in 1825, returned to Constantinople with the rank
of Ambassador.

He witnessed the overthrow of the Janissaries by
Sultan Mahmoud II., and had his own experience of
Turkish atrocities in the massacre which followed.   He
took a prominent part in the creation of the modern kingdom
of Greece, and resigned his appointment in 1828, because
of a conflict of opinion with Lord Aberdeen in the early
stages of that movement.   Afterwards, he was gazetted
Ambassador to St. Petersburg ; but the Emperor Nicholas,
who by this time recognised the masterful qualities of the
man, refused to receive him—a conspicuous slight, which
Lord Stratford, who was as proud and irascible as the Czar,
never forgave.   Between the years 1842 and 1858 he again

filled his old position as Ambassador to Constantinople, and during those years he won a unique ascendency—unmatched in the history of diplomacy—over men and movements in Turkey. He brought about many reforms, and made it his special concern to watch over the interests of the Christian subjects at the Porte, who styled him the 'Padishah of the Shah,' and that title—Sultan of the Sultan—exactly hit off the authority which he wielded, not always wisely, but always with good intent. It was an unfortunate circumstance that Lord Stratford, after his resignation in 1852, should have been summoned back for a further spell of six years' tenure of power exactly at the moment when Nicholas, prompted by the knowledge of the absence from Constantinople of the man who had held him in check, and of the accession to power in Downing Street of a statesman of mild temper and friendly disposition to Russia, was beginning once more to push his claims in the East. Lord Stratford had many virtues, but he had also a violent and uncertain temper. He was a man of inflexible integrity, iron will, undeniable moral courage, and commanding force of character. Yet, for a great Ambassador, he was at times strangely undiplomatic, whilst the keenness of his political judgment and forecasts some-times suffered eclipse through the strength of his personal antipathies.

Meanwhile, Lord John Russell, who had expressly stipulated when the Cabinet was formed that he was only to hold the seals of the Foreign Office for a few weeks, convinced already that the position was untenable to a man of his views, insisted on being relieved of the office. The divergent views in the Cabinet on the Eastern Question were making themselves felt, and Lord Aberdeen's eminently charitable interpretation of the Russian demands was little to the minds of men of the stamp of Palmerston and Russell, neither of whom was inclined to pin his faith so completely to the Czar's assurances. When Parliament met in February, Lord John quitted the Foreign Office and led the House of Commons without portfolio. His quick recognition of Mr. Gladstone's great qualities as a responsible statesman was not the least pleasing incident of the moment. In April, Lord Aberdeen once more made no secret of his determination to retire at the end of the session, and this intimation no doubt had its influence with the more restive of his colleagues.

When Parliament rose, Lord John Russell's position in the country was admitted on all hands to be one of renewed strength, for, set free from an irksome position, he had thrown himself during the session with ardour into the congenial work of leader of the House of Commons. The resolution of the Cabinet to send Lord Stratford to Constantinople has already been stated. He received his instructions on February 25 ; in fact, he seems to have dictated them, for Lord Clarendon, who had just succeeded to the Foreign Office, made no secret of the circumstance that they were largely borrowed from the Ambassador's own notes. He was told that he was to proceed first to Paris, and then to Vienna, in order that he might know the minds of France and Austria on the issues at stake. Napoleon III. was to be assured that England relied on his cordial co-operation in maintaining the integrity and independence of the Turkish Empire. The young Emperor of Austria was to be informed that her Majesty's Government gladly recognised the fact that his attitude towards the Porte had not been changed by recent events, and that the policy of Austria in the East was not likely to be altered. Lord Stratford was to warn the Sultan and his advisers that the crisis was one which required the utmost prudence on their part if peace was to be preserved.

The Sultan and his Ministers were practically to be told by Lord Stratford that they were the authors of their own misfortunes, and that, if they were to be extricated from them, they must place the 'utmost confidence in the sincerity and soundness of the advice' that he was commissioned to give them. He was further to lay stress on palpable abuses, and to urge the necessity of administrative reforms. 'It remains,' added Lord Clarendon, 'only for me to say that in the event, which her Majesty's Government earnestly hope may not arise, of imminent danger to the existence of the Turkish Government, your Excellency will in such case despatch a messenger to Malta requesting the Admiral to hold himself in readiness; but you will not direct him to approach the Dardanelles without positive instructions from her Majesty's Government.' The etiquette of Courts has to be respected, especially by Ambassadors charged with a difficult mission, but Lord Stratford's diplomatic visits to Paris and Vienna were unduly prolonged, and occupied more time than was desirable at such a crisis. He arrived at Constantinople on April 5, and was received, to his surprise, with a remarkable personal ovation. In Kinglake's phrase, his return was regarded as that 'of a king whose realm had been suffered to fall into danger.'

The Czar's envoy, Prince Menschikoff, had already been on the scene for five weeks. If Russia meant peace, the choice of such a representative was unfortunate. Menschikoff was a brusque soldier, rough and impolitic of speech, and by no means inclined to conform to accepted methods of procedure. He refused to place himself in communication with the

Foreign Minister of the Porte ; and this was interpreted at Stamboul as an insult to the Sultan. The Grand Vizier, rushing to the conclusion that his master was in imminent danger, induced Colonel Rose, the British Chargé d'Affaires, to order the Mediterranean Fleet, then at Malta, to proceed to Vourla. The Admiral, however, refused to lend himself to the panic, and sent back word that he waited instructions from London, a course which was afterwards approved by the Cabinet. The commotion at Stamboul was not lost upon Napoleon, though he knew that the English Cabinet was not anxious to precipitate matters. Eager to display his newly acquired power, he promptly sent instructions to the French Fleet to proceed to Salamis. Meanwhile Prince Menschikoff, who had adopted a more conciliatory attitude on the question of the Holy Places, with the result that negotiations were proceeding satisfactorily, assumed shortly before the arrival of Lord Stratford a more defiant manner, and startled the Porte by the sudden announcement of new demands. He claimed that a formal treaty should be drawn up, recognising in the most ample, not to say abject, terms, the right of Russia to establish a Protectorate over the Christian subjects of the Porte. This meant, as Lord Clarendon pointed out at the time, that fourteen millions of people would henceforth regard the Czar as their defender, whilst their allegiance to the Sultan would become little more than nominal, and the position of the Turkish ruler would inevitably dwindle from independence to vassalage.

Lord Stratford at once took the bull by the horns. Acting on his advice, the Porte refused even to entertain such proposals until the question of the Holy Places was settled. Within a month, through Lord Stratford's firmness, Russia and Turkey came to terms over the original point in dispute ;

but on the following day Menschikoff placed an ultimatum before the Porte, demanding that, within five days, his master's claim for the acknowledgment of the Russian Protectorate over the Sultan's Greek subjects should be accepted. The Sultan's Ministers, who interpreted the dramatic return of Lord Stratford to mean that they had England at their back, declined to accede, and their refusal was immediately followed by the departure of Prince Menschikoff. Repulsed in diplomacy, the Czar, on July 2, marched forty thousand troops across the frontier river, the Pruth, and occupied Moldavia and Wallachia. The Imperial manifesto stated that it was not the Czar's intention to commence war, but only to obtain such security as would ensure the restoration of the rights of Russia. This was, of course, high ground to take, and a conference of the Great Powers was hastily summoned, with the result that the French view of the situation was embodied by the assembled diplomatists in the Vienna Note, which was despatched simultaneously to Russia and Turkey. Lord John Russell, even before the arrival of Lord Stratford at Constantinople, had come to the conclusion that the Emperor of Russia was determined to pick a quarrel with Turkey ; but Lord Aberdeen and his Peelite following were of another mind, and even Lord Clarendon seems for the moment to have been hoodwinked by the Czar's protestations.

A month or two later the Foreign Minister saw matters in a different light, for he used in the House of Lords, in the summer of 1853, an expression which has become historic : ' We are drifting into war.' The quarrel at this stage—for the susceptibilities of France and of Rome had been appeased by the settlement of the question of the Holy Places —lay between Russia and Turkey, and England might have compelled the peace of Europe if she had known her own mind, and made both parties recognise in unmistakeable terms what was her policy. Lord John Russell had a policy, but no power to enforce it, whilst Lord Aberdeen had no policy which ordinary mortals could fathom, and had the power to keep the Cabinet—though scarcely Lord Stratford de Redcliffe —from taking any decided course. The Emperor Nicholas, relying on the Protocol which Lord Aberdeen had signed— under circumstances which, however, bore no resemblance to existing conditions—imagined that, with such a statesman at the head of affairs, England would not take up arms against Russia. Lord Aberdeen, to add to the complica- tion, seemed unable to credit the hostile intentions of the Czar, even after the failure of the negotiations which fol- lowed the despatch of the Vienna Note. Yet as far back as June 19, Lord John Russell, in a memorandum to his colleagues, made a clear statement of the position of affairs. He held that, if Russia persisted in her demands and invaded Turkey, the interests of England in the East would compel us to aid the Sultan in defending his capital and his throne. On the other hand, if the Czar by a sudden movement seized Constantinople, we must be prepared to make war on Russia herself. In that case, he added, we ought to seek the alliance of France and Austria. France would willingly join ; and England and France together might, if it were worth while, obtain the moral weight, if not the material support, of Austria in their favour.

Lord Aberdeen responded with characteristic caution. He refused to entertain warlike forecasts, and wished for liberty to meet the emergency when it actually arose. Lord Palmerston, a week or two later, made an ineffectual attempt to persuade the Cabinet to send the Fleet to the Bosphorus without fur- ther delay. ' I think our position,' were his words on July 7, 'waiting timidly and submissively at the back door, whilst Russia is violently threatening and arrogantly forcing her way into the house, is unwise, with a view to a peaceful settlement.' Lord Aberdeen believed in the 'moderation' of a despot who took no pains to disguise his sovereign contempt for 'les chiens Turcs.' Lord Palmerston, on the other hand, made no secret of his opinion that it was the invariable policy of Russia to push forward her encroachment 'as fast and as far as the apathy or want of firmness' of other Governments would allow. He held that her plan was to 'stop and retire when she was met with decided resistance,' and then to wait until the next favourable opportunity arose to steal once more a march on Europe. There was, in short, a radical divergence in the Cabinet. When the compromise suggested in the Vienna Note was rejected, the chances of a European war were sensibly quickened, and all the more so because Lord Stratford, with his notorious personal grudge against the Czar, was more than any other man master of the situation. What that situation had become in the early autumn of 1853 is pithily expressed in a letter of Sir George Cornewall Lewis's to Sir Edmund Head : 'Everything is in a perplexed state at Constantinople. Russia is ashamed to recede, but afraid to strike. The Turks have collected a large army, and have blown up their fanaticism, and, reckoning on the support of England and France, are half inclined to try the chances of war. I think that both parties are in the wrong—Russia in making unjust demands, Turkey in resisting a reasonable settlement. War is quite on the cards, but I still persist in thinking it will be averted, unless some accidental spark fires the train.' [1]

---

[1] *Letters of Sir George Cornewall Lewis, Bart.*, edited by his brother, Canon Frankland Lewis, p. 270.

The Vienna Note was badly worded, and it failed as a scheme of compromise between the Porte and Russia. When it was sent in a draft form to St. Petersburg the Czar accepted it, doubtless because he saw that its statements were vague in a sense which might be interpreted to his advantage. At Constantinople the document swiftly evoked protest, and the Divan refused to sanction it without alteration. England, France, and Austria recognised the force of the amendments of Turkey, and united in urging Russia to adopt them. The Emperor Nicholas, however, was too proud a man to submit to dictation, especially from the Sultan, with Lord Stratford at his elbow, and declined to accede to the altered proposals. Lord John deemed that Turkey had a just cause of complaint, not in the mere fact of the rejection of her alterations to the Vienna Note, but because they were rejected after they had been submitted to the Czar. He told Lord Aberdeen that he hoped that Turkey would reject the new proposals, but he added that that would not wipe away the shame of their having been made. In a speech at Greenock, on September 19, Lord John said : ' While we endeavour to maintain peace, I certainly should be the last to forget that if peace cannot be maintained with honour, it is no longer peace. It becomes then but a truce—a precarious truce, to be denounced by others whenever they may think fit—whenever they may think that an opportunity has occurred to enforce by arms their unjust demands either upon us or upon our allies.'

England and France refused to press the original Vienna Note on Turkey ; but as Austria and Prussia thought that their reasons for abandoning negotiations were scarcely of sufficient force, they in turn declined to adopt the same policy. The concert of Europe was, in fact, broken by the failure of the Vienna Note, and the chances of peace grew suddenly remote. There is a saying that a man likes to believe what he wishes to be the fact, and its truth was illustrated at this juncture by both parties to the quarrel. The Czar persuaded himself that Austria and Prussia would give him their aid, and that England, under Aberdeen, was hardly likely to proceed to the extremity of war. The Sultan, on the other hand, emboldened by the movements of the French and English fleets, and still more by the presence and counsels of Lord Stratford, who was, to all intents and purposes, the master spirit at Constantinople, trusted—and with good reason as the issue proved—on the military support of England and France. It was plain enough that Turkey would go to the wall in a struggle with Russia, unless other nations which dreaded the possession of Constantinople by the Czar came, in their own interests, to her help. With the rejection by Russia of the Turkish amendments to the Vienna Note, and the difference of opinion which at once arose between the four mediating Powers as to the policy which it was best under the altered circumstances to pursue, a complete deadlock resulted.

Lord John's view of the situation was expressed in a memorandum which he placed before the Cabinet, and in which he came to these conclusions : 'That if Russia will not make peace on fair terms, we must appear in the field as the auxiliaries of Turkey ; that if we are to act in conjunction with France as principals in the war, we must act not for the Sultan, but for the general interests of the population of European Turkey. How, and in what way, requires much further consideration, and concert possibly with Austria, certainly with France.' He desired not merely to resist Russian aggression, but also to make it plain to the

Porte that we would in no case support it against its Christian subjects. The Cabinet was not prepared to adopt such a policy, and Lord John made no secret of his opinion that Lord Aberdeen's anxiety for peace and generous attitude toward the Czar were, in reality, provoking war. He believed that the Prime Minister's vacillation was disastrous in its influence, and that he ought, therefore, to retire and make way for a leader with a definite policy. The Danube, for the moment, was the great barrier to war, and both Russia and Turkey were afraid to cross it. Lord John believed that energetic measures in Downing Street at this juncture would have forestalled, and indeed prevented, activity of a less peaceful kind on the Danube. Meanwhile, despatches, projects, and proposals passed rapidly between the Great Powers, for never, as was remarked at the time by a prominent statesman, did any subject produce so much writing. Turkey—perhaps still more than Russia—was eager for war. Tumults in favour of it had broken out at Constantinople ; and, what was more to the purpose, the finances and internal government of the country were in a state of confusion. Therefore, when the concert of the four Powers had been shattered, the Turks saw a better chance of drawing both England and France into their quarrel. At length, on October 10, the Porte sent an ultimatum to the commander of the Russian troops which had invaded Moldavia and Wallachia, demanding that they should fall back beyond the Pruth within fifteen days. On October 22 the war-ships of England and France passed the Dardanelles in order to protect and defend Turkish territory from any Russian attack. The Czar met what was virtually a declaration of war by asserting that he would neither retire nor act on the aggressive. Ten days after the expiration of the

stipulated time, Omar Pacha, the Ottoman commander in
Bulgaria, having crossed the Danube, attacked and van-
quished the Russians on November 4 at Oltenitza. The
Czar at once accepted the challenge, and declared that he
considered his pledge not to act on the offensive was no
longer binding. The Russian fleet left Sebastopol, and,
sailing into the harbour of Sinope, on the southern coast of
the Black Sea, destroyed, on November 30, the Turkish
squadron anchored in that port, and slew four thousand
men.

A significant light is thrown on the crisis in Sir Theodore Martin's 'Life of the Prince Consort,'[1] where it is stated
that the Czar addressed an autograph letter to the Queen,
'full of surprise that there should be any misunderstanding
between her Majesty's Government and his own as to the
affairs of Turkey, and appealing to her Majesty's "good
faith" and "wisdom" to decide between them.' This letter,
it is added, was at once submitted to Lord Clarendon for
his and Lord Aberdeen's opinion. The Queen replied that
Russia's interpretation of her treaty obligations in the particular instance in question was, in her Majesty's judgment
and in the judgment of those best qualified to advise her,
'not susceptible of the extended meaning' put upon it. The
Queen intimated in explicit terms that the demand which the
Czar had made was one which the Sultan could hardly con-
cede if he valued his own independence. The letter ended
with an admission that the Czar's intentions towards Turkey
were 'friendly and disinterested.' Sir Theodore Martin states
that this letter, dated November 14, was submitted to Lord
Aberdeen and Lord Clarendon, and was by them 'thought
excellent.' Scarcely more than a fortnight elapsed when

[1] Sir Theodore Martin's *Life of the Prince Consort*, ii. 530, 531.

Russia's ' friendly and disinterested ' feelings were displayed in her cruel onslaught at Sinope, and the statesmen who had prompted her Majesty's reply received a rude awakening.   It became plain in the light of accomplished events that the wisdom which is profitable to direct had deserted her Majesty's chief advisers.

Lord Aberdeen always made haste slowly, and when other statesmen had abandoned hope he continued to lay stress on the resources of diplomacy.   He admitted that he had long regarded the possibility of war between England and Russia with the ' utmost incredulity ; ' but even before Sinope his confidence in a peaceful solution of the difficulty was beginning to waver.   He distrusted Lord Stratford, and yet he refused to recall him ; he talked about the ' indignity ' which Omar Pacha had inflicted on the Czar by his summons to evacuate the Principalities, although nothing could justify the presence of the Russian troops in Moldavia and Wallachia, and they had held their ground there for the space of three months.   Even Lord Clarendon admitted that the Turks had displayed no lack of patience under the far greater insult of invasion.   The ' indignity ' of notice to quit was, in fact, inevitable if the Sultan was to preserve a vestige of self-respect. Lord Aberdeen was calmly drafting fresh plans of pacification, requiring the Porte to abstain from hostilities ' during the progress of the negotiations undertaken on its behalf ' [1] a fortnight after Turkey had actually sent her ultimatum to Russia ; and the battle of Oltenitza was an affair of history before the despatch reached Constantinople.   Lord Stanmore is inclined to blame Lord John Russell for giving the Turks a loophole of escape by inserting in the document the qualifying words ' for a reasonable time ; ' but his argu-

____
[1] Lord Stanmore's *Earl of Aberdeen*, p. 234.

ment falls to the ground when it is remembered that this despatch was written on October 24, whilst the Turkish ultimatum had been sent to Russia on October 10. Sinope was a bitter surprise to Lord Aberdeen, and the 'furious passion' which Lord Stanmore declares it aroused in England went far to discredit the Coalition Ministry.

Unfortunately, all through the crisis Lord Aberdeen appears to have attached unmerited weight to the advice of the weak members of his own Cabinet—men who, to borrow a phrase of Lord Palmerston's, were 'inconvenient entities in council,' though hardly conspicuous either in their powers of debate or in their influence in the country. Politicians of the stamp of the Duke of Newcastle, Mr. Sidney Herbert, and Sir James Graham played a great part in Downing Street, whilst for the moment men of superior ability like Palmerston and Russell found their advice unheeded. More than any other man, Sir James Graham, now almost a forgotten statesman, was Lord Aberdeen's trusted colleague, and the wisdom of his advice was by no means always conspicuous ; for rashness and timidity were oddly blended in his nature. 'The defeat of the Turks at Sinope upon our element, the sea,' wrote the Prince Consort to Baron Stockmar, 'has made the people furious ; it is ascribed to Aberdeen having been bought over by Russia.'[1] The rumour which the Prince mentions about Lord Aberdeen was, of course, absurd, and everyone who knew the lofty personal character of the Prime Minister laughed it at once to scorn. Nevertheless, the fact that the Prince Consort should have thought such a statement worth chronicling is in itself significant; and though no man of brains in the country held such a view, at least two-thirds of the educated opinion of the nation

[1] Sir Theodore Martin's *Life of the Prince Consort*, ii. 534.

regarded the Prime Minister with increasing disfavour, as a man who had dragged England, through humiliating negotiations, to the verge of war.

The destruction of the Turkish squadron at Sinope under the shadow of our fleet touched the pride of England to the quick. The nation lost all patience—as the contemptuous cartoons of 'Punch' show—with the endless parleyings of Aberdeen, and a loud and passionate cry for war filled the country. Lord Stanmore thinks that too much was made in the excitement of the 'massacre' of the Turkish sailors, and perhaps he is right. However that may be, the fact remains that the Russians at Sinope continued to storm with shot and shell the Turkish ships when those on board were no longer able to act on the defensive—a naval engagement which cannot be described as distinguished for valour. Perhaps the indignation might not have been so deep and widespread if the English people had not recognised that the Coalition Government had strained concession to the breaking point in the vain attempt to propitiate the Czar. All through the early autumn Lord Palmerston was aware that those in the Cabinet who were jealous of Russia had to reckon with 'private and verbal communications, given in all honesty, but tinctured by the personal bias of the Prime Minister,' to Baron Brunnow, which were doing 'irreparable mischief' at St. Petersburg.[1] The nation did not relish Lord Aberdeen's personal friendship with the Czar, and now that Russia was beginning to show herself in her true colours, prejudice against a Prime Minister who had sought to explain away difficulties was natural, however unreasonable. The English people, moreover, had not forgotten that Russia ruthlessly crippled Poland

[1] *Life of Lord Palmerston*, by the Hon. Evelyn Ashley, ii. 282.

in 1831, and lent her aid to the subjugation of Hungary in 1849. If the Sultan was the Lord of Misrule to English imagination in 1853, the Czar was the embodiment of despotism, and even less amenable to the modern ideas of liberty and toleration. The Manchester School, on the other hand, had provoked a reaction. The Great Exhibition had set a large section of the community dreaming, not of the millennium, but of Waterloo. Russia was looked upon as a standing menace to England's widening heritage in the East, and neither the logic of Cobden nor the rhetoric of Bright was of the least avail in stemming the torrent of national indignation.

When the Vienna Note became a dead letter Lord Aberdeen ought either to have adopted a clean-cut policy, which neither Russia nor Turkey could mistake, or else have carried out his twice-repeated purpose of resignation. Everyone admits that from the outset his position was one of great difficulty, but he increased it greatly by his practical refusal to grasp the nettle. He was not ambitious of power, but, on the contrary, longed for his quiet retreat at Haddo. He was on the verge of seventy and was essentially a man of few, but scholarly tastes. There can be no doubt that considerable pressure was put upon him both by the Court and the majority of his colleagues in the Cabinet, and this, with the changed aspect of affairs, and the mistaken sense of duty with regard to them, determined his course. His decision ' not to run away from the Eastern complication,' as Prince Albert worded it, placed both himself and Lord John Russell in somewhat of a false position. If Lord Aberdeen had followed his own inclination there is every likelihood that he would have carried out his arrangement to retire in favour of Lord John. His

colleagues were not in the dark in regard to this arrangement when they joined the Ministry, and if not prepared
to fall in with the proposal, they ought to have stated
their objections at the time. There is some conflict of
opinion as to the terms of the arrangement ; but even if we
take it to be what Lord Aberdeen's own friends represent it
—not an absolute but a conditional pledge to retire— Lord
Aberdeen was surely bound to ascertain at the outset
whether the condition was one that could possibly be
fulfilled.   If the objection of his colleagues to retain office
under Lord John as Prime Minister was insurmountable,
then the qualified engagement to retire—if the Government
would not be broken up by the process —was worthless, and
Lord John was being drawn into the Cabinet by assurances
given by the Prime Minister alone, but which he was powerless to fulfil without the co-operation of his colleagues. Lord
Aberdeen was therefore determined to remain at his post,
because Lord John was unpopular with the Cabinet, and
Palmerston with the Court, and because he knew that the
accession to power of either of them would mean the
adoption of a spirited foreign policy.

CHAPTER XI

WAR HINDERS REFORM

1854–1855

A Scheme of Reform —Palmerston's attitude—Lord John sore let and
hindered—Lord Stratford's diplomatic triumph—The Duke of Newcastle and the War Office—The dash for Sebastopol—Procrastination and its deadly work —The Alma—Inkerman —The Duke's
blunder —Famine and frost in the trenches.

ALL through the autumn of 1854 Lord John Russell was busy
with a scheme of Parliamentary reform. The Government
stood pledged to bring forward the measure, though a section
of the Cabinet, and, notably Lord Palmerston, were opposed
to such a course. As leader of the House, Lord John had
announced that the question would be introduced to Parliament in the spring, and the Cabinet, therefore, took the
subject into consideration when it resumed its meetings
in November. A special committee was appointed, and
Lord John placed his proposals before it. Every borough
with less than three hundred electors was to be disfranchised,
and towns with less than five hundred electors were to lose
one of their representatives. Seventy seats, he argued,
would be gained by this plan, and he suggested that they
should be divided between the largest counties and the great
towns. He proposed greatly diminishing the qualifications
alike in counties and boroughs. He laid stress on the

necessity of calling into existence triangular constituencies, in which no elector should have the power to vote for more than two of the three candidates, and wished also to deprive the freemen of their guild qualification. Lord Palmerston had no relish for the subject. His predilections, in fact, leaned in quite the opposite direction. If his manner was genial, his temper was conservative, and he was inclined to smile, if not to scoff, at politicians who met such problems of government with other than a light heart. He was therefore inclined at this juncture to adopt Lord Melbourne's attitude, and to meet Lord John with that statesman's famous remark, 'Why can't you let it alone?'

Devotion to one idea, declared Goethe, is the condition of all greatness. Lord John was devoted from youth to age to the idea of Parliamentary reform, and in season and out was never inclined to abandon it. Probably Lord Palmerston would have adopted a less hostile attitude if he had been in his proper element at the Foreign Office ; but being Home Secretary, he was inclined to kick against a measure which promised to throw into relief his own stationary position on one of the pet subjects of the party of progress. Whilst the Cabinet was still engaged in thrashing the subject out, tidings of the battle of Sinope reached England, and the popular indignation against Russia, which had been gathering all the autumn, burst forth, as has already been stated, into a fierce outcry against the Czar. Two days after the news of Russia's cowardly attack had been confirmed, Palmerston saw his opportunity, and promptly resigned. Doubtless such a step was determined by mixed motives. Objections to Lord John's proposals for Parliamentary reform at best only half explains the position, and behind such repugnance lay hostility to Lord Aberdeen's vacillating policy on the Eastern Question. The nation accepted Lord Palmerston's resignation in a matter-of-fact manner, which probably surprised no one more than himself. The Derbyites, oddly enough, made the most pother about the affair; but a man on the verge of seventy, and especially one like Lord Palmerston with few illusions, is apt to regard the task of forming a new party as a game which is not worth the candle. The truth is, Palmerston, like other clever men before and since, miscalculated his strength, and on Christmas Eve was back again in office. He had received assurances from his colleagues that the Reform proposals were still open to discussion; and, as the Cabinet had taken in his absence a decision on Turkish affairs which was in harmony with the views that he had persistently advocated, he determined to withdraw his resignation.

The new year opened darkly with actual war, and with rumours of it on a far more terrible scale. 'My expectation is,' wrote Sir G. C. Lewis on January 4, 'that before long England and France will be at war with Russia; and as long as war lasts all means of internal improvement must slumber. The Reform Bill must remain on the shelf—if there is war; for a Government about to ask for large supplies and to impose war taxes, cannot propose a measure which is sure to create dispersion and to divide parties.' France, in spite of the action of the Emperor over the question of the Holy Places, had not displayed much interest in the quarrel; but a contemptuous retort which Nicholas made to Napoleon III.'s final letter in the interests of peace put an end to the national indifference. The words ' Russia will prove herself in 1854 what she was in 1812,' cut the national pride to the quick, and the cry on that side of the Channel as on this, was for war with Russia. The Fleets were ordered to enter the

Black Sea, and on February 27 England and France sent a joint ultimatum to St. Petersburg, demanding that the Czar's troops should evacuate the Principalities by April 30.

The interval of suspense was seized by Lord John to place the Reform proposals of the Government before the House of Commons ; but the nation was by this time restless, dissatisfied, and preoccupied, for the blast of the trumpet seemed already in the air. The second reading of the measure was fixed for the middle of March ; but the increasing strain of the Eastern Question led Lord John to announce at the beginning of that month that the Government had decided not to bring forward the second reading until the end of April. This announcement led to a personal attack, and one member, whose name may be left in the oblivion which has overtaken it, had the audacity to hint that the leader of the House had never intended to proceed with the measure. Stung into sudden indignation by the taunt, Lord John promptly expressed his disdain of the opinion of a politician who had no claim whatever to speak in the name of Reform, and went on, with a touch of pardonable pride, to refer to his own lifelong association with the cause. When he turned to his opponent with the words, ' Does the honourable gentleman think he has a right to treat me——,' the House backed and buried his protest with its generous cheers. Lord John Russell, in power or out of it, was always jealous for the reputation of the responsible statesmen of the nation, and he did not let this occasion pass without laying emphasis on that point. ' I should be ashamed of myself if I were to prefer a concern for my own personal reputation to that which I understood to be for the interests of my country. But it seems to me that the character of the men who rule this country—whether they be at the moment in office or in opposition—is a matter of the utmost interest to the people of this country, and that it is of paramount importance that full confidence should be reposed in their character. It is, in fact, on the confidence of the people in the character of public men that the security of this country in a great degree depends.'

A few days later it became plain that war was at hand, and a strong feeling prevailed in Parliament that the question of Reform ought to be shelved for a year.   Lord John's position was one of great difficulty.   He felt himself pledged on the subject, and, though recognising that a great and unexpected emergency had arisen, which altered the whole political outlook, he knew that with Lord Palmerston and others in the Ministry the question was not one of time, but of principle. The sinews of war had to be provided.   Mr. Gladstone proposed to double the income tax, and Lord John urged that a period of increased taxation ought to be a period of widened political franchise.   He therefore was averse to postponement, unless in a position to assure his Radical following that the Government recognised that it was committed to the question.   Lord Aberdeen was only less anxious than Lord John for the adoption of a progressive and enlightened home policy ; in fact, his attitude in his closing years on questions like Parliamentary reform was in marked contrast to his rigidly conservative views on foreign policy. He therefore determined to sound the Cabinet advocates of procrastination as to their real feeling about Reform, with the result that he saw clearly that Lord John Russell's fears were not groundless, since Lord Palmerston and Lord Lansdowne bluntly declared that they meant to retire from office if the Government went forward with the Bill.

Lord John felt that he could not withdraw the Bill unconditionally, and therefore resignation seemed the only honourable course which was left. After deliberate consideration he could see no other choice in the matter, and, on April 8, relinquished his seat in the Cabinet. The Court, the Prime Minister and his colleagues saw at once the gravity of the position, for the Liberal party were restive enough under Lord Aberdeen, without the withdrawal from his Cabinet of a statesman of the first rank, who was not anxious for peace at any price. Lord John's position in the country at the moment rendered it probable that a quarrel with him would bring about the downfall of the Government. His zeal for Reform won him the respect and support of the great towns, and the determination which he shared with Palmerston to resist the intolerable attitude of the Czar made him popular with the crowd. A recent speech, delivered when Nicholas had recalled his Ambassador from London, had caught, moreover, the sympathies of all classes of the community. 'For my part, if most unexpectedly the Emperor of Russia should recede from his former demands, we shall all rejoice to be spared the pain, the efforts, and the burdens of war. But if peace is no longer consistent with our duty to England, with our duty to Europe, with our duty to the world, we can only endeavour to enter into this contest with a stout heart. May God defend the right, and I, for my part, shall be willing to bear my share of the burden and the responsibility.'

John Leech, in one of his inimitable cartoons in ' Punch,' caught the situation with a flash of insight which almost amounted to genius, and Lord John became the hero of the hour. One verse out of a spirited poem entitled 'God defend the Right,' which appeared in ' Punch ' at the time, may be quoted in passing, especially as it shows the patriotic fervour and the personal enthusiasm which Lord John Russell's speech evoked in the country :

' From humble homes and stately domes the cry goes through the air,
  With the loftiness of challenge, the lowliness of prayer,
Honour to him who spoke the words in the Council of the Land,
  To find faith in old England's heart, force in old England's hand.'

A week before the appearance of these lines, the cartoon in ' Punch ' represented Lord Aberdeen, significantly arrayed in Windsor uniform, vainly attempting to hold back the struggling British lion, which sees the Russian bear in the distance, and exclaiming, ' I *must* let him go.'

Lord John's resignation meant much, perhaps everything, to the Government. Great pressure was put upon him. The Queen and the Cabinet alike urged him to abandon his intention of retirement ; whilst Lord Palmerston, with that personal chivalry which was characteristic of him, declared that in a moment of European crisis he could be better spared, and was ready to resign if Lord John insisted upon such terms, as the price for his own continuance in office. Every day the situation abroad was becoming more critical, and Lord John saw that it might imperil greater interests than any which were bound up with the progress of a party question to resist such appeals. He, therefore, on April 11 withdrew his resignation, and received an ovation in the House of Commons when he made it plain that he was willing to thrust personal considerations aside in the interests of his colleagues, and for the welfare of his country. Mr. Edward Miall has described the scene. ' " If it should be thought that the course he was taking would damage the cause of Reform "—the noble Lord paused, choked with the violence of his own emotions. Then arose a cheer from

both sides of the House, loud and long continued. . . .
'Every eye was glistening with sudden moisture, and every
heart was softened with genuine sympathy. . . . The effect
was electric. Old prejudices long pent up, grudges, accumulated discontents, uncharitable suspicions, all melted
away before that sudden outburst of a troubled heart." ' [1]

Throughout the spring diplomacy was still busy, though
it became every week more and more apparent that hostilities
were inevitable. Lord Stratford achieved, what Lord Clarendon did not hesitate to term, a ' great diplomatic triumph '
when he won consent from the Porte to fresh terms in the
interests of peace, which met with the approval, not only of
England and France, but also of Austria and Prussia. The
Czar began at length to realise the gravity of the situation
when Austria moved in February fifty thousand men to the
frontier of the territory which Russia had seized. When the
Russian troops, a few months later, evacuated the Principalities, Austria and Prussia, whose alliance had been formed
in defence of the interests of Germany, were no longer
directly concerned in the quarrel. Thus the war which England and France declared at the end of March against Russia
was one which they were left to pursue, with the help of
Turkey, alone. Lord John Russell urged that it should be
short and sharp, and with characteristic promptitude sketched
out, with Lord Panmure's help, a plan of campaign. He
urged that ten thousand men should at once be raised for
the Army, five thousand for the Navy, and that the services
of fifteen thousand more be added to the Militia. He laid
stress on the importance of securing the active aid of
Austria, for he thought that her co-operation might make the
difference between a long and a short war. He proposed

<hr>

[1] *Life of Edward Miall, M.P.*, by A. Miall, p. 179.

that Sweden should be drawn into the Alliance, with the view of striking a blow at Russia in the North as well as on her southern frontier. He also proposed that English and French troops should be massed at Constantinople, and submitted a plan of operations for the consideration of the Cabinet.

Lord John knew perfectly well that radical changes were imperative in the administration of the Army. The Secretary for War was, oddly enough, Secretary for the Colonies as well, and there was also a Secretary at War, who controlled the finances at the bidding of the Commander-in-Chief. The Ordnance Department was under one management, the Commissariat under another, whilst the Militia fell within the province of a third, in the shape of the Home Office. Lord John Russell had seen enough of the outcome of divided counsels in the Cabinet, and insisted, in emphatic terms, on the necessity of separating the duties of the War and Colonial Departments, and of giving the Minister who held the former post undisputed control over all branches of the executive.

It was perhaps an undesigned coincidence, but none the less unfortunate, that the statesmen in the Aberdeen Government who were directly concerned with the war were former colleagues of Sir Robert Peel. Lord Aberdeen's repugnance to hostilities with Russia was so notorious that the other Peelites in the Cabinet fell under the suspicion of apathy; and the nation, exasperated at the Czar's bombastic language and high-handed action, was not in the mood to make fine distinctions. The Duke of Newcastle and his riend, Mr. Sidney Herbert, were regarded, perhaps unjustly, as lukewarm about the approaching campaign; but it was upon the former that the brunt of public censure ultimately fell. The Duke was Secretary for War and the Colonies. It was an odd combination of offices which had existed for more than half a century. The tradition is that it had been brought about in order that the Secretary for the Colonies, who at the beginning of the century had comparatively little to do, but who possessed large patronage, might use that patronage on behalf of deserving military men.

In the immediate prospect of hostilities, it was felt to be imperative that two posts of such responsibility should not be held by the same Minister ; but the Duke was adverse to the proposed change. It was, however, brought about in the early summer, and the Duke was given his choice of the two posts. He decided to relinquish the Colonies, and thus the burden of the approaching conflict fell upon him by his own deliberate act. Sir George Grey was appointed to the vacant office. The Duke of Newcastle's ambition outstripped his ability, and the choice which he made was disastrous both to himself and to the nation. Because some men are born great, they have greatness of another kind thrust upon them ; and too often it happens that responsibility makes plain the lack of capacity, which the glamour neither of rank nor of place can long conceal. The Duke of Newcastle was born to greatness—for in the middle of the century the highest rank in the Peerage counted for more in politics than it does to-day—but he certainly did not achieve it as War Minister.

There is no need to relate here the more than twice-told story of the Crimean War. Its incidents have been described by historians and soldiers ; and, of late, gallant officers who took part in it have retraced its course and revived its memories. In one sense it is a glorious chapter in the annals of the Queen's reign, and yet there are circumstances connected with it which every Englishman, worthy of the name, would gladly forget. Although the nation did not take up arms with a light heart, its judgment was clouded by passion ; and the first great war since Waterloo caught the imagination of the people, especially as Lord Raglan, one of the old Peninsular heroes, was in command of the Army of Invasion. England and France were not satisfied merely to blockade the Black Sea and crush the commerce of Russia. They determined to strike at the heart of the Czar's power in the East, and therefore the Allies made a dash at the great arsenal and fort of Sebastopol. It did not enter into their reckoning that there might be a protracted siege. What they anticipated was a swift march, a sudden attack, and the capture of the stronghold by bombardment. The allied forces 25,000 English soldiers, 23,000 French, and about 5,000 Turks - landed in the Crimea in September, 1854, and stormed the heights of the Alma on the 20th of that month. Then they hesitated, and their chance of reducing Sebastopol that autumn was lost. 'I have been very slow to enter into this war,' said Lord Aberdeen to an alderman at a banquet in the City. 'Yes,' was the brusque retort, 'and you will be equally slow to get out of it.'

Divided counsels prevailed in the camp as well as in the Cabinet. Cholera attacked the troops, and stores began to fail. Prince Menschikoff, defeated at Alma, seized the opportunity which the delay gave him to render the harbour of Sebastopol impassable to hostile ships ; and General Todleben brought his skill as an engineer to the task of strengthening by earthworks the fortifications of the Russian stronghold. The Allies made the blunder of marching on Sebastopol from the southern instead of the northern side of the harbour, and this gave time to the enemy to receive strong reinforcements, with the result that 120,000 men were massed behind the Russian fortifications. Meanwhile a rumour that Sebastopol had fallen awakened short-lived rejoicings in England and France. The tidings were contradicted in twenty-four hours, but most people thought, on that exciting 3rd of October, that the war was virtually at an end. The Emperor Napoleon announced the imaginary victory of their comrades in arms to his assembled troops. Even Mr. Gladstone was deceived for the moment, and there is a letter of his in existence to one of the most prominent of his colleagues, full of congratulation at such a result. The chagrin of the nation was great when it learnt that the Russians were not merely holding their own, but were acting on the aggressive; whilst the disappointment was quickened by the lack of vigour displayed by the Cabinet. The Allies fought, on October 25, the glorious yet indecisive battle of Balaclava, which was for ever rendered memorable by the useless but superb charge of the Light Brigade. Less than a fortnight later, on November 5, the Russians renewed the attack, and took the English by surprise. A desperate hand-to-hand struggle against overwhelming odds ensued. Then the French came to the aid of the English troops, and the battle of Inkerman was won.

As the winter approached, the position of the Allies grew perilous, and it seemed likely that the plans of the invaders would miscarry, and the besieging Allies be reduced to the position of the besieged. Before the middle of November winter set in with severity along the shores of the Black Sea, and a hurricane raged, which destroyed the tents of the troops, and wrecked more than a score of ships, which were carrying stores of ammunition and clothing. As the winter advanced, with bleak winds and blinding snow, the shivering, ill-fed soldiers perished in ever-increasing numbers under the twofold attack of privation and pestilence. The Army had been despatched to the Crimea in the summer, and, as no one imagined that the campaign would last beyond the early autumn, the brave fellows in the trenches of Sebastopol were called to confront the sudden descent of winter without the necessary stores. It was then that the War Office awoke slowly to the terrible nature of the crisis. Lord John Russell had made his protest months before against the dilatory action of that department, and, though he knew that personal odium was sure to follow, endeavoured at the eleventh hour to persuade Lord Aberdeen to take decisive action. 'We are in the midst of a great war,' were his words to the Premier on November 17. 'In order to carry on that war with efficiency, either the Prime Minister must be constantly urging, hastening, completing the military preparations, or the Minister of War must be strong enough to control other departments.' He went on to contend that the Secretary of State for War ought to be in the House of Commons, and that he ought, moreover, to be a man who carried weight in that assembly, and who brought to its debates not only vigour of mind but experience of military details. 'There is only one person belonging to the Government,' added Lord John, 'who combines these advantages. My conclusion is that before Parliament meets Lord Palmerston should be entrusted with the seals of the War Department.'

This was, of course, an unwelcome proposition to Lord Aberdeen, and he met it with the declaration that no one man was competent to undertake the duties of Secretary of State for War and those of Secretary at War. He considered that the latter appointment should be held in connection with the finances of the Army, and in independence of the Secretary for the War Department. Lord John replied that either the Prime Minister must himself be the acting and moving spirit of the whole machine, or else the Secretary for War must have delegated authority to control other departments,' and added, ' neither is the case under the present *régime*.' Once more, nothing came of the protest, and, when Parliament met on December 12, to indulge in the luxury of dull debates and bitter personalities, the situation remained unchanged, in spite of the growing sense of disaster abroad and incapacity at home. The Duke of Newcastle in the Lords made a lame defence, and his monotonous and inconclusive speech lasted for the space of three hours. ' The House went to sleep after the first half hour,' was the cynical comment of an Opposition peer. As the year ended the indignation in the country against the Duke of Newcastle grew more and more pronounced, and he, in common with Lord Aberdeen, was thought in many quarters to be starving the war. The truth was, the Duke was not strong enough for the position, and if he had gone to the Colonial Office, when that alternative was offered him, his reputation would not now be associated with the lamentable blunders which, rightly or wrongly, are laid to his charge. It is said that he once boasted that he had often kept out of mischief men who, he frankly admitted, were his superiors in ability. However that may be, the Duke of Newcastle ignominiously failed, at the great crisis in his public career, to keep out of mischief men who were his subordinates in position, and, in consequence, to arrest the fatal confusion which the winter campaign made on the military resources of the nation. Lord Hardinge, who on the death of the Duke of Wellington had succeeded to the post of Commander-in-

Chief, assured Lord Malmesbury in January 1855 that the Duke of Newcastle had never consulted him on any subject connected with the war.   He added, with considerable heat, that not a single despatch had been submitted to him ; in fact, he had been left to gather what the War Minister was doing through the published statements in the newspapers.

The Duke of Newcastle was a sensible, well-intentioned man, but allowed himself to be involved in the management of the details of his office, instead of originating a policy and directing the broad course of affairs with vigour and determination.   He displayed a degree of industry during the crisis which was praiseworthy in itself, and quite phenomenal in the most exalted branch of the Peerage, but he lacked the power of initiative, and had not sufficient force and decision of character to choose the right men for the emergency.

The Cabinet might falter and the War Office dawdle, the faith of the soldiers in the authorities might be shaken and their hopes of personal succour be eclipsed, but the charity of womanhood failed not to respond to the call of the suffering, or to the demands of self-sacrifice.   Florence Nightingale, and the nurses who laboured at her side in the hospital at Scutari not only soothed the dying and nursed the sick and wounded, but thrilled the heart of England by their modest heroism and patient devotion.

Before Parliament met in December, Lord John Russell, in despair of bringing matters to a practical issue, informed his colleagues that, though he was willing to remain in the Cabinet, and to act as Leader of the House during the short session before Christmas, it was his intention to relinquish office at the close of the year.   The objection was raised that it was unconstitutional for him to meet Parliament in a responsible position if he had arrived at this fixed but unannounced resolution. He met this expression of opinion by requesting Lord Aberdeen to submit his resignation to the Queen on December 7. The correspondence between Lord Lansdowne and Lord John, and the important memorandum which the latter drew up on December 30, which Mr. Walpole has printed, speak for themselves.[1] It will be seen that Lord John once more insisted that the Secretary of State for the War Department ought immediately to be invested with all the more important functions hitherto exercised by the Secretary at War, and he again laid stress on the necessity in such a crisis that the War Minister should be a member of the House of Commons. He complained that, though he was responsible in the Commons, Lord Aberdeen did not treat him with the confidence which alone could enable a Leader of the House to carry on the business of the Government with satisfaction. He declared that Lord Grey treated Lord Althorp in a different fashion, and that Lord Melbourne, to bring the matter nearer home, had shown greater consideration towards himself. He added that he felt absolved from the duty of defending acts and appointments upon which he had not been consulted.

Lord Lansdowne succeeded for the moment in patching up an unsatisfactory peace, but it was becoming every day more and more obvious that the Aberdeen Government was doomed. The memorandum which Lord John drew up, at the suggestion of Lord Lansdowne, describes in pithy and direct terms the privations of the soldiers, and the mortality amongst men and horses, which was directly due to hunger and neglect. He shows that between the

---

[1] *Life of Lord John Russell*, by Spencer Walpole, vol. ii. 232–235.

end of September and the middle of November there was
at least six weeks when all kinds of supplies might have
been landed at Balaclava, and he points out that the
stores only needed to be carried seven or eight miles
to reach the most distant division of the Army.   He
protested that there had been great mismanagement, and
added: 'Soldiers cannot fight unless they are well fed.'
He stated that he understood Lord Raglan had written
home at the beginning of October to say that, if the Army
was to remain on the heights during the winter, huts would
be required, since the barren position which they held did
not furnish wood to make them.   Nearly three months had,
however, passed, and winter in its most terrible form had
settled on the Crimea, and yet the huts still appeared not to
have reached the troops, though the French had done their
best to make good the discreditable breakdown of our commissariat.   'There appears,' concludes Lord John, 'a want
of concert among the different departments.   When the
Navy forward supplies, there is no military authority to
receive them ; when the military wish to unload a ship, they
find that the naval authority has already ordered it away.
Lord Raglan and Sir Edmund Lyons should be asked to
concert between them the mode of remedying this defect.
Neither can see with his own eyes to the performance of
all the subordinate duties, but they can choose the best men
to do it, and arm them with sufficient authority.   For on the
due performance of these subordinate duties hangs the welfare of the Army.   Lord Raglan should also be informed
exactly of the amount of reinforcements ordered to the
Crimea, and at what time he may expect them.   Having
furnished him with all the force in men and material which
the Government can send him, the Government is entitled

to expect from him in return his opinion as to what can be done by the allied armies to restore the strength and efficiency of the armies for the next campaign. Probably the troops first sent over will require four months' rest before they will be able to move against an enemy.' Procrastination was, however, to have its perfect work, and Lord John, chilled and indignant, told Lord Aberdeen on January 3 that nothing could be less satisfactory than the result of the recent Cabinets. 'Unless,' he added, 'you will direct measures, I see no hope for the efficient prosecution of the war ;' for by this time it was perfectly useless, he saw, to urge on Lord Aberdeen the claims of Lord Palmerston.

CHAPTER XII

THE VIENNA DIFFICULTY

1855

Blunders at home and abroad—Roebuck's motion—'General Février turns traitor'—France and the Crimea—Lord John at Vienna—The pride of the nation is touched—Napoleon's visit to Windsor—Lord John's retirement—The fall of Sebastopol—The Treaty of Paris.

PARLIAMENT met on January 23, and the general indignation at once found expression in Mr. Roebuck's motion—the notice of which was cheered by Radicals and Tories alike—to 'inquire into the condition of our Army before Sebastopol, and into the conduct of those Departments of the Government whose duty it has been to minister to the wants of that Army.' Lord John, in view of the blunders at home and abroad, did not see how such a motion was to be resisted, and at once tendered to Lord Aberdeen his resignation. His protests, pointed and energetic though they had been, had met with no practical response. Even the reasonable request that the War Minister should be in the Commons to defend his own department had passed unheeded. Peelites, like Sir James Graham and Mr. Sidney Herbert, might make the best of a bad case, but Lord John felt that he could not honestly defend in Parliament a course of action which he had again and again attacked in the Cabinet. Doubtless it would have been better both for himself and for his colleagues if he had adhered to his earlier intention of resigning ; and his dramatic retreat at this juncture unquestionably gave a handle to his adversaries. Though prompted by conscientious motives, sudden flight, in the face of what was, to all intents and purposes, a vote of censure, was a grave mistake. Not unnaturally, such a step was regarded as a bid for personal power at the expense of his colleagues. It certainly placed the Cabinet in a most embarrassing position, and it is easy to understand the irritation which it awakened. In fact, it led those who were determined to put the worst possible construction on Lord John's action to hint that he wished to rid himself of responsibility and to stand clear of his colleagues, so that when the nation grew tired of the war he might return to office and make peace. Nothing could well have been further from the truth.

Lord John's retirement was certainly inopportune ; but it is almost needless to add—now that it is possible to review his whole career, as well as all the circumstances which marked this crisis in it—that he was not actuated by a self-seeking spirit. Looking back in after life, Lord John frankly admitted that he had committed an error in resigning office under Lord Aberdeen at the time and in the manner in which he did it. He qualified this confession, however, by declaring that he had committed a much greater error in agreeing to serve under Lord Aberdeen as Prime Minister : 'I had served under Lord Grey and Lord Melbourne before I became Prime Minister, and I served under Lord Palmerston after I had been Prime Minister. In no one of these cases did I find any difficulty in allying subordination with due counsel and co-operation. But, as it is proverbially said, " Where there is a will there is a way," so in political affairs the converse is true, " Where there is no will there is no way." '   He explained his position in a personal statement in the House of Commons on the night of Mr. Roebuck's motion.   ' I had to consider whether I could fairly and honestly say, " It is true that evils have arisen.   It is true that the brave men who fought at the Alma, at Inkerman, and at Balaclava are perishing, many of them from neglect ; it is true that the heart of the whole of England throbs with anxiety and sympathy on this subject ; but I can tell you that such arrangements have been made—that a man of such vigour and efficiency has taken the conduct of the War Department, with such a consolidation of offices as to enable him to have the entire control of the whole of the War Offices—so that any supply may be immediately furnished, and any abuse instantly remedied."   I felt I could not honestly make such a declaration ; I therefore felt that I could come only to one conclusion, and that as I could not resist inquiry—by giving the only assurances which I thought sufficient to prevent it— my duty was not to remain any longer a member of the Government.'   In the course of a powerful speech Lord John added that he would always look back with pride on his association with many measures of the Aberdeen Government, and more particularly with the great financial scheme which Mr. Gladstone brought forward in 1853.

He refused to admit that the Whigs were an exclusive party, and he thought that such an idea was refuted by the fact that they had consented to serve in a Coalition Government. ' I believe that opinion to have been unjust, and I think that the Whig party during the last two years have fully justified the opinion I entertained.   I will venture to say that no set of men ever behaved with greater honour or with more dis- interested patriotism than those who have supported the

Government of the Earl of Aberdeen. It is my pride, and it will ever be my pride to the last day of my life, to have belonged to a party which, as I consider, upholds the true principles of freedom ; and it will ever be my constant endeavour to preserve the principles and to tread in the paths which the Whig party have laid down for the guidance of their conduct.' Lord John made no attempt to disguise the gravity of the crisis, and the following admission might almost be said to have sealed the fate of the Ministry : ' Sir, I must say that there is something, with all the official knowledge to which I have had access, that to me is inexplicable in the state of our army. If I had been told, as a reason against the expedition to the Crimea last year, that your troops would be seven miles from the sea, and that—at that seven miles' distance—they would be in want of food, of clothing, and of shelter to such a degree that they would perish at the rate of from ninety to a hundred a day, I should have considered such a prediction as utterly preposterous, and such a picture of the expedition as entirely fanciful and absurd. We are all, however, forced to confess the notoriety of that melancholy state of things.' Three days later, after a protracted and heated debate, Mr. Roebuck's motion was carried in a House of 453 members by the sweeping majority of 157. ' The division was curious,' wrote Greville. ' Some seventy or eighty Whigs, ordinary supporters of Government, voted against them, and all the Tories except about six or seven.' There was no mistaking the mandate either of Parliament or of the people. Lord Aberdeen on the following day went down to Windsor and laid his resignation before the Queen, and in this sorry fashion the Coalition Government ignominiously collapsed, with hardly an expression of regret and scarcely a claim to remembrance.

The Queen's choice fell upon Lord Derby, but his efforts
to form an Administration proved unavailing. Lord Lansdowne was next summoned, and he suggested that Lord John
Russell should be sent for, but in his case, also, sufficient
promises of support were not forthcoming. In the end
Her Majesty acquiesced in the strongly-expressed wish of
the nation, and Lord Palmerston was called to power on
February 5. For the moment Lord John was out of office,
and Lord Panmure took the place of the Duke of Newcastle
as War Minister, but all the other members of the defeated
Administration, except, of course, Lord Aberdeen, entered
the new Cabinet. Lord Palmerston knew the feeling of the
country, and was not afraid to face it, and, therefore, determined to accept Mr. Roebuck's proposals for a searching
investigation of the circumstances which had attended the
conduct of the war. Loyalty to their late chief, as well as
to their former colleague, the Duke of Newcastle, led Sir
James Graham, Mr. Sidney Herbert, Mr. Gladstone, and
other Peelites to resign. Lord John, urged by Lord
Palmerston, became Colonial Secretary. Palmerston
shared Lord Clarendon's view that no Government calling
itself Liberal had a chance of standing without Lord John.
Sir G. C. Lewis succeeded Mr. Gladstone as Chancellor of
the Exchequer, and Sir Charles Wood took Sir James
Graham's vacant place at the Admiralty.

Changes of a more momentous character quickly followed. Early in the winter, when tidings of the sufferings
of the Allies reached St. Petersburg, the Emperor Nicholas
declared, with grim humour, that there were two generals
who were about to fight for him, ' Janvier et Février ; '
but the opening month of the year brought terrible privations to the Russian reinforcements as they struggled

painfully along the rough winter roads on the long march
to the Crimea. The Czar lost a quarter of a million of
men before the war ended, and a vast number of them fell
before the cold or the pestilence. Omar Pasha defeated
the Russian troops at Eupatoria in the middle of February.
The fact that his troops had been repulsed by the hated
Turks touched the pride of Nicholas to the quick, and is
believed to have brought on the fatal illness which seized
him a few days later. On February 27, just after the
Emperor had left the parade-ground on which he had been
reviewing his troops, he was struck down by paralysis, and,
after lingering in a hopeless condition for a day or two,
died a baffled and disappointed man. The irony of the
situation was reflected with sombre and dramatic realism in
a political cartoon which appeared in 'Punch.' It represented a skeleton in armour, laying an icy hand, amid the
falling snow, on the prostrate Czar's heart. The picture—
one of the most powerful that has ever appeared, even in
this remarkable mirror of the times—was entitled, 'General
Février turned Traitor,' and underneath was the dead Emperor's cruel boast, 'Russia has two generals on whom she can
confide—Generals Janvier and Février.' Prior to the resignation of the Peelites the second Congress of Vienna
assembled, and Lord John Russell attended it as a plenipotentiary for England ; and France, Austria, Turkey, and
Russia were also represented. The 'four points' which
formed the basis of the negotiations were that Russia should
abandon all control over Moldavia, Wallachia, and Servia ;
that the new Czar, Alexander II., should surrender his
claim to command the entrance of the Danube ; that
all treaties should be annulled which gave Russia supremacy in the Black Sea ; and that she should dismiss her

pretensions to an exclusive right to protect in her own fashion the Christians in the Ottoman Empire. Nicholas, though at one time favourable to this scheme as a basis of peace, eventually fell back on the assertion that he would not consent to any limitation of his naval power in the Black Sea. Though the parleyings at Vienna after his death were protracted, the old difficulty asserted itself again, with the result that the second Congress proved, as spring gave way to summer, as futile as the first.

Although subjects which vitally affected the Turkish Empire were under consideration, the Turkish Ambassador at Vienna had received anything but explicit directions, and Lord John was forced to the conclusion that the negotiations were not regarded as serious at Constantinople. Indeed, he had, in Mr. Spencer Walpole's words, 'reason to suspect that the absence of a properly credited Turk was not due to the dilatory character of the Porte alone but to the perverse action of Lord Stratford de Redcliffe.'[1] Lord Clarendon did not hesitate to declare that Lord Stratford was inclined to thwart any business which was not carried on in Constantinople, and the English Ambassador kept neither Lord John in Vienna nor the Cabinet in Downing Street acquainted with the views of the Porte. Lord John declared that the Turkish representative at Vienna, from whom he expected information about the affairs of his own country, was 'by nature incompetent, and by instruction silent.' Two schemes, in regard to the point which was chiefly in dispute, were before the Congress ; they are best stated in Lord John's own words : 'One, called limitation, proposed that only four ships of the line should be maintained in the Black Sea by Russia, and two each by the

<hr>

[1] *Life of Lord John Russell*, vol. ii. p. 251.

allies of Turkey. The other mode, proposed by M. Drouyn de Lhuys, contemplated a much further reduction of force —namely, to eight or ten light vessels, intended solely to protect commerce from pirates and perform the police of the coast.' Although a great part of the Russian fleet was at the bottom of the sea, and the rest of it hemmed in in the harbour of Sebastopol, Prince Gortschakoff announced, with the air of a man who was master of the situation, that the Czar entirely refused to limit his power in the Euxine.

At this juncture Count Buol proposed a compromise, to the effect that Russia should maintain in the Black Sea a naval force not greater than that which she had had at her disposal there before the outbreak of the war ; that any attempt to evade this limitation should be interpreted as a *casus belli*, by France, England, and Austria, which were to form a triple treaty of alliance to defend the integrity and independence of Turkey in case of aggression. Lord Palmerston believed, to borrow his own phrase, that Austria was playing a treacherous game, but that was not the opinion at the moment either of Lord John Russell or of M. Drouyn de Lhuys. They appear to have thought that the league of Austria with England and France to resist aggression upon Turkey would prove a sufficient check on Russian ambition, and did not lay stress enough on the objections, which at once suggested themselves both in London and Paris. The Prince Consort put the case against Count Buol's scheme in a nutshell : 'The proposal of Austria to engage to make war when the Russian armaments should appear to have become excessive is of no kind of value to the belligerents, who do not wish to establish a case for which to make war hereafter, but to obtain a security upon which they can conclude peace now.'

Lord John Russell, in a confidential interview with Count Buol, declared that he was prepared to recommend the English Cabinet to accept the Austrian proposals. It seemed to him that, if Russia was willing to accept the compromise and to abandon the attitude which had led to the war, the presence of the Allies in the Crimea was scarcely justifiable. M. Drouyn de Lhuys took the same view, and both plenipotentiaries hastened back to urge acquiescence in proposals which seemed to promise the termination of a war in which, with little result, blood and treasure had already been lavishly expended.

Lord Palmerston and Lord Clarendon, backed by popular sentiment, refused to see in Russia's stubborn demand about her fleet in the Black Sea other than a perpetual menace to Turkey. They argued that England had made too heavy a sacrifice to patch up in this fashion an inglorious and doubtful peace. The attitude of Napoleon III. did more than anything else to confirm this decision. The war in the Crimea had never been as popular in France as it was in England. The throne which Napoleon had seized could only be kept by military success, and there is no doubt whatever that personal ambition, and the prestige of a campaign, with England for a companion-in-arms, determined the despatch of French troops to the Crimea. On his return, Lord John at once saw the difficulty in which his colleagues were landed. The internal tranquility of France was imperilled if the siege of Sebastopol was abandoned. 'The Emperor of the French,' he wrote, 'had been to us the most faithful ally who had ever wielded the sceptre or ruled the destinies of France. Was it possible for the English Government to leave the Emperor to fight unaided the battle of Europe, or to force him to join us in a peace which would have sunk his reputation with his army and his people?' He added, that this consideration seemed to him so weighty that he ceased to urge on Lord Palmerston the acceptance of the Austrian terms, and Lord Clarendon therefore sent a reply in which Count Buol's proposals were rejected by the Cabinet. Lord Palmerston laid great stress on Lord John's presence in his ministry, and Mr. Walpole has shown that the latter only consented to withdraw his resignation after not merely an urgent, but a thrice-repeated personal request from the Premier.

He ought unquestionably, at all hazards to Lord Palmerston's Government, to have refused to remain a member of it when his colleagues intimated that they were not in a position to accept his view of the situation without giving mortal offence to the Emperor of the French. Under the circumstances, Lord Palmerston ought not to have put the pressure on Lord John. The latter stayed in order to shield the Government from overthrow by a combined Radical and Tory attack at a moment when Palmerston was compelled to study the susceptibilities of France and Napoleon III.'s fears concerning his throne. There is a published letter, written by the Prince Consort at this juncture to his brother the Duke of Saxe-Coburg, which throws light on the situation. The Prince hints that the prospects of the Allies in the Crimea had become more hopeful, just as diplomatic affairs at Vienna had taken an awkward turn. He states that in General Pélissier the French 'have at last a leader who is determined and enterprising, and who will once more raise the spirit of the army, which has sunk through Canrobert's mildness.' He adds that the English troops 'are again thirty thousand men under arms, and their spirit is excellent. At home, however, Gladstone and the

Peelites are taking up the cry for peace, and declaring them-
selves against all further continuation of the war ; whilst
Lord Derby and the Protectionists are all for making
common cause with Layard and others, in order to overthrow
Palmerston's Ministry.' Disraeli, significantly adds the
Prince, has been 'chiefly endeavouring to injure' Lord
John Russell.

Towards the end of May, Mr. Disraeli introduced a
resolution condemning the conduct of the Government,
and calling attention to Lord John Russell's attitude at
the Vienna Conference. Lord John had fulfilled the
promise which he had given to Count Buol before leaving
Vienna ; but Lord Palmerston was determined to maintain the alliance with France, and therefore, as a member
of his Government, Lord John's lips were sealed when he
rose to defend himself. He stated in a powerful speech the
reasons which had led to the failure of the Conference, and
ended without any allusion to the Austrian proposals or
his own action in regard to them. Irritated at the new turn
of affairs, Count Buol disclosed what had passed behind the
scenes in Vienna, and Lord John found himself compelled
to explain his explanations. He declared that he had
believed before leaving Vienna that the Austrian scheme
held out the promise of peace, and, with this conviction in
his mind, he had on his return to London immediately
advised its acceptance by Lord Palmerston. He was not
free, of course, to state with equal frankness the true reason
of its rejection by the Cabinet, and therefore was compelled to fall back on the somewhat lame plea that it had
been fully considered and disallowed by his colleagues.
Moreover he felt, as a plenipotentiary, it was his duty to
submit to the Government which had sent him to Vienna,

and as a member of the Cabinet it was not less his duty to yield to the decision of the majority of his colleagues.

Lord John's explanations were not deemed satisfactory. He was in the position of a man who could only defend himself and make his motives plain to Parliament and the country by statements which would have embarrassed his colleagues and have shattered the French alliance at a moment when, not so much on national as on international grounds, it seemed imperative that it should be sustained. The attacks in the Press were bitter and envenomed ; and when Lord John, in July, told Lord Palmerston it was his intention to retire, the latter admitted with an expression of great regret that the storm was too strong to be resisted, though, he added, 'juster feelings will in due time prevail.' A few days later Lord John, in a calm and impressive speech, anticipated Sir E. B. Lytton's hostile motion on the Vienna Conference by announcing his intention to the House. Though he still felt in honour obliged to say nothing on the real cause of his withdrawal, his dignified attitude on that occasion made its own impression, and all the more because of the sweeping abuse to which he was at the moment exposed. It was of this speech that Sir George Cornewall Lewis said that it was listened to with attention and respect by an audience partly hostile and partly prejudiced. He declared that he was convinced it would go far to remove the imputations, founded on error and misrepresentation, under which Lord John laboured. He added, with a generosity which, though characteristic, was rare at that juncture : ' I shall be much surprised if, after a little time and a little reflection, persons do not come to the conclusion that never was so small a matter magnified beyond its true porportions.'

Within twenty-four hours of his resignation Lord John had an opportunity of showing that he bore no malice towards former colleagues. Mr. Roebuck, with characteristic denunciations, attacked the Government on the damaging statements contained in the report of the Sebastopol Committee. He proposed a motion censuring in severe terms every member of the Cabinet whose counsels had led to such disastrous results. Whatever construction might be placed on Lord John's conduct of affairs in Vienna, he at least could not be charged with lukewarmness or apathy in regard to the administration of the army and the prosecution of the war. He had, in fact, irritated Lord Aberdeen and the Duke of Newcastle by insisting again and again on the necessity of undivided control of the military departments, and on the need of a complete reorganisation of the commissariat. A less magnanimous man would have seized the opportunity of this renewed attack to declare that he, at least, had done his best at great personal cost to prevent the deplorable confusion and collapse which had overtaken the War Office. He disdained, however, the mean personal motive, and made, what Lord Granville called, a 'magnificent speech,' in which he declared that every member without exception remained responsible for the consequences which had overtaken the Expedition to the Crimea. Mr. Kinglake once asserted that, though Lord John Russell was capable of coming to a bold, abrupt, and hasty decision, not duly concerted with men whose opinions he ought to have weighed, no statesman in Europe surpassed him on the score of courage or high public spirit. The chivalry which he displayed in coming to the help of the Government on the morrow of his own almost compulsory retirement from office was typical of a man who made many mistakes, but was never guilty, even when wounded to the quick, of gratifying the passing resentments of the hour at the expense of the interests of the nation.

During the summer of 1855 the feeling of the country grew more and more warlike. The failure of the negotiations at Vienna had touched the national pride. The State visit in the spring to the English Court of the Emperor Napoleon, and his determination not to withdraw his troops from the Crimea until some decisive victory was won, had rekindled its enthusiasm. The repulse at the Redan, the death of Lord Raglan, and the vainglorious boast of Prince Gortschakoff, who declared 'that the hour was at hand when the pride of the enemies of Russia would be lowered, and their armies swept from our soil like chaff blown away by the wind,' rendered all dreams of diplomatic solution impossible, and made England, in spite of the preachers of peace at any price, determined to push forward her quarrel to the bitter end. The nation, to borrow the phrase of one of the shrewdest political students of the time, had now begun to consider the war in the Crimea as a 'duel with Russia,' and pride and pluck were more than ever called into play, both at home and abroad, in its maintenance. The war, therefore, took its course. Ample supplies and reinforcements were despatched to the troops, and the Allies, under the command of General Simpson and General Pélissier, pushed forward the campaign with renewed vigour. Sardinia and Sweden had joined the alliance, and on August 16 the troops of the former, acting in concert with the French, drove back the Russians, who had made a sortie along the valley of the Tchernaya. After a month's bombardment by the Allies, the Malakoff, a redoubt which commanded Sebastopol, was taken by the French ; but the English troops were twice repulsed in their attack on the Redan. Gortschakoff and Todleben were no longer able to withstand the fierce and daily renewed bombardment. The forts on the south side were, therefore, blown up, the ships were sunk, and the army which had gallantly defended the place retired to a position of greater security with the result that Sebastopol fell on September 8, and the war was virtually over. Sir Evelyn Wood lately drew attention to the fact that forty out of every hundred of the soldiers who served before Sebastopol in the depth of that terrible winter of 1854 lie there, or in the Scutari cemetery—slain, not by the sword, but by privation, exposure, disease, and exertions beyond human endurance.

France was clamouring for peace, and Napoleon was determined not to prolong the struggle now that his troops had come out of the siege of Sebastopol with flying colours. Russia, on her part, had wellnigh exhausted her resources. Up to the death of the Emperor Nicholas, she had lost nearly a quarter of a million of men, and six months later, so great was the carnage and so insidious the pestilence, that even that ominous number was doubled. The loss of the Allies in the Crimean war was upwards of eighty-seven thousand men, and more than two-thirds of the slain fell to France. Apart from bloodshed, anguish, and pain, the Crimean war bequeathed to England an increase of 41,000,000*l.* in the National Debt. No wonder that overtures for the cessation of hostilities now met with a welcome which had been denied at the Vienna Conference. After various negotiations, the Peace of Paris was signed on March 30, 1856. Russia was compelled to relinquish her control over the Danube and her protectorate over the

Principalities, and was also forbidden to build arsenals on the shores of the Black Sea, which was declared open to all ships of commerce, but closed to all ships of war. Turkey, on the other hand, confirmed, on paper at least, the privileges proclaimed in 1839 to Christians resident in the Ottoman Empire; but massacres at Damascus, in the Lebanon, and later in Bulgaria, and recently in Armenia, have followed in dismal sequence in spite of the Treaty of Paris. The neutrality of the Black Sea came to an end a quarter of a century ago, and the substantial gains—never great even at the outset—of a war which was costly in blood and treasure have grown small by degrees until they have almost reached the vanishing point.

CHAPTER XIII

LITERATURE AND EDUCATION

Lord John's position in 1855 – His constituency in the City—Survey of his work in literature—As man of letters—His historical writings - Hero-worship of Fox – Friendship with Moore Writes the biography of the poet —' Don Carlos '—A book wrongly attributed to him — Publishes his ' Recollections and Suggestions '— An opinion of Kinglake's—Lord John on his own career—Lord John and National Schools—Joseph Lancaster's tentative efforts— The formation of the Council of Education—Prejudice blocks the way—Mr. Forster's tribute.

MEN talked in the autumn of 1855 as if Lord John Russell's retirement was final, and even his brother, the Duke of Bedford, considered it probable that his career as a responsible statesman was closed. His health had always been more or less delicate, and he was now a man of sixty-three. He had been in Parliament for upwards of forty years, and nearly a quarter of a century had passed since he bore the brunt of the wrath and clamour and evil-speaking of the Tories at the epoch of Reform. He had been leader of his party for a long term of difficult years, and Prime Minister for the space of six, and in that capacity had left on the statute book an impressive record of his zeal on behalf of civil and religious liberty. No statesman of the period had won more distinction in spite of ' gross blunders,' which he himself in so many words admitted.   He was certainly entitled to rest on his laurels; but it was nonsense for anyone to suppose that the animosity of the Irish, or the indignation of the Ritualists, or the general chagrin at the collapse—under circumstances for which Lord John was by no means alone responsible—of the Vienna Conference, could condemn a man of so much energy and courage, as well as political prescience, to perpetual banishment from Downing Street.

There were people who thought that Lord John was played out in 1855, and there were many more who wished to think so, for he was feared by the incompetent and apathetic of his own party, as well as by those who had occasion to reckon with him in honourable but strenuous political conflict. The great mistake of his life was not the Durham Letter, which has been justified, in spite of its needless bitterness of tone, by the inexorable logic of accomplished events. It was not his attitude towards Ireland in the dark years of famine, which was in reality far more temperate and generous than is commonly supposed. It was not his action over the Vienna Conference, for, now that the facts are known, his reticence in self-defence, under the railing accusations which were brought against him, was magnanimous and patriotic. The truth is, Lord John Russell placed himself in a false position when he yielded to the importunity of the Court and the Peelites by consenting to accept office under Lord Aberdeen.   The Crimean War, which he did his best to prevent, only threw into the relief of red letters against a dark sky the radical divergence of opinion which existed in the Coalition Government.

For nearly four years after his retirement from office Lord John held an independent political position, and there is evidence enough that he enjoyed to the full this respite from the cares of responsibility. He gave up his house in town, and the quidnuncs thought that they had seen the last of him as a Minister of the Crown, whilst the merchants and the stockbrokers of the City were supposed to scout his name, and to be ready to lift up their heel against him at the next election.

Meanwhile, Lord John studied to be quiet, and succeeded. He visited country-houses, and proved a delightful as well as a delighted guest. He travelled abroad, and came back with new political ideas about the trend in foreign politics. He published the final volume of his 'Memoirs and Correspondence of Thomas Moore,' and busied himself over his 'Life and Times of Charles James Fox,' and other congenial literary tasks. He appeared on the platform and addressed four thousand persons in Exeter Hall, in connection with the Young Men's Christian Association, on the causes which had retarded moral and political progress in the nation. He went down to Stroud, and gave his old constituents a philosophic address on the study of history. He spoke at the first meeting of the Social Science Congress at Birmingham, presided over the second at Liverpool, and raised in Parliament the questions of National Education, Jewish Disabilities, the affairs of Italy, besides taking part, as an independent supporter of Lord Palmerston, in the controversies which arose from time to time in the House of Commons. His return to office grew inevitable in the light of the force of his character and the integrity of his aims.

It is, of course, impossible in the scope of this volume to describe at any length Lord John Russell's contributions to literature, even outside the range of letters and articles in the press and that almost forgotten weapon of controversy, the political pamphlet. From youth to age Lord John not merely possessed the pen of a ready writer, but employed it freely in history, biography, criticism, *belles-lettres*, and verse. His first book was published when George III. was King, and his last appeared when almost forty years of Queen Victoria's reign had elapsed. The Liverpool Administration was in power when his biography of his famous ancestor, William, Lord Russell, appeared, and that of Mr. Disraeli when the veteran statesman took the world into his confidence with 'Recollections and Suggestions.' It is amusing now to recall the fact that two years after the battle of Waterloo Lord John Russell feared that he could never stand the strain of a political career, and Tom Moore's well-known poetical ' Remonstrance ' was called forth by the young Whig's intention at that time to abandon the Senate for the study. When Lord Grey's Ministry was formed in 1830 to carry Reform, Lord John was the author of several books, grave and gay, and had been seventeen years in Parliament, winning already a considerable reputation within and without its walls. It was a surprise at the moment, and it is not even yet quite clear why Russell was excluded from the Cabinet. Mr. Disraeli has left on record his interpretation of the mystery : ' Lord John Russell was a man of letters, and it is a common opinion that a man cannot at the same time be successful both in meditation and in action.' If this surmise is correct, Lord John's fondness for printer's ink kept him out of Downing Street until he made by force his merit known as a champion of popular rights in the House of Commons. Literature often claimed his pen, for, besides many contributions in prose and verse to periodicals, to say nothing of writings which still remain in manuscript and prefaces to the books of other people, he published about twenty works, great and small. Yet, his strength lay elsewhere.

His literary pursuits, with scarcely an exception, represent his hours of relaxation and the manner in which he sought relief from the cares of State. In the pages of 'William, Lord Russell,' which was published in 1819, when political corruption was supreme and social progress all but impossible, Lord John gave forth no uncertain sound. 'In these times, when love of liberty is too generally supposed to be allied with rash innovation, impiety, and anarchy, it seems to me desirable to exhibit to the world at full length the portrait of a man who, heir to wealth and title, was foremost in defending the privileges of the people ; who, when busily occupied in the affairs of public life, was revered in his own family as the best of husbands and of fathers ; who joined the truest sense of religion with the unqualified assertion of freedom ; who, after an honest perseverance in a good cause, at length attested, on the scaffold, his attachment to the ancient principles of the Constitution and the inalienable right of resistance.' The interest of the book consists not merely in its account—gathered in part at least from family papers at Woburn and original letters at Longleat—of Lord Russell, but also in the light which is cast on the period of the Restoration, and the policy of Charles II. and the Duke of York.

Two years later, Lord John published an ' Essay on the History of the English Government and Constitution,' which, in an expanded form, has passed through several editions, and has also appeared in a French version. The book is concerned with constitutional change in England from the reign of Henry VII. to the beginning of the nineteenth century. Lord John made no secret of his conviction that, whilst the majority of the Powers of Europe needed revolutionary methods to bring them into sympathy with the aspirations of the people, the Government of England was not in such an evil case, since its 'abuses easily admit of reforms consistent with its spirit, capable of being effected without injury or danger, and mainly contributing to its preservation.' The historical reflections which abound in the work, though shrewd, can scarcely be described as remarkable, much less as profound. The 'Essay on English Government' is, in fact, not the confessions of an inquiring spirit entangled in the maze of political speculation, but the conclusions of a young statesman who has made up his mind, with the help of Somers and Fox.

Perhaps, however, the most important of Lord John's contributions to the study of the philosophy of history was 'Memoirs of the Affairs of Europe from the Peace of Utrecht.' It describes at considerable length, and often with luminous insight, the negotiations which led to the treaty by which the great War of the Spanish Succession was brought to an end. It also throws light on men and manners during the last days of Louis XIV., and on the condition of affairs in France which followed his death. The closing pages of the second volume are concerned with a survey of the religious state of England during the first half of the eighteenth century. Lord John in this connection pays homage to the work of Churchmen of the stamp of Warburton, Clarke, and Hoadly; but he entirely fails to appreciate at anything like their true value the labours of Whitfield and Wesley, though doing more justice to the great leaders of Puritanism, a circumstance which was perhaps due to the fact that they stand in the direct historical succession, not merely in the assertion of the rights of conscience, but in the ordered growth of freedom and society.

Amongst the most noteworthy of Lord John Russell's literary achievements were the two works which he published concerning a statesman whose memory, he declared, ought to be 'consecrated in the heart of every lover of freedom throughout the globe'—Charles James Fox, a master of assemblies, and, according to Burke, perhaps the greatest debater whom the world has ever seen. The books in question are entitled 'Memorials and Correspondence,' which was published in four volumes at intervals between the years 1853 and 1857, and the more important 'Life and Times of Charles James Fox,' which appeared in three volumes between the years 1859 and 1866. This task, like so many others which Lord John accomplished, came unsought at the death of his old friend, Lady Holland, in 1845. It was the ambition of Lord Holland, 'nephew of Fox and friend of Grey,' as he used proudly to style himself, to edit the papers and write the life of his brilliant kinsman. Politics and society and the stately house at Kensington, which, from the end of last century until the opening years of the Queen's reign, was the chief *salon* of the Whig party, combined, with an easy procrastinating temperament, to block the way, until death ended, in the autumn of 1840, the career of the gracious master of Holland House. The materials which Lord Holland and his physician, librarian, and friend, Dr. John Allen, had accumulated, and which, by the way, passed under the scrutiny of Lord Grey and Rogers, the poet, were edited by Lord John, with the result that he grew fascinated with the subject, and formed the resolution, in consequence, to write 'The Life and Times' of the great

Whig statesman. He declared that it was well to have a hero, and a hero with a good many faults and failings.

Fox did more than any other statesman in the dull reign of George II. to prepare the way for the epoch of Reform, and it was therefore fitting that the statesman who more than any other bore the brunt of the battle in 1830 32 should write his biography. Lord Russell's biography of Fox, though by no means so skilfully written as Sir George Otto Trevelyan's vivacious description of 'The Early History of Charles James Fox,' is on a more extended scale than the latter. Students of the political annals of the eighteenth century are aware of its value as an original and suggestive contribution to the facts and forces which have shaped the relations of the Crown and the Cabinet in modern history. Fox, in Lord John's opinion, gave his life to the defence of English freedom, and hastened his death by his exertion to abolish the African Slave Trade. He lays stress, not only on the great qualities which Fox displayed in public life, but also on the simplicity and kindness of his nature, and the spell which, in spite of grievous faults, he seemed able to cast, without effort, alike over friends and foes.

One of the earliest, and certainly one of the closest, friendships of Lord John Russell's life was with Thomas Moore. They saw much of each other for the space of nearly forty years in London society, and were also drawn together in the more familiar intercourse of foreign travel. It was with Lord John that the poet went to Italy in 1819 to avoid arrest for debt, after his deputy at Bermuda had embezzled 6,000*l.* Moore lived, more or less, all his days from hand to mouth, and Lord John Russell, who was always ready in a quiet fashion, in Kingsley's phrase, to help lame dogs over stiles, frequently displayed

towards the light-hearted poet throughout their long friendship delicate and generous kindness. He it was who, in
conjunction with Lord Lansdowne, obtained for Moore
in 1835 a pension of 300*l.* a year, and announced the
fact as one which was 'due from any Government, but
much more from one some of the members of which
are proud to think themselves your friends.' Moore died
in 1852, and when his will was read it had been made
when Lord John was still comparatively unknown—it
was discovered that he had, to give his own words, 'confided to my valued friend, Lord John Russell (having
obtained his kind promise to undertake the service for
me), the task of looking over whatever papers, letters, or
journals I may leave behind me, for the purpose of forming
from them some kind of publication, whether in the shape
of memoirs or otherwise, which may afford the means of
making some provision for my wife and family.' Although
Lord John was sixty, and burdened with the cares of State,
if not with the cares of office, he cheerfully accepted the
task. Though it must be admitted that he performed
some parts of it in rather a perfunctory manner, the eight
volumes which appeared between 1853 and 1856 of the
'Memoirs, Journal, and Correspondence of Thomas Moore'
represent a severe tax upon friendship, as well as no ordinary
labour on the part of a man who was always more or less
immersed in public affairs.

Lord John also edited the 'Correspondence of John,
fourth Duke of Bedford,' and prefaced the letters with a
biographical sketch. Quite early in his career he also
tried his hand at fiction in 'The Nun of Arrouca,' a story
founded on a romantic incident which occurred during his
travels in the Peninsula. The book appeared in 1822,

and in the same year—he was restless and ambitious of literary distinction at the time, and had not yet found his true sphere in politics—he also published 'Don Carlos,' a tragedy in blank verse, which was in reality not merely a tirade against the cruelties of the Inquisition, but an impassioned protest against religious disabilities in every shape or form. 'Don Carlos,' though now practically forgotten, ran through five editions in twelve months, and the people remembered it when its author became the foremost advocate in the House of Commons of the repeal of the Test and Corporation Acts. Amongst other minor writings which belong to the earlier years of Lord John Russell, it is enough to name 'Essays and Sketches of Life and Character,' 'The Establishment of the Turks in Europe,' 'A Translation of the Fifth Book of the Odyssey,' and an imitation of the Thirteenth Satire of Juvenal, as well as an essay on the 'Causes of the French Revolution,' which appeared in 1832.

It is still a moot point whether 'Letters Written for the Post, and not for the Press,' an anonymous volume which appeared in 1820, and which consists of descriptions of a tour in Scotland, interspersed with dull moral lectures on the conduct of a wife towards her husband, was from his pen. Mr. George Elliot believes, on internal evidence, too lengthy to quote, that the book—a small octavo volume of more than four hundred pages—is erroneously attributed to his brother-in-law, and the Countess Russell is of the same opinion. Mr. Elliot cites inaccuracies in the book, and adds that the places visited in Scotland do not correspond with those which Lord John had seen when he went thither in company with the Duke and Duchess in 1807 ; and there is no evidence that he made another pilgrimage north of the Tweed between that date and the appearance of the book. He adds that his father took the trouble to collect everything which was written by Lord John, and the book is certainly not in the library at Minto. Moreover, Mr. Elliot is confident that either Lord Minto or Lord John himself assured him that he might dismiss the idea of the supposed authorship.

After his final retirement from office, Lord John published, in 1868, three letters to Mr. Chichester Fortescue on 'The State of Ireland,' and this was followed by a contribution to ecclesiastical history in the shape of a volume of essays on 'The Rise and Progress of the Christian Religion in the West of Europe to the Council of Trent.' The leisure of his closing years was, however, chiefly devoted to the preparation, with valuable introductions, of selections from his own 'Speeches and Despatches ; ' and this, in turn, was followed, after an interval of five years, by a work entitled ' Recollections and Suggestions, 1813–1873,' which appeared as late as 1875, and which was of singular personal interest as well as of historical importance. It bears on the title-page two lines from Dryden, which were often on Lord John's lips in his closing years :

> Not Heaven itself upon the past has power,
> But what has been has been, and I have had my hour.

The old statesman's once tenacious memory was failing when he wrote the book, and there is little evidence of literary arrangement in its contents. If, however, Lord John did not always escape inaccuracy of statement or laboured discursiveness of style, the value not only of his political reminiscences, but also of his shrewd and often pithily expressed verdicts on men and movements, is unquestionable, and, on the whole, the vigour of the book is as remarkable as its noble candour. Mr. Kinglake once declared that 'Lord John Russell wrote so naturally that it recalled the very sound of his voice ;' and half the charm of his 'Recollections and Suggestions' consists in the artlessness of a record which will always rank with the original materials of history, between the year in which Wellington fought the battle of Vittoria and that in which, just sixty years later, Napoleon III. died in exile at Chislehurst. In speaking of his own career, Lord Russell, writing at the age of eighty-one, uses words which are not less manly than modest :

'I can only rejoice that I have been allowed to have my share in the task accomplished in the half-century which has elapsed from 1819 to 1869. My capacity, I always felt, was very inferior to that of the men who have attained in past times the foremost place in our Parliament and in the councils of our Sovereign. I have committed many errors, some of them very gross blunders. But the generous people of England are always forbearing and forgiving to those statesmen who have the good of their country at heart. Like my betters, I have been misrepresented and slandered by those who know nothing of me ; but I have been more than compensated by the confidence and the friendship of the best men of my own political connection, and by the regard and favourable interpretation of my motives, which I have heard expressed by my generous opponents, from the days of Lord Castlereagh to these of Mr. Disraeli.'

There were few questions in which Lord John Russell was more keenly interested from youth to age than that of National Education. As a boy he had met Joseph Lancaster, during a visit of that far-seeing and practical friend of poor children to Woburn, and the impression which the humble Quaker philanthropist made on the Duke of Bedford's quick-witted as well as kind-hearted son was retained, as one of his latest speeches show, to the close of life. At the opening of the new British Schools in Richmond in the summer of 1867, Lord John referred to his father's association with Joseph Lancaster, and added: 'In this way I naturally became initiated into a desire for promoting schools for the working classes, and I must say, from that time to this I never changed my mind upon the subject. I think it is absolutely necessary our schools should not merely be secular, but that they should be provided with religious teaching, and that religious teaching ought not to be sectarian. There will be plenty of time, when these children go to church or chapel, that they should learn either that particular form of doctrine their parents follow or adopt one more consistent with their conscientious feelings; but I think, while they are young boys and girls at school, it ought to be sufficient for them to know what Christ taught, and what the apostles taught; and from those lessons and precepts they may guide their conduct in life.'

Lord John put his hand to the plough in the day of small things, and, through good and through evil report, from the days of Lancaster, Bell, and Brougham, to those of Mr. Forster and the great measure of 1870, he never withdrew from a task which lay always near to his heart. It is difficult to believe that at the beginning of the present century there were less than three thousand four hundred schools of all descriptions in the whole of England, or that when the reign of George III. was closing one-half of the children of the nation still ran wild without the least pretence of education. At a still later period the marriage statistics revealed the fact that one-third of the men and one-half of the women were unable to sign the register. The social elevation of the people, so ran the miserable plea of those who assuredly were not given to change, was fraught with peril to the State. Hodge, it was urged, ought to be content to take both the Law and the Commandments from his betters, since a little knowledge is a dangerous thing. As for the noisy, insolent operatives and artisans of the great manufacturing towns, was there not for them the strong hand of authority, and, if they grew too obstreperous, the uplifted sabre of the military as at Peterloo? It was all very well, however, to extol the virtues of patience, contentment, and obedience, but the sense of wrong and of defiance rankled in the masses, and with it—in a dull and confused manner—the sense of power.

The Reform Bill of 1832 mocked in many directions the hopes of the people, but it at least marked a great social as well as a great political departure, and with it came the dawn of a new day to modern England. As the light broadened, the vision of poets and patriots began to be realised in practical improvements, which came home to men's business and bosom ; the standard of intelligence rose, and with it freedom of thought, and the, sometimes passionate, but more often long-suffering demand for political, social, and economic concessions to justice. It was long before the privileged classes began to recognise, except in platform heroics, that it was high time to awake out of sleep and to ' educate our masters ; ' but the work began when Lord Althorp persuaded the House of Commons to vote a modest sum for the erection of school buildings in England ; and that grant of 20,000*l.* in

1832 was the ' handful of corn on the top of the mountains ' which has brought about the golden harvest of to-day. The history of the movement does not, of course, fall within the province of these pages, though Lord John Russell's name is associated with it in an honourable and emphatic sense. The formation, chiefly at his instance, in 1839 of a Council of Education paved the way for the existing system of elementary education, and lifted the whole problem to the front rank of national affairs.

He was the first Prime Minister of England to carry a measure which made it possible to secure trained teachers for elementary schools ; and his successful effort in 1847 to ' diminish the empire of ignorance,' as he styled it, was one of the events in his public life on which he looked back in after years with the most satisfaction. During the session of 1856 Lord John brought forward in the House of Commons a bold scheme of National Education. He contended that out of four million children of school age only one-half were receiving instruction, whilst not more than one-eighth were attending schools which were subject to inspection. The vast majority were to be found in schools where the standard of education, if not altogether an unknown quantity, was deplorably low. He proposed that the number of inspectors should be increased, and that a rate should be levied by the local authorities for supplying adequate instruction in places where it was unsatisfactory. He contended that the country should be mapped out in school districts, and that the managers should have the power to make provision for religious instruction, and, at the same time, should allow the parents of the children a voice in the matter. Prejudices ecclesiastical and social blocked the way, however, and Lord John was compelled to abandon the scheme, which suggested, and to a large extent anticipated Mr. Forster's far-reaching measure, which in 1870 met with a better fate, and linked the principles of local authority and central supervision in the harmonious working of public education. When the victory was almost won Mr. Forster, with characteristic kindliness, wrote to the old statesman who had laboured for the people's cause in years of supreme discouragement :—'As regards universal compulsory education, I believe we shall soon complete the building. It is hard to see how there would have been a building to complete, if you had not, with great labour and in great difficulty, dug the foundations in 1839.' Happily Lord John lived to witness the crowning of the edifice by the Gladstone Administration.

CHAPTER XIV

COMING BACK TO POWER

1857-1861

Lord John as an Independent Member—His chance in the City—The Indian Mutiny—Orsini's attempt on the life of Napoleon—The Conspiracy Bill—Lord John and the Jewish Relief Act—Palmerston in power—Lord John at the Foreign Office—Cobden and Bright— Quits the Commons with a Peerage.

LORD JOHN came prominently to the front in public affairs in the brief session of 1857, which ended in Lord Palmerston's appeal to the country. He spoke against the Government during the discussions in the House of Commons on the conduct of the Persian War, and he exercised his independence in other directions. Even shrewd and well-informed observers were curiously oblivious, for the moment, of the signs of the times, for Greville wrote on February 27 : ' Nobody cares any longer for John Russell, everybody detests Gladstone ; Disraeli has no influence in the country, and a very doubtful position with his own party.' Yet scarcely more than a fortnight later this cynical, but frank scribe added : ' Some think a reaction in favour of John Russell has begun. He stands for the City, and is in very good spirits, though his chances of success do not look bright ; but he is a gallant little fellow, likes to face danger, and comes out well in times of difficulty.' Between these two statements the unexpected had happened. Cobden had brought forward a motion censuring the conduct of the Government in the affair of the lorcha, 'Arrow,' at Canton, and the three statesmen on whom Greville had contemptuously pronounced judgment—Russell, Gladstone, and Disraeli—had supported the Manchester school, with the result that the Government, on March 4, suffered defeat by a majority of sixteen votes. Parliament was dissolved in the course of the month, and the General Election brought Lord Palmerston back to power, pledged to nothing unless it was a spirited foreign policy.

The personal ascendency of Lord Palmerston, whom Disraeli cleverly styled the Tory chief of a Radical Cabinet, carried the election, for there was a good deal of truth in the assertion that nobody cared a straw for his colleagues. The Peace party suffered defeat at the polls, and, amongst others, Cobden himself was turned out at Huddersfield, and Bright and Milner Gibson were his companions in misfortune at Manchester. A vigorous attempt was made to overthrow Lord John in the City, and his timid friends in the neighbourhood of Lombard Street and the Exchange implored him not to run the risk of a contested election. He was assured in so many words, states Lady Russell, that he had as much chance of being elected Pope as of being elected member for the City; and the statement roused his mettle. He was pitted against a candidate from Northampton, and the latter was brought forward with the powerful support of the Registration Association of the City of London, and in a fashion which was the reverse of complimentary to the old statesman.

Lord John was equal to the occasion, and was by no means inclined to throw up the sponge. He went down to the City, and delivered not merely a vigorous, but vivacious speech, and in the course of it he said, with a jocularity which was worthy of Lord Palmerston himself : 'If a gentleman were disposed to part with his butler, his coachman, or his gamekeeper, or if a merchant were disposed to part with an old servant, a warehouseman, a clerk, or even a porter, he would say to him, "John— (laughter)—I think your faculties are somewhat decayed ; you are growing old, you have made several mistakes, and I think of putting a young man from Northampton in your place." (Laughter and cheers.)   I think a gentleman would behave in that way to his servant, and thereby give John an opportunity of answering that he thought his faculties were not so much decayed, and that he was able to go on, at all events, some five or six years longer.   That opportunity was not given to me.   The question was decided in my absence, without any intimation to me ; and I come now to ask you and the citizens of London to reverse that decision.' He was taken at his word, and the rival candidate from Northampton was duly sent to the neighbouring borough of Coventry.

The summer of 1857 was darkened in England by tidings of the Indian Mutiny and of the terrible massacre at Cawnpore.   In face of the disaster Lord John not merely gave his hearty support to the Government, but delivered an energetic protest against the attack of the Opposition at such a crisis, and moved an address assuring the Crown of the support of Parliament, which was carried, in spite of Disraeli, without a division.   At the same time Lord John in confidential intercourse made it plain that he recognised to the full extent the need of reform in the administration of India, and he did not hesitate to intimate that, in his view, the East India Company was no longer

equal to the strain of so great a responsibility. He brought
no railing accusations against the Company, but, on the
contrary, declared that it must be admitted they had 'con-
ducted their affairs in a wonderful manner, falling into errors
that were natural, but displaying merits of a high order.
The real ground for change is that the machine is worn
out, and, as a manufacturer changes an excellent engine of
Watt and Boulton made fifty years ago for a new engine
with modern improvements, so it becomes us to find a new
machine for the government of India.'

Before the upheaval in India had spent its force fresh
difficulties overtook Lord Palmerston's Government. Count
Orsini, strong in the conviction that Napoleon III. was the
great barrier to the progress of revolution in Italy, determined
to rid his countrymen of the man who, beyond all others,
seemed bent on thwarting the national aspirations. With other
conspirators, he threw three bombs on the night of January
14, 1858, at the carriage of the Emperor and Empress as they
were proceeding to the Opera, and, though they escaped un-
hurt, ten persons were killed and many wounded. The bombs
had been manufactured in England, and Orsini—who was
captured and executed—had arranged the dastardly outrage
in London, and the consequence was a fierce outbreak of
indignation on the other side of the Channel. Lord
Palmerston, prompted by the French Government, which
demanded protection from the machinations of political
refugees, brought forward a Conspiracy Bill. The feeling
of the country, already hostile to such a measure, grew pronounced when the French army, not content with congratu-
lating the Emperor on his escape, proceeded to refer to
England in insulting, and even threatening, terms. Lord
John, on high constitutional grounds, protested against the

introduction of the measure, and declared that he was determined not to share in such 'shame and humiliation.' The Government were defeated on the Conspiracy Bill, on February 19, by nineteen votes. Amongst the eighty-four Liberals in the majority occur the names, not merely of Lord John Russell and Sir James Graham, but Mr. Cardwell and Mr. Gladstone. Lord Palmerston promptly resigned, and Lord Derby came into office. Disraeli, as Chancellor of the Exchequer and leader of the House of Commons, proceeded with characteristic audacity and a light heart to educate the new Conservative Party in the art of dishing the Whigs.

The new Ministry was short-lived. Lord Derby was in advance of his party, and old-fashioned Tories listened with alarm to the programme of work which he set before them. For the moment Lord John was not eager for office, and he declared that the ' new Ministers ought not to be recklessly or prematurely opposed.' He added that he would not sanction any cabal among the Liberal party, and that he had no intention whatever of leading an alliance of Radicals and Peelites. Impressed with the magnitude of the issues at stake, he helped Lord Derby to pass the new India Bill, which handed the government of that country over to the Crown. He held that the question was too great to be made a battle-field of party, but thorough-paced adherents of Lord Palmerston did not conceal their indignation at such independent action. Lord John believed at the moment that it was right for him to throw his influence into the scale, and therefore he was indifferent to the passing clamour. The subsequent history of the English in India has amply justified the patriotic step which he took in scorn of party consequences. The Jewish Relief Act became law

in 1858, and Lord John at length witnessed the triumph of
a cause which he had brought again and again before
Parliament since the General Election of 1847, when Baron
Rothschild was returned as his colleague in the representation of the City.   Scarcely any class of the community
showed themselves more constantly mindful of his services
on their behalf than the Jews.   When one of them took an
opportunity of thanking him for helping to free a once
oppressed race from legal disabilities, Lord John replied :
' The object of my life has been not to benefit a race alone,
but all nationalities that suffered under civil and religious
disabilities.'   He used to relate with evident appreciation the
reply which Lord Lyndhurst once gave to a timid statesman
who feared a possible Hebrew invasion of the woolsack.   The
man who was appointed four times to that exalted seat re-
torted : ' Well, I see no harm in that ; Daniel would have made
a good Lord Chancellor.'

Everyone recognised that the Derby Administration
was a mere stop-gap, and, as months passed on, its
struggle for existence became somewhat ludicrous.   They
felt themselves to be a Ministry on sufferance, and, according to the gossip of the hour, their watchword was ' Anything for a quiet life.'   There were rocks ahead, and at
the beginning of the session of 1859 they stood revealed in
Mr. Disraeli's extraordinary proposals for Reform, and in
the war-cloud which was gathering rapidly over Europe in
consequence of the quarrel between France and Austria about
the affairs of Italy.   Mr. Disraeli's Reform Bill taxed the
allegiance of his party to the breaking point, and when its
provisions were disclosed two of his colleagues resigned—
Mr. Spencer Walpole the Home Office, and Mr. Henley the
Board of Trade, rather than have part or lot in such a

measure. There is no need here to describe in detail a scheme which was foredoomed by its fantastic character to failure. It confused great issues ; it brought into play what Mr. Bright called fancy franchises ; it did not lower the voting qualification in boroughs ; its new property qualifications were of a retrograde character ; and it left the working classes where it found them. It frightened staid Tories of the older school, and excited the ridicule, if not the indignation, of all who had seriously grappled with the problem.

The immediate effect was to unite all sections of the Liberal Party. Lord John led the attack, and did so on the broad ground that it did not go far enough ; and on April 1, after protracted debate, the measure was defeated by a majority of thirty-nine votes in a House of six hundred and twenty-one members. Parliament was prorogued on April 19, and the country was thrown into the turmoil of a General Election. Lord John promptly appealed to his old constituents in the City, and in the course of a vigorous address handled the 'so-called Reform Bill' in no uncertain manner. He declared that amongst the numerous defects of the Bill ' one provision was conspicuous by its presence and another by its absence.' He had deemed it advisable on the second reading to take what seemed to be the ' most clear, manly, and direct ' course, and that was the secret of his amendment. The House of Commons had mustered in full force, and the terms of the amendment had been carried. The result of the General Election was that three hundred and fifty Liberals and three hundred and two Conservatives were returned to Westminster. Parliament met on May 31, and Lord Hartington moved an amendment to the Address which amounted to an expression of want of confidence. The amendment was carried by a majority of thirteen on June 12, and Lord Derby's Administration came the same night to an end. The result of the division took both parties somewhat by surprise. The astonishment was heightened when her Majesty sent for Lord Granville, an action which, to say the least, was a left-handed compliment to old and distinguished advisers of the Crown. Happily, though the sovereign may in such high affairs of State propose, it is the country which must finally dispose, and Lord Granville swiftly found that in the exuberance of political youth he had accepted a hopeless commission. He therefore relinquished an impossible task, and the Queen sent for Lord Palmerston.

In the earlier years of Lord John's retirement from office after the Vienna Conference his relations with some of his old colleagues, and more particularly with Lord Clarendon and Lord Palmerston, were somewhat strained. The blunders of the Derby Government, the jeopardy in India, the menacing condition of foreign politics, and, still more, the patriotism and right feeling of both men, gradually drew Palmerston and Russell into more intimate association, with the result that in the early summer of 1859 the frank intercourse of former years was renewed. More than twelve years had elapsed since Lord John had attained the highest rank possible to an English statesman. In the interval he had consented, under strong pressure from the most exalted quarters, to waive his claims by consenting to serve under Lord Aberdeen ; and the outcome of that experiment had been humiliating to himself, as well as disastrous to the country. He might fairly have stood on his dignity—a fool's pedestal at the best, and one which Lord John was too sensible ever to mount—at the present juncture, and have declined to return to the responsibilities of office, except as Prime Minister. The leaders of the democracy, Mr. Bright and Mr. Cobden, were much more friendly to him than to Lord Palmerston. Apart from published records, Lady Russell's diary shows that at the beginning of this year Mr. Bright was in close communication with her husband. Lord John good-humouredly protested that Mr. Bright alarmed timid people by his speeches; whereupon the latter replied that he had been much misrepresented, and declared that he was more willing to be lieutenant than general in the approaching struggle for Reform. He explained his scheme, and Lord John found that it had much in common with his own, from which it differed only in degree, except on the question of the ballot. 'There has been a meeting between Bright and Lord John,' was Lord Houghton's comment, 'but I don't know that it has led to anything except a more temperate tone in Bright's last speeches.' Mr. Cobden, it is an open secret, would not have refused to serve under Lord John, but his hostility to Lord Palmerston's policy was too pronounced for him now to accept the offer of a seat in the new Cabinet. He assured Lord John that if he had been at the head of the Administration the result would have been different. Both Mr. Cobden and Mr. Bright felt that Lord Palmerston blocked the way to any adequate readjustment in home politics of the balance of power, and they were inspired by a settled distrust of his foreign policy. Lord John, on the other hand, though he might not move as swiftly as such popular leaders thought desirable, had still a name to conjure with, and was the consistent advocate, though on more cautious lines, of an extension of the franchise. Moreover, Lord John's attack on Palmerston's Government in regard to the conduct of the Chinese war, his vigorous protest against the Conspiracy Bill, and his frank sympathy with Mazzini's dream of a United Italy, helped to bring the old leader, in the long fight for civil and religious liberty, into vital touch with younger men of the stamp of Cobden, Bright, and Gladstone, of whom the people justly expected great things in the not distant future. Lord John knew, however, that the Liberal camp was full of politicians who were neither hot nor cold—men who had slipped into Parliament on easy terms, only to reveal the fact that their prejudices were many and their convictions few. They sheltered themselves under the great prestige of Lord Palmerston, and represented his policy of masterly inactivity, rather than the true sentiments of the nation. Lord Palmerston was as jaunty as ever ; but all things are not possible even to the ablest man, at seventy-five.

Although Lord John was not willing to serve under Lord Granville, who was his junior by more than a score of years, he saw his chance at the Foreign Office, and therefore consented to join the Administration of Lord Palmerston. In accepting office on such terms in the middle of June, he made it plain to Lord Palmerston that the importance of European affairs at the moment had induced him to throw in his lot with the new Ministry. The deadlock was brought to an end by Lord John's patriotic decision. Mr. Gladstone became Chancellor of the Exchequer, Lord Granville President of the Council ; and amongst others in the Cabinet were Sir G. C. Lewis, Mr. Milner Gibson, Sir George Grey, and the Duke of Argyll. Though Cobden would not accept a place in the Government, he rendered it important service by negotiating the commercial treaty with France, which came into force at the beginning of 1860. Next to the abolition of the Corn Laws, which he more than any other man brought about, it was the great achievement of his career. Free Trade, by liberating commerce from the bondage under which it groaned, gave food to starving multitudes, redressed a flagrant and tyrannical abuse of power, shielded a kingdom from the throes of revolution, and added a new and magical impetus to material progress in every quarter of the globe. The commercial treaty with France, by establishing mercantile sympathy and intercourse between two of the most powerful nations of the world, carried forward the work which Free Trade had begun, and, by bringing into play community of interests, helped to give peace a sure foundation.

Parliament met on January 24, and in the Speech from the Throne a Reform Bill was promised. It was brought forward by Lord John Russell on March 1 — the twenty-ninth anniversary of a red-letter day in his life, the introduction of the first Reform Bill. He proposed to reduce the county franchise to 10l. qualification, and the borough to 6l.; one member was to be taken from each borough with a population of less than seven thousand, and in this way twenty-five seats were obtained for redistribution. Political power was to be given where the people were congregated, and Lord John's scheme of re-distribution gave two seats to the West Riding, and one each to thirty other counties or divisions, and five to boroughs hitherto unrepresented. The claims of Manchester, Liverpool, Birmingham, and Leeds were recognised by the proposal to add another representative in each case; and the claims of culture were not forgotten, for a member was given to London University. Gallio-like, Lord Palmerston cared for none of these things, and he made no attempt to conceal his indifference. One-half of the

Cabinet appear to have shared his distaste for the measure, and two or three of them regarded it with aversion. If Cobden or Bright had been in the Cabinet, affairs might have taken a different course ; as it was, Lord John and Mr. Gladstone stood almost alone.

The Radicals, though gaining ground in the country, were numerically weak in the House of Commons, and the measure fell to the ground between the opposition of the Tories and the faint praise with which it was damned by the Whigs. Even Lord John was forced to confess that the apathy of the country was undeniable. A more sweeping measure would have had a better chance, but so long as Lord Palmerston was at the head of affairs it was idle to expect it. Lord John recognised the inevitable after a succession of dreary debates, and the measure was withdrawn on June 11. Lord John's first important speech in the House of Commons was made in the year of Peterloo, when he brought forward, thirteen years before the Reform Bill of 1832 was passed, proposals for an extension of the franchise ; and his last great speech in the House of Commons at least showed how unmerited was the taunt of ' finality,' for it sought to give the working classes a share in the government of the country.

Early in the following year, Lord John was raised to the peerage as Earl Russell of Kingston-Russell and Viscount Amberley and Ardsalla. 'I cannot despatch,' wrote Mr. Gladstone, ' as I have just done, the Chiltern Hundreds for you, without expressing the strong feelings which even that formal act awakens. They are mixed, as well as strong ; for I hope you will be repaid in repose, health, and the power of long-continuing service, for the heavy loss we suffer in the House of Commons.

Although you may not hereafter have opportunities of adding to the personal debt I owe you, and of bringing it vividly before my mind by fresh acts of courage and kindness, I assure you, the recollection of it is already indelible.' Hitherto, Lord John—for the old name is the one under which his family and his friends still like to apply to him—had been a poor man ; but the death, in the spring of this year, of his brother the Duke of Bedford, with whom, from youth to age, his intercourse had been most cordial, placed him in possession of the Ardsalla Estate, and, indeed, made possible his acceptance of the proffered earldom. Six months later, her Majesty conferred the Garter upon him, as a mark of her 'high approbation of long and distinguished services.' Lord John had almost reached the age of three score and ten when he entered the House of Lords. He had done his work in 'another place,' but he was destined to become once more First Minister of the Crown, and, as Mr. Froude put it, to carry his reputation at length off the scene unspotted by a single act which his biographers are called upon to palliate.

CHAPTER XV

UNITED ITALY AND THE DIS-UNITED STATES

1861–1865

Lord John at the Foreign Office—Austria and Italy—Victor Emmanuel and Mazzini—Cavour and Napoleon III.—Lord John's energetic protest—His sympathy with Garibaldi and the struggle for freedom —The gratitude of the Italians—Death of the Prince Consort—The 'Trent' affair—Lord John's remonstrance—The 'Alabama' difficulty—Lord Selborne's statement—The Cotton Famine.

FOREIGN politics claimed Lord John's undivided attention throughout the four remaining years of the Palmerston Administration. It was well for the nation that a statesman of so much courage and self-reliance, cool sagacity, and wide experience, controlled the Foreign Office in years when wars and rumours of war prevailed alike in Europe and in America. He once declared that it had always been his aim to promote the cause of civil and religious liberty, not merely in England, but in other parts of the world, and events were now looming which were destined to justify such an assertion. It is not possible to enter at length into the complicated problems with which he had to deal during his tenure of the Foreign Office, but the broad principles which animated his policy can, in rough outline at least, be stated. It is well in this connection to fall back upon his own words : 'In my time very difficult questions arose. During the period I held the seals of the Foreign Office I had to discuss the question of the independence of Italy, of a treaty regarding Poland made by Lord Castlereagh, the treaty regarding Denmark made by Lord Malmesbury, the injuries done to England by the republic of Mexico, and, not to mention minor questions, the whole of the transactions arising out of the civil war in America, embittered as they were by the desire of a party in the United States to lay upon England the whole blame of the insurrection, the " irrepressible conflict " of their own fellow-citizens.'   Both of these questions were far-reaching and crucial, and in his attitude towards Italy and America, when they were in the throes of revolution, Lord Russell's generous love of liberty and vigour of judgment alike stand revealed.

Prince Metternich declared soon after the peace of 1815 that Italy was 'only a geographical expression.'   The taunt was true at the time, but even then there was a young dreamer living who was destined to render it false.   'Great ideas,' declared Mazzini, 'create great nations,' and his whole career was devoted to the attempt to bring about a united Italy.   The statesmanship of Cavour and the sword of Garibaldi were enlisted in the same sacred cause.   The petty governments of the Peninsula grew suddenly impossible, and Italy was freed from native tyranny and foreign domination.   Austria, not content with the possession of Lombardy, which was ceded to her by the treaty of 1815, had made her power felt in almost every direction, and even at Naples her authority prevailed.   The Austrians were not merely an alien but a hated race, for they stood between the Italian people and their dream of national independence and unity, and native despotism could always count on their aid in quelling any outbreak of the revolutionary spirit.   The governments of the country,

Austria and the Vatican apart, were rendered contemptible by the character of its tyrannical, incapable, and superstitious rulers, but with the sway of such powers of darkness Sardinia presented a bright contrast. The hopes of patriotic Italians gathered around Victor Emmanuel II., who had fought gallantly at Novara in 1849, and who possessed more public spirit and common-sense than the majority of crowned heads. Victor Emmanuel ascended the throne of Sardinia at the age of twenty-eight, immediately after the crushing disaster which seemed hopelessly to have wrecked the cause of Italian independence. Although he believed, with Mazzini, that there was only room for two kinds of Italians in Italy, the friends and the enemies of Austria, he showed remarkable self-restraint, and adopted a policy of conciliation towards foreign Powers, whilst widening the liberties of his own subjects until all over the land Italians came to regard Sardinia with admiration, and to covet 'liberty as it was in Piedmont.'

He gathered around him men who were in sympathy with modern ideas of liberty and progress. Amongst them was Count Cavour, a statesman destined to impress not Italy alone, but Europe, by his honesty of purpose, force of character, and practical sagacity. From 1852 to 1859, when he retired, rather than agree to the humiliating terms of the Treaty of Villafranca, Cavour was supreme in Sardinia. He found Sardinia crippled by defeat, and crushed with debt, the bitter bequest of the Austrian War; but his courage never faltered, and his capacity was equal to the strain. Victor Emmanuel gave him a free hand, and he used it for the consolidation of the kingdom. He repealed the duties on corn, reformed the tariff, and introduced measures of free trade. He encouraged public works, brought about the construction of railways and telegraphs, and advanced perceptibly popular education. He saw that if the nation was to gain her independence, and his sovereign become ruler of a united Italy, it was necessary to propitiate the Western Powers. In pursuance of such a policy, Cavour induced Piedmont to join the Allies in the Crimean War, and the Italian soldiers behaved with conspicuous bravery at the battle of Tchernaya. When the war closed Sardinia was becoming a power in Europe, and Cavour established his right to a seat at the Congress of Paris, where he made known the growing discontent in Italy with the temporal power of the Papacy.

In the summer of 1858 Napoleon III. was taking the waters at Plombières, where also Count Cavour was on a visit. The Emperor's mood was leisured and cordial, and Cavour took the opportunity of bringing the Court of Turin into intimate but secret relations with that of the Tuileries. France was to come to the aid of Sardinia under certain conditions in the event of a war with Austria. Napoleon was not, of course, inclined to serve Victor Emmanuel for naught, and he therefore stipulated for Savoy and Nice. Cavour also strengthened the position of Sardinia by arranging a marriage between the Princess Clotilde, daughter of Victor Emmanuel, and the Emperor's cousin, Prince Napoleon. Alarmed at the military preparations in Sardinia, and the growth of the kingdom as a political power in Europe, Austria at the beginning of 1859 addressed an imperious demand for disarmament, which was met by Cavour by a curt refusal. The match had been put to the gunpowder and a fight for liberty took place. The campaign was short but decisive. The Austrian army crossed in force the Ticino, then hesitated and was lost. If they had acted promptly they might have crushed the troops of Piedmont, whom they greatly outnumbered, before the soldiers of France could cross the Alps. The battle of Magenta, and the still more deadly struggle at Solferino between Austria and the Allies, decided the issue, and by the beginning of July Napoleon, for the moment, was master of the situation.

The French Emperor, with characteristic duplicity, had only half revealed his hand in those confidential talks at Plombières. Italy was the cradle of his race, and he too wished to create, if not a King of Rome, a federation of small States ruled by princes of his own blood. The public rejoicings at Florence, Parma, Modena, and Bologna, and the ardent expression of the populace at such centres for union with Sardinia, made the Emperor wince, and showed him that it was impossible, even with French bayonets, to crush the aspirations of a nation. Napoleon met Francis Joseph at Villafranca, and the preliminaries of peace were arranged on July 11 in a high-handed fashion, and without even the presence of Victor Emmanuel. Lombardy was ceded to Sardinia, though Austria was allowed to keep Venetia and the fortress of Mantua. France afterwards took Nice and Savoy ; and the Grand Duke of Tuscany and the Duke of Modena were restored to power. The Treaty of Zürich ratified these terms in the month of November. Meanwhile it was officially announced that the Emperor of Austria and the Emperor of the French would ' favour the creation of an Italian Confederation under the honorary presidency of the Holy Father.'

The Countess Martinengo Cesaresco, in a brilliant book published within the last few months on ' The Liberation

of Italy,' in describing Lord John Russell's opposition
to the terms of peace at Villafranca, and the vigorous
protest which, as Foreign Minister, he made on behalf
of England, says : ' It was a happy circumstance for Italy
that her unity had no better friends than in the English
Government during those difficult years.   Cavour's words,
soon after Villafranca, " It is England's turn now,"
were not belied.'[1]   With Lord John at the Foreign
Office, England rose to the occasion.   Napoleon III.
wished to make a cat's-paw of this country, and was
sanguine enough to believe that Her Majesty's Government would take the proposed Italian Confederation
under its wing.   Lord Palmerston, Mr. Gladstone, and Lord
John Russell, were not, however, the men to bow to his
behests, and the latter in particular could scarcely conceal
his contempt for the scheme of the two emperors.   'We
are asked to propose a partition of the peoples of Italy,' he
exclaimed, 'as if we had the right to dispose of them.'

Lord John contended that if Austria, by virtue of her
presence on Italian soil, was a member of the suggested confederation, she, because of the Vatican, the King of Naples,
and the two dukes, would virtually rule the roost. He wrote to
the British Minister at Florence in favour of a frank expression on the part of the people of Tuscany of their own
wishes in the matter, and declared in the House of
Commons that he could have neither part not lot with any
attempt to deprive the people of Italy of their right to choose
their own ruler.   He protested against the presence in Italy
of foreign troops, whether French or Austrian, and in despatches to Paris and Vienna he made the French and

---

[1] *The Liberation of Italy*, 1815–1870, by the Countess Evelyn
Martinengo Cesaresco (Seeley and Co. 1895), p. 252.

Austrian Governments aware that England was altogether opposed to any return to that 'system of foreign interference which for upwards of forty years has been the misfortune of Italy and the danger of Europe.' Lord John urged that France and Austria should agree not to employ armed intervention for the future in the affairs of Italy, unless called upon to do so by the unanimous voice of the five Great Powers of Europe. He further contended that Napoleon III. should arrange with Pius IX. for the evacuation of Rome by the troops of France. He protested in vain against the annexation of Savoy and Nice by France, which he regarded as altogether a retrograde movement. In March 1860, in a speech in the House of Commons, he declared that the course which the Emperor Napoleon had taken was of a kind to produce great distrust all over Europe. He regarded the annexation of Savoy, not merely as in itself an act of aggression, but as one which was likely to 'lead a nation so warlike as the French to call upon its Government from time to time to commit other acts of aggression.' England wished to live on the most friendly terms with France. It was necessary, however, for the nations of Europe to maintain peace, to respect not merely each others' rights, but each others' boundaries, and, above all, to restore, and not to disturb that 'commercial confidence which is the result of peace, which tends to peace, and which ultimately forms the happiness of nations.' When Napoleon patched up a peace with Francis Joseph, which practically ignored the aspirations of the Italian people, their indignation knew no bounds, and they determined to work out their own redemption.

Garibaldi had already distinguished himself in the campaign which had culminated at Solferino, and he now

took the field against the Bourbons in Naples and Sicily,
whilst insurrections broke out in other parts of Italy.
France suggested that England should help her in arrest-
ing Garibaldi's victorious march, but Lord John was too
old a friend of freedom to respond to such a proposal.
He held that the Neapolitan Government—the iniquities of
which Mr. Gladstone had exposed in an outburst of righteous
indignation in 1851—must be left to reap the consequences
of 'misgovernment which had no parallel in all Europe.'
Garibaldi, carried thither by the enthusiasm of humanity
and the justice of his cause, entered Naples in triumph on
September 7, 1860, the day after the ignominious flight of
Francis II. Victor Emmanuel was proclaimed King of
Italy two days later, and when he met the new Parliament
of his widened realm at Turin he was able to declare :
' Our country is no more the Italy of the Romans, nor the
Italy of the Middle Ages : it is no longer the field for every
foreign ambition, it becomes henceforth the Italy of the
Italians.'

Lord John's part in the struggle did him infinite credit.
He held resolutely to the view all through the crisis, and
in the face of the censure of Austria, France, Prussia, and
Russia, that the Italians were the best judges of their own
interests, and that the Italian revolution was as justifiable
as the English revolution of 1688. He declared that, far
from censuring Victor Emmanuel and Count Cavour, her
Majesty's Government preferred to turn its eyes to the
' gratifying prospect of a people building up the edifice of
their liberties, and consolidating the work of their independence, amid the sympathies and good wishes of Europe.'
Foreign Courts might bluster, protest, or sneer, but England
was with her Foreign Minister ; and ' Punch ' summed up

the verdict of the nation in generous words of doggerel
verse :

> ' Well said, Johnny Russell !   That latest despatch
> You have sent to Turin is exactly the thing ;
> And again, my dear John, you come up to the scratch
> With a pluck that does credit to you and the King.'

The utmost enthusiasm prevailed in Italy when the
terms of Lord John's despatch became known.   Count
Cavour and General Garibaldi vied with each other in
emphatic acknowledgments, and Lord John was assured
that he was ' blessed night and morning by twenty millions
of Italians.'   In the summer of 1864 Garibaldi visited
England, and received a greater popular ovation in the
streets of the metropolis than that which has been accorded
to any crowned head in the Queen's reign.   He went down
to Pembroke Lodge to thank Lord John in person for the
help which he had given to Italy in the hour of her greatest
need.   Lord John received a beautiful expression of the
gratitude of the nation, in the shape of an exquisite marble
statue by Carlo Romano, representing Young Italy holding
in her outstretched arms a diadem, inscribed with the arms
of its united States.   During subsequent visits to Florence and
San Remo he was received with demonstrations of popular
respect, and at the latter place, shortly after his final retirement from office in 1866, he said, in reply to an address : ' I
thank you with all my heart for the honour you have done
me. I rejoice with you in seeing Italy free and independent,
with a monarchical government and under a patriotic king.
The Italian nation has all the elements of a prosperous
political life, which had been wanting for many centuries.
The union of religion, liberty, and civil order will increase
the prosperity of this beautiful country.'

A still more delicate problem of international policy, and one which naturally came much nearer home to English susceptibilities, arose in the autumn of 1861—a year which was rendered memorable on one side of the Atlantic by the outbreak of the Civil War, and on the other by the national sorrow over the unexpected death, at the early age of forty-two, of the Prince Consort. The latter event was not merely an overwhelming and irrevocable loss to the Queen, but in an emphatic sense a misfortune—it might almost be said a disaster—to the nation. It was not until the closing years of his life that the personal nobility and political sagacity of Prince Albert were fully recognised by the English people. Brought up in a small and narrow German Court, the Prince Consort in the early years of her Majesty's reign was somewhat formal in his manners and punctilious in his demands. The published records of the reign show that he was inclined to lean too much to the wisdom, which was not always 'profitable to direct,' of Baron Stockmar, a trusted adviser of the Court, of autocratic instincts and strong prejudices, who failed to understand either the genius of the English constitution or the temper of the English race. It is an open secret that the Prince Consort during the first decade of the reign was by no means popular, either with the classes or the masses. His position was a difficult one, for he was, in the words of one of the chief statesmen of the reign, at once the 'permanent Secretary and the permanent Prime Minister' of the Crown ; and there were undoubtedly occasions when in both capacities he magnified his office. Even if the Great Exhibition of 1851 had been memorable for nothing else, it would have been noteworthy as the period which marked a new departure in the Prince's relations with all grades of her Majesty's subjects. It not only brought him into touch with the people, but it brought into view, as well as into play, his practical mastery of affairs, and also his enlightened sympathy with the progress in art and science, no less than in the commercial activities, of the nation. It was not, however, until the closing years of his life, when the dreary escapades of the Coalition Ministry were beginning to be forgotten, that the great qualities of the Prince Consort were appreciated to any adequate degree. From the close of the Crimean War to his untimely death, at the beginning of the Civil War in America, was unquestionably the happiest as well as the most influential period in a life which was at once sensitive and upright.

It ought in common fairness to be added that the character of the Prince mellowed visibly during his later years, and that the formality of his earlier manner was exchanged for a more genial attitude towards those with whom he came in contact in the duties and society of the Court. Mr. Disraeli told Count Vitzthum that if the Prince Consort had outlived the 'old stagers' of political life with whom he was surrounded, he would have given to England —though with constitutional guarantees—the 'blessing of absolute government.' Although such a verdict palpably overshot the mark, it is significant in itself and worthy of record, since it points both to the strength and the limitations of an illustrious life. There are passages in Lady Russell's diary, of too personal and too sacred a character to quote, which reveal not only the poignant grief of the Queen, but the manner in which she turned instinctively in her burst of need to an old and trusted adviser of the Crown. High but artless tribute is paid in the same pages to the Queen's devotion to duty under the heart-breaking strain of a loss which overshadowed with sorrow every home in England, as well as the Palace at Windsor, at Christmas, 1861.

The last act of the Prince Consort of an official kind was to soften certain expressions in the interests of international peace and goodwill in the famous despatch which was sent by the English Government, at the beginning of December, to the British Ambassador at Washington, when a deadlock suddenly arose between England and the United States over the 'Trent' affair, and war seemed imminent. Hostilities had broken out between the North and the South in the previous July, and the opinion of England was sharply divided on the merits of the struggle. The bone of contention, to put the matter concisely, was the refusal of South Carolina and ten other States to submit to the authority of the Central Government of the Union. It was an old quarrel which had existed from the foundation of the American Commonwealth, for the individual States of the Union had always been jealous of any infringement of the right of self-government ; but slavery was now the ostensible root of bitterness, and matters were complicated by radical divergences on the subject of tariffs. The Southern States took a high hand against the Federal Government. They seceded from the Union, and announced their independence to the world at large, under the style and title of the Confederate States of America. Flushed by the opening victory which followed the first appeal to the sword, the Confederate Government determined to send envoys to Europe. Messrs. Mason and Slidell embarked at Havana, at the beginning of November, on board the British mail-steamer 'Trent,' as representatives to the English and French Governments respectively. The 'Trent' was stopped on her voyage by the American man-of-war 'San Jacinto,' and

Captain Wilkes, her commander, demanded that the Confederate envoys and their secretaries should be handed over to his charge. The captain of the 'Trent' made a vigorous protest against this sort of armed intervention, but he had no alternative except to yield, and Messrs. Mason and Slidell were carried back to America and lodged in a military fortress.

The 'Trent' arrived at Southampton on November 27, and when her captain told his story indignation knew no bounds. The law of nations had been set at defiance, and the right of asylum under the British flag had been violated. The clamour of the Press and of the streets grew suddenly fierce and strong, and the universal feeling of the moment found expression in the phrase, 'Bear this, bear all.' Lord John Russell at once addressed a vigorous remonstrance to the American Government on an 'act of violence which was an affront to the British flag and a violation of international law.' He made it plain that her Majesty's Ministers were not prepared to allow such an insult to pass without 'full reparation ;' but, at the same time, he refused to believe that it could be the 'deliberate intention' of the Government of the United States to force upon them so grave a question. He therefore expressed the hope that the United States of its own accord would at once 'offer to the British Government such redress as alone could satisfy the British nation.' He added that this must take the form of the liberation of the envoys and their secretaries, in order that they might again be placed under British protection, and that such an act must be accompanied by a suitable apology. President Lincoln and Mr. Seward reluctantly gave way ; but their decision was hastened by the war preparations in England, and the protests which France, Austria, Prussia, Russia, and Italy made against so wanton an outrage.

The war took its course, and it seemed on more than one occasion as if England must take sides in a struggle which, it soon became apparent, was to be fought out to the bitter end. Thoughts of mediation had occurred, both to Lord Palmerston and Lord Russell, and in 1862 they contemplated the thankless task of mediation, but the project was abandoned as at least premature.	Feeling ran high in England over the discussion as to whether the 'great domestic institution' of Negro slavery really lay at the basis of the struggle or not, and public opinion was split into hostile camps. Sympathy with the North was alienated by the marked honours which were paid to the commander of the 'San Jacinto : ' and the bravery with which the South fought, for what many people persisted in declaring was merely the right of self-government, kindled enthusiasm for those who struggled against overwhelming odds.	In the summer of 1862 a new difficulty arose, and the maintenance of international peace was once more imperilled.	The blockade of the Southern ports crippled the Confederate Government, and an armed cruiser was built on the Mersey to wage a war of retaliation on the high seas against the merchant ships of the North.	When the 'Alabama' was almost ready the Federal Government got wind of the matter, and formally protested against the ship being allowed to put to sea.

The Cabinet submitted the question to the law officers of the Crown ; delay followed, and whilst the matter was still under deliberation the 'Alabama,' on the pretext of a trial trip, escaped, and began at once her remarkable career of destruction. The late Lord Selborne, who at that time was Solicitor-General, wrote for these pages the following detailed and, of course, authoritative statement of what transpired, and the facts which he recounts show that Lord Russell, in spite of the generous admission which he himself made in his ' Recollections,' was in reality not responsible for a blunder which almost led to war, and which when submitted to arbitration at Geneva cost England—besides much irritation—the sum of 3,000,000*l*.

' It was when Lord Russell was Secretary of State for Foreign Affairs, during the American Civil War, and when I was one of the Law Officers of the Crown, that I first became personally well acquainted with him ; and from that time he honoured me with his friendship. In this way I had good opportunities of knowledge on some subjects as to which he has been at times misrepresented or misunderstood ; and perhaps I may best do honour to his memory by referring to those subjects.

' There can be no idea more unfounded than that which would call in question his friendliness towards the United States during their contest with the Confederates. But he had a strong sense, both of the duty of strictly observing all obligations incumbent on this country as a neutral Power by the law of nations, and of the danger of innovating upon them by the admission of claims on either side, not warranted by that law as generally understood, and with which, in the then state both of our own and of the American Neutrality Laws, it would have been practically impossible for the Government of a free country to comply. As a general principle, the freedom of commercial dealings between the citizens of a neutral State and belligerents, subject to the right of belligerents to protect themselves against breach of blockade or carriage of contraband, had been universally allowed, and by no nation more insisted on than by the United States. Lord Russell did not think it safe or expedient to endeavour to restrict that liberty.

When asked to put in force Acts of Parliament made for the better protection of our neutrality, he took, with promptitude and with absolute good faith, such measures as it would have been proper to take in any case in which our own public interests were concerned ; but he thought (and in my judgment he was entirely right in thinking) that it was not the duty of a British Minister, seeking to enforce British statute law, to add to other risks of failure that of unconstitutional disregard of the securities for the liberty of the subject, provided by the system on which British laws generally are administered and enforced.

'It was not through any fault or negligence of Lord Russell that the ship "Alabama," or any other vessel equipped for the war service of the Confederate States, left the ports of this country. The course taken by him in all those cases was the same. He considered that some *prima facie* evidence of an actual or intended violation either of our own law or of the law of nations (such as might be produced in a court of justice) was necessary, and that in judging whether there was such evidence he ought to be guided by the advice of the Law Officers of the Crown. To obtain such evidence, he did not neglect any means which the law placed in his power. If in any case the Board of Customs may have been ill-advised, and omitted (as Sir Alexander Cockburn thought) to take precautions which they ought otherwise to have taken, this was no fault of Lord Russell ; still less was he chargeable with the delay of three or four days which took place in the case of the " Alabama," in consequence of the illness of the Queen's Advocate, Sir John Harding ; without which that vessel might never have gone to sea.

'Lord Russell stated to Mr. Adams, immediately afterwards, that Sir John Harding's illness was the cause of that delay. No one then called that statement in question, which could not have been made without good foundation. But after a lapse of many years, when almost everybody who had known the exact circumstances was dead, stories inconsistent with it obtained currency. Of these, the most remarkable was published in 1881, in a book widely read, the " Reminiscences " of the late Thomas Mozley. The writer appears to have persuaded himself (certainly without any foundation in fact) that " there was not one of her Majesty's Ministers who was not ready to jump out of his skin for joy when he heard of the escape of the 'Alabama.' "[1] He said that he met Sir John Harding "shortly after the 'Alabama' had got away," and was told by him that he (Sir John) had been expecting a communication from Government anxiously the whole week before, that the expectation had unsettled and unnerved him for other business, and that he had stayed in chambers rather later than usual on Saturday for the chance of hearing at last from them. He had then gone to his house in the country. Returning on Monday, when he was engaged to appear in court, he found a large bundle of documents in a big envelope, without even an accompanying note, that had been dropped into the letter-box on Saturday evening. To all appearance, every letter and every remonstrance and every affidavit, as fast as it arrived from Liverpool, had been piled in a pigeon-hole till four or five o'clock on Saturday, when the Minister, on taking his own departure for the country, had directed a clerk to tie up the whole heap and carry it to Doctors' Commons.

'The facts are, that in the earlier stage of that business,

[1] Second edition, 1892, chap. xcii.

before July 23, the Attorney- and Solicitor-General only were consulted, and Sir John Harding knew nothing at all about it. No part of the statement said by Mr. Mozley to have been made to him could possibly be true ; because during the whole time in question Sir John Harding was under care for unsoundness of mind, from which he never even partially recovered, and which prevented him from attending to any kind of business, or going into court, or to his chambers, or to his country house. He was in that condition on July 23. 1862 (Wednesday, not Saturday) when the depositions on which the question of the detention of the " Alabama " turned were received at the Foreign Office. Lord Russell, not knowing that he was ill, and thinking it desirable, from the importance of the matter, to have the opinion of all the three Law Officers (of whom the Queen's Advocate was then senior in rank), sent them on the same day, with the usual covering letter, for that opinion ; and they must have been delivered by the messenger, in the ordinary course, at Sir John Harding's house or chambers. There they remained till, the delay causing inquiry, they were re- covered and sent to the Attorney-General, who received them on Monday, the 28th, and lost no time in holding a con- sultation with the Solicitor-General. Their opinion, advising that the ship should be stopped, was in Lord Russell's hands early the next morning ; and he sent an order by telegraph to Liverpool to stop her ; but before it could be executed she had gone to sea.

'Some of the facts relating to Sir John Harding's illness remained, until lately, in more or less obscurity, and Mr. Mozley's was not the only erroneous version of them which got abroad. One such version having been mentioned, as if authentic, in a debate in the House of Commons on

March 17, 1893, I wrote to the " Times " to correct it ; and in confirmation of my statement the gentleman who had been Sir John Harding's medical attendant in July 1862 came forward, and by reference to his diary, kept at the time, placed the facts and dates beyond future controversy.

'In the diplomatic correspondence, as to the " Alabama " and other subjects of complaint by the United States, Lord Russell stood firmly upon the ground that Great Britain had not failed in any duty of neutrality ; and Lord Lyons, the sagacious Minister who then represented this country at Washington, thought there would be much more danger to our future relations with the United States in any departure from that position than in strict and steady adherence to it. But no sooner was the war ended than new currents of opinion set in. In a debate on the subject in the House of Commons on March 6, 1868, Lord Stanley (then Foreign Secretary), who had never been of the same mind about it with his less cautious friends, said that a " tendency might be de- tected to be almost too ready to accuse ourselves of faults we had not committed, and to assume that on every doubtful point the decision ought to be against us." The sequel is well known. The Conservative Government consented to refer to arbitration, not all the questions raised by the Government of the United States, but those arising out of the ships alleged to have been equipped or to have received augmentation of force within the British dominions for the war service of the Confederate States ; and from that concession no other Government could recede. For a long time the Government or the Senate of the United States objected to any re- ference so limited, and to the last they refused to go into an open arbitration. They made it a condition, that new Rules should be formulated, not only for future observance, but for retrospective application to their own claims. This condition, unprecedented and open in principle to the gravest objections, was accepted for the sake of peace with a nation so nearly allied to us ; not, however, without an express declaration, on the face of the Treaty of Washington, that the British Government could not assent to those new Rules as a statement of principles of international law which were in force when the claims arose.

' While the Commissioners at Washington were engaged in their deliberations, I was in frequent communication both with Lord Granville and other members of the Cabinet, and also with Lord Russell, who could not be brought to approve of that way of settling the controversy. He had an invincible repugnance to the reference of any questions affecting the honour and good faith of this country, or its internal administration, to foreign arbitrators ; and he thought those questions would not be excluded by the proposed arrangement. He felt no confidence that any reciprocal advantages to this country would be obtained from the new Rules. Their only effect, in his view, would be to send us handicapped into the arbitration. He did not believe that the United States would follow the example which we had set, by strengthening their Neutrality Laws ; or that they would be able, unless they did so, to prevent violations of the Rules by their citizens in any future war in which we might be belligerent and they neutral, any more than they had been able in former times to prevent the equipment of ships within their territory against Spain and Portugal. It was not without difficulty that he restrained himself from giving public expression to those views ; but, from generous and patriotic motives, he did so. The sequel is not likely to have convinced him that his apprehensions were groundless. The character of the " Case" presented on the part of the United States, with the "indirect claims," and the arguments used to support them, would have prevented the arbitration from proceeding at all, but for action of an unusual kind taken by the arbitrators. In such of their decisions as were adverse to this country, the arbitrators founded themselves entirely upon the new Rules, without any reference to general international law or historical precedents ; and the United States have done nothing. down to this day, to strengthen their Neutrality Laws, though certainly requiring it, at least as much as ours did before 1870.'

Lord Russell then held resolutely to the view that her Majesty's Government had steadily endeavoured to maintain a policy of strict neutrality, and so long as he was in power at the Foreign Office, or at the Treasury, the demands of the United States for compensation were ignored. Meanwhile, there arose a mighty famine in Lancashire through the failure of the cotton supply, and 800,000 operatives were thrown, through no fault of their own, on the charity of the nation, which rose splendidly to meet the occasion. All classes of the community were bound more closely together in the gentle task of philanthropy, as well as in admiration of the uncomplaining heroism with which privation was met by the suffering workpeople.

CHAPTER XVI

SECOND PREMIERSHIP

1865–1866

The Polish Revolt—Bismarck's bid for power—The Schleswig-Holstein
difficulty—Death of Lord Palmerston—The Queen summons Lord
John—The second Russell Administration—Lord John's tribute to
Palmerston—Mr. Gladstone introduces Reform—The 'Cave of
Adullam'—Defeat of the Russell Government—The people accept
Lowe's challenge—The feeling in the country.

LORD JOHN, in his conduct of foreign affairs, acted with
generosity towards Italy and with mingled firmness and
patience towards America. It was a fortunate circumstance,
for the great interests at stake on both sides of the Atlantic,
that a man of so much judgment and right feeling was in
power at a moment when prejudice was strong and passion
ran high. Grote, who was by no means consumed with enthusiasm for the Palmerston Government, did not conceal
his admiration of Lord John's sagacity at this crisis. 'The
perfect neutrality of England in the destructive civil war
now raging in America appears to me almost a phenomenon
in political history. No such forbearance has been shown
during the political history of the last two centuries. It is
the single case in which the English Government and
public, generally so meddlesome, have displayed most
prudent and commendable forbearance in spite of great

temptations to the contrary.' Lord John had opinions, and the courage of them ; but at the same time he showed himself fully alive to the fact that no greater calamity could possibly overtake the English-speaking race than a war between England and the United States.

Europe was filled at the beginning of 1863 with tidings of a renewed Polish revolt. Russia provoked the outbreak by the stern measures which had been taken in the previous year to repress the growing discontent of the people. The conspiracy was too widespread and too deep-rooted for Alexander II. to deal with, except by concessions to national sentiment, which he was not prepared to make, and, therefore, he fell back on despotic use of power. All able-bodied men suspected of revolutionary tendencies were marked out for service in the Russian army, and in this way, in Lord John's words, the ' so-called conscription was turned into a proscription.' The lot was made to fall on all political suspects, who were to be condemned for life to follow the hated Russian flag. The result was not merely armed resistance, but civil war. Poland, in her struggle for liberty, was joined by Lithuania ; but Prussia came to the help of the Czar, and the protests of England, France, and Austria were of no avail. Before the year ended the dreams of self-government in Poland, after months of bloodshed and cruelty, were again ruthlessly dispelled.

One diplomatic difficulty followed another in quick succession. Bismarck was beginning to move the pawns on the chess-board of Europe. He had conciliated Russia by taking sides with her against the Poles in spite of the attitude of London, Paris, and Vienna. He feared the spirit of insurrection would spread to the Poles in

Prussia, and had no sympathy with the aspirations of oppressed nationalities. His policy was to make Prussia strong—if need be by 'blood and iron'—so that she might become mistress of Germany. The death of Frederick VII. of Denmark provoked a fresh crisis and revived in an acute form the question of succession to the duchies of Schleswig-Holstein. The Treaty of London in 1852 was supposed to have settled the question, and its terms had been accepted by Austria and Prussia. The integrity of Denmark was recognised, and Prince Christian of Glucksburg was accepted as heir-presumptive of the reigning king. The German Diet did not regard this arrangement as binding, and the feeling in the duchies themselves, especially in Holstein, was against the claims of Denmark. But the Hereditary Prince Frederick of Augustenburg disputed the right of Christian IX. to the Duchies, and Bismarck induced Austria to join Prussia in the occupation of the disputed territory.

It is impossible to enter here into the merits of the quarrel, much less to describe the course of the struggle or the complicated diplomatic negotiations which grew out of it. Denmark undoubtedly imagined that the energetic protest of the English Government against her dismemberment would not end in mere words. The language used by both Lord Palmerston and Lord John Russell was of a kind to encourage the idea of the adoption, in the last extremity, of another policy than that of non-intervention. Bismarck, on the other hand, it has been said with truth, had taken up the cause of Schleswig-Holstein, not in the interest of its inhabitants, but in the interests of Germany, and by Germany he meant the Government of Berlin and the House of Hohenzollern. He represented not merely other ideas, but other methods than those which prevailed with statesmen who were old enough to recall the wars of Napoleon and the partition of Europe to which they gave rise. It must be admitted that England did not show to advantage in the Schleswig-Holstein difficulty, in spite of the soundness of her counsels; and Bismarck's triumph in the affair was as complete as the policy on which it was based was bold and adroit. Lord Palmerston and Lord John were embarrassed on the one hand by the apathy of Russia and France and on the other by the cautious, not to say timid, attitude of their own colleagues. 'As to Cabinets,' wrote Lord Palmerston, with dry humour, in reply to a note in which Lord John hinted that if the Prime Minister and himself had been given a free hand they could have kept Austria from war with Denmark, 'if we had had colleagues like those who sat in Pitt's Cabinet, such as Westmoreland and others, or such men as those who were with Peel, like Goulburn and Hardinge, you and I might have had our own way in most things. But when, as is now the case, able men fill every department, such men will have opinions and hold to them. Unfortunately, they are often too busy with their own department to follow up foreign questions so as to be fully masters of them, and their conclusions are generally on the timid side of what might be the best.'[1]

Lord John wrote to Foreign Courts—was Mr. Bagehot's shrewd criticism—much in the same manner as he was accustomed to speak in the House of Commons. In other words, he used great plainness of speech, and,

---

[1] *Life and Correspondence of Viscount Palmerston*, by the Hon. Evelyn Ashley, vol. ii. p. 438.

because of the very desire to make his meaning clear, he,
was occasionally indiscreetly explicit and even brusque.
Sometimes it happened that the intelligent foreigner grew
critical at Lord John's expense. Count Vitzthum, for example, laid stress on the fact that Lord John 'looked on the
British Constitution as an inimitable masterpiece,' which
less-favoured nations ought not only to admire but adopt,
if they wished to advance and go forward in the direction
of liberty, prosperity, and peace. There was just enough
truth in such assertions to render them amusing, though
not enough to give them a sting. There were times when
Lord John was the 'stormy petrel' of foreign politics, but
there never was a time when he ceased to labour in season
and out for what he believed to be the honour of England.
'I do not believe that any English foreign statesman, who
does his duty faithfully by his own countrymen in difficult
circumstances, can escape the blame of foreign statesmen,'
were his own words, and he assuredly came in for his full
share of abuse in Europe. One of Lord John Russell's
subordinates at the Foreign Office, well known and distinguished in the political life of to-day, declares that Lord
John, like Lord Clarendon, was accustomed to write many
drafts of despatches with his own hand, but as a rule did not
go with equal minuteness into the detail of the work. It
sometimes happened that he would take sudden resolutions
without adequate consideration of the points involved ; but
he would always listen patiently to objections, and when
convinced that he was wrong was perfectly willing to
modify his opinion. In most cases, however, Lord John
did not make up his mind without due reflection, and
under such circumstances he showed no vacillation. No
tidings from abroad, however startling or unpleasant, seemed

able to disturb his equanimity.   He was an extremely considerate chief, but, though always willing to listen to his subordinates, kept his own counsel and seldom took them much into his confidence.

The year 1865 was rendered memorable both in England and America by the death of statesmen of the first rank. In the spring, that great master of reason and economic reform, Richard Cobden, died in London, after a few days' illness, in the prime of life ; and almost before the nation realised the greatness of such a loss, tidings came across the Atlantic that President Abraham Lincoln had been assassinated at Washington, in the hour of triumph, by a cowardly fanatic. The summer in England was made restless by a General Election. Though Bright denounced Lord Palmerston, and Mr. Gladstone lost his seat at Oxford, to stand 'unmuzzled' a few days later before the electors of South-West Lancashire, the predicted Conservative reaction was not an accomplished fact.   Lord Palmerston's ascendency in the country, though diminished, was still great, and the magic of his name carried the election. 'It is clear,' wrote Lord John to the plucky octogenarian Premier, when the latter, some time before the contest, made a fighting speech in the country, 'that your popularity is a plant of hardy growth and deep roots.' Quite suddenly, in the spring of 1865, Lord Palmerston began to look as old as his years, and as the summer slipped past, it became apparent that the buoyant elasticity of temperament had vanished. On October 18 the great Minister died in harness, and Lord John Russell, who was only eight years younger, was called to the helm.

The two men, more than once in mid-career, had serious misunderstandings, and envious lips had done their best to widen their differences. It is pleasant to think now that Palmerston and Russell were on cordial and intimate terms during the critical six years, when the former held for the last time the post of First Minister of the Crown, and the latter was responsible for Foreign Affairs. It is true that they were not of one mind on the question of Parliamentary Reform ; but Lord John, after 1860 at least, was content to waive that question, for he saw that the nation, as well as the Prime Minister, was opposed to a forward movement in that direction, and the strain of war abroad and famine at home hindered the calm discussion of constitutional problems. Lord Lyttelton used to say that Palmerston was regarded as a Whig because he belonged to Lord Grey's Government, and had always thrown in his lot with that statesman's political posterity. At the same time, Lord Lyttelton held—even as late as 1865 – that a 'more genuine Conservative, especially in home affairs, it would not be easy to find.' Palmerston gave Lord John Russell his active support in the attitude which the latter took up at the Foreign Office on all the great questions which arose, sometimes in a sudden and dramatic form, at a period when the power of Napoleon III., in spite of theatrical display, was declining, and Bismarck was shaping with consummate skill the fortunes of Germany.

The day after Palmerston's death her Majesty wrote in the following terms to Lord John : 'The melancholy news of Lord Palmerston's death reached the Queen last night. This is another link with the past that is broken, and the Queen feels deeply in her desolate and isolated condition how, one by one, tried servants and advisers are taken from her. . . . The Queen can turn to no other than Lord Russell, an old and tried friend of hers, to undertake the arduous duties of Prime Minister, and to carry on the Government.' Such a command was met by Lord John with the response that he was willing to act if his colleagues were prepared to serve under him. Mr. Gladstone's position in the country and in the councils of the Liberal Party had been greatly strengthened by his rejection at Oxford, and by the subsequent boldness and fervour of his speeches in Lancashire. He forestalled Lord John's letter by offering, in a frank and generous spirit, to serve under the old Liberal leader. Mr. Gladstone declared that he was quite willing to take his chance under Lord John's 'banner,' and to continue his services as Chancellor of the Exchequer. This offer was of course accepted, and Mr. Gladstone also took Lord Palmerston's place as Leader of the House of Commons. Lord Cranworth became Lord Chancellor, Lord Clarendon took Lord John's place at the Foreign Office, the Duke of Argyll and Sir George Grey resumed their old positions as Lord Privy Seal and Home Secretary. After a short interval, Mr. Goschen and Lord Hartington were raised to Cabinet rank ; while Mr. Forster, Lord Dufferin, and Mr. Stansfeld became respectively Under-Secretaries for the Colonies, War, and India ; but Lord John, in spite of strong pressure, refused to admit Mr. Lowe to his Cabinet.

At the Lord Mayor's banquet in November, Lord John took occasion to pay a warm tribute to Palmerston : ' It is a great loss indeed, because he was a man qualified to conduct the country successfully through all the vicissitudes of war and peace.' He declared that Lord Palmerston displayed resolution, resource, promptitude, and vigour in the conduct of foreign affairs, showed himself also able to maintain internal tranquillity, and, by extending commercial relation-

ships, to give to the country the ' whole fruits of the blessings
of peace.'   He added that Lord Palmerston's heart never
ceased to beat for the honour of England, and that his mind
comprehended and his experience embraced the whole field
which is covered by the interests of the nation.

The new Premier made no secret of his conviction that, if
the Ministry was to last, it must be either frankly Liberal or
frankly Conservative.   As he had the chief voice in the
matter, and was bent on a new Reform Bill, it became, after
certain changes had been effected, much more progressive
than was possible under Palmerston.   Parliament was
opened on February 1, 1866, by the Queen in person, for
the first time since the death of the Prince Consort, and
the chief point of interest in the Speech from the Throne
was the guarded promise of a Reform Bill.   The attention
of Parliament was to be called to information concerning the
right of voting with a view to such improvements as might
tend to strengthen our free institutions and conduce to
the public welfare.   Lord John determined to make haste
slowly, for some of his colleagues were hardly inclined to
make haste at all, since they shared Lord Palmerston's
views on the subject and distrusted the Radical cry which
had arisen since the industrial revolution.   The Premier
and Mr. Gladstone—for they were a kind of Committee
of Two—were content for the moment to propose a
revision of the franchise, and to leave in ambush for another
session the vexed question involved in a redistribution of
seats.   'It was decided,' states Lord John, 'that it would
be best to separate the question of the franchise from that
of the disfranchisement of boroughs.   After much inquiry,
we agreed to fix the suffrages of boroughs at an occupation
of 7*l.* value.'

The House of Commons was densely packed when Mr. Gladstone introduced the measure on March 12, but, in spite of his powers of exposition and infectious enthusiasm, the Government proposals fell undeniably flat. Broadly stated, they were as follows. The county franchise was to be dropped to 14*l.*, and that of the borough, as already stated, to half that amount, whilst compound householders and lodgers paying 10*l.* a year were to possess votes. It was computed at the time that the measure would add four hundred thousand new voters to the existing lists, and that two hundred thousand of these would belong to what Lord John termed the 'best of the working classes.' Mr. Bright, and those whom he represented, not only in Birmingham, but also in every great city and town in the land, gave their support to the Government, on the principle that this was at least an 'honest' measure, and that half a loaf, moreover, was better than no bread. At the same time the country was not greatly stirred one way or another by the scheme, though it stirred to panic-stricken indignation men of the stamp of Mr. Lowe, Mr. Horsman, Lord Elcho, Earl Grosvenor, Lord Dunkellin, and other so-called, but very indifferent, Liberals, who had attached themselves to the party under Lord Palmerston's happy-go-lucky and easy auspices. These were the men who presently distinguished themselves, and extinguished the Russell Administration by their ridiculous fear of the democracy. They retired into what Mr. Bright termed the 'political cave of Adullam,' and, as Lord John said, the 'timid, the selfish, and those who were both selfish and timid' joined the sorry company.

The Conservatives saw their opportunity, and, being human, took it. Lord Grosvenor brought forward an amendment calling attention to the omission of a redistribution scheme. A debate, which occupied eight nights, followed, and when it was in progress, Mr. Gladstone, in defending his own conduct as Leader of the House, incidentally paid an impressive tribute to the memorable and protracted services in the Commons of Lord John :—

'If, sir, I had been the man who, at the very outset of his career, wellnigh half a century ago, had with an almost prophetic foresight fastened upon two great groups of questions, those great historic questions relating to the removal of civil disabilities for religious opinions and to Parliamentary Reform ; if I had been the man who, having thus in his early youth, in the very first stage of his political career, fixed upon those questions and made them his own, then went on to prosecute them with sure and unflagging instinct until the triumph in each case had been achieved ; if I had been the man whose name had been associated for forty years, and often in the very first place of eminence, with every element of beneficent legislation—in other words, had I been Earl Russell, then there might have been some temptation to pass into excess on the exercise of authority, and some excuse for the endeavour to apply to this House a pressure in itself unjustifiable. But, sir, I am not Earl Russell.'

In the end, Lord Grosvenor's amendment was lost by a majority equal only to the fingers of one hand. Such an unmistakeable expression of opinion could not be disregarded, and the Government brought in a Redistribution of Seats Bill at the beginning of May. They proposed that thirty boroughs having a population of less than eight thousand should be deprived of one member, whilst nineteen other seats were obtained by joint representation in smaller boroughs. After running the gauntlet of much hostile criticism, the bill was read a second time, but the Government were forced to refer it and the franchise scheme to a committee, which was empowered to deal with both schemes. Lord Stanley, Mr. Ward Hunt, and Mr. Walpole assailed with successive motions, which were more or less narrowly rejected, various points in the Government proposals, and the opposition grew more and more stubborn. At length Lord Dunkellin (son of the Earl of Clanricarde) moved to substitute rating for rental in the boroughs ; and the Government, in a House of six hundred and nineteen members, were defeated on June 18 by a majority of eleven. The excitement which met this announcement was extraordinary, and when it was followed next day by tidings that the Russell Administration was at an end, those who thought that the country cared little about the question found themselves suddenly disillusioned.

Burke declared that there were moments when it became necessary for the people themselves to interpose on behalf of their rights. The overthrow of the Russell Administration took the nation by surprise. Three days after Lord John's resignation there was a historic gathering in Trafalgar Square. In his speech announcing the resignation of his Ministry, Lord John warned Parliament about the danger of alienating the sympathy of the people from the Crown and the aristocracy. He reminded the Peers that universal suffrage prevailed not only in the United States but in our own Colonies ; and he took his stand in the light of the larger needs of the new era, on the assertion of Lord Grey at the time of the Reform Bill that only a large measure was a safe measure. 'We have made the attempt,' added Lord John, 'sincerely and anxiously to perform the duties of reconciling that which is due to the Constitution of the country with that which is due to the growing intelligence, the increasing wealth, and the manifest forbearance, virtue, and order of the people.' He protested against a niggardly and ungenerous treatment of so momentous a question.

Lord Russell's words were not lost on Mr. Bradlaugh. He made them the text of his speech to the twenty thousand people who assembled in Trafalgar Square, and afterwards walked in procession to give Mr. Gladstone an ovation in Carlton House Terrace. About three weeks later another great demonstration was announced to take place in Hyde Park, under the auspices of the Reform League. The authorities refused to allow the gathering, and, after a formal protest, the meeting was held at the former rendezvous. The mixed multitude who had followed the procession to the Park gates took the repulse less calmly, with the result that, as much by accident as by design, the Park railings for the space of half a mile were thrown down. Force is no remedy, but a little of it is sometimes a good object-lesson, and the panic which this unpremeditated display occasioned amongst the valiant defenders of law and order was unmistakeable.

Mr. Lowe had flouted the people, and had publicly asserted that those who were without the franchise did not really care to possess it. Forty-three other so-called Liberals in the House of Commons were apparently of the same way of thinking, for the Russell Administration was defeated by forty-four ' Liberal ' votes. This in itself shows that Lord John, up to the hour in which he was driven from power, was far in advance of one section of his followers. The great towns, and more particularly Birmingham, Manchester, and Leeds, promptly took up the challenge ; and in those three centres alone half a million of people assembled

to make energetic protest against the contemptuous dismissal
of their claims. The fall of the Park railings appealed to
the fear of the classes, and aroused the enthusiasm of the
masses. It is scarcely too much to say that if they had been
demolished a month earlier the Russell Government would
have carried its Reform proposals, and Disraeli would have
lost his chance of 'dishing the Whigs.' The defeat of
Lord John Russell was a virtual triumph. He was driven
from power by a rally of reactionary forces at the very
moment when he was fighting the battle of the people.[1] The
Tories were only able to hold their own by borrowing a leaf
from his book, and bringing in a more drastic measure of
reform.

[1] In a letter written in the spring of 1867, Lord Houghton refers to
Mr. Gladstone as being ' quite awed ' for the moment by the ' diabolical
cleverness of Dizzy.' He adds : ' Delane says the extreme party for
Reform are now the grandees, and that the Dukes are quite ready to
follow Beale into Hyde Park.'— *The Life, Letters, and Friendships of
Lord Houghton*, by Sir Wemyss Reid, vol. ii. pp. 174–5.

CHAPTER XVII

OUT OF HARNESS

1867-1874

Speeches in the House of Lords—Leisured years—Mr. Lecky's reminiscences—The question of the Irish Church—The Independence of Belgium—Lord John on the claims of the Vatican—Letters to Mr. Chichester Fortescue—His scheme for the better government of Ireland—Lord Selborne's estimate of Lord John's public career—Frank admissions—As his private secretaries saw him.

LORD JOHN never relinquished that high sense of responsibility which was conspicuous in his attitude as a Minister of the Crown. Although out of harness from the summer of 1866 to his death, twelve years later, he retained to the last, undiminished, the sense of public duty. He took, not merely a keen interest, but an appreciable share in public affairs ; and some of the speeches which he delivered in the House of Lords after his retirement from office show how vigorous and acute his intellect remained, and how wide and generous were his sympathies. The leisured years which came to Lord John after the fall of the second Russell Administration enabled him to renew old friendships, and gave him the opportunity for making the acquaintance of distinguished men of a younger generation. His own historical studies—the literary passion of a lifetime—made him keenly appreciative of the work of others in that direction, and kindred tastes drew him into intimate relations with

Mr. W. E. H. Lecky. Few of the reminiscences, great or small, which have been written for these pages, can compare in interest with the following statement by so philosophic a critic of public affairs and so acute a judge of men :—

'It was, I think, in 1866, and in the house of Dean Milman, that I had the privilege of being introduced to Lord Russell. He at once received me with a warmth and kindness I can never forget, and from this time till near the end of his life I saw him very frequently. His Ministerial career had just terminated, but I could trace no failure in his powers, and, whatever difference of opinion there might be about his public career, no one, I believe, who ever came in contact with him failed to recognise his singular charm in private life. His conversation differed from that of some of the more illustrious of his contemporaries. It was not a copious and brilliant stream of words, dazzling, astonishing, or overpowering. It had no tendency to monologue, and it was not remarkable for any striking originalities either of language, metaphor, or thought. Few men steered more clear of paradox, and the charm of his talk lay mainly in his admirable terseness and clearness of expression, in the skill with which, by a few happy words, he could tell a story, or etch out a character, or condense an argument or statement. Beyond all men I have ever known, he had the gift of seizing rapidly in every question the central argument, the essential fact or distinction ; and of all his mental characteristics, quickness and soundness of judgment seemed to me the most conspicuous. I have never met with anyone with whom it was so possible to discuss with profit many great questions in a short time. No one, too, could know him intimately without being impressed with his high sense of honour, with his transparent purity of motive, with the fundamental kindliness of his disposition, with the remarkable modesty of his estimate of his own past. He was eminently tolerant of difference of opinion, and he had in private life an imperturbable sweetness of temper that set those about him completely at their ease, and helped much to make them talk their best. Few men had more anecdotes, and no one told them better—tersely, accurately, with a quiet, subdued humour, with a lightness of touch which I should not have expected from his writings. In addition to the experiences of a long and eventful life, his mind was stored with the anecdotes of the brilliant Whig society of Holland House, of which he was one of the last repositories. It is much to be regretted that he did not write down his " Recollections " till a period of life when his once admirable memory was manifestly failing. He was himself sadly conscious of the failure. " I used never to confuse my facts," he once said to me ; " I now find that I am beginning to do so."

' He has mentioned in his " Recollections " as one of the great felicities of his life that he retained the friendship of his leading opponents, and his private conversation fully supported this view. Of Sir Robert Peel he always spoke with a special respect, and it was, I think, a matter of peculiar pleasure to him that in his old age his family was closely connected by marriage with that of his illustrious rival. His friendship with Lord Derby, which began when they were colleagues, was unbroken by many contests. He spoke of him, however, as a man of brilliant talent, who had not the judgment or the character suited for the first place ; and he maintained that he had done much better both under Lord Grey and under Sir Robert Peel than as Prime Minister. Between Lord Russell and Disraeli there was, I believe, on both sides much kindly feeling, though no two men could be less like, and though there was much in Disraeli's ways of looking at things that must have been peculiarly trying to the Whig mind. Lord Russell told me that he once described him in Parliament by quoting the lines of Dryden :—

> 'He was not one on picking work to dwell.
> He fagotted his notions as they fell ;
> And if they rhymed and rattled, all was well.'

'Of his early chiefs, he used to speak with most reverence of Lord Grey. Lord Melbourne, he said, greatly injured his Government by the manner in which he treated deputations. He never could resist the temptation of bantering and snubbing them. Two men who flourished in his youth surpassed, Lord Russell thought, in eloquence any of the later generation. They were Canning and Plunket, and as an orator the greater of these was Plunket. Among the statesmen of a former generation, he had an especial admiration for Walpole, and was accustomed to maintain that he was a much greater statesman than Pitt. His judgment, indeed, of Pitt always seemed to me much warped by that adoration of Fox which in the early years of the century was almost an article of religion in Whig circles. Lord Russell had also the true Whig reverence for William III., and, I am afraid, he was by no means satisfied with some pages I wrote about that sovereign.

'Speaking of Lord Palmerston, I once said to him that I was struck with the small net result in legislation which he accomplished considering the many years he was in power. "But during all these years," Lord Russell replied, "he kept the honour of England very high ; and I think that a great thing."

'The Imperialist sentiment was one of the deepest in
his nature, and few things exasperated him more than the
school which was advocating the surrender of India and
the Colonies. "When I was young," he once said to me,
"it was thought the work of a wise statesman that he had
turned a small kingdom into a great empire.   In my old age
it seems to be thought the object of a statesman to turn a
great empire into a small kingdom."   He thought we
had made a grave mistake, when conceding self-government
to the Colonies, in not reserving the waste lands and free
trade with the Mother Country ; and he considered that
the right of veto on legislation, which had been reserved,
ought to have been always exercised (as he said it was
under Lord Grey) when duties were imposed on English
goods.   In Irish politics he greatly blamed Canning, who
agreed with the Whigs about Catholic Emancipation, though
he differed from them about Reform.   The former question,
he said, was then by far the more pressing, and if Canning
had insisted on making it a first-class ministerial question he
would have carried it in conjunction with the Whigs.   "My
pride in Irish measures," he once wrote to me, " is in the
Poor Law, which I designed, framed, and twice carried."
Like Peel, he strongly maintained that the priests ought to
have been paid.   He would gladly have seen the principle
of religious equality in Ireland carried to its furthest consequences, and local government considerably extended ;
but he told me that any statesman who proposed to repeal
the Union ought to be impeached, and in his "Recollections,"
and in one of his published letters to the present Lord
Carlingford, he has expressed in the strongest terms his
inflexible hostility to Home Rule.

'Though the steadiest of Whigs, Lord Russell was by no

means an uncompromising democrat. The great misfortune, he said, of America was that the influence of Jefferson had eclipsed that of Washington. One of her chief advantages was that the Western States furnished a wide and harmless field for restless energy and ambition. In England he was very anxious that progress should move on the lines of the past, and he was under the impression that statesmen of the present generation studied English history less than their predecessors. He was one of the earliest advocates of the Minority Vote, and he certainly looked with very considerable apprehension to the effects of the Democratic Reform Bill of 1867. He said to me that he feared there was too much truth in the saying of one of his friends that " the concessions of the Whigs were once concessions to intelligence, but now concessions to ignorance."

'When the Education Act was carried, he was strongly in favour of the introduction of the Bible, accompanied by purely undenominational teaching. This was, I think, one of his last important declarations on public policy. I recollect a scathing article in the " Saturday Review," demonstrating the absurdity of supposing that such teaching was possible. But the people of England took a different view. The great majority of the School Boards adopted the system which Lord Russell recommended, and it prevailed with almost perfect harmony for more than twenty years.

'In foreign politics he looked with peculiar pleasure to the services he had rendered to the Italian cause. Italy was always very dear to him. He had many valued friends there, and he spoke Italian (as he also did Spanish) with much fluency. Among my most vivid recollections are those of some happy days I spent with him at San Remo.'

Two years before the disestablishment of the Irish Church, Lord John Russell, knowing how great a stumbling-block its privileges were to the progress of the people, moved for a Commission to inquire into the expenditure of its revenues. The investigation was, however, staved off, and the larger question was, in consequence, hastened. He supported Mr. Gladstone in a powerful speech in 1870, and showed himself in substantial agreement with Mr. Forster over his great scheme of education, though he thought that some of its provisions bore heavily upon Nonconformists. The outbreak of war between France and Germany seemed at first to threaten the interests of England, and Lord John introduced a Militia Bill, which was only withdrawn when the Government promised to take action. The interests of Belgium were threatened by the struggle on the Continent, and Lord John took occasion to remind the nation that we were bound to defend that country, and had guaranteed by treaty to uphold its independence : —

' . . . I am persuaded that if it is once manfully declared that England means to stand by her treaties, to perform her engagements—that her honour and her interest would allow nothing else— such a declaration would check the greater part of these intrigues, and that neither France nor Prussia would wish to add a second enemy to the formidable foe which each has to meet. . . . When the choice is between honour and infamy, I cannot doubt that her Majesty's Government will pursue the course of honour, the only one worthy of the British people. . . . I consider that if England shrank from the performance of her engagements— if she acted in a faithless manner with respect to this matter —her extinction as a Great Power must very soon follow.'

Lord John's vigorous protest did not go unheeded, and

the King of the Belgians sent him an autograph letter in acknowledgment of his generous and opportune words. On the other hand, Lord John Russell resented the determination of Mr. Gladstone to submit the ' Alabama ' claims to arbitration, and also opposed the adoption of the Ballot and the abolition of purchase in the Army. The conflict which arose in the autumn of 1872 between the Emperor of Germany and Pius IX. was a matter which appealed to all lovers of liberty of conscience. Lord John, though now in his eighty-second year, rose promptly to the occasion, and promised to preside at a great public meeting in London, called to protest against the claims of the Vatican. At the last moment, though the spirit was willing, the flesh was weak, and, yielding to medical advice, he contented himself with a written expression of sympathy. This was read to the meeting, and brought him the thanks of the Kaiser and Prince Bismarck. Lord John's letters, declared Mr. Kinglake seem to carry with them the very ring of his voice ; and the one which was written from Pembroke Lodge on January 19, 1874, was full of the old fire of enthusiasm and the resolution which springs from clean-cut convictions :—
' I hasten to declare with all friends of freedom, and I trust with the great majority of the English nation, that I could no longer call myself a lover of civil and religious liberty were I not to proclaim my sympathy with the Emperor of Germany in the noble struggle in which he is engaged.'

Lord John Russell's pamphlets, published in 1868-9—in the shape of letters to Mr. Chichester Fortescue—show that in old age and out of office he was still anxious to see justice done to the legitimate demands of Ireland. He declared that he witnessed with alarm the attempt to involve the whole Irish nation in a charge of disaffection, conspiracy, and treason.   He contended that Englishmen ought to seek to rid their minds of exaggerated fears and national animosities, so that they might be in a position to consider patiently all the facts of the case.   'We ought to weigh with care the complaints that are made, and examine with still more care and circumspection the remedies that are proposed, lest in our attempts to cure the disease we give the patient a new and more dangerous disorder.'   In his 'Life of Fox' Lord John Russell maintained that the wisest system that could be devised for the conciliation of Ireland had yet to be discovered ; and in his third letter to Mr. Chichester Fortescue, published in January 1869, he made a remarkable allusion to Mr. Gladstone as a statesman who might yet seek to 'perform a permanent and immortal service to his country' by endeavouring to reconcile England and Ireland. If, added Lord John, Mr. Gladstone should 'undertake the heroic task of riveting the union of the three kingdoms by affection, even more than by statute ; if he should endeavour to efface the stains which proscription and prejudice have affixed on the fair fame of Great Britain, then, though he may not reunite his party . . . he will be enrolled among the noblest of England's statesmen, and will have laid the foundations of a great work, which either he or a younger generation will not fail to accomplish.'

The proposals Lord John Russell made in the columns of the 'Times,' on August 9, 1872, for the better government of Ireland have been claimed as a tentative scheme of Home Rule. 'It appears to me, that if Ireland were to be allowed to elect a representative assembly for each of its four provinces of Leinster, Ulster, Munster, and Connaught, and if Scotland in a similar manner were to be divided into Lowlands and Highlands, having for each province a representative assembly, the local wants of Ireland and Scotland might be better provided for than they are at present.' Lord John went on to say that the Imperial Parliament might still retain its hold over local legislation, and added that it was his purpose to explain in a pamphlet a policy which he thought might be adopted to the 'satisfaction of the nation at large.' The pamphlet, however, remained unwritten, and the scheme in its fulness, therefore, was never explained. Evidently Lord Russell's mind was changing in its attitude towards the Irish problem; but, as Mr. Lecky points out in the personal reminiscences with which he has enriched these pages, though in advance of the opinion of the hour he was not prepared to accept the principle of Home Rule. Although Mr. Lecky does not mention the year in which Lord John declared that any statesman who 'proposed to repeal the Union ought to be impeached,' Lord Russell himself in his published 'Recollections' admits that he saw no hope that Ireland would be well and quietly governed by the adoption of Home Rule. In fact, he makes it quite clear that he was in sympathy with the view which Lord Althorp expressed when O'Connell demanded the repeal of the Union—namely, that such a request amounted to a dismemberment of the Empire. On the other hand, Lord John was wont in his latest years to discuss the question in all its bearings with an Irish representative who held opposite views. There can be no doubt that he was feeling his way to a more generous interpretation of the problem than that which is commonly attributed to him. His own words on this point are : 'I should have been very glad if the leaders of popular opinion in Ireland had so modified and mollified their demand for Home Rule as to make it consistent with the unity of the Empire.' His mind, till within a few years of his death, was clear, and did not stand still. Whether he would have gradually become a Home Ruler is open to question, but in 1874 he had gone quite as far in that direction as Mr. Gladstone.

Lord John, though the most loyal of subjects, made it plain throughout his career that he was not in the least degree a courtier. His nephew, Mr. George Russell, after stating that Lord John supported, with voice and vote, Mr. Hume's motion for the revision of the Civil List under George IV., and urged in vigorous terms the restoration of Queen Caroline's name to the Liturgy, as well as subscribing to compensate an officer, friendly to the Queen, whom the King's animosity had driven from the army, adds : 'It may well be that some tradition of this early independence, or some playful desire to test the fibre of Whiggery by putting an extreme case, led in much later years to an embarrassing question by an illustrious personage, and gave the opportunity for an apt reply. "Is it true, Lord John, that you hold that a subject is justified, under certain circumstances, in disobeying his Sovereign's will ?" "Well," I said, "speaking to a Sovereign of the House of Hanover, I can only say that I suppose it is !"' [1]

Looking back in the autumn of last year on the length and breadth of Earl Russell's public career, the late Earl Selborne sent for these pages the following words, which gather up his general, and, alas ! final impressions of his old friend and colleague : ' I have tried to imagine in what words an ancient Roman panegyrist might have summed up such a public and private character as that of Lord Russell. "Animosa juventus," and "jucunda senectus," would not inaptly have

[1] *Contemporary Review*, vol. 56, p. 814.

described his earlier and his latter days.   But for the life of long and active public service which came between, it is difficult to find any phrase equally pointed and characteristic. Always patriotic, always faithful to the traditions associated with his name, there was, as Sydney Smith said, nothing which he had not courage to undertake.   What he undertook he did energetically, and generally in a noble spirit ; though sometimes yielding to too sudden impulses.   As time went on, the generosity and sagacity of his nature gained strength ; and, though he had not always been patient when the control of affairs was in other hands, a successful rival found in him the most loyal of colleagues.   Any estimate of his character would be imperfect which omitted to recognise either his appreciative and sympathetic disposition towards those who differed from him, even on points of importance, when he believed their convictions to be sincere and their conduct upright, or the rare dignity and magnanimity with which, after 1866, he retired from a great position, of which he was neither unambitious nor unworthy, under no pressure from without, and before age or infirmity had made it necessary for him to do so.'

Lord Selborne's allusion to Lord John's sympathetic disposition to those who differed from him, even on points of importance, is borne out by the terms in which he referred to Lord Aberdeen in correspondence—which was published first in the 'Times,' and afterwards in a pamphlet—between himself and Sir Arthur Gordon over statements in the first edition of 'Recollections and Suggestions.'   Lord John admitted that, through lapse of memory, he had fallen into error, and that his words conveyed a wrong impression concerning Lord Aberdeen.   He added : 'I believe no man has entered public life in my time more pure in his personal views, and more free from grasping ambition or selfish consideration. I am much grieved that anything I have written should be liable to an interpretation injurious to Lord Aberdeen.' It is pleasant in this connection to be able to cite a letter, written by Lord Aberdeen to the Duke of Bedford, when the Crimean War was happily only a memory. The Duke had told Lord Aberdeen that his brother admitted his mistake in leaving the Coalition Government in the way in which he did. Lord Aberdeen in his reply declared that he did not doubt that Lord John entered the Government on generous and high-minded motives, or that, in consequence of delay, he might have arrived at the conclusion that he was in a somewhat false position. Any appearance of lack of confidence in Lord John, Lord Aberdeen remarked, was 'entirely the effect of accident and never of intention.' He hints that he sometimes thought Lord John over-sensitive and even rash or impracticable. He adds : ' But these are trifles. We parted with expressions of mutual regard, which on my side were perfectly sincere, as I have no doubt they were on his. These expressions I am happy in having this opportunity to renew ; as well as with my admiration of his great powers and noble impulses to assure you that I shall always feel a warm interest in his reputation and honour.' Lord Stanmore states that his father 'steadily maintained that Lord John was the proper head of the Liberal party, and never ceased to desire that he should succeed him as Prime Minister.' Rashness and impatience are hard sayings to one who looks steadily at the annals of the Coalition Government. Lord Aberdeen and the majority of his Cabinet, were, to borrow a phrase from Swift, ' huge idolators of delay.' Their policy of masterly inactivity was disastrous, and, though Lord John made a mistake in quitting the

Ministry in face of a hostile vote of censure, his chief mistake arose from the 'generous and high-minded motives' which Lord Aberdeen attributes to him, and which led him to join the Coalition Government.

His personal relations with his political opponents, from the Duke of Wellington to Lord Salisbury, were cordial. His friendship with Lord Derby was intimate, and he visited him at Knowsley, and in his closing years he had much pleasant intercourse with Lord Salisbury at Dieppe. His association with Lord Beaconsfield was slight ; but one of the kindest letters which Lady Russell received on the death of her husband was written by a statesman with whom Lord Russell had little in common. Sir Robert Peel, in spite of the encounters of party warfare, always maintained towards Lord John the most friendly attitude. 'The idea which the stranger or casual acquaintance,' states his brother-in-law and former private secretary, Mr. George Elliot, 'conceived of Lord Russell was very unlike the real man as seen in his own home or among his intimates. There he was lively, playful, and uniformily good-humoured, full of anecdote, and a good teller of a story. . . . In conversation he was easy and pleasant, and the reverse of disputatious. Even in the worst of his political difficulties— and he had some pretty hard trials in this way—he had the power of throwing off public cares for the time, and in his house retained his cheerfulness and good-humour. . . . In matters of business he was an easy master to serve, and the duties of his private secretary were light as compared to others in the same position. He never made work and never was fussy, and even at the busiest times never seemed in a hurry. . . . Large matters he never neglected, but the difficulty of the private secretary was to get him to attend to

the trifling and unimportant ones with which he had chiefly
to deal.'

The Hon. Charles Gore, who was also private secretary to
Lord John when the latter held the Home Office in the
Melbourne Administration, gives in the following words his
recollections : 'Often members of Parliament and others
used to come into my room adjoining, after their interview
with Lord John, looking, and seeming, much dissatisfied
with their reception. His manner was cold and shy, and,
even when he intended to comply with the request made, in
his answer he rather implied no than yes. He often used to
say to me that he liked to hear the laugh which came to him
through the door which separated us, as proof that I had
been able to soothe the disappointed feelings with which his
interviewer had left him. As a companion, when not feeling shy, no one was more agreeable or full of anecdote than
Lord John—simple in his manner, never assuming superiority, and always ready to listen to what others had to say.'
This impression is confirmed by Sir Villiers Lister, who
served under Lord John at the Foreign Office. He states
that his old chief, whilst always quick to seize great problems, was somewhat inclined to treat the humdrum details
of official life with fitful attention.

CHAPTER XVIII

PEMBROKE LODGE

1847–1878

Looking back—Society at Pembroke Lodge—Home life—The house
and its memories—Charles Dickens's speech at Liverpool—Literary
friendships—Lady Russell's description of her husband—A packet
of letters—His children's recollections—A glimpse of Carlyle—A
witty impromptu—Closing days—Mr. and Mrs. Gladstone—The
jubilee of the Repeal of the Test and Corporation Acts—' Punch ' on
the ' Golden Wedding '—Death—The Queen's letter—Lord Shaftesbury's estimate of Lord John's career—His great qualities.

PEACE with honour—a phrase which Lord John used long
before Lord Beaconsfield made it famous—sums up the
settled tranquillity and simple dignity of the life at Pembroke Lodge. No man was more entitled to rest on his
laurels than Lord John Russell. He was in the House of
Commons, and made his first proposals for Parliamentary
redress, in the reign of George III. His great victory
on behalf of the rights of conscience was won by the
repeal of the Test and Corporation Acts in the reign of
George IV. He had piloted the first Reform Bill through
the storms of prejudice and passion which had assailed
that great measure in the reign of William IV. He was
Home Secretary when Queen Victoria's reign began, and
since then he had served her Majesty and the nation
with unwearied devotion for almost the life-time of a generation. He was Secretary for the Colonies during a period

when the expansion of England brought delicate constitutional questions to the front, and was Minister of Foreign Affairs when struggling nationalities looked to England, and did not seek her help in vain. Twice Prime Minister in periods of storm and stress, he had left his mark, directly or indirectly, on the statute-book in much progressive legislation, and, in spite of mistakes in policy, had at length quitted office with the reputation of an honest and enlightened statesman.

Peel at the age of fifty-eight had judged himself worthy of retirement ; but Russell was almost seventy-four, and only his indomitable spirit had enabled him to hold his own in public life against uncertain health during the whole course of his career. In this respect, at least, Lord John possessed that 'strong patience which outwearies fate.' He was always delicate, and in his closing years he was accustomed to tell, with great glee, those about him an incident in his own experience, which happened when the century was entering its teens and he was just leaving his own. Three physicians were summoned in consultation, for his life appeared to be hanging on a thread. He described how they carefully thumped him, and put him through the usual ordeal. Then they looked extremely grave and retired to an adjoining room. The young invalid could hear them talking quite plainly, and dreaded their return with the sentence of death. Presently the conversation grew animated, and Lord John found, to his surprise, they were talking about anything in the world except himself. On coming back, all the advice they gave was that he ought to travel abroad for a time. It jumped with his mood, and he took it, and to the end of his days travel never failed to restore his energies.

'For some years after his retirement from Ministerial life,' says Mr. Lecky, 'he gathered round him at Pembroke Lodge a society that could hardly be equalled—certainly not surpassed—in England. In the summer Sunday afternoons there might be seen beneath the shade of those majestic oaks nearly all that was distinguished in English politics and much that was distinguished in English literature, and few eminent foreigners visited England without making a pilgrimage to the old statesman. Unhappily, this did not last to the end. Failing memory and the weakness of extreme old age at last withdrew him completely from the society he was so eminently fitted to adorn, but to those who had known him in his brighter days he has left a memory which can never be effaced.'

Pembroke Lodge, on the fringe of Richmond Park, was, for more than thirty years, Lord John Russell's home. In his busiest years, whenever he could escape from town, the rambling, picturesque old house, which the Queen had given him, was his chosen and greatly loved place of retreat. 'Happy days,' records Lady Russell, 'so full of reality. The hours of work so cheerfully got through, the hours of leisure so delightful.' When in office much of each week was of necessity passed at his house in Chesham Place, but he appreciated the freedom and seclusion of Pembroke Lodge, and took a keen delight in its beautiful garden, with its winding walks, magnificent views, and spreading forest trees—truly a haunt of ancient peace, as well as of modern fellowship. There, in old age, Lord Russell loved to wander with wife or child or friend, and there, through the loop-holes of retreat amid his books and flowers, he watched the great world, and occasionally sallied forth, so long as strength remained, to bear his part in its affairs.

Lord John Russell in his closing years thoroughly distrusted Turkish rule in Europe. He declared that he had formerly tried with Lord Palmerston's aid to improve the Turks, but came to the conclusion that the task was hopeless, and he witnessed with gladness the various movements to throw off their control in South-Eastern Europe. He was one of the first to call attention to the Bulgarian atrocities, and he joined the national protest with the political ardour which moral indignation was still able to kindle in a statesman who cherished his old ideals at the age of eighty-four. Two passages from Lady Russell's journal in the year 1876 speak for themselves :—' August 18. My dearest husband eighty-four. The year has left its mark upon him, a deeper mark than most years .... but he is happy, even merry. Seventy or eighty of our school children came up and sang in front of his window. They had made a gay flag on which were written four lines of a little poem to him. He was much pleased and moved with the pretty sight and pretty sound. I may say the same of Lord Granville, who happened to be here at the time.' Two months later occurs the following entry: ' Interesting visit from the Bulgarian delegates, who called to thank John for the part he has taken. They utterly deny the probability of civil war or bloodshed between different Christian sects, or between Christian and Mussulman, in case of Bulgaria and the other insurgent provinces obtaining self-government. Their simple, heart-felt words of gratitude to John were touching to us all.'

History repeats itself at Pembroke Lodge. On May 16, 1895, a party of Armenian refugees went thither on the ground that ' the name of Lord John Russell is honoured by every Christian under the rule of the Turk.' It recalled to Lady

Russell the incident just recorded, and the interview, she states, was 'a heart-breaking one, although gratitude for British sympathy seemed uppermost in what they wished to express. After they were gone I thought, as I have often thought before, how right my husband was in feeling and in saying, as he often did, that Goldsmith was quite wrong in these two lines in "The Traveller" :

> 'How small of all that human hearts endure
> That part which laws or kings can cause or cure !

He often recited them with disapproval when any occurrence made him feel how false they were.'

Lord John's manner of life, like his personal tastes, was simple. He contrived to set the guests who gathered around him at his wife's receptions perfectly at their ease, by his old-fashioned gallantry, happy humour, and bright, vigorous talk. One room in Pembroke Lodge, from the windows of which a glorious view of the wooded valley is obtained, has been rendered famous by Kinglake's description [1] of a certain drowsy summer evening in June 1854, when the Aberdeen Cabinet assembled in it, at the very moment when they were drifting into war. Other rooms in the house are full of memories of Garibaldi and Livingstone, of statesmen, ambassadors, authors, and, indeed, of men distinguished in every walk of life, but chiefly of Lord John himself, in days of intellectual toil, as well as in hours of friendly intercourse and happy relaxation.

[1] *History of the War in the Crimea*, by A. W. Kinglake, vol. ii. sixth edition, pp. 249–50.

Lady Russell states that Lord John used to smile at Kinglake's rhetorical exaggeration of the scene. Her impression is that only two of the Cabinet, and not, as the historian puts it, 'all but a small minority,' fell asleep. The Duke of Argyll or Mr. Gladstone can alone settle the point at issue.

Charles Dickens, speaking in 1869 at a banquet in Liverpool, held in his honour, over which Lord Dufferin presided, refused to allow what he regarded as a covert sneer against the House of Lords to pass unchallenged. He repelled the insinuation with unusual warmth, and laid stress on his own regard for individual members of that assembly. Then, on the spur of the moment, came an unexpected personal tribute. He declared that 'there was no man in England whom he respected more in his public capacity, loved more in his private capacity, or from whom he had received more remarkable proofs of his honour and love of literature than Lord John Russell.' The compliment took Lord Russell by surprise; but if space allowed, or necessity claimed, it would be easy to prove that it was not undeserved. From the days of his youth, when he lived under the roof of Dr. Playfair, and attended the classes of Professor Dugald Stewart in Edinburgh, and took his part, as a *protégé* of Lord Holland, in the brilliant society of Holland House, Lord John's leanings towards literature, and friendship with other literary men had been marked. As in the case of other Prime Ministers of the Queen's reign, and notably of Derby, Beaconsfield, and Mr. Gladstone, literature was his pastime, if politics was his pursuit, for his interests were always wider than the question of the hour. He was the friend of Sir James Mackintosh and of Sydney Smith, who playfully termed him 'Lord John Reformer,' of Moore and Rogers, Jeffrey and Macaulay, Dickens and Thackeray, Tyndall and Sir Richard Owen, Motley and Sir Henry Taylor, Browning and Tennyson, to mention only a few representative men.

When the students of Glasgow University wished, in 1846, to do him honour, Lord John gracefully begged them to appoint as Lord Rector a man of creative genius, like Wordsworth, rather than himself. As Prime Minister he honoured science by selecting Sir John Herschel as Master of the Mint, and literature, by the recommendation of Alfred Tennyson as Poet Laureate. When Sir Walter Scott was creeping back in broken health from Naples to die at Abbotsford it was Lord John who cheered the sad hours of illness in the St. James's Hotel, Jermyn Street, by a delicately worded offer of financial help from the public funds. Leigh Hunt, Christopher North, Sheridan Knowles, Father Mathew, the widow of Dr. Chalmers, and the children of Tom Hood are names which suggest the direction in which he used his patronage as First Minister of the Crown. He was in the habit of enlivening his political dinner parties by invoking the aid of literary men of wit and distinction, and nothing delighted him more than to bring, in this pleasant fashion, literature and politics to close quarters. The final pages of his ' Recollections and Suggestions ' were written in Lord Tennyson's study at Aldworth, and his relations with Moore at an earlier stage of his life were even more intimate.

Lord John Russell was twice married : first, on April 11, 1835, to Adelaide, daughter of Mr. Thomas Lister, of Armitage Park, Staffordshire, the young widow of Thomas, second Lord Ribblesdale ; and second, on July 20, 1841, to Lady Frances Anna Maria Elliot, second daughter of Gilbert, second Earl of Minto. By his first wife he had two daughters, the late Lady Victoria Villiers, and Lady Georgiana Peel ; and by his second three sons and one daughter—John, Viscount Amberley, the Hon. George William Gilbert, formerly of the 9th Lancers, the Hon. Francis Albert Rollo, and Lady Mary Agatha. Viscount Amberley married, on November 8, 1864, the fifth daughter of Lord

Stanley of Alderley. Lord Amberley died two years before his father, and the peerage descended to the elder of his two sons, the present Earl Russell.

Lady Russell states : ' Our way of life during the session, from the time we first settled in Pembroke Lodge till John ceased to take any active part in politics, was to be there from Wednesday to Thursday and from Saturday to Monday. This made him spend much time on the road ; but he always said the good it did him to snatch all he could of the delight of his own quiet country home, to breathe its pure air, and be cheered by the sight of his merry children, far outweighed the time and trouble it cost him. When he was able to leave town tolerably early, he used sometimes to ride down all the way ; but he oftener drove to Hammersmith Bridge, where his horse, and such of our children as were old enough to ride met him, and how joyfully I used to catch the first sight of the happy riders—he on his roan " Surrey " and they on their pretty ponies—from the little mount in our grounds ! He was very fond of riding, and in far later days, when age and infirmity obliged him to give it up, used often to say in a sad tone, pointing to some of his favourite grassy rides, as we drove together in the park, " Ah ! what pleasant gallops we used to have along there ! " ' Lord John was seen to great advantage in his own home and with his children. Even when the cares of State pressed most heavily on him he always seemed to the children about him to have leisure to enter with gay alacrity into their plans and amusements. When at home, no matter how urgent the business in hand, he always saw them either in the house or the garden every day, and took the liveliest interest in the round of their life, alike in work and play. He had conquered the art of bearing care lightly. He seldom allowed

public affairs to distract him in moments of leisure. He
was able to throw aside the cares of office, and to enter with
vivacity and humour into social diversions. His equable
temper and placid disposition served him in good stead amid
the turmoil and excitement of political life.

Sorrows, neither few nor light, fell upon the household
at Pembroke Lodge in the closing years of Lord Russell's
life ; but 'trials,' as Lady Russell puts it in her journal, 'had
taught Lord John to feel for others, and age had but
deepened his religion of love.' In reply to a birthday letter
from Mr. Archibald Peel, his son-in-law, and nephew of his
great political rival he said : 'Thanks for your good wishes.
Happy returns ! I always find them, as my children are so
affectionate and loving ; " many " I cannot expect, but I have
played my part.' Two or three extracts from a packet of
letters addressed by Lord John to his daughter, Lady Georgiana Peel, will be read with interest. The majority of them
are of too intimate and personal a kind for quotation. Yet
the whole of them leave the impression that Lord John, who
reproaches himself in one instance as a bad correspondent,
was at least a singularly good father. They cover a considerable term of years, and though for the most part dealing with private affairs, and often in a spirit of pleasant
raillery, here and there allusions to public events occur in
passing. In one of them, written from Gotha in the autumn
of 1862, when Lord John was in attendance on her Majesty,
he says : 'We have been dull here, but the time has never
hung heavy on our hands. Four boxes of despatches and
then telegrams, all requiring answers, have been our daily
food.' He refers touchingly to the Queen's grief, and there
is also an allusion to the minor tribulation of a certain
little boy in England who had just crossed the threshold

of school-life.   Probably Lord John was thinking of his own harsh treatment at Westminster, more than sixty years before, when he wrote : 'Poor Willy ! He will find a public school a rough place, and the tears will come into his eyes when he thinks of the very soft nest he left at home.'

Ecclesiastical affairs never lost their interest to the author of the Durham Letter, and the following comments show his attitude on Church questions. The first is from a letter written on May 23, 1867 : 'The Church has been greatly disturbed. The Bishop of Salisbury has claimed for the English clergy all the power of the Roman priests. The question whether they are to wear white surplices, or blue, green, yellow, or red, becomes a minor question in comparison. Of course the Bishop and those who think with him throw off the authority of our excellent Thirty-nine Articles altogether, and ought to leave the Church to the Protestant clergy and laity.' England just then, in Carlyle's judgment, was 'shooting Niagara,' and Disraeli's reform proposals were making a stir in the opposite camp. In the letter above quoted Lord John says :   'Happily, we are about to get rid of the compound householder. I am told Dizzy expects to be the first President of the British Republic.' Mr. Gladstone, according to Lord Houghton, seemed at the same moment 'quite awed with the diabolical cleverness of Dizzy.' The second bears date Woburn Abbey, September 29, 1868 : 'Dr. Temple is a man I greatly admire, and he has become more valuable to his country since the death of our admirable Dean of St. Paul's. If I had any voice in the appointment, Temple is the man I should wish to see succeed to Milman ; but I suppose the "Essays and Reviews" will tell heavily against him.' 'We lead a very quiet life here and a very happy one. I sometimes regret not seeing my old political friends a little oftener.' 'In June [1869] I expect Dickens to visit us. We went to see him last night in the murder of Nancy by Sikes, and Mrs. Gamp. He acts like a great actor, and writes like a great author. Irish Church is looming very near in the Commons, and, in June, in the Lords. The Archbishops and Bishops do not wish to oppose the second reading, but Lord Cairns is prepared to hack and hew in committee.'

The recollections of Lord John's children reveal, by incidents too trivial in themselves to quote, how completely he entered into their life. Lady Georgiana Peel recalls her childish tears when her father arrived too late from London one evening to see one of the glorious sunsets which he had taught her to admire. 'I can feel now his hand on my forehead in any childish illness, or clasping mine in the garden, as he led me out to forget some trifling sorrow.' She lays stress on his patience and serene temper, on his tender heart, and on the fact that he always found leisure on the busiest day to enter into the daily life of his little girls. Half heartedness, either in work or play, was not to his mind. '*Do* what you are doing' was the advice he gave to his children.

One of the elder children in far-off days at Pembroke Lodge, Mrs. Warburton, Lord John's step-daughter, recalls wet days in the country, when her father would break the tedium of temporary imprisonment indoors by romping with his children. 'I have never forgotten his expression of horror when in a game of hide-and-seek he banged the door accidentally in my elder sister's face and we heard her fall. Looking back to the home life, its regularity always astonishes me. The daily walks, prayers, and meals regular and punctual as a rule. . . . He was shy and we were shy, but I think we spoke quite freely with him, and he seldom said more than " Foolish child " when we ventured on any startling views on things. Once I remember rousing his indignation when I gave out, with sententious priggishness, that the Duke of Wellington laboured under great difficulties in Spain caused by the " factious opposition at home ; " that was beyond " Foolish child," but my discomforted distress was soon soothed by a pat on the cheek, and an amused twinkle in his kind eyes.' Lord Amberley, four days before his death, declared that he had all his life ' met with nothing but kindness and gentleness ' from his father. He added: ' I do earnestly hope that at the end of his long and noble life he may be spared the pain of losing a son.'

Mr. Rollo Russell says : ' My father was very fond of history, and I can remember his often turning back to Hume, Macaulay, Hallam, and other historical works. He read various books on the French Revolution with great interest. He had several classics always near him, such as Homer and Virgil ; and he always carried about with him a small edition of Horace. Of Shakespeare he could repeat much, and knew the plays well, entering into and discussing the characters. He admired Milton very greatly and was fond of reading " Paradise Lost." He was very fond of several Italian and Spanish books, by the greatest authors of those countries. Of lighter read ing, he admired most, I think, " Don Quixote," Sir Walter Scott's novels, Miss Evans' (" George Eliot ") novels, Miss Austen's, and Dickens and Thackeray. Scott especially he loved to read over again. He told me he bought " Waverley " when it first came out, and was so interested in it that he sat up a great part of the night till he had finished it.'

Lady Russell states that Grote's ' History of Greece ' was

one of the last books her husband read, and she adds : 'Many of his friends must have seen its volumes open before him on the desk of his blue armchair in his sitting-room at Pembroke Lodge in the last year or two of his life. It was often exchanged for Jowett's "Plato," in which he took great delight, and which he persevered in trying to read, when, alas ! the worn-out brain refused to take in the meaning.'

Lord John was a delightful travelling companion, and he liked to journey with his children about him. His cheerfulness and merriment on these occasions is a happy memory. Dr. Anderson, of Richmond, who has been for many years on intimate terms at Pembroke Lodge, and was much abroad with Lord John in the capacity of physician and friend, states that all who came in contact personally with him became deeply attached to him. This arose not only from the charm of his manner and conversation, but from the fact that he felt they trusted him implicitly. 'I never saw anyone laugh so heartily. He seemed almost convulsed with merriment, and he once told me that after a supper with Tom Moore, the recollection of some of the witty things said during the course of the evening so tickled him, that he had to stop and hold by the railings while laughing on his way home. I once asked which of all the merry pictures in "Punch" referring to himself amused him the most, and he at once replied : "The little boy who has written 'No Popery' on a wall and is running away because he sees a policeman coming. I think that was very funny !"' Dr. Anderson says that Lord John was generous to a fault and easily moved to tears, and adds : 'I never knew any one more tender in illness or more anxious to help.' He states that Lord John told him that he had encountered Carlyle one day in Regent Street. He stopped, and asked him if he had seen a paragraph in that morning's 'Times' about the Pope. 'What!' exclaimed Carlyle, 'the Pope, the Pope! The back of ma han' for that auld chimera!'

Lady Russell says: 'As far as I recollect he never but once worked after dinner. He always came up to the drawing-room with us, was able to cast off public cares, and chat and laugh, and read and be read to, or join in little games, such as capping verses, of which he was very fond.' Lord John used often to write prologues and epilogues for the drawing-room plays which they were accustomed to perform. Space forbids the quotation of these sparkling and often humorous verses, but the following instance of his ready wit occurred in the drawing-room at Minto, and is given on the authority of Mr. George Elliot. At a game where everyone was required to write some verses, answering the question written on a paper to be handed to him, and bringing in a word written on the same, the paper that fell to the lot of Lord John contained this question : 'Do you admire Sir Robert Peel?' and 'soldier' the word to be brought in. His answer was :

> ' I ne'er was a soldier of Peel,
>   Or ever yet stood at his back ;
> For while he wriggled on like an eel,
>   I swam straight ahead like a *Jack.*'

Mr. Gladstone states that perhaps the finest retort he ever heard in the House of Commons was that of Lord John in reply to Sir Francis Burdett. The latter had abandoned his Radicalism in old age, and was foolish enough to sneer at the 'cant of patriotism.' 'I quite agree, said Lord John, 'with the honourable baronet that the cant of patriotism is a bad thing. But I can tell him a worse— the *recant* of patriotism—which I will gladly go along with him in reprobating whenever he shows me an example of it.'

Lord John Russell once declared that he had no need to go far in search of happiness, as he had it at his own doors, and this was the impression left on every visitor to Pembroke Lodge. Lord Dufferin states that all his recollections gather around Lord John's domestic life. He never possessed a kinder friend or one who was more pleasant in the retirement of his home. Lord Dufferin adds: 'One of his most charming characteristics was that he was so simple, so untheatrical, so genuine, that his existence, at least when I knew him, flowed at a very high level of thought and feeling, but was unmarked by anything very dramatic. His conversation was too delightful, full of anecdote ; but then his anecdotes were not like those told by the ordinary *raconteur*, and were simple reminiscences of his own personal experience and intercourse with other distinguished men. Again, his stories were told in such an unpretending way that, though you were delighted with what you had heard, you were still more delighted with the speaker himself.'

The closing years of Lord Russell's career were marked by settled peace, the consciousness of great tasks worthily accomplished, the unfaltering devotion of household love, the friendship of the Queen, the confidence of a younger race of statesmen, and the respect of the nation. Deputations of working men found their way to Pembroke Lodge to greet the old leader of the party of progress, and school children gathered about him in summer on the lawn, and were gladdened by his kindly smile and passing word. In good report and in evil report, in days of power and in days of weakness, the Countess Russell cheered, helped, and solaced him, and brought not only rare womanly devotion, but unusual intellectual gifts to his aid at the critical moments of his life, when bearing the strain of public responsibility, and in the simple round of common duty. The nation may recognise the services of its great men, but can never gauge to the full extent the influences which sustained them. The uplifting associations of a singularly happy domestic life must be taken into account in any estimate of the forces which shaped Lord John Russell's career. It is enough to say—indeed, more cannot with propriety be added —that through the political stress and strain of nearly forty years Lady Russell proved herself to be a loyal and noble-hearted wife.

There is another subject, which cannot be paraded on the printed page, and yet, since religion was the central principle of Lord John Russell's life, some allusion to his position on the highest of all subjects becomes imperative. His religion was thorough ; it ran right through his nature. It was practical, and revealed itself in deeds which spoke louder than words. ' I rest in the faith of Jeremy Taylor,' were his words, ' Barrow, Tillotson, Hoadly, Samuel Clarke, Middleton, Warburton, and Arnold, without attempting to reconcile points of difference between these great men. I prefer the simple words of Christ to any dogmatic interpretation of them.' Dean Stanley, whom he used to call his Pope—always playfully adding, ' but not an infallible one ' —declared shortly before Lord Russell's death that ' he was a man who was firmly convinced that in Christianity, whether as held by the National Church or Nonconformist, there was something greater and vaster than each of the particular communions professed and advocated, something which made it worth while to develop those universal principles of religion that are common to all who accept in any real sense the fundamental truths of Christianity.'

Mr. Spurgeon, in conversation with the writer of these pages, related an incident concerning Lord John which deserves at least passing record, as an illustration of his swift appreciation of ability and the reality of his recognition of religious equality. Lord John was upwards of sixty at the time, and the famous Baptist preacher, though the rage of the town, was scarcely more than twenty. The Metropolitan Tabernacle had as yet not been built. Mr. Spurgeon was at the Surrey Music Hall, and there the great congregation had gathered around this youthful master of assemblies. One Sunday night, at the close of the service, Lord John Russell came into the vestry to speak a kindly word of encouragement to the young preacher. One of the children of the ex-Prime Minister was with him, and before the interview ended Lord John asked the Nonconformist minister to give his blessing to the child. Mr. Spurgeon never forgot the incident, or the bearing of the man who came to him, amid a crowd of others, on that Sunday night.

In opening the new buildings of Cheshunt College in 1871, Lord John alluded to the foundress of that seat of theological learning, Lady Huntingdon, as a woman who was far in advance of her times, since, a century before the abolition of University tests, she made it possible to divinity students to obtain academical training without binding themselves at the outset to any religious community.

During the early months of 1878 Lord John's strength failed rapidly, and it became more and more apparent that the plough was nearing the end of the furrow. His old courage and calmness remained to the end. Mr. and Mrs. Gladstone called at Pembroke Lodge on April 20, and he

sent down word that he wished to see them. 'I took them to
him for a few minutes,' relates Lady Russell. 'Happily, he was
clear in his mind, and said to Mr. Gladstone, " I am sorry you
are not in the Ministry," and kissed her affectionately, and was
so cordial to both that they were greatly touched.' He told
Lady Russell that he had enjoyed his life. 'I have made
mistakes, but in all I did my object was the public good !'
Then after a pause : 'I have sometimes seemed cold to my
friends, but it was not in my heart.' A change for the worse
set in on May 1, and the last sands of life were slipping
quietly through the glass when the Nonconformist deputation
came on the 9th of that month to present Lord Russell
with an address of congratulation on the occasion of the
jubilee of the Repeal of the Corporation and Test Acts.[1]
Lady Russell and her children received the Deputation. In
the course of her reply to the address Lady Russell said that
of all the 'victories won by that great party to which in his
later as in his earlier years Lord John had been insepar-
ably attached,' there was none dearer to his memory at that
moment than that which they had called to remembrance.
'It was a proud and a sad day,' is the entry in Lady Russell's
journal. 'We had hoped some time ago that he might perhaps see the Deputation for a moment in his room, but he
was too ill for that to be possible.'

A few days later, there appeared in the columns of
'Punch' some commemorative verses entitled 'A Golden

[1] Amongst those who assembled in the drawing-room of Pembroke
Lodge on that historic occasion were Mr. Henry Richard, M.P., Mr.
Samuel Morley, M.P., Mr. Edward Baines, Sir Charles Reed, Mr.
Carvell Williams, M.P., who came on behalf of the Protestant Dissent-
ing Deputies. The Congregationalists were represented by such men
as the Rev. Baldwin Brown and the Rev. Guinness Rogers ; the Baptists
by Dr. Underhill ; the Presbyterians by Dr. McEwan ; and the Uni
tarians by Mr. Middleton Aspland.

Wedding.' They expressed the feeling that was uppermost in the heart of the nation, and two or three verses may here be recorded :—

The Golden Wedding of Lord John and Liberty his love—
'Twixt the Russells' House and Liberty, 'twas ever hand and glove—
His love in those dark ages, he has lived through with his bride,
To look back on them from the sunset of his quiet eventide.

His love when he that loved her and sought her for his own
Must do more than suit and service, must do battle, trumpet blown,
Must slay the fiery dragons that guarded every gate
On the roads by which men travelled for work of Church and State.

Now time brings its revenges, and all are loud to own
How beautiful a bride she was, how fond, how faithful shown ;
But she knows the man who loved her when lovers were but few,
And she hails this golden wedding—fifty years of tried and true.

Look and listen, my Lord Russell : 'tis your golden wedding-day ;
We may not press your brave old hand, but you hear what we've to say.
A blessing on the bridal that has known its fifty years,
But never known its fallings-out, delusions, doubt, or fears.

The end came softly. 'I fall back on the faith of my childhood,' were the words he uttered to Dr. Anderson. The closing scene is thus recorded in Mr. Rollo Russell's journal : 'May 28 [1878].—He was better this morning, though still in a very weak state. He spoke more distinctly, called me by my name, and said something which I could not understand. He did not seem to be suffering . . . and has, all through his long illness, been cheerful to a degree that surprises everybody about him, not complaining of anything, but seeming to feel that he was being well cared for. About midday he became worse . . . but bore it all calmly. My mother was with him continually. . . . Towards ten he was much worse, and in a few minutes, while my mother was holding his hand, he breathed out gently the remainder of life.' Westminster Abbey was offered as a place of burial, but, in accordance with his own expressed wish, Lord John Russell was gathered to his fathers at Chenies. The Queen's sympathy and her sense of loss were expressed in the following letter :—

'Balmoral : May 30, 1878.

'DEAR LADY RUSSELL,—It was only yesterday afternoon that I heard through the papers that your dear husband had left this world of sorrows and trials peacefully and full of years the night before, or I would have telegraphed and written sooner. You will believe that I truly regret an old friend of forty years' standing, and whose personal kindness in trying and anxious times I shall *ever* remember. "Lord John," as I knew him best, was one of my *first* and *most distinguished* Ministers, and his departure recalls many eventful times.

'To you, dear Lady Russell, who were ever one of the most devoted of wives, this must be a terrible blow, though you must have for some time been prepared for it. But one is *never* prepared for the blow when it comes, and you have had such trials and sorrows of late years that I most truly sympathise with you. Your dear and devoted daughter will, I know, be the greatest possible comfort to you, and I trust that your grandsons will grow up to be all you could wish.

'Believe me always, yours affectionately,

'VICTORIA R. AND I.'

Lord Shaftesbury wrote in his journal some words about Lord Russell which speak for themselves. After recording that he had reached the ripe age of eighty-six, and that he had been a conspicuous man for more than half a century, he added that to have 'begun with disapprobation, to have fought through many difficulties, to have announced, and acted on, principles new to the day in which he lived, to have filled many important offices, to have made many speeches, and written many books, and in his whole course to have done much with credit, and nothing with dishonour, and so to have sustained and advanced his reputation to the very end, is a mighty commendation.'

When some one told Sir Stafford Northcote that Lord John was dead, the tidings were accompanied by the trite but sympathetic comment, 'Poor Lord Russell!' 'Why do you call him poor?' was the quick retort. 'Lord Russell had the chance of doing a great work and—he did it.'

Lord John was not faultless, and most assuredly he was not infallible. He made mistakes, and sometimes was inclined to pay too little heed to the claims of others, and not to weigh with sufficient care the force of his own impetuous words. The taunt of 'finality' has seldom been less deserved. In most directions he kept an open mind, and seems, like Coleridge, to have believed that an error is sometimes the shadow of a great truth yet behind the horizon. Mr. Gladstone asserts that his old chief was always ready to stand in the post of difficulty, and possessed an inexhaustible sympathy with human suffering.

It is at least certain that Lord John Russell served England—the country whose freedom, he once declared, he 'worshipped'—with unwearied devotion, with a high sense of honour, with a courage which never faltered, with an integrity which has never been impeached. He followed duty to the utmost verge of life, and—full himself of moral susceptibility —he reverenced the conscience of every man.

B B

INDEX